CW01498718

The moral right of the author has been asserted.
ASIN: B006ZML9X4
ISBN 10: 1484150244
ISBN 13: 978-1484150245

To those that have fallen.

To Dickie,

Best Wishes.

[signature]

Chapter 1

Between the land of the living and that of the dead, I only just exist. Barely able to touch either world, I am detached and frequently reflect on my passing as I drift further from those I love. My isolation increased with the death of each day and the conclusion of each season. Obscured by a creeping cloud of chlorine, I disappeared from view and slowly dissolved in agony until the corrosive gas denatured my nerve endings and the pain was gone, as was my viability. Tipping point of being crossed, I could do no more than wait; wait until I am gone forever.

It started with diminished responses to my communications. Telephone calls, e-mails and text messages went increasingly unanswered until they ceased altogether, leaving me calling into the unresponsive abyss. Time spent in the company of others became rarer and rarer as my decent into the darkness accelerated. Insidious isolation drew its impenetrable cloak about me and I became, as its other vassals, lost to the world we previously knew and alone.

All that was once me has gone, only the past exists and I retain nothing save one thing, a single hope. That hope is that out there, in the impenetrable forest, she is searching for me, carrying with her my old life. Eagerly she is seeking to re-unite us so that the sun would return and banish the dense shadow that has engulfed me for the past three years.

Day after day, I wander the once familiar streets, now alien to me or am I alien to them? Either way, we are not on the friendly terms that we once were. Passing from one display to another, I casually peruse, with my eyes, the goods that I would have bought for myself when I was alive. Very occasionally, I recall the emotions of love or desire when my attention is captured by a child's toy, smart suit, beautiful frock or crotch twitching lingerie. I try not to linger at those displays because the memories fade rapidly, replaced by terrible feelings of loss. Invariably however, I do linger and then, like a suddenly orphaned child, I limp away struggling with emotions that I cannot understand or control.

Today the sky is its usual battleship grey, crossed periodically by vapour trails from aeroplanes that ferry the living from city to city across land, seas and oceans. It has been a long time since I have seen a horizon. The tops of buildings frame the sky, a cold grey strip above my head. It will pour rain onto me in order to soak my inadequate clothing and assure my discomfort.

Deliciously unhealthy smells ooze from the fast food outlets to torture my aching stomach. Hunger is a gnawing pain that begins with mild discomfort and rapidly grows to a racking agony that ties you in a knot at the middle and burns your extremities. 'One billion people on The Earth go to bed hungry every night', is a statistic. It is probably true in every regard but one, I doubt all of them have a bed to go to, I do not.

With envy in my soul, I watch a youth munching on a large burger. The salad and dressing is hanging from the sinister side of the bun as he chomps into the dexter. Dropping nearly one third of the sandwich back into the Styrofoam container, he then wipes the relish from his chops and moves towards the litterbin. Unseeingly conscious of my presence and of my desire for his leftovers, he snorts and hawks all that he can muster onto the remnant of his meal, and then closing the container, he neatly places it on top of the bin. Walking away, a smile on his face and a swagger in his gait, he leaves me with a quandary.

A mosaic of grey concrete slabs forms the ground, on which my fellow pedestrians and I walk. Between the twin facades of the shopping precinct, a young woman in a blue skirt suit totters by in clear discomfort; the source of her unease is obviously the very high-heeled shoes she wears. When she had chosen to wear the shoes her judgement must have been that the admiring glances, drawn from the opposite sex by her artificially long legs and protruding bottom, would be more than adequate compensation for the pain her footwear would inflict. My shoes are old, worn and sensible, yet equally uncomfortable. They have holes in the soles and my feet hurt all the time from fatigue, the effect of excessive perspiration and cold. Over the last two or three years I have developed a curiously random shuffle. As I walk, my gait follows a

4

complex asymmetrical pattern resembling the progress of a clown's car into the ring of a circus. The body, when allowed to naturally adapt, will always avoid as much pain as it can and my perambulatory style is a result of that natural law.

When I complete my tour of each street, I sit and rest awhile before continuing my patrol of the retail nucleus of this Royal Borough. Sitting invisibly alone allows me the luxury of voyeurism. Respectable middle-aged ladies will pick their noses, young men adjust the dressing of their packages, smart young business ladies pull their knickers from between the cheeks of their bottoms and teenage girls will sit together on the walls by the shopping centre; flashing their tiny thongs through the passage of their thighs and skirts. This simple pleasure is the only comfort that purgatory affords me, and constantly I seek its distraction.

When the days grow old, the streets become more unfriendly. The daytime shoppers and welfare dependent drinkers gradually disperse, replaced by the office workers who rush homeward through the streets that they will promenade at their leisure come the weekend. A brief lull follows the office workers procession, then the shop workers bid farewell to each other and make their ways home. Grills pulled down and alarms are set before the retail outlets' Duty Managers walk away from the city centre, passing the first of the night's drinkers arriving to begin the celebrations.

The drinkers are usually young and excited, groups of males pushing each other about and making a volume of noise inversely proportional to their intellect. Nearly an hour later, groups of females following the same rules of 'street' culture/intellectual proportionality. During this period of the day, I retreat to the relative security of a charity shop doorway where I watch the second wave of revellers make their way to the starting point of the evening's festivities. The heels of their shoes click on the concrete as they wiggle in tight trousers, knickers showing above the waistband, or short skirts, curved young buttocks showing from beneath as they hurry towards the courting grounds.

The invisibility of the dead only protects me from the attentions of the ordinary and established people. The young, feral and drunk can see me, so as the night grows to a close, I

5

take sanctuary near the commercial wheelie bins by the multi-storied car park where the shadows protect me. In the darkness, I wait in the hope that I can indulge my voyeuristic pleasure.

Deep in the corners that street lighting cannot penetrate, I lay out my cardboard groundsheet, pull on the second jumper from my bag, pull my overcoat back on and settle down in the hope of entertainment. Feeling the thrill of theatre my anticipation heightens as urgently whispered voices draw near. Eventually the players take the stage; he leads her to the recessed fire escape doorway opposite my vantage point, and pulls her to him. They kiss passionately as his hands grope at her fleshy backside encased in unfeasibly tight denim. Her hand, drawn from his shoulder, begins to rub at his crotch, an act that immediately initiates his pelvic mating movements.

Slipping my hand into my, already open, trousers, I rub myself as I watch her undo the front of her beau's jeans and pull his eager cock from within. She plays with it for a while before bending over and taking its throbbing urgency into her mouth. Evidently she is keen to show off her prowess in the act of felatio but he fears that his part in this love story is about to come to a premature end and pulls her upright by the breasts. He fumbles at the fastenings of her jeans until they release, then with obvious effort, pulls them down to her ankles. As he turns her for penetration, she bleats at him for protection and with reluctance, he delays coitus.

They stand together in the doorway awkwardly, he fumbling to fit a condom, she staring into the darkness hugging her chest. She almost assumes an air of dignity with her demeanour but to no immediate end as her trousers round her ankles and the pink knickers, ruffled to one side of her crotch, deny any form of respectability. Unperturbed she holds her head high and gazes out of the doorway as though she were only mildly interested in a room full of people who dance for her pleasure. Moving her weight from one foot to the other, her impatience visibly grows until she casts a sharp look in the direction of her immediate lover.

Satisfied with the fitting of his prophylactic he turns her once again into the mating position and inserts himself. As he pumps away at her from behind, I stroke my erection in time with his movements. Experience has taught me to be able to bring myself to climax at the same time as my leading man achieves the same. I spill my seed onto the cardboard between my legs as he unloads his into the rubber teat of his sheath.

Doing his trousers up with one hand and discarding the latex tube with the other, he hazards a coy 'thank you' then after a pause adds, "that was good". She struggles to fit her bottom half back into her jeans, "that's ok I was gagging for it too" she lies and audibly breathes in to fasten the top button. Patting her clothes down with both hands, she instructs him to walk her to the taxi rank. Checking his flies, he breathes out and they break cover. Heading back to the light they walk towards the city thoroughfares, him holding her hand, somewhat more reluctantly than before.

The curtain falls on tonight's performance and the voices of my cast recede into the normal world. I sit still for a while savouring the images in my head as I process them from the short to the long-term memory. Then fastening my trousers and gathering up my groundsheet I set off for home, where I shall re-join the dead.

When the living desert the streets, the dead walk abroad from the shadows. In the hours of the others, I rarely see my own kind and in our time, we are everywhere, manifest in doorways, on park benches or drifting as heavy clouds on a brisk breeze through the deserted streets. Rarely acknowledging each other, we prefer to pass silently by. Only when some need demands, we mark the meeting with a nodded head or the briefest of grunts.

Rustling nylon and moving shadows from a nearby bus shelter followed by murmured voices. Two of my fellows had clearly decided to pass the bitter night together, sharing their fetid breaths under an old square-necked sleeping bag. Their passing passions will serve only to temporarily remind them of what it was to be alive and by the time the living hours return to the streets, they will become invisible again, even to each other.

We are a peculiar people, drifting through our individual purgatories wrapped in the security of our imperceptibility. Through unspoken consent, we have a universal agreement to follow the same rules the living apply to us; only conflict will bring another of our kind into full focus. We have few needs and those needs will cause conflict between us: food, alcohol and a place to sleep or the means with which to acquire any of these.

Billowing clouds of condensation from my mouth are demonstrative of the falling temperature. My coat is old and offers only limited protection from the now biting wind so I quicken my shambling gait and take less notice of my environment as I hasten for home. In the distance I can see the high stonewall that bounds the garden of the dead; my home.

Slipping through the broken gates like a grotesque shadowy panther, I move silently into the darkness. The outer garden is, on occasion, frequented by the delinquent living. They can be dangerous so I push quickly past the memorials to the long dead. Monoliths collected and arranged in symmetrical patterns devised by the living like some plantation of stunted and deformed trees. In the darkest corner of the garden is my home, a broken down mausoleum built to house the bodies of a family that died during the reign of William IV. They have long since completed, if indeed they were ever required to endure, their purgatories and so I live here alone.

Fumbling in the dark, I find the black bin bag at the back of the shelter where I had hidden it under some dead leaves. Then I eagerly rifle the contents of the bag and find my gloves and blanket. With my hands warming in the gloves and the blanket over my shoulders, I lay out the cardboard on top of the sarcophagus. This serves as my bed and I sit on the edge shivering in the cold.

Though I am the single occupant of my sanctuary, I do share the garden with others. In the darkness beyond the doorway, I can hear her walking in the long grass. Throughout purgatory from beginning to end, our invisibility increases and she must be very close to completion as I have never seen her, though I hear her outside my door every night. Just beyond the doorway, she stands quietly in the black air as though she is waiting for me to come and join her. When I first came here, I would leave my hermitage to seek closer contact, only to hear her walking away as I searched the shadows. Now, I just listen to her and she seems content to stand and listen to me. If undisturbed, we can sit in our distant company for hours, but tonight the breathing comes early and she takes to her heels, as she always does, when It is prowling our garden.

He brushes his flanks down the exterior wall of my home and stands by the door panting sheets of condensing warm air across the aperture. Then he speaks to me in heaving breaths of rasping poison. I do not listen, It comes every night to corrupt me and by that corruption prolong my purgatory. I hold my gloved hands over my ears and sing 'Bah Bah Black Sheep' until he tires and prowls off in search of other prey. I listen to him move away, like a snake with legs, through the overgrown graveyard. Once I am sure he has passed from my territory, I suck in great gulps of night air in order to calm my racing chest. I can still smell his acrid scent, a mixture of rotting flesh and goats cheese; choking in my throat as I struggle to control the gag reflex and fill my chest with the damp night air.

The Garden of The Dead is a strange place, there are its more permanent residents such as myself, my friend and It, and there are transients who may stay for weeks or simply pass through in the night. Some nights I have seen silent processions of souls passing through, though since It has become more predacious, the transients tend to move as quickly as possible in groups of two or three through the forest of headstones. Those transients who opt to stay a while face competition for the few sanctuaries there are here, The Order of The Garden will not allow any to usurp my dwelling or the home of any other settled resident, it is their code; a law by which we, the lost, must live.

The Order is powerful in so much as they are a conduit to greater knowledge. To incur their wrath is to sever yourself from knowledge and without knowledge none will navigate a course from this forest of darkness. They rarely make themselves known directly to us; usually it is in the coincidental, accidental, circumstantial that they are manifest. The most obvious of their mediums are their acolytes The Willow Monks; they are never seen but are frequently heard from the darkest corner of The Garden. I for one would never draw too close to that corner for I fear The Order.

Lying on my back, I listen to the Willow Monks chanting away in the garden corner. Their song is at first a complex mixture of sounds that vary in pitch from the deep rumbling of the moving Earth to the piercing siren of a high-pressure leak. I like it when they chant, it is peaceful and re-assuring, they know me and they know my predicament. Then it comes to me, I understand the language they are using, they are telling me how to shorten my purgatory; for the greater good of man, sacrifices must be made. It seems reasonable that I should be rewarded, if I contribute in a meaningful way to the greater good. Then with this revelation, the chanting of the Monks fades and a glorious reverie fills my soul as I drift off to sleep.

During the night the rain begins to fall, washing 'The Capital' and the garden of the dead with bitter tasting drops. Morning dawned cold and grey as the relentless rain fell from the dense clouds above. The greyness of the new day is tangible to every sense, so dense and uncompromising it can be touched. Through the thick, damp air, a dark figure lurched with purpose through the gravestones towards the gates, his shabby coat and trousers receiving a soaking from the long grass as he goes. In the distance, the growing sound of traffic can be heard and the clatter of unloading delivery vehicles punctuates the omni-present grey of the local morning air.

Chapter 2

Less than a second after he had pushed the 'start' button the BMW 650's powerful engine growled into life. The clinical fluorescent lights of the dull underground car park stroked the gleaming body of the sports car as it negotiated the turns and ramps that would bring it to the surface. Grand office buildings line the broad street in stark contrast to the grim functionality of the subterranean parking facility. Abdul Hadi blinked in the early evening light as he emerged and pushed the nose of his car out into the traffic. He crept forward until there was sufficient road space under his tyres to pull legitimately out into the pedestrian-paced traffic flow.

Stop-start progress eventually brought his car to a more consistently flowing thoroughfare where Abdul relaxed a little. He hated the traffic in London and resented that he had to pay for the privilege of entering the central knot of congestion every day. He was convinced that London was the most vehicle unfriendly city in the world and would frequently hold forth his view at dinner parties and other social gatherings, much to the annoyance of his wife who would squirm with irritation in her seat when he turned to the subject towards his favourite social rant.

For a short distance, his BMW's velocity nearly reached thirty miles per hour before a string of red brake lights forced him to slow to a stop. As he sat fuming behind the wheel, Abdul consoled himself by considering the alternatives. Every time he returned home, complaining of the traffic his wife, Samira, would tell him that it was his own fault and that he should use The Tube. He tried to commute by public transport once and it had been a truly awful affair. Stinking unclean bodies all cramped together in a stifling metal box that rattled between juddering halts and erratic starts, throwing the passengers at each other. The experience had convinced him that, whilst driving in London was only marginally preferable to self-harming it was infinitely preferable to public transport.

His anxiety increased as he pulled forward towards the green traffic signal. On the island that anchored the lights, there was a group of teenaged Eastern Europeans armed with washing up liquid bottles and squeegee blades. They were waiting for the signal to turn red again when they would issue forth at pace to cover the windscreens of the waiting vehicles with soapy water, which they would scrape from the glass with their blades then stand begging for money from the drivers. He cursed when the vehicle before him refused to run the amber light. Abdul forced to stop, knew that he would have to prepare to repel the window washers.

Two young girls, eyes the colour and effervescence of highly polished mahogany, ran towards his big black sports car. They moved with forced enthusiasm from the traffic island, waving at Abdul and blowing him kisses. He waved his hands frantically signally his unwillingness to purchase their services. One of the girls, who could have been no more than fourteen years old, stood by the driver's side window and made begging motions towards him, petite olive skinned hands extending from between her already ample breasts, in a flamboyant pose of utter submission. As he gesticulated and shouted "no thank you", the other child sprayed his windscreen with soapy water.

Frustrated by their actions and pleasant refusal to comprehend his clearly articulated wishes, Abdul activated his windscreen wipers just as the young girl leaned over with her squeegee, causing her to jump backward in alarm. Her sudden movement drew the attention of two older boys who watched over the younger children. They looked at each other briefly, as if to confirm their air of menace, before advancing towards the BMW where Abdul sat rigidly clutching the steering wheel studiously peering at the traffic lights.

Much to Abdul's relief the light array changed to indicate green, "come on, come on, come on you son of a dog" he muttered as the car in front of him slowly pulled away. He stared straight ahead until he was clear of the lights and the occupants of its island, then glancing in the rear view mirror he saw the youths staring after him and the children dodging through the traffic back to their island base. Relieved for the moment but only too well aware that he would have to face the same ordeal on the following day, he settled into the relatively comfortable remainder of his commute.

Climate control set to the optimum level for the weather conditions, Beethoven's Ninth on the sound system and the traffic now flowing freely enhanced Abdul's mood. He loved his car, its sumptuous leather interior made an unequivocal statement of refinement whilst the eye-watering performance it could conjure up would excite a corpse. It was almost with regret that he pulled the vehicle off the leafy residential road onto his drive.

Parking the car behind his wife's Mercedes, he killed the engine and gathered his belongings from the cockpit before stepping out onto the gravel drive and locking the car door. He walked to the front door, each step accompanied by the snow crunch noise of the gravel moving to accommodate every footfall. The familiar sound, issuing from under his feet, filled him with the warmth that only home could bring.

Tree Tops was a beautiful house, Abdul had bought it three years previously when Samara was heavily pregnant with Aesha. His wife occasionally reminisced about their city apartment, which had overlooked The Thames, but he never thought about it. He was much happier in this extensive and well-appointed house with its driveway, six bedrooms, five bathrooms, three reception rooms and large mature garden. This was a home suitable to raise children in and a city centre apartment was not.

An impressive house in a well-regarded neighbourhood of North London, was not an inconsiderable purchase. To buy the house, he had raised what he could from the sale of the apartment and borrowed from his father to gather together fifty five percent of the purchase price. Shari'ah law prohibited the payment or acceptance of interest fees for the lending or acceptance of money. His father's loan would be free of charge and so quite acceptable however, in order to raise the additional funds he required to buy the house, he had utilised a Murabaha. This had not been difficult as he arranged it through the bank that he worked at and after all, arranging acceptable funding for house purchases was his own area of expertise.

A Murabaha is an arrangement where an Islamic Bank will purchase the house at the agreed price and then sell it to the client at a higher price. The client would pay part of that higher price upfront, in Abdul's case fifty five percent, and pay the remainder with monthly instalments spread over a number of years. In this way the transaction was compliant with Shari'ah Law, the bank made a profit and adequate funding was provided to the observant. It would have been possible to arrange the Murabaha with as little as thirty five percent of the price, fifty five percent was a significant amount of cash and represented all of the free liquid assets of both Abdul and his father. Both men reasoned that, as the cash was not required for any other pressing financial purpose, the family's interests were served best by realising the cost savings on the purchase price the bank would ask for Tree Tops.

Family was important to Abdul just as it was to the global Islamic community. Without the support of his family, he would never have achieved all that he had and for that reason, he would always honour his parents, siblings and extended family. The bedrock of any family is a man and a woman, together they form the steady hub around which children can flourish and the dynasty can grow. Even in the parts of The Islamic World where polygamy is accepted, the honour in those marital relationships must remain pure. From his early childhood, his mother had taught him to honour women and to be a good Muslim man. When he came to marry, his father had begged him on his knees the night before the ceremony to be a good Muslim and never to bring dishonour on the family again. With absolute purity in his heart, Abdul had helped his father to his feet, embraced him and promised to be a good Muslim.

In the large hallway, Samira stood on the authentic Agra rug, holding baby Zaynab in her arms. Her eldest daughter, Aesha, stood by her side clutching a small pink teddy bear. When Abdul stepped through the door Aesha ran forward to greet him with hugs and kisses. He swept her, shrieking delightedly, into his arms and kissed her warmly. His heart leapt and a tingling afterglow flowed out through his body as he looked into her perfectly sweet face. Shining back at him was unadulterated innocence and love, proof, if proof were needed, that Allah loves us all.

Joining his wife and youngest child on the rug he kissed them both and told all of his girls that he loved them deeply and that if Allah willed, he always would. "Allah always will, my beautiful husband" Samira stated confidently. "You know the mind of God, wife" mocked Abdul? He switched Aesha into his right arm and placed his left about his wife. She smiled at him adoringly and with a playfully faux coyness cooed, "of course not, light of my life".

Laughing together, they carried the children upstairs to their bedrooms where they rotated between the two, tucking them in and administering goodnight kisses. Once the girls settled with teddies and beakers of water, Abdul retired to the master bedroom to change and pray whilst Samira crept back down the staircase and walked through to the kitchen to prepare her husband's supper.

When he sat at the large country-style table in the kitchen, he relaxed and watched his wife as she brought their meal to the table. It had been an arranged marriage and his family had chosen well. Samira was a model wife and Abdul had grown to love her absolutely. She in return, had admired and grown to love Abdul with all of her heart, from the day of their marriage. Sitting by her husband she looked deep into his brown eyes and said simply "I love you", then without hesitation began to fill his plate. He thought about returning the declaration but decided against it as the moment could not be made more perfect than it was. She had not spoken those words seeking confirmation of any kind; it had been a simple statement of fact. He decided to bring her flowers when he returned from work the following day and tell her how much he loved her then.

As they ate together, she asked him for the details of his day and he in turn asked her for the day's news of his children and her plans for the following days. They discussed some domestic matters, she informed him that she had extended the hours of the domestic help in order to free up more of her time to focus on Aesha's education and that the first service was due on her car. He nodded his agreement knowing that it was only out of courtesy and respect that she shared this information with him, he made the money, she ran the house, that was the way of things and he would not have it any other way.

After dinner, Abdul sat in the lounge watching television whilst his wife loaded the dishwasher in the kitchen before joining him. When she sat by him on the large sofa, they took each other's hand and watched a film together in silence. Only when the film was finished did she speak "remember we have the family party on Sunday at your father's house". Almost startled by his wife's voice Abdul sat up and paused before replying, "yes I eh... had actually forgotten, do we have gifts to take"? She smiled at him then reassuringly patted his hand "yes Darling I bought them all last week". Visibly relaxing, he put his head on her shoulder and nuzzled her neck. Samira's hair smelt of jasmine, a scent he had come to associate with his wife and so indirectly with love, her familiar warmth comforted him as it oozed through their clothing to caress his skin. The giving of body heat, love and attention the bedrock of humanity and the truest gift that is shared, only in the purest of relationships. They sat peacefully content with their lot, passing the time until they prepared for bed.

Prior to climbing beneath the duvet together, they prayed in separate rooms. He begged forgiveness for cursing the other driver and gave thanks for his family. She gave thanks for her husband and children.

That night they made gentle love together for nearly twenty minutes until, satisfied, they lay on their respective sides of the bed. They stared at the ceiling whilst he gently played with her hair and softly recited a love poem, some tale of adoration from one, long dead, lover to another.

After blessing each other's sleep they lay on their sides facing away from the centre of the bed. She thought of her hopes for her daughters and he thought of his desire for a son, then sleep took them both.

Chapter 3

Rising early, as he always did on a workday, Abdul had showered, prayed and dressed even before Zaynab roused from her slumber to call her mother with needy cries. Dressed in her house robe Samira brought her children downstairs to their father who sat drinking coffee in the kitchen. "You know that you should not drink that" she chided him cheerfully as Aesha toddled to him and began to try climbing onto his lap. She sat by the table, pulled her right breast from the robe and presented it to Zaynab "shall I fix you herbal tea instead"? Lifting Aesha onto his lap he grumbled "no thanks" to his wife then changed his tone as he smiled at Aesha "how is Daddy's little angel this morning?" She stuttered through her limited morning vocabulary to confirm that she was in good spirits.

"Busy day today darling" she asked Abdul once her youngest child had latched and began to suckle hungrily? "Not especially but we lose two hours to the mosque today so we will have to work that bit harder to catch up" he replied gloomily then leaned away from his daughter as he took a gulp of his coffee. "Now now you should not say it in such a way" she reprimanded her husband. "I know sorry darling, I'm just not a great morning person, as you know and I am really not looking forward to this party on Sunday". She smiled indulgingly at him then turned her attention to the baby in her arms and looked adoringly down at Zaynab, still suckling away.

He sighed heavily then spoke to his wife again "you know that I always enjoy seeing my parents and my brothers but I just do not want to listen to Uncle Mohammed banging on about 'back to basics' Islam and how wonderfully pious his sons are. God I hope they will not be there". Her attention now returned to her husband "who?" she enquired. "Al qasim and Abrahim they bore me without even trying and despite my promise to God and you I cannot stop hating Al qasim" he muttered rather huffily with an edge of darkness. "They will be there and you will be polite to them," she said rather sternly, then blushing slightly she returned her attention to the infant on her breast. He lifted the coffee mug once again and muttered into it "suppose" before draining the last of the warm bitter beverage and replacing the mug on the table.

Kissing Aesha on the forehead he lifted her down from his lap then standing he adjusted his cufflinks and tucked his shirt tightly into the top of his trousers. "Are you leaving now," asked Samira as she looked up at him? "Yes darling" he said to his wife before looking to Aesha and explaining, "Daddy needs to earn pennies for us all". She toddled about the kitchen asking her mother for something to eat "yes darling once Zaynab has had her breakfast" her mother answered, then raised her face to receive Abdul's kiss. He then bent over his wife and kissed Zaynab, who continued to enjoy her breakfast and refused to be distracted by her father's attention. Pulling his jacket on he called "I love you all" as he headed for the front door with Samira calling "we love you too" after him.

Walking quickly through the rain to his car, Abdul activated the remote unlocking mechanism and pulled the driver side door open. He removed his jacket and placed it on the passenger seat as he slipped behind the wheel. The start button brought the coupé to life and Abdul selected drive on the automatic gear box, tuned the radio to Radio 4 then released the parking break and eased his right food off the break peddle.

Effortlessly the black BMW accelerated away from the leafy suburb into the ever-thickening commuter traffic. Within the hour, Abdul manoeuvred his car into his designated parking space beneath The Albion Islamic Bank. Locking his car door remotely, he waved at some colleagues who had also just completed their morning drive to work and walked towards the elevator.

After running the gauntlet of morning greetings, he gained the privacy of his own office. When he unlocked the drawers of his desk he retrieved his laptop from the top drawer and fitted it into the docking station on his desk then turned it on. Taking advantage of the time that the machine took to start up he left his office to bring back a plastic beaker of chilled water from the water cooler. His standard day began with this routine followed by him logging-on and checking his e-mail. Just like all of the senior staff at the bank, he carried a

Blackberry but tried never to look at his inbox outside of working hours.

Abdul Hadi had worked at The Albion Islamic Bank for nearly eight years and had risen rapidly from a junior position to Head of Domestic Property Funding. The bank was bucking recent trends in the financial services industry by enjoying growth in both revenues and profits.

Islamic financing pre-dated capitalism and was, for a number of years, almost eradicated when the Europeans dominated trade throughout the known world and then the years of Empire that occupied all Islamic lands. From the seventeenth century of the Common Era, Westerners had ruthlessly promoted capitalism at the expense of any human ethics. This approach was contrary to the values of Islam, which forbade certain commercial activities because of the potential they presented for exploitation. Primarily the Qur'an proscribed 'riba', generally accepted to be interest; the charging of a set amount of premium on capital lent to others. The practice of money lending, considered intolerably prone to the exploitation of the borrower by the lender, was therefore prohibited.

With the large-scale migration of Muslims to North America and Europe a need for a Shari'ah compliant banking services was established. The near catastrophic banking crises of the Eighties and early Nineties increased the desire for a more ethical banking system and from there a large market for Islamic Banking grew in the Western World.

Idiotic lending and greed led to the creation of a perverse property market in The UK and many other Western Countries. Feeble-minded house purchasers paid ridiculously over-inflated prices for their homes in the dual and equally erroneous beliefs that property would always increase in value and that their own wealth would increase with it. When cheap easy lending disappeared with the exposure of The Western Banking World's greedy and shabby practices, the deluded homeowners and the unsuspecting taxpayers paid the price. It was now a boom time for Abdul and his colleagues in the domestic property Islamic finance industry, as they had not been tarnished by the malfeasance of their Capitalist counterparts.

Recent clients of Abdul were of a greater eclectic nature than they had ever been. He counted Christians, Muslims, Zoroastrians and Hindus amongst those he recently helped purchase their homes. With very few exceptions, a Murabaha or an Ijana agreement could fulfill their needs. The properties purchased, varied from a two bedroom flat in Ealing to a twenty eight million pound mansion on Bishop's Avenue.

As midday approached, the office began to empty. The faithful from all over The City descended on the Whitechapel Road, to join in Friday prayers at the mosque. Abdul enjoyed the walk, the feelings of brotherhood increasing as the pedestrians about him became increasingly Muslim and all moving in the same direction.

When he came within sight of the mosque, his left foot slid in something and he had to react quickly to avoid falling over. He had been too wrapped up in his own thoughts to notice the repetitive pattern of rapid side steps ahead of him in the pedestrian traffic. He therefore was not aware of the hazard before he placed his foot in the dog turd on the pavement. The schadenfreude experienced by his fellow Muslims, who passed on their procession to the mosque, was almost tangible. He surveyed the immediate vicinity of the incident whilst trying to establish the best recovery strategy.

According to Muslim tradition, dogs are unclean animals and Abdul had always subscribed to that tradition. He was upset about the dog shit incident and stood for several minutes scraping the sole of his shoe on the edge of the curb before continuing his progress to prayer. When he arrived at the mosque, he gingerly removed his shoes then went inside to join his observant brothers.

Walking back to the office, he considered the English and their peculiar love of dogs. It appeared to him that most natives did not consider a family complete without a dog. The Government had tried to tackle the problem of dogs fouling the public areas of the wider community by passing laws designed to force owners to clean up after their animals. Unfortunately, there remained a significant hardcore who actively sought to avoid their social, legal and hygiene responsibilities.

Curiously, this love affair with canines was not class dependent, as many things were in England. The overweight shaven-headed Saxons, driving the streets of London in their vans, loved the animals just as much as their Norman overlords did. The conquering classes preferred to employ their hounds, usually in some unnecessary pursuit of prey where their social underlings had no purpose for the animals save to sleep, eat, walk and defecate.

Chapter 4

Detective Inspector Mac Gregor took nearly an hour to hand over the case to his Sergeant. It was a relatively straightforward case involving stolen goods and illegal drugs. They were close to a result and Detective Sergeant Willox was more than capable of completing the work however, Mac Gregor wanted to ensure that every detail was covered before he left to concentrate on a priority incident. Willox sat listening, with obvious irritation, to his boss as he ran through the familiar details of the case. He liked Mac Gregor and knew him to be an excellent detective but he occasionally frustrated him with his pedantry nature.

Once he was satisfied that he had covered everything, and conscious of the time, Mac Gregor took his leave from his relieved subordinate and headed for the car park. He opened the passenger door and climbed into the vehicle. Detective Sergeant Thomas Gayle sat behind the steering wheel waiting for him.

"Morning Tommo," Mac Gregor delivered in his customary gruff manner.

"Morning Guv, we ready for the off then?"

"Aye let's go have a wee look see at this crime scene".

The unmarked vehicle left the compound and was immediately caught up in the usual crawling traffic of The Capital.

"Fuck this, hit the blues and twos," commanded Mac Gregor.

Without a word, Tommo activated the covert blue lights and two-tone siren and the surrounding traffic awkwardly began to edge out of their way.

As they repeatedly accelerated and decelerated through the crawling vehicles Mac Gregor pulled a cigarette pack from his jacket pocket and fished about for his lighter in the same pocket.

"Sorry Guv, no smoking in these cars now," Tommo cautioned his senior officer.

"You're no gonna tell anyone are yea," Mac Gregor said as he placed a cigarette in his mouth and cracked the car window open.

"Guv I don't smoke and I hate the habit," persisted Tommo.

Perceiving his companions resolve, the senior officer removed the cigarette from his mouth, placed it back into the packet and closed the window. He placed the pack back into his jacket pocket and then turning in his seat, Mac Gregor fixed Tommo with a constant gaze and farted loudly.

"There, I take it that's no been banned yet?"

They continued the journey in silence, DS Gayle trying to breathe through his mouth, occasionally gasping air from the clean stream blowing in through his now fully open window. He was confident that they both knew as little as each other about the priority case, to which they had been rapidly seconded. Turning onto the, usually pedestrian thoroughfare of the retail area, they drove to the collection of other emergency services vehicles clustered about the entrance to a small service road and parked the car. Leaving his window open Tommo immediately killed the engine and leapt from the interior, relieved to plunge into the relatively fresh air free from the rancid gaseous residue of Mac Gregor's last meal.

Mac Gregor introduced himself and his Sergeant to the uniformed Officer that stood by the tape marking the boundary of the crime scene then ducked under the tape, obligingly lifted by uniformed officers to allow them to pass. Inside the taped cordon was a white nylon tent where white suited Scenes of Crime Officers busied themselves gathering what available evidence there was.

Recognising the Coroner, Mac Gregor walk directly to him and greeted him.

"Mr Collins what have we got?"

"Ah Inspector Mac Gregor, have they given this one to you then?"

"Aye for my sins they have taken me off my other case and dropped me in for this one. This is Detective Sergeant Gayle he is my side-kick for this show."

"Well Mac Gregor they like to give you the strange ones don't they?"

"Aye I might start to take it personally if this continues. What have we got then?"

"White female found dead this morning in there. Preliminary examination suggests she was killed by several blows to the back of the head with a heavy instrument similar to a hammer."

"Was it a prolonged attack?"

"No I don't think so, she had been struck about five times but due to the severity of the blows I would say she was unconscious by the third or fourth blow and she will have subsequently died no more than five minutes after that."

"Can you give us an approximate time of death?"

"Well rigor has passed and judging by her pallor and blood coagulation I would say she died probably about two or three o'clock this morning."

"Any sexual interference?"

"She does have her underwear pulled down to her ankles and her skirt has been raised to her waist. The patterns in the blood would suggest that the body was moved to leave it in the rather revealing pose in which it was found. There is however, no indication of rape or sexual assault. I will be able to say for certain once I have had a chance to examine the body back at the morgue."

"Anything else you can tell us at his stage?"

"Not really, I've taken blood samples and will have the preliminary report ready by tomorrow."

"Well thanks for your help Mr Collins, I look forward to your report."

Nodding his farewells, the Coroner passed the two Detectives and headed for his car. Mac Gregor watched him go then turned to his Sergeant "let's go have a look then". They walked the short distance to the white tent and pulled the door flap aside. Their entrance drew the fleeting attention of the Officers working inside.

The victim lay on her back, dark empty eyes staring unseeingly at the canopy of the tent. A dark corona of drying blood framed her head and shoulders in crimson. Her knees were wide apart revealing the ashen white flesh of her shaved pubic area. Further into the recessed doorway, there were sprays of dark blood on the walls and ground. Approximately

24

three feet from where the body lay, there was a large damp patch on the grey paving slabs and a semi-liquid pile of faeces.

"Christ" remarked Tommo once he had taken in the scene. Mac Gregor scanned the area with cold eyes and without expression, he focussed his attention on the clothing and blood stains. Her hand was the colour of lilies; it lay across her chest like some Victorian actress, in a posed faint, the deep orange of her wedding band contrasting with the deathly pallor of her flesh. The dead girl had been a pretty girl probably in her early thirties with a slightly chubby, not unattractive figure.

The senior Scene of Crime Officer introduced himself to Mac Gregor and Tommo.

"Inspector Mac Gregor, Tommo you two working on this one then?"

"Aye we are Charlie. What you got for us?"

"You spoken with Collins Sir?"

"Aye just had a wee chat outside. What can you add?"

"There are no signs of robbery, her bag is lying over there and appears to be complete with money and cards. Despite her pose Collins does not think she has been raped or interfered with."

"He also said that the body was moved after the attack."

"Yes, judging by the shape of the wounds and the blood patterns over here by the fire escape she was struck from behind and collapsed onto her hands and knees where she was struck again and dropped face first onto the ground where she was struck at least once more. She was then dragged shortly after the attack to the position she was found in."

"What is that," Mac Gregor asked as he indicated the faeces with a jutting of his chin?

"Probably hers, the first blow will have caused a loss of control both to the bladder and bowel."

"Poor wee girl, life and dignity lost. Was her clothing adjusted after she was moved?"

"I don't think so, there is some blood on her underwear which probably got there as she was being moved. Her skirt only has blood stains that have soaked down as she

25

was laid on her back and shows no signs of being pushed up into the blood pool. Additionally there is no trace of faeces on her undergarments."

"Are you saying she had her knickers round her ankles and her skirt up round her waist before she was attacked?"

"Yes that is what I believe happened."

"What evidence have you found?"

"There are some partial footprints in the blood and that is about it."

"Did she fight back?"

"Don't think she got the chance."

"Not a lot to go on then."

"This whole scene is a nightmare, obviously popular with local lovers, there are several used condoms lying about, numerous cigarette ends and when the lovers are not here others use it as a public toilet."

"Ok let's get this wrapped up as soon as possible then we can pull everything together back at the station. Thanks for your help Charlie."

"Come on Tommo let's take a wee look around the wider area."

Standing outside the tent, Mac Gregor lit a cigarette, stared upwards at a multi-storied car park, and exhaled a long stream of smoke. Tommo walked over to the industrial wheelie bins opposite the white tent then standing between two bins looked back towards Mac Gregor. "Good vantage of that doorway from over here" Tommo called to his senior Officer. Mac Gregor wandered over to his Sergeant whilst he concentrated on his cigarette, then as he stood in front of him asked:

"Why would a bonnie wee thing like that be standing aboot in a piss stained doorway wae her knickers roond her ankles and why would some psycho bash her heid in wi a hammer?"

"I don't know Guv, maybe she was under duress when she was taken there, pervert or jilted boyfriend?"

"Maybe Tommo, there is a story here and it's oor job tae piece it together. C'mon let's get back tae the station and see whit we can find oot aboot the victim."

They returned to the tent and took the woman's handbag and the contents of her pockets away in plastic evidence bags before climbing into the car and beginning the journey back to the station. Again, the men sat in silence, this time content to sit in the slow moving traffic as they collected their thoughts. Mac Gregor considered his approach to the case; he concluded that the first item on the agenda should be to find out as much as possible about the victim. It did not take Sherlock Holmes to deduce the key to this case would lie in her private life. Sergeant Gayle drove the vehicle with deliberate purpose and thinly disguised excitement at the prospect of working on a potentially high profile murder case, this had the potential to put him 'on the map' and promote his career, both professionally and politically.

Chapter 5

Mac Gregor's gruff deadpan demeanour served him well in his professional life. At work he was a hard man to know, constantly cynical and seemingly detached from all individuals, victims, colleagues or perpetrators. No matter how dreadful the events he uncovered or experienced, he refused to reveal any emotion. At home, he was a loving husband and father who focussed his care onto his family with absolute diligence. He always compartmentalised his life, finding things easier to deal with if boundaries were clearly defined and the relevant demons and angels were segregated.

Early in their relationship, Mary McGregor had learned not to ask her husband about his work. Mac Gregor never discussed the cases he was working on at home; he never allowed those two worlds to meet. In his modest bungalow, he had led a quiet life with Mary for over twenty years, watching television, eating his meals and enjoying the occasional glass of single malt. They had lived in the house since their first daughter had been born; she had left home and married a pleasant enough lad who worked in IT. Their youngest daughter, now eighteen, lived with them for the present however, she was planning to leave later that year, to go to university.

It was a comfort to him; those close to him at home were fully apart from the ugliness of the world that he knew in his professional life. With those he loved safely cocooned in his mind, Mac Gregor could focus on his job.

A room was allocated at the station, to serve as the investigation's base, the Incident Room, and a team of detectives detailed to assist Mac Gregor to find the murderer. The previous occupants had left loose papers and empty coffee cups littering the room. Inspector Mac Gregor and Sergeant Gayle wandered through the debris for a moment before the senior man told Tommo: "get someone to tidy this mess up".

Occupying the office attached to the Incident Room, Mac Gregor sat behind the desk and began to sift through the evidence that they had removed from the scene of crime. He then made telephone calls to various departments to order the support he would need for the case. When he had finished he replaced the handset and returned to the Incident Room where a cleaner and Tommo were gathering all the rubbish from the desks into black bin bags.

"Right Tommo, oor victims name is Shirley Babcock. She is not known tae us and we are waiting for a National Database check to come back. We have an address where she lived wi her husband and daughter let's get started by talking tae her husband."

"Ok Guv, has he been informed?"

"Yes uniform visited him this morning."

Together they walked from the room with renewed purpose.

It was a modest two bedroom terraced house in a non-descript suburb. They sat in the car observing the neighbourhood. The entire area looked as though it had been built all at once, back in the nineteen seventies. Uneven and broken paving slabs with blades of grass growing from between them constituted the narrow pavement that separated the front door from the kerb. Half-bare trees clustered in back gardens visible from the road. Functional brick boxes, provided shelter for young families, old people and the occasional middle aged families or couples for whom life had not delivered its initial promise. No birdsong could be heard over the constant racket of screaming children and barking dogs. Mac Gregor broke the silence "come on let's go".

As they climbed from the car they became aware of the attention their presence had drawn from the neighbours, many were staring as they deposited bin bags into the wheelie bins parked outside of their houses, others gazed from beyond net curtains. In his usual brusque manner, Mac Gregor strode up to the front door and pressed the doorbell for what seemed to Tommo an unnecessarily long time. He stood back from the door and fished in his jacket for his warrant card, his Sergeant following suit.

The door opened to reveal a man dressed in a tracksuit, his face was drawn with eyes that looked like they had been dowsed in vinegar, red and raw.

"Mr Babcock," enquired Mac Gregor in his most detached voice?

Without looking at the proffered Warrant cards, the man simply said with absolute resignation, "you had better come in" and stood away from the door, leaving the Police Officers to close it behind them.

On the floor, a small child was playing with a plastic lorry and small plastic figures. She looked up with curiosity at the strange men that had just entered the room with her father. Struggling to her feet, she tottered towards Tommo holding one her plastic toys towards him and chattering excitedly. "Hello there, what's that?" he condescended to the child. Her father checked her progress by swinging her up into his arms where he held her tight and kissed her cheek. The child giggled and struggled to release herself, but her father held her firmly to him.

"Are you Mr Charles Babcock?"
"Yes I am."
The man replied as he sat on a threadbare and stained armchair with his daughter on his lap.

"Is there someone you can call to look after your daughter," asked Tommo?
"I won't let her go, I need her right now."
The Police Officers exchanged vexed glances. Mac Gregor then informed Babcock that they were going to interview him about his wife's death and that Sergeant Gayle would be taking notes. Babcock nodded his acceptance then indicated a sofa that matched his armchair for them to sit on. Whilst the officers sat down he turned the television on and selected a channel showing children's programmes. The child's attention drawn completely to the screen, she sat on the carpet where her father placed her and began to watch quietly.

"I am Detective Inspector Mac Gregor and this is Detective Sergeant Gayle, it is our job to find out what happened to your wife."
Mac Gregor would annunciate carefully when speaking with members of the public, not wishing his Scots accent to hinder the communication.

"She was murdered wasn't she?"
"It is too early tae say until we have the Coroner's report."

"I know she has been murdered, if it were an accident or natural causes I would have been told already."

"Our condolences for your loss."

"Just get the bastard that did this."

"We may have to ask you to come down to the station at a later date to take a statement but I would like to ask you some preliminary questions for now, if you feel up to it?"

"Ok."

"Do you know where your wife went last night?"

"No, she said she was out with her friend Jodi but I called her today and she said that she had not seen her for over a week."

"We will need to speak to Jodi. Do you have an address for her?"

"Yes."

"Sergeant Gayle will take a note of the address when we have finished. Do you know why she might have lied about where she was going?"

"No. We trusted each other and I have no idea why she would do that."

"Did she often go out without you?"

"Maybe once every two weeks with her friends."

"Would you be able to give us a list of her friends?"

"Yes I can but I have spoken with them all on the telephone this morning and they all say they did not see her last night."

"Would any of them have any reason to lie about seeing her last night?"

"Not to my knowledge."

"Do you have any idea or suspicion why she would not tell you the truth about her whereabouts last night?"

"None whatsoever, maybe she was having an affair."

"Did you have reason to believe she was having an affair?"

"No I did not but it does seem like a possibility now."

"If she were, who would you suspect she was seeing?"

"No-one I know, probably one of her mates off the internet."

"She used the internet a lot then?"

"Every night, when she wasn't out that is."

"How did she access it?"

"When she was here on her laptop and she has one of those fancy i-phone things."

"Do you use the internet."

"No never really seen the point. If I want to chat to someone I go down to the pub and have a few pints with my mates."

"Is that what she used the internet for, to chat to people?"

"Yes all the time she was never off the bloody thing. I could hardly get a word out of her when she was on-line."

"Do you know who she chatted with on-line?"

"Not really, she just said it was her mates and old friends from school etcetera."

"We will have to take her laptop away with us, do you have it here?"

"Yeah it's there by the side of the sofa."

"Has there been anything strange about her behaviour lately?"

"No nothing, she was the same old Shirley."

"Do you know of anybody who bore her a grudge or would want to hurt her?"

"Not a soul, as far as I was concerned she did not have an enemy in the world."

"Ok thank you for that you have been very helpful Mr Babcock. May I take a look at your wife's personal documents and belongings whilst you give Sergeant Gayle the information about her friends that we require?"

"Sure but she didn't keep a diary or anything like that, all her stuff is in drawers by her side of the bed and her clothes are in the top three drawers of the chest in our bedroom and hung up in of the wardrobe."

"May I have a look?"

"By all means, she slept on the left of the bed, go up and have a look."

Mac Gregor took his leave and climbed the narrow staircase that lead from the front room to the next floor of the house. Tommo drew Mr Babcock's attention to providing the list of his wife's friends and their details. The child, peering at the television, giggled, strange little creatures were chasing each other about a garden. Happy for the moment, she was unaware that she would never see her mother again.

The furniture was all too large for the bedroom, its modest dimensions made even more constrictive by its oversized furnishings. Mac Gregor had to edge his way round the bed to the victim's side then donning a pair of latex gloves from his jacket pocket opened the top drawer. He found nothing unusual: some old perfume bottles; make up, tissues, hairbrush and assorted female paraphernalia. The small cupboard beneath the bedside drawer held a collection of lightweight literature produced exclusively for the female market and an old landline telephone, probably stored there as a backup to one currently in use.

Backing out of the narrow confine, he manoeuvred himself to the other side of the bed where there was only just enough space to open the wardrobe doors. There was a male suit and a jacket hanging on the left hand end of the rail. The rest of the space in the wardrobe was full of female clothing. She had an extensive wardrobe Mac Gregor thought to himself as he checked the top shelf for hidden boxes or files but there was nothing. He then turned his attention to the chest of drawers; each drawer stuffed with female clothing even the underwear drawer was difficult to open due to its bulging contents. Her underwear was all of a titillating nature. Mrs Babcock had clearly had a strong preference for pretty rather than functional underwear. Again, he found nothing that would suggest that she had something to hide, so closing the drawer with difficulty he left the bedroom and joined his sergeant downstairs.

Waving to the others to ignore him, Mac Gregor left the house and went to the car where he retrieved a large evidence bag and returned to the front room. Mr Babcock was just completing the list of information that they had asked for as Mac Gregor took the laptop from the side of the stained sofa and placed it in the bag. Then he waited for Tommo to conclude the information gathering before he spoke.

"That's all for now Mr Babcock, we will be taking this laptop with us and Sergeant Gayle will require a signature

33

from you for that, he will give you a receipt. Thank you for all your help so far."

"That's fine; just get the bastard who did this."

"We will do oor best. Just one last question for now, did you and your wife go out much together?"

"No hardly ever, not since our little one arrived. I see my friends down at the local and she would go out with her friends."

"Ok sorry to have troubled you, we will be in touch if we need any more information."

Inspector Mac Gregor paused by the front door then turned to Charles Babcock.

"I am sorry to have to ask you this but I am afraid it is important, where were you last night?"

"I was here all night looking after my child."

He replied steadily as he returned the policeman's piercing gaze. With calm determination Mac Gregor pressed on.

"Can anyone else verify that Mr Babcock?"

"No inspector, because my wife was not here, she was elsewhere as you know, but I can tell you my little angel over there" he indicated his child with a nod of his head "would have missed me if I had been anywhere else."

As he nodded his head, Mac Gregor reminded him that they would have to speak to him again.

Both Policemen said their goodbyes to Mr Babcock and his daughter then returned to their car. Mac Gregor put the laptop into the boot of the car and joined Tommo as he started the engine.

"Well what do you make of that Guv?"

"She liked her clothes, the sort of clothes a woman wears for a man but she hardly ever went out with her husband. So the question in my mind is: who she was wearing those clothes for?"

They returned to the Incident Room in silence, both men deep in thought as they evaluated what they had learnt about Shirley Babcock and her life.

Chapter 6

The minicab navigated the seemingly endless domicile streets of provincial Greater London in the dark wee hours of the morning. On the back seat of the cab Richard and Becky locked in a passionate embrace, he had his arm about her and his hand down the back of her jeans whilst she rested her hand on his crotch, gently rubbing his erection. He explored the interior of her mouth with his tongue, occasionally stroking his free hand over her body and up to her breasts.

They had met that evening in a bar, she was out celebrating her friend's birthday with a group of females and he was out with his best friend, drinking and looking for likely sexual conquests. Becky had that 'available look' when she turned from her friends and surveyed the collective clientele of the establishment. Their eyes had met and to his satisfaction he had held her gaze long enough to confirm that she was interested. He moved confidently over the relatively small distance between them and asked, with a cheeky smile, if he could buy her a drink, she readily accepted and their liaison began.

After Richard had taken the pint of lager and the Pernod and Coke from the bar, the barmaid returned to the corner of the gantry where she resumed to her vigil. Every Friday night was the same, groups of intoxicated males and females would seek congress with each other. It was her role to feed their desires with a supply of alcohol on demand. The paired up lovers standing before the bar rarely looked suited and the number of familiar faces she saw each week pursuing the opposite sex, confirmed that few of the liaisons begun in that place would last more than one night.

It had not taken long for the conversation to reach a natural break which, supported by the furtive pre-ambling physical contacts, facilitated the first kiss. First oral contact was a gentle brushing kiss on the lips initiated by him, this was reciprocated by Becky with longer contact that invited him to push is tongue through her yielding lips. Most of the remaining evening spent entwined with each other; his

35

protective arms about her and his hands constantly gravitating to the curvature of her buttocks. She leaned in closely to him and thrilled at the pressure of his erect penis through their clothing.

During the brief periods when they were not passionately kissing, they exchanged the edited facts of their lives and he would check his mobile telephone. Becky told him that she was a single mother, who worked in an office and lived in her own place further out towards The London Orbital but for tonight, she was staying at her mother's house. Richard told her that he was a plumber who lived with a housemate near where she lived and that he was single.

When the evening's festivities came to an end, the clientele of the bar issued out onto the street and began to disperse. Becky spoke with her friends to confirm that it was okay to leave her, as she would get a taxi with her newfound beau. Richard stood by her side with his arm around her checking his 'phone. With vicarious excitement and faux concern, her friends said their goodbyes and set off into the night.

After several minutes of kissing and groping, they formulated their plan for homeward travel. With his hand down the back of her jeans where he played with the large lacy knickers she wore, Richard suggested that they get a taxi together. They could have the driver drop her at her mother's house then take him onto his home. Becky readily agreed to the plan and with their arms about each other, they walked drunkenly to the taxi rank.

Her friends were at the front of the queue for taxis and there were several groups, mainly couples, between them and her friends. Becky's friends shouted hellos and encouragement from the front of the queue then turned into each other and giggled before turning their attention outward again, towards their friend and the man she had found. Eventually, much to Richard's relief, a minicab came and drove the cackling Harpies away. Left alone in the line of people they passed the time kissing and caressing until a cab was at their disposal.

Changing gear the minicab pulled into a cul-de-sac lined with neat houses and then pulled up in front of a bungalow. They parted their lips from each other and she spoke quietly as she looked him in the eye, "well this is me." He leaned towards her and asked,

"Am I not even getting invited in for a coffee?"

Through an affected coy smile, she chided, "it's not coffee you really want is it?"

It was his turn to smile.

"No, I guess not".

"Remember this is my mum's place so you will have to be quiet and quick."

"I will be, promise."

She pulled the leaver to open her door and began to climb out as Richard leaned forward to the taxi driver.

"Here's twenty mate, wait for me," Richard instructed as he handed over a note, checked his mobile and then pushed the cab door open.

Giggling together, they rushed towards the front door as quietly as they could. Becky opened the door and pushed through into the interior where she pacified the excited Springer Spaniel, roused by their arrival. Richard followed her indoors and closed the door behind him. Leading him by the hand, she led him to the spare bedroom and stealthily shut the door, turned on the light and kicked off her shoes. Shrugging her jacket off, she cast it onto the chair in the corner and dumped her handbag onto the bed. She lay on the bed whilst Richard checked his watch and the screen of his mobile telephone before throwing his jacket on top of hers and joining her on the bed.

Kissing her passionately, he fumbled at the buckle of her belt until she assisted him to release it and undo the front of her jeans. Kneeling by her side, he pulled down her blue jeans and black knickers until she was able to kick her feet out of them. She lay with her naked bottom half on full display and her top half fully clothed. He manoeuvred his head between her thighs where he lapped hungrily at her pussy. She smelt a little musty and vaguely of sweat, Richard recognised and ignored the distinct taste of urine as he pleasured his conquest. He toiled with his tongue and thought smugly to himself, 'this will be one to share with the boys how he fucked the girl he picked up that night, in her mother's house whilst his taxi waited outside for a quick getaway'.

Becky rested her hands on his head where she stroked the soft, closely cropped hair and pushed her crotch up into his face. A warm, moist tingling spread through her groin from her clitoris. The sensation intensified when he inserted his fingers and probed for her 'G' spot. She always enjoyed sex when her men went down on her. It gave a positive indication that he was a lover who aimed to please her as well as himself. Conscious of the time and her immediate accommodation arrangements, she reluctantly pulled his face up towards hers then kissed his wet mouth before undoing his trousers.

When she pulled his boxer shorts down to his knees, she marvelled at his impressive penis, standing fully to attention before her. Congratulating herself on her choice, she pulled her hand down the length of his cock several times before fishing in her handbag for a condom.

"Here wear this," she told Richard as she handed him the small foil package. Pulling herself to the centre of the bed, she rested on her elbows with her legs wide apart and watched him.

With his trousers and pants about his knees, he jumped onto the bed and lay next to her, showing off his bare erection. She moaned in sexually excited admiration of his tool and made her hips writhe as if he were already inside her. He waited as long as he could before it became apparent that she was not going to return the compliment of oral sex then fitted the condom. Taking his manhood in her left hand, she reached out to Richard with her right and pushed his shoulder back onto the bed. Then cocking her leg she straddled his groin and positioned the tip of his cock between her labia.

Pressing down with her hips, she felt the glorious sensation of him filling her, he felt even larger that he had looked. Inward panic rose until with reluctant relief she felt her backside pressing onto his loins. She began gradually pulling and pushing her pelvis as he slid in and out of her, his hands rubbing her flanks and thighs, then with practiced skill pushing her smock top up over her breasts and undoing the bra clip with one hand he freed her tits. She leant down to him and they kissed passionately as their coitus continued, then she straightened her back and presented her breasts to his eager mouth as she held her top up out of the way. Holding both tits

38

in his hands from beneath the loose bra, he sucked alternatively on them, pulling as much of the glorious flesh into his mouth and teasing her erect nipples with his teeth and tongue. Their mutual excitement increased as did the pace of their lovemaking, he forced harder and longer into her as she slid her pelvis faster and faster over his groin.

Pumping her hard he felt his balls begin to tingle, then his sphincter tightened and the rushing relief of climax surged through him as he pushed himself all of the way into her. After orgasm he moved in and out of her slowly for a short while then, flopped her onto the bed next to him with a twist of his hips. She rolled onto her side and stroked his chest through his shirt. Richard removed the condom and checked his watch.

"What shall I do with this," he asked?

"Just leave it on the bed, I will get rid of it later," she answered softly.

He placed the condom on the bottom of the bed and raised his legs so he could retrieve his mobile telephone from his trouser pocket and check the screen for information.

"You've got a girlfriend, haven't you" asked Becky?

"What makes you say that," he countered?

"You've been checking your watch and 'phone all evening".

There was a pregnant pause until he answered.

"It's complicated."

Their mutual objective had been achieved, the purpose of the entire evenings courtship and flirtation fulfilled. They had satisfied their accumulated lust in a hurried and functional manner covered only with a thin veneer of affection. Standing up from the bed she pulled her trousers on and adjusted her smock, Richard followed suite when he struggled off the bed. Then with no exchange of telephone numbers or future arrangements made, they parted on the doorstep with a brief kiss. He swaggered off into the night to join his waiting taxi and she returned to the bedroom to dispose of the evidence and then to sleep.

Waiting for sleep to come, she lay in bed enjoying the wonderful feelings that promiscuity and inappropriate wildcat sexual behaviour aroused in her. It had been her intention from the early evening to finish the night with a man inside her and she had succeeded. Careful to wear a matching bra and knickers, her favourite perfume and to pack some condoms into her bag, she had prepared before leaving home. Tonight's result had not held any of the trappings of accepted sexual social behaviours: coffee, sofa seduction, coy retirement to the bedchamber, nakedness and lovemaking between the sheets. In reality, it had been marginally more sophisticated than it would have been in a toilet cubicle at the pub or a town centre alleyway. Becky did not care, in the morning she would report to the girls with all the sordid details of her conquest and to award him the 'good fuck' accolade to the audience of her friends, even though she had failed to reach climax herself.

Shortly before sleep took her, she considered what it was that really she sought and allowed herself a fleeting twinge of disappointment. Her shallow objective had achieved, though her cardinal need remained unfulfilled.

At ten o'clock the following morning, her mother opened the bedroom door to admit her three year old grandson. He cheerfully ran to the bed and climbed on to join his mother, waking her with shrill calls.

"Mummy, Mummy."

Through screwed up eyes and with a parched pallet, Becky croaked, "Morning Darling, how are you?"

Thomas snuggled into his mother and listened as his grandmother spoke with her.

"Are you getting up today, we have been up for hours?"

Ignoring the question, she spoke to her mother whilst keeping her attention on her son.

"Did he sleep well last night?"

"Yes, he did," her mother, replied rather pointedly.

She addressed the child, "Come on Darling let's get some juice and let mummy get ready."

Becky sat at the kitchen table, hair still wet from the shower, drinking her second cup of coffee in silence. Thomas was playing with a toy garage and cars in the front room whilst the dog ran backwards and forwards between the two occupied rooms. Her mother busied herself about the kitchen. Becky began to feel uneasy as she recognised her mother's behavioural pattern. Whenever she was worried or angry she would pretend to be, fully employed in seemingly innocuous tasks, usually in the kitchen. Avoiding the confrontation she gave the dog the attention that it was seeking, an act that only made her mother's activity all the more furious.

It was her way, to always avoid difficult conversations by pretending to be engrossed in some other activity. Her husband occasionally called her 'Jack', short for Stonewall Jackson. Her maiden name had been Jackson and he had identified this characteristic 'stonewalling' early in their relationship. It was also one of his favourite characters from American history, which was a subject, that he had a passing interest in as he had spent much of his earlier life in the USA.

Reluctantly recognising her mother's persistence, she decided to cease her 'stonewalling' and grasp the nettle, Becky spoke in a weary voice.

"Is something the matter Mother?"
Freezing mid-surface wipe, her mother leaned on the worktop and drew breath before spinning round to confront her daughter.

"Did you bring someone back here last night?"
Becky felt a hot glow rising up her neck towards her face.

"He just came back for a coffee, it was an old friend from work that I hadn't seen for ages and he gave me a lift home."
Furious at this lie, the older woman raised her voice.

"Don't lie to me Becky I heard you in the bedroom!"

"Yes I took him in there to show him some old photographs I have with me in my bag."
With obvious effort, her mother regained her composure to avoid drawing Thomas's attention from the other room before continuing.

"Don't treat me like an idiot! I heard exactly what you were doing in there and it wasn't looking through photo albums."

The silence that followed those sharp words was truly agonising, both mother and daughter frozen in rage and mortification respectively. The only action in the room was the witless dog scampering about seeking attention from either woman.

When eventually Becky composed herself, she spoke calmly and evenly in a clipped monotone.

"Are you going to tell Brian?"

Through controlled rage, the older woman explained.

"No, of course I am not going to tell him. I have to think of Thomas, the last thing in the world that I want to see is his Mummy and Daddy splitting up. You should think about that before you carry on like a drunken slapper. Your baby boy was sleeping in the room just across the hall. I brought you up better than that. I won't say anything this time but don't you dare do anything like that ever again in my home."

Hugging her rage to her chest, she waited for her daughter's response.

Realising that a defendable moral redoubt was beyond her grasp, Becky could only mumble apologies and issue the reassurances that her mother demanded. When some grudging acceptance was granted, she fled the house after rapidly packing her overnight bag and gathering her son from amid his toys on the front room carpet. She hurried to her blue Honda Civic, parked directly in front of the bungalow, and fitted her protesting child into the seat in the rear before getting behind the wheel. After bringing the machine to life, she slumped in the driver's seat and groaned to herself as she considered the damage the previous night's dalliance had done to her relationship with her mother. She did not regret the sex and even managed a little smile when she hazily recalled the events that had played out in the spare bedroom. Then engaging first gear, she pulled away to drive the few miles home.

She pulled the Civic over to the side of the road close to her home and checked her mobile telephone for the first time that day. It was on silent mode and the display told her that she had thirteen missed calls from her friends. For now her nosey friends could wait, she had a family to get back to. Deleting the call list, she returned the 'phone to her bag and completed her journey.

Brian sat in the armchair watching television. She was surprised that he was out of bed, left on his own for a night she would have expected him to be in bed nursing a hangover.

Thomas yelled "Daddy" and wriggled to be released from his mother's grip. She set him on the floor and he ran to his father, arms held up for love. Bending down he scooped his son into his arms, set him on his knee and smothered him in kisses.

"Good night last night Darling," enquired Brian?

"Yes not bad dear, the usual you know, girls complaining about their other halves."

"Well I hope you did not do too much complaining."

"What about you, my lovely husband? Never."

She smiled at him and kissed his cheek before sitting on the sofa and resting her overnight bag on the floor. Then looking over at them, she told her boys that she loved them both very much and that she had missed them. They both smiled back at her.

That evening she prepared the family meal and considered when she might manage her next illicit sexual encounter. She was never short of offers from randy men of all descriptions over the internet and anytime she went out with her friends she would 'pull', as in truth would any woman willing to give herself for gratuitous sexual satisfaction with no complications.

Brian was not a good husband and she did not love him but she had never been able to kick the habit of being his wife. There was a demon in her mind, 'Jack' refused to confront, she knew it was there and its origin; terrible insecurity and low self-esteem. Her reasoning for the 'stonewalling' was simple, others had caused her insecurity and so it was not the business of others as to how she chose to live her life. She would persist until she found what it really was that she was seeking.

Chapter 7

They took the Mercedes, it was the more practical choice when driving the children about. Abdul drove the car gently as Samira sat in the passenger seat, frequently turning round to check on the girls sitting on the back seat. This was the day Abdul had been dreading, the family party for which, his wife had prepared both him and their offerings. As he steered the car onto his father's drive he steeled himself for the ordeal to come, 'God please give me the strength to endure and bless me with peace in my heart when I meet him' he prayed to himself before bringing the vehicle to a complete halt. The engine fell silent and they began to arrange themselves before approaching the impressive front door of his father's home.

The expansive driveway was full of expensive quality motorcars, predominantly Mercedes and Lexuses.

"Looks like we are the last to arrive," Samira observed as she climbed from the passenger seat.

"Yup looks like the gang's all here," Abdul replied in a fake American accent. Samira giggled.

"I love you so much."

"I love you too," came his immediate response.

He moved to the rear door, opened it and ushered Aesha from the back seat. Once he had helped her down, she toddled a few paces on the gravel and waited for further instructions from either parent. When Samira had gathered up Zaynab and the bags full of equipment, required to support a child on the move, she swung her hips into the car door to close it and then as a family, they moved towards the front door.

Abdul's father answered the door with shouted blessings and welcomes, his arms wide to embrace his family. He embraced and kissed Abdul first, then Samira and Zaynab. With a bellowing call of faux surprise, he bent down and swept Aesha into his arms.

"Well what do we have here? A true princess if ever I have seen one."

Aesha giggled with joy and weakly kicked her legs as her grandfather smothered her with kisses and hugged her close.

"Come in, come in and welcome to my humble abode," the Patriarch commanded the dearest members of his tribe.

They squeezed past into the interior where Abdul remembered the gifts he had left in the boot of the car. With begging apologies, he took his leave and returned to the Mercedes at pace where he grabbed the large bag of gifts and returned to the, still open, front door. When he re-entered his father's house Uncle Mohammed was in the entrance hall with his sons.

Taking a deep breath Abdul adopted a broad smile and approached his relatives to greet them. "Uncle Mohammed, Al qasim and Abrahim blessings be on you, how are you all"? His relatives took turns to embrace Abdul and bless him as they did. Collectively Abdul's father ushered them all through to the main reception room announcing, "come, join the party" as he waved his arms about.

Dutifully they all wandered through to where the women and children had gathered. Samira and Abdul distributed the gifts they had brought and then took their seats on the comfortable furnishings of the room. Uncle Mohammed sat next to Abdul and smiled superciliously at him before surveying the assembled company in the room. Then with obvious satisfaction, he turned back to Abdul and spoke with his eyes closed.

"How is your family?"

"They are well, praise be to Allah."

Abdul replied courteously, even though his uncle's habit of talking with his eyes closed really irritated him.

"And have you considered marriages for you daughters yet?"

Again, with his eyes closed.

"Not yet uncle there is plenty of time for that."

"It is always best to seek a suitable husband as soon as you can, in my experience."

An unseeing Uncle Mohammed persisted.

He knew that he would have to ask for forgiveness when he prayed for the thoughts he instinctually felt when his uncle insisted on lecturing him. It was with great relief to Abdul when his uncle eventually finished his oratory and left to pick on some other unfortunate member of the family. When he judged it safe to follow his uncle, Abdul rose from the sofa and moved through the room chatting happily with his relatives. Everyone he spoke with congratulated him on his family. He watched Samira interacting with the others and her children playing among the children of his extended family and felt very proud, almost smug.

When eventually Abdul returned to his seat he found himself sitting next to Abrahim, the apple of Uncle Mohammed's eye.

"Hey, how are you Abrahim?"
He asked cheerfully. Abrahim paused as though collecting his thoughts and then turned to his cousin.

"How pure are your thoughts Brother?"

"Eh well, I am a good Muslim and I believe that me and my family are clean."
Abdul responded uncertainly.

"You live amongst the unclean does that not worry you?"
Abrahim stated with growing intensity.

"Well not really, you live amongst them too does that worry you?"

"Yes it does. I have been back to Pakistan, as you have, and met with great minds, minds that have shown me the light."
Abrahim's growing intensity unsettled Abdul and he immediately wanted to terminate the conversation. In order to extricate himself he opened his exit plan.

"Well that must have been good for you. I must go to speak with…"

"They are a filthy people, family means nothing to them, they are sexually promiscuous and they dishonour Allah."
Now feeling very uneasy Abdul eased himself off the sofa and moved away scattering a collection of platitudes in his cousin's direction as he went.

"Wow that Abrahim is a very intense individual," Abdul gasped as he found his wife in the kitchen.

"Yes but he is very observant and unlike his brother he is a good man," she cooed back to her husband.

46

"I know but he is hard work."

"You must be tolerant when dealing with family; it is the only way that all families stay together."

"I suppose," Abdul replied with his head down and hands in his pockets. Samira thought that he looked like a huffy schoolboy who had just been told that he had to play with his little sister.

"Look, cheer up and take this drink to your mother," she said as she handed him a glass of fruit juice.

He dutifully took the glass and left the kitchen.

Passing from the kitchen into the hallway Abdul found himself confronted by Abrahim who seemed to have been waiting for him. He felt a flush when he considered the prospect that Abrahim had overheard his conversation with Samira and found it difficult to hold eye contact with his cousin as he tried to manoeuvre past him in the relatively confined space of the passage. As he moved to his right Abrahim moved closer almost forcing him into the wall. They stood face to face, his cousin having successfully blocked his escape route. He felt very uncomfortable with the close proximity of his ambusher and was about to ask him 'what he thought he was doing' when Abrahim spoke.

"You love your family as do we all. The heart of our faith is our dedication and commitment to our families. We respect family and our women, they do not. They will fornicate at will, caring not for the costs to their families; they will divorce and leave mothers with children but no father. This is not our way and it is against the word of God. The Prophet Mohammed, peace be upon him, teaches us that this behaviour is an insult to God and those that insult God must die."

Feeling extremely uncomfortable, Abdul simply said, "excuse me," and tried to squeeze past his cousin but Abrahim moved to block him again. Speaking with his mouth only inches from Abdul's face:

"Are you listening to me brother?"

Al qasim's intervention was a welcome distraction for Abdul, even though he hated the man. His cousin proclaimed in a jocular manner "hey there Fire Brand let old White Eye go, he has no wish to hear you right now."

Without breaking eye contact Abrahim backed away sufficiently to allow his cousin to escape.

Without a word, Abdul walked quickly away to deliver the fruit juice to his mother. He was disturbed by the lecture he had just received and wondered if Abrahim was directly referencing Abdul's wild years when at university. Those were dark days and Abdul was not proud of them. He had been weak and had given himself to thoughtless pleasures, including alcohol and promiscuous people. He had, on occasion, paid for the pleasures of others' bodies and on equal occasion, simply seduced with alcohol and lies. Abdul feared that his cousin was working up to something. If he were to be plotting, the consequences were potentially devastating.

When Al qasim had used his old nickname 'White Eye' it had brought back memories of how his cousins had teased him as a child. The purpose of the name was to make a young Abdul feel like an outsider and that exclusion had upset him for many of his younger years. A 'White Eye' is a Middle Eastern slang term for a European and Abdul's lighter skin colour had made it easy for others to pick on him. It was maintained, by his hectoring cousins that Abdul would easily pass as a European and that perhaps there had been a mix up at the hospital when he had been born. "Who are you and what have you done with our cousin Abdul?" they teased him mercilessly.

His mother greeted him warmly as he entered the large ornately decorated room. Many of the younger women had gathered about the matriarch and sat demurely listening to the wise words that she bestowed on them.

"The light of my life and God's greatest blessing on me, my only son," she announced to the assembled then extended her hand to receive the glass that he held out to her.

"Abdul your father must speak with you. He is waiting for you in his office, so please do not keep him waiting," his mother instructed him and then returned her attention to the women in the room.

Taking the re-focus of her attention as his leave to depart the room, Abdul backed away from his mother and left, curious as to what gravity of matter could warrant his summons to his father's office.

The office was located on the first floor and was very much his father's domain. No one was allowed to enter the room without the Patriarch's express permission. The office was primarily used to run the family's financial interests and to hold court on matters that would affect any part of the family in a significant way. Abdul walked on the dense first floor hallway carpet to the door of his father's office, knocked and waited for permission to enter. He was about to knock again when his father's voice sounded from within "enter". To Abdul's surprise, he found his father sitting on one of the leather sofas opposite Uncle Mohammed. "Father, Uncle" he acknowledged before taking a seat on the sofa indicated by his father.

"What is this about is there some difficulty?"

"No not at all my Son. Mohammed has spoken to me on a matter that is of great importance and I believe that it is proper that you hear what has been said."

"I see."

Abdul positioned himself so that he could give his attention equally to both men. Uncle Mohammed closed his eyes and began to deliver his message:

"As you know Al qasim has been promised a bride from our homeland. Unfortunately, she has not been heard of since the earthquakes that destroyed much of her region. I have since been informed that her family acknowledge her death. This is why I have spoken with your father. We believe that it would be a positive thing for the family, if Aesha were to be betrothed to Al qasim."

Abdul was shocked by the content of his uncle's speech and disappointed by his father's willingness to consider the proposition. "She is only a child," Abdul protested as he gesticulated with his hands open towards them. She was still a baby in his eyes and it had never occurred to him that it was even remotely appropriate that such matters should be considered now or for the foreseeable future.

"It is wisdom that makes us consider this. Al qasim needs a wife and Aesha will need a husband. In a little over ten years we can send them home to be wed and our family will grow stronger."

Mohammed stated with complete conviction of his propriety.

"It is too soon." Abdul retorted in an absolute manner.

"If it is a question of dowry then I can…"

"Dowry has nothing to do with this I cannot believe what I am hearing she is barely past her third birthday."
Abdul interrupted his Uncle. The breach of protocol solicited an awkward silence that was only broken by his father's eventual intervention.

"Abdul we do not have to decide immediately. Matters such as this, are best considered with an open mind and with time to reflect. I ask only that you consider this and discuss it with me when you have had sufficient time to gather your thoughts."

After apologising to his uncle for the interruption Abdul took his leave and returned to the party where he wrestled with the problem of whether or not he should discuss the proposed arrangement with his wife. His greatest desire was to ignore the matter but he knew that neither his uncle nor his father would let it be forgotten. He went to the room where the children were playing and stood, watching his daughter happily engaged with a large soft toy that she threw on the floor and then jumped on top of it before rolling onto the carpet and repeating the action.

Chapter 8

It has always struck me as curious that, the closer people were to death the less sleep they seemed to need or want. Perhaps they feared that sleep was a state so close to death that dark hands could simply reach out and take them at will. From my vantage point, on the bench, next to the oak trees, in the local park, I watched the few dark hunched figures wandering in the mist of dawn with their dogs. Every one of my fellow early morning park patrons were well beyond retirement age.

Driven by the mission of redemption, revealed to me during the previous night in the song of The Willow Monks, I had issued forth from the garden of the dead earlier than was my custom. Through the grey wet morning, I lurched with purpose to my current position. I had been watching an old woman with a Yorkshire terrier for nearly ten minutes when I found what I was looking for, a transgression.

Shaking as it defecated; the terrier completed its business then made a token effort of scraping some grass over the scat to cover it. The dog's owner contemplated the steaming pile of shit for a moment then with a quick glance about her, hurried away from the offending pile on the grass.

It happened very quickly, I broke cover and came from my invisibility, as a shadow cast by something flying across the Sun. Stamping it downward, the heel of my right boot crushed the small dog's skull with a satisfying 'crack'. Then I was gone, leaving a shocked little old lady struggling to comprehend what had just happened.

Euphoria rushed through my soul as I savoured a rare moment of personal effect in the world of the living. Moving as quickly as I could, using all the available natural cover the park had to offer, I made my way to the opposite end of the recreation ground seeking my next sinner to slay.

The old man looked bemused as I pushed him to the ground and kicked his dog in the head. His facial expression changed to a look of abject horror and anger as I rained blows with my feet onto the animal's head. It expired with my final blow, a running kick that made contact under the beast's chin and broke its neck. I looked down at the owner with triumphal satisfaction. He still lay, appropriately, in the foulness his animal had made.

I could not remain in the park any longer and so decided to make for another, nearly a mile and a half away, in pursuit of further work to do. Unfortunately, by the time I had made the second park, the morning was maturing and there were too many people about for me to, successfully, execute another vengeance. I could not rest with only two events and had to think of another approach quickly so that I could harvest this day as fully as was possible.

In the shopping streets, I used my invisibility to acquire a heavy claw hammer from a large DIY store. More lethally prepared than before, I passed the office workers walking in the opposite direction to me and moved to the quieter residential streets of the surrounding area.

Barking had drawn me to the house, a modest terraced residence similar to the hundreds of others that surrounded it. Drifting unseen past the little front gardens in varying states of repair, I identified it by the persistent noise of the animal coming from the back garden. When I rounded the terraced block I realised that I was in luck, the gardens backed onto a railway track. With little difficulty, I made my way through the undergrowth that served as a border between the railway verge and the private gardens until I found my quarry.

It was a big beast, probably a rottweiler, and having sensed my cautious approach was straining on its chain and barking threateningly towards my hidden position. I waited long enough to ensure that no humans were taking any notice of it and to wrap my jumper about my left hand and forearm. When I felt the moment was right, I climbed over the low broken-down fence and waded through the long grass towards the dog. The entire back garden was strewn with dog shit. The smell was repellent to my senses.

Swinging my left arm at the creature, I allowed it to lock its jaws around my padded forearm and brought the hammer down with all my strength onto the flat-topped head. It took me three blows to kill it. With my customary imperceptibility I slid away to find more of its kind before returning to the busy streets to witness the nightly procession of revelling drunks, making their way to the numerous bars and clubs.

I was back in my more customary haunts of the city. It had been a fruitful day. The population of those revolting creatures, The Willow Monks would have me destroy, had been reduced by seven animals. From a familiar doorway, I enjoyed my voyeurism through a reverie of significant achievement.

Following my standard routine for the evening, I found myself again sat on cardboard between the wheelie bins. It had been such a successful day I held high hopes that tonight's show would be an excellent performance. It seemed that I was not going to be disappointed when I heard the furtive voices approach. Undoing the front of my trousers I settled in for the show.

In purgatory, you learn to be adaptable and seek what little pleasure you can from any circumstance. The two young men jogged excitedly to the recessed fire escape doorway where they threw themselves into a close embrace. Kissing each other passionately, they pulled at their clothing until both of them stood with their trousers and pants about their ankles. The blond one bobbed down onto his haunches and took the other's penis in his mouth. As my excitement grew, I felt my own manhood hardening and began to massage it inside my trousers.

Suddenly my excited breath caught in my throat causing me to convulse as I struggled to stifle the rising cough. My hacking exhalations ended the amorous activities of the two homosexuals. When I had recovered most of my composure, I looked up to see the young lovers advancing on my position, violent resolve in their eyes. I fastened my trousers up as fast as I could and was regaining my feet when the first blow struck.

My invisibility had failed and they subjected me to a savage and prolonged beating. Curled up into a ball I could hear them shouting "dirty old bastard" and "fucking pervert" as they took turns kicking me. When they tired of assaulting me, one of them, I do not know which, urinated on my beaten body and together they wandered off into to the night; no doubt to continue their passionate liaison with renewed vigour elsewhere.

Pain is a fundamental component of purgatory and I must accept it. Each bruise on my body took every opportunity to remind me of its existence as I staggered through the streets towards the sanctuary of the garden of death. Orange night air and the grey structures of man surround me as I press on through the world that has cast me out. The physical pain is of no great consequence to me, it is the internal pain that throws me about and tatters my emotions. I long so much to be alive again or fully dead. The state I am in is torture to the body and the soul. I had woken this morning with a euphoric feeling that something great would happen and that my existence had a purpose again. Hope has cheated me, as it has done many times before, and now I am cast back into that deep pit of dreadful despair.

A year or so before, my friend in the garden had told me that the secret to enduring purgatory was to lose hope. It is much easier for her to do without hope, as she is so much closer to deliverance from here than I am. I suppose it is the fault of my inherent weakness and my burning desire for redemption, that I am always seduced by the lies that hope offers. A drowning man will clutch at a straw, a bankrupt man will buy a lottery ticket and a beaten woman will accept the apologies of her abusive husband, all of them only to feel the bitter and inevitable evisceration of crushing disappointment.

Memories of regret and pain from my living years blind my mind as I stumble into the garden, the familiar monuments to the dead surrounding me. The sound of my friend running through the undergrowth passed me on the right. She passes close to me but, as usual, I could not see her. Resisting the urge to follow her I press on towards my home. It annoys me when I use the term 'home' when I refer to the place I stay; home is where the heart is and it has been many years since I have had a home.

Loss is a powerful and painful tutor. It has taught me much in the years that we have been on intimate terms, not least of which 'the meaning of life'. The great and the good of mankind, have struggled to understand the purpose of our existence. I know what all the polymaths of the world do not, and through that knowledge I understand the fundamental nature of man. The meaning of life is to have someone to love and we seek it wisely or unwisely. If we are unwise, our lives will never be complete and we shall destroy ourselves seeking what we will never find. To possess the wisdom we must understand love and recognise that we have to focus our desires through 'The One' and not on ourselves. Enlightenment when it arrives too late is just another form of pain.

My philosophic reflections are rudely interrupted, as I feel his breath on the back of my neck. Distracted as I have been by my pain and my thoughts, I had failed to sense It coming, and due to the beating I took earlier, I am returning later to my sanctuary than I usually do. Caught in the open I freeze as I struggle inwardly to control the rising panic. It's rasping voice began and I have nowhere to hide; forced to listen to its words I feel the corruption flowing into me.

At first, his voice sounds like a low and complex scream, with each oratory it subjects you to, his voice becomes increasingly discernible. As a veteran of It's oral violations I am now proficient in its language and understand every word he diminishes me with. Without strength, I fall to the ground and allow It to feed on my soul, every torn mouthful pulling me further down into the darkness.

When I came to my senses I was lying in the long grass, the early morning dew had soaked my clothes and I shivered uncontrollably in the grey light of dawn. As I rolled onto my knees the pain in my ribs and back racked my body with spasms of agony then as I tried to stand my leg buckled and sent me sprawling into the wet grass again. I felt ravaged, bereft of all substance, totally alone with no hope of deliverance from my purgatory and hopelessness. As I wept in the grass, I longed for the salvation of a helping hand, the warmth of human kindness and beyond all hope, the hand that belonged to the woman who had once loved me like no other.

As the sun slowly rose behind the clouds, it began to rain. I continued to weep whilst Mother Nature pissed on me. My shivering intensified and the physical pain diminished to the extent that, to attempt movement was both possible and necessary. With aching determination, I gained my hands and knees where I breathed as deeply as my aching ribs allowed. The blood of my soul hung heavy in the air that I breathed, It had brought carnage to the garden when he fed on me and now the stripped carcass that remained struggled to gain an upright posture. Once gained, that posture allowed me to stagger from monument to monument until I recovered to the stone shelter of my crib.

With effort, I drew my blanket from beneath the leaves and collapsed onto the stone byre under the limited protection of the threadbare travel accessory. The familiar sound of the Willow Monks came, floating on the heavy early morning air, soothing me to sleep with orchestrated pitch and verbs.

It was beyond noon when I woke. I had rarely seen the interior of my sanctuary bathed in sunlight. It looked awful and its appearance served only to increase my despair. Pausing to hide the belongings that I would not carry with me, I left the mausoleum and set off on my rounds. The day had improved since its genesis and few clouds occupied the skies when I set forth back into the world of the living.

Steep sided unreality defined my state of mind as I approached the busy streets where the people gathered and the retail empires tout their goods. Through my physical pain, I struggled along my familiar route. Through my emotional pain, I observed the living.

Nervously I hoped my invisibility was fully functional when I saw the blue lights of the Police cars. There were two patrol cars parked by the entrance to the narrow service road, blue and white tape stretched across the road. Mesmerised by the flashing lights and the activity of the white suit-clad officers, busying themselves with the details of the fire escape doorway; approximately thirty metres down the service road. I stood transfixed. It was only the look of surprise on the face of a fellow observer, that alerted me to the approaching vehicle. Diving to the pavement only served to increase the levels of physical discomfort that I felt as the impressive black sports car drove through the space I had previously occupied on the road.

The vanguard of approaching concerned onlookers consisted of an attractive woman, probably in her early thirties. Her small but well-formed breasts bouncing in her smock top as she jogged across the road. Her brown/green eyes fixed on my prone carcass spread on the pavement.

Rather than suffer the attentions of strangers, I pulled myself to my feet and limped away from the advancing crowd who seemed intent on a Samaritan role. With a degree of nervousness, I noted the attention of the Police Officers who watched me depart the scene, with an intensity that was more than I was used to and certainly more than I found comfortable.

Curiosity followed me all day until I was able to scavenge a copy of 'The Standard' from a wastepaper bin where. The front page carried the headline: 'Woman Found Murdered', eagerly I read the article. There was little information beyond the headline contained within the article apart from the fact that, a body had been found at approximately seven thirty this morning.

Pushing the newspaper into the pocket of my overcoat, I wandered to the park, where I sat on a bench and considered the events. There was a familiarity about the victim, maybe I had seen her perform in the fire escape doorway or maybe I knew her in my living years but I was certain that we had some connection.

Driven by curiosity, I returned to the scene of the crime. This time rather than join the morbid crowd gathered by the entrance to the service road, I walk to the multi-storied car park next door and climb to the first level where I can overlook the fire escape. As I approach my preferred vantage point, I notice a stranger occupying the position. My disappointment is short lived as he departs the vantage point the moment he became aware of my approach.

There was little to observe, the Police Officers in white suits had completed their work and now only a single uniformed officer stood at either end of the service road to guard the crime scene. My curiosity was not going to gain further satisfaction this evening and painfully aware of the previous night's events, I decided to return to the garden where I would hopefully be able to enjoy her company for a short time before It came abroad.

Chapter 9

Surprised and confused she stood awkwardly holding the telephone handset towards him.

"It's Vanya Byrd for you."

Matt swung his legs off the sofa and sat bolt upright, visibly startled.

"What does she want?"

"I don't know, she just asked to speak with you."

Struggling to control his racing heart, he stood up and took the cordless handset from his wife. Through the windows of their attractive front room, he could see that the sun continued to shine on the extensive garden beyond, yet darkening storm clouds were gathering rapidly about his heart. With cautious reluctance, he held the handset to his ear, aware of his wife's constant attention.

"Hello."

………………………………..

"No I'm sorry I can't help you."

………………………………...

"No you must call the Duty Manager, he will be able to arrange that."

………………………………

"No no I'm sorry this is my private number and I am currently not working."

………………………………

"Again sorry, you will just have to call the Duty Manager."

………………………………

"You have the number, please just…"

………………………………..

"Ok sorry again, bye."

She could hear the voice on the other end of the line but Lily could not understand what it was saying. Her husband had turned so that the handset was on the other side of his head from her. She watched him press the button to disconnect the line and replace the handset in its cradle. His pallor was ashen, there was perspiration on his forehead and his hands were shaking. Before she could speak, he spoke with affected calmness.

"Bloody cheek I will have to have a word in the office about giving out Managers' personal telephone numbers. That was Vanya Byrd! The main lifts in The Central Building are on the 'fritz' and she wants an engineer to fix them this weekend."

Unconvinced but with no reason to doubt him, she nodded her acceptance and returned to her seat. Relaxing, Matt felt comfortable enough to take large steps towards normality and away from the peculiar 'danger zone' that had unexpectedly clutched the, previously peaceful, morning.

"Can I get you another cup of coffee Darling?"

Nodding she held her cup up; he took it with a smile then set off down the lengthy hallway towards the kitchen. When he had taken the cup, Lily noticed that his hand continued to tremble.

Half way to the kitchen, he heard the telephone ring again. 'Shit' he thought to himself as the panic rose again, with a vengeance. The nearest handset was back in the front room and he would never reach that before Lily. Placing the cups he carried onto the windowsill, he moved almost at a run towards the front room. As he pulled up into the room, he saw Lily standing by the telephone cradle holding the handset.

"It's her again and she is being very insistent."

"Right leave it to me."

He held his shaking hand towards his pregnant wife. She gave him the handset and continued to watch him as he put the handset to his head and immediately spoke.

"Look I thought that I had explained earlier."

Matt's anxiety increased tenfold when a male voice answered him.

"You fucking shit!"

He left the room sweating and white as a ghost, the handset was pinned to his head by a shaking hand. Lily had been unable to understand what the other voice was saying but she could tell that this time it was a man speaking. When Matt returned to the front room, she confronted him.

"What's going on?"

He replaced the handset in its cradle and turned to her.

"That bloody Vanya, won't take 'no' for an answer."

"It was Vanya when I answered it but that was a man speaking when you took it." "Yeah well she put her Chief Building Engineer on to try and persuade me."

"Why are you sweating?"

"Oh it just makes me so angry that people think they can disturb others like that." "That's not like you, you are usually strong and calm with difficult people."

"Let's just have that coffee then we can go out to that garden centre where you saw those hanging baskets."
Reluctantly she agreed and sat down to consider the strange events of the morning.

They took her Boxster and put the roof down before taking to the country roads of Kent. The little Porsche's engine growled and Matt drove it hard towards the garden centre, concentrating single-mindedly on the road ahead. Lily sat quietly in the passenger seat contemplating the implied possibilities of the strange telephone calls and her husband's subsequent odd behaviour. There was one conclusion that her thought processes constantly returned to and she really did not want that to be the truth.

It had the silent air that was suitable for the horticultural equivalent of a library. Couples of all ages beyond their thirtieth birthdays wandered the various beds of plants and racks of outdoor utility tools. They whispered to each other as they debated the wisdom of each potential purchase. Lily busied herself with the selection of hanging baskets as Matt loitered beyond her peripheral vision. He planned his next move and covering stories with the intensity of a senior military commander constructing his battle plan.

"What do you think of these two?"
Lily asked as she held up two hanging baskets of varied coloured trailing petunias.

"Yes darling they are lovely."

"Ok let's get these. Shall we stop somewhere for lunch on the way back?"

"That's a good idea we could stop at The Swan."
With tacit approval from Lily, they set off for the check-out counter with their baskets of flowers.

Behind the counter there was a girl of approximately seventeen years, she wore a green pinafore that strained at the fasteners as it struggled to contain her ample body. She finished scanning the barcodes.

"Is that all?"

"Yes. Why do you think we should buy more?"

Matt responded with the sarcasm that Lily had grown to expect from her husband. Lily told the girl to pay him no mind and paid for the items with her card. The fat girl smiled at Lily and asked when she was due.

"I am due in two months, all going well."

With standard courtesies exchanged, they left the counter and walked to their car where they had to manoeuvre the baskets behind the seats, as they would not fit into the modest boot of the Boxster.

The beer garden was busy. They had been lucky to arrive just as a small family group vacated a table. Lily sat in the sun whilst Matt went to the bar to order the food and drink. He returned after a short wait at the bar with a pint of lager and a glass of orange juice, which he placed in front of his wife before sitting to join her at the table.

"Do you want to tell me the truth about the 'phone calls this morning now?"

Lily asked without pre-amble. Frantically trying to recall his plan of action from earlier, Matt stumbled some nonsense from his mouth before he took a deep breath and looked deep into his wife's eyes. He could see her eyes searching his face for an answer.

Trying to speak, he took a breath and opened his mouth, but the words did not come so he broke eye contact with her and tried another deep breath before he looked back to his wife and opened his mouth. Eventually he strung together a response to her question.

"Listen I eh…have to tell you something."

Taking pity on her struggling husband Lily decided to help him.

"You've been having an affair with Vanya Byrd, haven't you?"

Matt felt relieved when his wife had said it for him and smiled, which he immediately recognised as an inappropriate reaction. Feeling the gravity of the situation, he pulled a sullen face and confirmed "yes" to his wife. The following silence was broken only to thank the Waitress, who brought their sandwiches to the table. Sensing an atmosphere, she did not hang about to deliver the usual customer service speech, preferring to retreat to the interior of The Swan, leaving Matt and Lily alone.

During the return journey home neither Matt nor Lily spoke, both deep in thought. When they pulled up onto their drive, she looked directly at him.

"Was that her husband that spoke to you this morning on the telephone?"

He turned the engine off and turned to her.

"Yes it was."

"What did he say?"

"What you would expect him to say. He is going to kill me and I have ruined his life."

"Is he dangerous?"

"I don't know. I don't think so."

They put the top up on the car and went indoors.

Home was an extensive bungalow set in rural Kent. They both loved the place with its large garden of mature flowerbeds. The surrounding woodland ensured that the daylight hours filled with the sound of birdsong. Ideal surroundings they had thought in which to raise a family. They had enjoyed their earlier years together as a high earning professional couple without children but had decided when they bought this house that it was the right time to have children.

Lily went to put her feet up in the front room whilst Matt brought her a cool drink from the kitchen. She thanked him when he handed her the glass and watched him until he sat down in his armchair. He sat looking sheepish as he returned her gaze, waiting for her reaction to the earlier revelation. Outside the sun was shining and the birds' songs twittered through the glass doors that led out into the garden.

Swinging her legs down Lily moved forward on the sofa and farted. Immediately she stared at Matt and caught him stifling a laugh. Lily hated being pregnant, her figure was bent out of shape and she had lost the usual control of her normal bodily functions. This was her moment, she was in control, her husband had been found out and she was furious. Lily wanted to maintain an air of composure as she interrogated the philandering bastard and just as she was about to strike, her body had let her down. Previously in control she was now very angry, obviously with him but now with herself.

"So how long have you been sleeping with her?"
Lily spoke in a seething monotone. Matt considered lying but then thought better of it.

"Just over a year."
The ugly truth now had to be shared, and she lost no time in bombarding him with questions:

"Where did you go with her?"

"Hotels mainly."

"Mainly, where else did you go?"

"Her place once or twice."

"Did you fuck her here?"

"No never" he lied.

"Are you sure?"

"Yes" he lied again.

"Her place; did you fuck her in her bed, the one she shares with her husband?"

"Ehh, yes I did."

"Dirty pair of dogs!"

She sat glaring at Matt for several minutes before she continued.

"Why, why the fuck did you go and do that?"

"What sleep with her in her bed?"

"No you prick, just sleeping with that cow full stop."

"I am sorry."

"Sorry? Fucking sorry, you son of a bitch I am pregnant and just discovered my husband has been fucking a black bitch from work for over a year and all you can say is sorry."

"I don't know what else to say."

"Ok why did you sleep with Vanya?"

"I don't know I just felt like I was being cool you know, the big shot business professional with his mistress."

"You think that is something to aspire to do you?"

"Well not really but I kind of got caught up in the whole thing."

"When was the first time?"

"At The Facilities Management Conference in Chancery Lane."

"I remember. So how often did you see each other?"

"Maybe once or twice a month."

"What was she like?"

"What do you mean?"

"I mean was she a good fuck, did she suck it on demand, did she take it up the arse? Well?"

"Yes."

They spoke together as the sun went down and the room became dark. The pattern of the conversation remained the same throughout, she fired questions at him and he answered them as honestly as he could. She cried, shouted, screamed and raged at him and The Universe. Matt slowly became aware of a very important door in his life, closing. He could feel the aching loss that came when a part of a person's soul is lost. They sat together in the dark, both emotionally exhausted. Silence had fallen when she could think of no more questions to fire at him and the awfulness of what had been revealed, came fully into focus. Eventually, she spoke in a weak voice. "So what now?"

Chapter 10

"Sophistidates! What kind of bloody name is that? I can see nothing sophisticated in what they peddle," growled Detective Inspector Mac Gregor as he tossed the beige card file onto the, already cluttered, desk before Tommo Gayle. Tommo looked up from the transcribed statements he was reading and followed Mac Gregor to his office with his eyes before audibly groaning and rising to his feet. He paused briefly to inspect the contents of the file, which had been abruptly dropped onto his desk. Tucking the file under his arm, he walked to the Inspector's office.

Standing just inside the office doorway Tommo squinted as the early afternoon sun shone through the filthy windows. In the absence of an immediate acknowledgement, he shuffled two feet to his left where his eyes were able to gain the sanctuary of shadow whilst he waited for the Inspector to focus attention on him.

When Mac Gregor felt inclined to raise his eyes from the post-it notes on his desk, he saw Detective Sergeant Gayle standing in his office doorway, holding the beige file out in his left hand with a quizzical expression on his face.

"What's this Guv?"

"It is the report from the Techies on the contents of oor victim's laptop computer."

"Turn up anything interesting?"

"Aye we now know where she was going the night she died and who she was meeting."

"Well Guv? Don't keep me in suspense."

"She had a date wi Sean."

"Sean who and what are we waiting for? Let's go pick him up for a chat."

"No that easy Tommo, no that easy Son."

Before he actually spoke, Tommo closed his mouth again and moved to the scuffed plastic chair by Mac Gregor's desk. He sat down and placed the file on the desk between them. He leafed through the pages within as his boss detailed what had been found on Shirley Babcock's laptop.

The laptop held a number of e-mail addresses, the majority of which, traced to friends and family members of the victim. She was a member of two social networking sites and used several on-line lingerie-shopping sites. The most frequently visited internet sites were two amateur pornography sites and a subscription-dating site. The dating site was, 'Sophistidates' a specialist site for matching married individuals who were seeking extra-marital liaisons. Analysis of the files recovered from the hard drive revealed that Mrs Shirley Babcock had arranged to meet twelve men through the site. Follow up files confirmed that she had met with eight of these men. The contents of those files strongly implied, and in many cases stated categorically, that she had had sex with those men.

A man known as Sean was the last man she had arranged to meet. The history on her Sophistidates profile account traced the liaison from the first electronic meeting through to the final arrangement. Unusually there had been no exchange of mobile telephone numbers or e-mail addresses, they had simply agreed on a date, time and location where they would meet. The correspondence graphically detailed the congress that they wished to perform with each other. Her final message to Sean was 'Looking forward to seeing you tomorrow Babe xxx'. His had simply read 'likewise Sexy x'.

As Mac Gregor had suspected the victim was no angel however, much as he found her behaviour repellent he felt angry that someone had taken her life. It had always been those wrongs and injustices, which made him such an obstinate and dogged Police Officer. When the writhing nausea, which cruel injustice provoked in his stomach, took hold of him, Mac Gregor resolved to seek recompense on behalf of all decent people. To him it became a personal matter, those who sought to slow his pursuit or bind his activity with due process, became as much a malignant factor as the perpetrator of whatever injustice it was that he meant to address.

That morning, he had spent arguing with the Techies and The Chief Inspector, about what should logically be done and what they maintained could not be done. It irked Mac Gregor that he had to explain the Anti-Meridian vexations to his

Sergeant before they could begin to move forward with the new evidence.

"Look Tommo son, A ken whit yer sayin' bit yon Sean is just a screen name. That web site is run fea Bulgaria an' were no able tae force them tae co-operate wi us. We cannae access thir records frem here an' they winnae tak tae us, wiv tried tae ca'em an' they winnae gee us anything. The Chief has pit a request intae Interpol bit disnae think they will git anae firther than us. They people that use thit site pay weel fir the privilege an discretion is wan o' the guarantees they offer."

Explained Mac Gregor; his accent growing stronger with his own agitation.

Both men sat momentarily in silence, staring unseeingly at the cluttered desk top. Tommo sighed loudly and raised his head.

"What shall we do with this then?"

He asked as he pushed the beige folders an inch towards the other side of the desk. His composure regained, Mac Gregor fixed Tommo with a steady look and spoke in clipped syllables.

"We shall set up several dummy accounts on this web site and see if we can draw oor man, Sean, oot".

"Do you think this is our man Guv?"

"Ah would say he has tae be our prime suspect at the moment. It's not the husband, she had nae known enemies and this was no random attack, it was staged for someone's purpose though Lord only knows whit that is. I also think oor man is going to strike again, so the sooner we get that bastard behind bars the better."

As Mac Gregor finished talking, he fixed his Sergeant with a solid gaze that left Tommo in no doubt of his Boss's resolve, a resolve that made him feel uneasy. Tommo had great ambition though he was not confident his own resolve could ever match that of his Inspectors.

Unusually they worked together for the remainder of the afternoon in the same office, co-ordinating the dummy web site accounts and administering the sifting of reams of evidence that had been gathered. As the natural light faded, they instructed a departing Detective Constable to switch the office light on as they hypothesised about the facts known to them.

"Why would someone smash that wee girl's brains oot when she was clearly willing to gee him all he had been asking for?"

"Maybe she was taunting him, Guv."

"Aye maybe, but she seems to have been in a willing posture when she had been killed."

"Could there have been a third party?"

"No evidence for that Tommo and besides whit was Sean's role if the third party just gate crashed the party and killed his wee bit?"

"We could be dealing with a pair of sickos, Guv."

"Sick enough to risk a lifetime behind bars for the thrill of luring a woman to a piss stained doorway and bashing her brains in?"

"Gov you know as well as I do there are some sick types out there."

"Valid point Tommo but ah think there is more to oor man's motive than that."

"Like what Guv?"

"Tommo this is a crime of hate, there was something that he hated aboot the victim."

"Well she was blonde, slightly chubby, pretty and promiscuous."

"Aye Tommo and she was guilty of infidelity."

"So we could suppose the motive was religion, morals or personal vendetta."

"Those would be the most logical motives to hate her, enough to kill her Tommo. That or we are dealing with a random psychopath."

"I hope we are dealing one of the former Guv or we will have all those profiling psychologist bastards crawling all over the place."

"Aye Tommo and the former will be far easier to predict."

Together they worked through the possibilities that the facts would allow them to explore. The night grew old and the building emptied but for the control room staff. The nightshift personnel came and went as their duties dictated and the curious silence, unique to the silent hours of any facility that operated twenty-four seven, fell. Both men agreed to resume their work early the following morning and with a fonder farewell than had been customary in their relationship, they bade each other a goodnight.

It was Mary, who stirred first under the protective warmth of their duvet, when his mobile telephone began to ring.

"It's your 'phone Darling."

She said in a sleepy voice.

"Bollocks."

He growled as he struggled to a sitting position before groping in the darkness for the offending communications device.

"Don't swear Dear."

She reprimanded as she returned to her previous position.

"Sorry Dear."

He said before pressing the answer key and putting the 'phone to his ear.

"Mac Gregor."

He growled into the device as he blinked to bring his eyes into focus in the darkness of the bedroom.

Assuring the caller that he was on his way, he then disconnected the call and relaxed into his pillow and his thoughts. As Mary began to turn over, he selected a name from the contacts list on his mobile and pressed dial.

"Tommo there's been another, see you in the Incident Room soon as you can and we'll go together".

Mac Gregor terminated the call and turned to his wife.

"Everything alright Dear?"

She asked.

"Yes Darling, I need to go in."

He explained as he leaned towards her, placing his big hand on her ample upper arm and kissing her shoulder.

"I love you Mirren, see you tonight for dinner."

He spoke softly to her.

Chapter 11

"Hey! Jack, quit stonewalling."
Brian spoke with determination as he stared at his wife, who sat on the armchair in the corner of the room.

"What the hell are these doing in your bag?"
He persisted as he held three unopened condoms up in his left hand. She sat with her eyes fixed on the screen of the laptop that balanced on her thighs as she busied herself tapping at the keys of the device.

"Just a minute dear, I need to finish this then I will be with you."
She spoke in a casual distracted manner. He stood fuming for a few moments before he raised his voice again.

"The hell I will, you answer my question now!"
Reluctantly, she raised her gaze from the machine and fixed him with her soft brown eyes.

From the moment he had met Becky he had felt a curious stirring in the pit of his stomach every time she fixed her beautiful eyes on him. From the very instance her gaze initiated that physical sensation he had known that he would love her eternally. They had met on a Friday night in a bar full of mirrors and lights that faded from one primary colour to another, the precocious ambitions of the designer evident even to the partially sighted.

She had been there with a group of her friends and he was accompanying his cousin who had insisted that they visit the local 'Meat Market'. Brian had found it difficult to chat with the girls in England, having spent most of his childhood, adolescence and teenage years in America. His mother had married an American, ten years her senior. A year after the marriage they had moved across the Atlantic, Brian was five years old, to a mid-west city that was to be his home for the next thirteen years.

His accent would draw interest from the girls. They would encourage him to repeat ridiculous statements then fall about laughing with each other as they tried to imitate his pronunciation. This irked him and he chastised himself inwardly, every time the scenario replayed itself, for having played along. It had taken him many experiences, to develop the necessary resolve to refuse their requests. This was achieved only when he was fully convinced that his compliance would not get them into bed. His early unsuccessful attempts at seduction in England had made him more reserved and wary of the loud herds of mini-skirted trollops that trawled the bars seeking sponsorship for their drinks in exchange for insincere promises of sexual intimacy.

Finding himself alone at the bar when his cousin had led a fat girl onto the dance floor, Brian looked about and had seen Becky looking at him coyly. He had asked her if she wanted a drink, she did. When he returned from the bar with drinks, their hands had touched as she took the glass from him. It was then that her eyes, the colour of molten chocolate, had engulfed him and his heart was lost to her.

Becky had noticed what was in his hand when Brian had walked into the room. Her initial emotion was not one of fear; it was to recall the thrill of sex with a stranger in her mother's spare room only the weekend before. Brian had gone to bed an hour previously and she was enjoying some free time on the laptop. When she heard him moving in the bedroom and the clatter of something spilling onto the floorboards above she had immediately looked about for her bag. 'Shit' she thought to herself when her search confirmed her retuning memory, the handbag was in the bedroom hanging from the post on the footboard of the bed. After rapidly considering her options she began frantically closing the windows of the chat rooms on her computer and concocting reasons why she might have condoms in her handbag.

The screen of her laptop provided a barrier and the keyboard a distraction as her mind raced. With careful application of her practiced techniques, she stalled her husband for as long as she could to buy herself valuable minutes and seconds. Even she knew that on this occasion, there was limited time to be bought. His voice rapidly reached the level and tone that warned her, the next step was physical intervention.

When the last window closed on the screen before her, she raised her head with affected casualness and fixed her eyes on

Brian. She held him in her gaze for a moment, sensing the effect her eyes were having on him, before she spoke gently.

"What is it Dear? I thought you had gone to bed?"

"You heard me the first time, what are these doing in your handbag?"

Her confidence nearly failed her when she realised the extent of his resolve to open the matter up to the closest of scrutiny. She had long suspected that he knew of her regular infidelity and that he chose to ignore all the signs but his manner suggested her suspicions had been erroneous. Avoiding the direct question, she changed her tone to one of admonishment and feigned a flanking assault.

"Have you been snooping in my things?"

He had almost begun to defend himself before he saw the attack for what it was.

"Do not change the subject and answer the question."

Controlling his rising anger, Brian waited whilst Becky carefully closed her laptop and placed it into the bag at the side of the armchair. When she sat back she had a gentle smile on her face and soft look in her eye.

"Oh darling you don't think that I have been using them for that, do you? They were for Mary's desk at work last Friday. I told you we covered it in blown up condoms because she got married last Saturday."

He stood staring at her in disbelief for an uncomfortably long time before he spoke.

"You never told me about that and who the hell is Mary?"

Becky began to relax a little as she found her stride in deceit.

"She is the Scots one who joined our team last year, don't you remember, I told you she has got really bad breath? I did tell you about the condoms last weekend but I don't think you were listening."

"When did you tell me?"

She knew she had him now, his conviction was visibly fading away and his tone was softening.

"I told you when I was getting ready to go out last Saturday. You were clowning about with Thomas and I knew you were not listening even though you said that you were."

The resolve that had carried Brian down to the front room to confront his wife stuttered and failed. What she had said did have a strong credibility; he remembered playing with their son whilst she was packing to go to her mother's home. When she arranged these nights she would always rush about the house gathering things for herself and Thomas to take away for the night. It was equally true that he had not been listening to what she was saying as his focus had been entirely on their child. He had no recollection of a work colleague named Mary but he was never sure who comprised Becky's team at her work. The names always seemed to change and she only worked two days a week, which seemed too little for her to be so intimately involved in her colleagues' lives.

When Becky rose from the armchair and embraced him, he felt a sense of relief that allowed him to relax into his normal disposition.

"I am sorry darling, I was going for a pee when I knocked your bag off the end of the bed and found them. I was putting your stuff back in the bag."

"Never mind darling, it feels nice that you can still get jealous."

As he held her close, he remembered the pain and anger of the years in America.

His stepfather had been a serial adulterer and his poor mother had put up with it for years. He always wondered why she did and when he had eventually asked her she told him that they were two strangers in a foreign land and that she had made the decision for both of them to be there. Her reasoning had never made sense to him, especially when he could hear her crying from his bed when she was alone at night waiting for her wayward husband to return. Brian had hated his stepfather for the betrayal of his mother and when he repeatedly insisted that they change Brian's surname to match theirs he hated him more. To a young Brian it appeared that this vile man was trying to take everything including the final legacy of his dead father.

Testicular cancer made his mother a widow when Brian was only a baby and he had never known his father. In the darkest moments of his childhood, he would build his resilience by convincing himself that his father was watching

73

him from above and that he had to be strong for his Dad. He became stronger on the inside but never strong enough on the outside to protect his mother from the mental cruelty that the American inflicted on her. The pain and shame of that failing, stayed with Brian all of his life and his greatest fear was that he treat another or that he be treated, the way his mother had been.

High School graduation was a memorable day for two reasons: the tears of pride in his mother's eyes and their suitcases, thrown on the lawn of their home when they returned from the ceremony. The American had not come to the ceremony choosing instead to use the time to pack their stuff and throw it out of the front door to make way for the new girlfriend who was to take his mother's place. They had lived in a motel for two weeks before she managed to persuade her husband to give them enough money to return to The United Kingdom.

Kissing Becky on the top of the head, Brian spoke softly to her.

"Come on let's go to bed."

"I will be right up, you go ahead. I need to switch off the lights first, be with you in a minute."

She tidied the front room as she moved about switching lights off and checking that the French Widows were locked. Upstairs she could hear him urinating and then returning to bed. It had been a close run thing. She congratulated herself on her skills in diverting him from the truth, and thanked her luck, for him not having picked up on the fact that the condoms were the ribbed variety, not the product that anyone would purchase for a prank. She knew it was a dangerous game she played, if she had been discovered, this would not have been the first time.

When she had been eight months pregnant with Thomas, Brian walked into the front room of their home to find her on all fours with her lover of the time thrashing away at her from behind. It had been an ugly moment; Brian stood in stunned disbelief as her lover pulled out of her and struggled to pull his clothing back on. She could only roll onto her bottom and sit there cradling her heavily pregnant belly. Shouting followed and punches thrown, leaving both men with fat lips and

74

bruised egos. An uneasy period of days followed and would have resulted in a divorce had it not been for the accident.

She had been returning home from an overnight visit to her aunt's house in Kent and had been feeling uncomfortable driving. Distracted by the recent events, her attention had wandered away from the immediate function of controlling her vehicle. The impact and thudding noise of the front wheel hitting and mounting the pavement had brought her focus back to driving. Pulling the wheel to the right she had brought the front of the vehicle back onto a course that avoided the small child but not its father, who was struck hard and thrown into a garden wall. Panic had taken her and she had driven off without stopping. When she eventually reached the sanctuary of home, she had fallen into Brian's arms, weeping and begging for his help.

He had always been a loyal man and Brian did not let her down, he arranged for the car to be repaired, that afternoon, after he had checked it for traces of the victim. Time passed and the Police had not come to call. Over a relatively short period of time, they returned to a semblance of normality. When Thomas was born and the paternity test proved that Brian was Thomas's father, reconciliation became possible.

Through the early months she worked hard with her new born, and the delicate recovery of their marriage, until eventually the matter faded from every day conversation and thought. Normality restored, she was able to return to her indulgencies.

The headlights of passing cars occasionally shone through the slats of the Venetian blinds and across the ceiling of the bedroom. Brian lay, waiting for his wife to join him in bed. He watched the light display and thought of the confrontation, he felt much better now that normality had been re-established and he was once again in control of his emotions. Rolling onto his side, he pulled the duvet up around his ears. Waiting and wondering, he considered what had possessed him to go so close to uncovering the ugly truth.

In the room next door, their son sighed and moved under his covers before settling back into sleep, the sleep of the innocents watched over by Angels. His was an uncertain future, the legacy of his parents, volatile and potentially destructive. No prophet could foresee an assured future.

Chapter 12

Her mother gathered her energy and focussed it into one last push, accompanied with a primal scream that rose to a terrible crescendo then fell away to a spent throaty groan as Lucy was born. Matt stood helplessly holding his wife's hand and peering down between her knees as he watched the midwife gather his infant daughter up and skilfully work on the child until a brief coughing heralded the welcome sound of her crying. He waved the shears away as the midwife offered them to him to cut the umbilical cord. Turning from the father, she clamped off the cord and cut Lucy's last physical connection with her mother.

The child was taken, by an assistant, and cleaned under the heating lamp whilst the midwife supervised the passing of the placenta. Lily had asked for her child and was assured that, 'everything was fine'. She struggled to sit up and watch her child in the hands of a stranger at the other side of the room. Her anxiety only subsided when she was presented with the new-born wrapped in a warm clean towel. Lucy wriggled in slow motion in her mother's arms, as she relaxed into her first sleep beyond the womb, her mother gazing down with admiration and love.

Stunned, Matt felt nothing and everything at once. His emotional senses were overloaded. As a myriad of thoughts raced through his head, he slowly realised that he had not said a word since his daughter had opened her blue eyes. She had seemed to look directly at him, though he knew that not to be possible at her tender age. With forced effort, he broke free from his reverie and moved to his wife's side where he laid a supporting hand on her shoulder and kissed the top of her head. "I love you both so much" were his first words after his daughter's birth.

Since the revelation of Matt's affair with Vanya Byrd, Lily had found it difficult to re-capture the love and trust she had felt for her husband since the first day they met. His constant assurances that the affair was over and that Vanya had not meant any more to him than a release for his sexual desires, could not repair the damage to the fundamental fabric of their relationship. In the days and weeks that followed her husband's, forced, confession on that early summer's Sunday after the shattering telephone call from his lover, she could only focus on caring for herself and the child that she carried. She was numb to emotion and the light had gone from her eyes, he knew that something precious had died within his wife.

Regardless of the pain she had felt and the shame he carried they clung together through the advanced weeks of her pregnancy. It was close to her due date when they began to relate their emotions to each other in any meaningful way. That connection was abruptly curtailed, when Lily went into labour. The functionality that nature demands when a child is, cast out of the sanctuary of its mother's womb, took absolute attention and the parents' need to relate, relegated to an irrelevant status.

When they returned from the hospital, their home seemed strangely different. It was quieter and colder than Matt had remembered it. Only thirty-six hours previously, it had been full of action as he gathered Lily's overnight bag and ushered his frightened wife into his car for the journey to the maternity ward.

She walked slowly from the car to the comfort of the sofa as he carried their daughter in her car seat into the front room and after gently setting her on the floor, returned to the car to fetch the overnight bag. Closing the front door, he dropped the bag on the floor in the hallway and went to the kitchen where he filled the kettle and switched it on. By the time he returned to the front room Lucy had begun to cry and Lily was struggling to sit on her stitches as she tried to reach her crying child. Rushing forward he said, "let me do that, you just sit back". Almost reluctantly, she relaxed back into her previous posture and allowed him to free Lucy from the car seat then pass her gently over. "I'll make us a cup of tea," he said as Lily re-arranged her clothing and began to feed Lucy.

Removing the tea bags from the steaming mugs on the kitchen work surface, Matt allowed himself to consider the future. He could not face life without Lily and Lucy but did not know what he needed to do to put things right. Gazing out of the kitchen window, he saw his reflection in the glass as the gathering gloom of evening fell on the front garden and the woods beyond. He looked tired and worried. The birth of his daughter had gone well but that was not what worried him, the future worried him. Focussing through his image to the darkening woods, he felt deeply uneasy. Almost subconsciously, he sensed an insidious threat gathering in the dark shadows between the trees. As he stared into the advancing darkness he felt hope drain from his soul to be replaced with a sense of overwhelming dread.

A mug of tea in each hand, he walked from the kitchen through the dining room then down the lengthy 'L' shaped hallway to the front room where Lily was winding Lucy. She looked up blankly from her child at him as he entered the room. "I think she is nearly asleep. Will you put her in her basket?" she asked her husband. Without a word, Matt placed the mugs onto the coffee table and took his daughter from Lily then carried the yawning child to the Moses basket by their bed. Lucy was asleep by the time he placed the blanket carefully over her little body. He paused briefly to admire his child before turning to re-join his wife on the sofa.

Over the first weeks of Lucy's existence beyond the womb, the brace of hours her routine allowed between waking needs provided her parents the opportunity to communicate. Though the fatigue of caring for an infant hindered Lily's ambitions to relate with her husband, they did begin to build some meaningful mutual understanding. The progress of their reconciliation accelerated when their child began to sleep through the nights.

When months had passed from her birth, Lucy's parents had re-established some stability in their relationship. Her father had begun to hope that there was a future for his family and her mother felt a soothing to the ragged edges of her love. It was a difficult road for both of her parents and frequently they would stumble however, they held close enough to each other that they were able to check the fall of the other.

Time did not heal the wounds that Matt's affair had dealt her, but Lily was able to patch them sufficiently to allow them to hold together whenever they hit a pothole in the road of life. He was ever conscious of his failings and how closely they had taken him to losing all that he held dear. This consciousness drove Matt to be ever diligent to his wife's needs and to respond positively when an opportunity to support her presented itself. Gradually they patched their relationship back together.

At work, Matt had begun to relax back into his previous professional routine. He felt confident that the foundations of his home life was secure and that freed his mind from the anxiety of fear. It was a terrible fear of losing his home, a place where his woman, the harbour of his soul, would tend the hearth fire and welcome him when the day's work was complete. During the months of uncertainty, his work had suffered as the preoccupation of his worries distracted from the attention that his work required. Back in control of his life, he felt that he was back on top of the job and those that he had to work with. At the end of each day, it was a joy for him to climb into his car and begin the journey home to Lily and Lucy.

The responsibilities of motherhood had been a daunting prospect for Lily, especially when Matt had returned to work after his brief paternity leave. As their relationship had recovered, she felt more confident and soon settled into an effective routine of feeds, changes, bathing and bedtimes. The dark feelings of betrayal that had haunted her every waking moment for months soon began to recede. She was not sure of the point in time that they disappeared altogether and passed into a forgotten memory like a bad dream.

She enjoyed the new attentiveness that Matt lavished on her at every opportunity and continued to feel a rush of excitement when he would bring her flowers, which he did on a weekly basis. As the year passed from spring into summer, the sun returned to their lives and together they basked in their glorious togetherness. It became natural and comfortable for her to love her husband again.

Having regained control of his professional life, Matt found that the active demands of his working day reduced, freeing more time for the passive activity of thought. He used his thinking time to proactively prepare and manage contingencies for the future unknowns of his operation. In time he had prepared absolutely for the unknown and all that remained for him to do was to lead his people and react when the unforeseen occurred. It became increasing difficult to occupy his thoughts throughout the working day and his mind began to wander.

Sitting at his desk, Matt allowed himself to daydream; he replayed the most erotic experiences of his life in his mind. As he pretended to read a tender document, his mind was full of images of ecstatic carnal activities. On reflection, he recognised that many of his favourite erotic memories had been shared with Vanya. Casually he opened the top drawer of his desk and retrieved a small 'post it' note that was stuck to the inside of the drawer. He read the note then held his mobile 'phone and pondered the possible outcomes of his imminent actions. With obvious resolve, he began to type text into his 'phone then with a final flourish he pressed 'send' and cast the device onto his desk.

The loud trill of his desktop telephone shattered his reflective mood. Rousing from his slouched position in his chair, he snatched the handset from its cradle with apparent annoyance and held it to his ear. The velvet tones of Lesley, his secretary, introduced one of his many customers. "Put him through" he said in a resigned tone and waited for the whining nasal voice of his customer to begin. He drew pictures of stick men hanging by their necks on the pad in front of him as he listened to the customer bleating on about an issue, the importance of which he and his customer absolutely did not agree on. It had always infuriated Matt that the nature of business was that every matter, however trivial, could be exaggerated to any magnitude by a customer and that he, the supplier, would be expected to share that view.

The customer repeated himself for the third time and Matt, forced to repeat his own platitudes and undertakings to look into the matter, was becoming more and more irritated with the self-important pedant. The mobile telephone bleeped loudly indicating the reception of a text message. Glad of the distraction, he picked the mobile up and read the display screen. It informed him that Vanya had replied. Eager to escape the banality of his conversation with the customer, Matt added greater steel to his voice and reassured the whining fat man on the other end of the telephone conversation that he would look into the matter and get back to him. The fat customer persisted for a further two minutes before the meaningful silence at Matt's end of the conversation sunk in. With expedient politeness, the correspondence terminated.

Dropping the handset of the telephone back into its cradle Matt spat the word 'wanker' into the empty office and turned his attention to the mobile. Her text message read:

> *Missing you too*
> *want to meet for*
> *a drink?X*

He smiled to himself before composing a positive response on his 'phone and pressing 'send'.

Driving home, he had the roof of the Boxter down and played Skunk Anansie's 'Yes it's Fucking Political' on the stereo at high volume, several times. Matt felt a freedom in his soul that he had not felt for a long time and he was enjoying it. The Renault Clio in front of him was annoying him and it was with great satisfaction that he was able to select third gear as he left a roundabout and floored the accelerator. The Porsche tore past the hesitant Clio and he deliberately cut in sharply to alarm the aged driver of the small 'city runabout'.

Eventually the tree lined rural roads led to the village where he lived and Matt parked the convertible next to his own four-door saloon that he had left with Lily that morning. Once the roof was closed, he retrieved his jacket from the passenger seat and strode to the front door of his home. Inside Lily was waiting with a crying Lucy in her arms, "you're home. Good look after your daughter" she said as she thrust his child into his arms. Cradling Lucy in his arms Matt followed his wife to the front room as he tried to sooth the wailing infant. "You ok?" he asked when she threw herself onto the sofa. "Yes I am fine, just tired" she replied as she pulled her legs up onto the furniture and turned her attention to the television.

The evening passed as every evening seemed to pass for the previous months. Matt tended to his daughter until it was time for her bath when he would hand her back to Lily who would bathe the child and put her to bed after a goodnight kiss from her father. He would prepare the evening meal, which they ate in silence as she stared at the television and Matt drank from a bottle of red wine. By nine thirty in the evening, Lily was in bed, leaving her husband to his thoughts and a second bottle of red wine. They were comfortable with this routine, even though it fulfilled neither of them. When eventually he joined Lily in bed, Matt would listen to the ticking of the alarm clock as he thought of another life. The images of the other life with his wife, as she was before the revelation of his affair and the arrival of their child, would carry him into a dreamless sleep.

Chapter 13

Conscious of the attention he was drawing from the elderly people climbing from a car parked closer to the Pub, Matt took his mobile telephone from his jacket pocket and pretended to study the screen. Once they had passed into the pub, he put the 'phone away and stared down the approach road, looking for the familiar green sports car. Lily had been curt with him earlier when he had telephoned her to let her know that he would be working late. He knew she suspected nothing; her attitude was borne of resentment. She would be required to look after Lucy all the way through to bedtime.

His smile broadened as he followed the approach of the aging Alpha Romeo, it swung into the car park and pulled up next to Matt's saloon. Climbing from behind the wheel, Vanya Byrd smiled at him and blew a kiss in his general direction. Greeting each other in the car park with a light embrace and a brief kiss on the cheek, they turned and walked across the grey, broken, asphalt towards the Public House.

Entering the Pub to receive the lingering glances of the other patrons, Matt remembered with pleasure the attention that they, as a couple, had always drawn. He was tall, broad and handsome. She was curvaceous, pretty and black. Together they made a striking couple, if a little incongruous; business suit meets tight pants and busty blouses.

After purchasing drinks from the bar, they sat discreetly together, at a table near the window furthest from the bar and its other patrons. Initially the conversation was factual and of no great depth, then they began to discuss their affair and the feelings that they had experienced since they last met. There was an undeniable chemistry between them and Matt felt the full force of her sexuality, simply the smell of Vanya was sufficient to arouse him sexually. Her body language shouted at him, she wanted him and her body ached for his touch. The resentment he felt towards her for the selfish actions she had taken, that in turn had led to the exposure of their infidelity, melted away as he gazed into her dark eyes. It was inevitable, that they would touch, yet it was with a gleeful thrill that he

84

clasped the hand she placed on his thigh. It felt as though it were an unexpected gift. Without a word, they studied the interior of the bar as they kneaded each other's hand.

When they returned to their cars, Matt stopped and embraced Vanya closely. When he pulled away and focussed on her face, she presented her mouth. Without hesitation he pressed his mouth to hers and plunged his tongue inwards. They kissed passionately, she suggested that they sit in his car and eagerly he agreed.

She sat demurely in the passenger seat whist he took his place behind the wheel and turned to her. Without hesitation Matt placed his left arm across her shoulder and moved in towards her, she reciprocated by turning her face to him and they engaged in another passionate kiss. As they kissed, he let his right hand slip from her shoulder down onto her breast and waited with some trepidation for her reaction. To his relief, she reacted by kissing home more passionately and throwing her left arm across his waist. When their lips parted, Vanya whispered to Matt "I was hoping that was going to happen". He smiled at her and they began to kiss again. His mind filled with the endorphins of sexual arousal and he was unable to think any practical thoughts, his mind filled only with the aching need he had to increase their immediate intimacy.

He gasped with pleasure as Vanya slid her hand down to his crotch and began to rub his genitals. The more passionately he kissed her, the more frenetic her frottage. Grasping roughly at her chest he crudely undid the buttons on her blouse and freed a large breast from the bondage of its bra cup. Kissing her neck and chest, he made his way down to take her breast in his mouth and sucked on her as he used his tongue to stimulate the nipple. When he made to push his hand up between her thighs, she stopped him by placing a hand on his shoulder and gently pushing him away. Rising from his suckling, he fixed her with the look of an injured puppy. Vanya simply smiled at him and began to undo his trousers.

In the rear-view mirror, he watched the old couples returning to their vehicle, this time they paid no heed to him sitting in the driver's seat. When they were all aboard and the last door had swung shut he returned his attention to Vanya, whose head, with its glorious hair extensions, bobbed in his lap as she performed fellatio. His cock felt ready to explode and he grasped her shoulder and head as he ejaculated waves of his seed into her mouth. She continued to fondle his penis with her tongue, as it lost its rigidity, and swallowed several times to ensure she had ingested all of his sperm. With a loud sucking noise, she pulled away from his, now flaccid, manhood and sat correctly in the passenger seat. She smiled at Matt, lightly drawing a finger into each corner of her mouth to adjust any wayward lipstick.

"Did you enjoy that?" she asked smugly as she did up the buttons on her blouse. "Very much indeed" he replied as he fastened his trousers. They kissed again, sharing the vague saltiness of his semen, before saying their goodbyes and making promises that they would see each other again soon. Vanya climbed from his car and opened the door of her own vehicle then turned to see him go. Matt waved at her as he drove off in a hurry to return to his home and the waiting Lily.

On hearing his car pull up outside, she ceased pacing the room and composed herself into a relaxed seated position in front of the television. Matt entered the room with affected fluster and kissed his wife before regaling her with tales of how incompetent his people at work were. Sitting quietly, she watched his performance before seizing her moment to speak, just as he turned to leave the room, "you smell of drink". Spinning on his heels Matt faced Lily and smiled at her.

"I know Babes. I took some of my people out for a quick drink after we had finished working late. Hope you don't mind?"

"You know I don't like you drinking and driving" she said with a deadpan face and turned her attention back to the television set. He stood awkwardly for a moment before joining her on the sofa where he placed an arm about her and spoke softly to her.

"Shall I cook us something nice for dinner?"

"I'm not hungry. You sort yourself out if you like."

"Come on what's the matter Darling?"

With a sigh, she turned to face him and coldly articulated:

"Nothing I am just tired, now please leave me alone."

In the bedroom, Matt reflected on the carnal joy he had felt with Vanya in contrast to the stiff coldness he now felt in his own home. When he had changed out of the business suit, he had worn all day into a pair of jeans and a jumper he went to the kitchen where he prepared a light meal and opened a bottle of red wine. As he returned to the front room, he considered whether he should have offered, for a second time, to prepare Lily something but thought better of pestering her. By the time he reached his armchair in the front room he had begun to resent his wife's attitude, she in turn resented what she perceived as his lack of support. Together they sat watching television and quietly seething at each other.

When Lily had retired to bed, Matt opened a second bottle of wine and sat staring blankly at the television as he wondered what had gone wrong. Once they repaired their relationship, he had relaxed and she had become withdrawn. They rarely made love and she never showed him any overt affection in private or in company. He now began to wonder if he had done the right thing when he begged to save the marriage. If he had let it die, then he may be happy by now, maybe in the arms of a sexy woman like Vanya or even Vanya herself if she could be persuaded to leave her husband. He considered it unfair that he worked all day and did everything he could to pander to Lily's needs when she would show no gratitude or affection. Matt was tired of it, he felt that he had paid the price of his infidelity and he was now owed a comfortable life. As he drained the last of the wine from his glass, he resolved that he would improve things and make himself happier.

The months passed and Lily resigned herself to the life Matt and she had stuck back together; it was not the happy family life she had imagined for herself when she was a girl, but it was a life with a family. She struggled every day to forget the betrayal of her husband's infidelity. He was fundamentally a good man who had been led astray by his own vicious ego and she felt a responsibility to forgive the father of her child. Her hopes for complete redemption seemed to be frustrated only by the increasing distance that had begun to creep into their relationship. Increasingly Matt stayed away from home on business as he had done before when his affair with Vanya was in full swing. She had no reason to believe he was seeing her again but had no way of silencing the doubts that came to her every night she lay alone in their bed.

Lucy grew well. Within a year, she was an accomplished walker and by two years, her oratory was persistent, accurate and extensive. The large bungalow and its expansive garden was a wonderful world where she felt safe to explore unhindered by uncertainty or fear. All unwelcome surprises or minor injuries gained whilst advancing her boundaries, soothed away by her loving Mummy with soft warmth and the unshakable tones of a mother's reassurance. When her Daddy returned home from work, it was a moment of inexplicable excitement and joy. Lucy would writhe and giggle in his arms as she struggled to avoid his bristly chin when he would rub it against her cheeks. The halcyon period of each day was bedtime. She would snuggle under her quilt and listen to one of her parents reading a story. She loved both her Mummy and Daddy, but it was her father's soft deep voice, that gave her the warmest feelings when she drifted off to sleep at night.

Life out of the home was good, Matt enjoyed his job and the numerous liaisons he had with his mistress. Sex with Vanya was fantastic and the antipathy of his love life with Lily. Nights in hotel rooms at the expense of his employer had become the backbone of his relationship with his lover. During those nights, they confirmed the strength of their illicit relationship, her absolute sexual compliance and reinforced his conviction that he was irresistible to all women. Monday to Friday the evenings he spent at home had become mundane and he had given up any thoughts of anticipation when he left the office for the familiar drive home. The weekends were devoid of hedonistic pleasure. Matt would sit watching Lucy play on the floor of the front room, whilst his dowdy wife busied herself with domestic chores, thinking of the opportunities that the following week would afford him to meet with Vanya.

Sunday mornings were Matt's time to get up early to care for Lucy, it was not a duty he relished and usually he had a crippling hangover. It was a beautiful early spring morning and Lucy was happily playing with her soft toy as she sat on the sofa, next to her jaded looking father, watching children's television. Eventually he roused himself and after he had dressed; he dressed his daughter. They left the house to walk the short distance to the local shop, where he would purchase his newspaper and some sweets for Lucy.

She looked beautiful as she scampered back and forth before the shelves of confectionary. Matt stood patiently holding his newspaper whilst his daughter selected the sweets she wanted, and then they walked together to the service counter. He handed the money to his daughter and she happily offered it to the shop assistant, an act that provoked smiles and cooing approval from the ladies of a certain age in the queue.

Hand in hand, they left the shop and walked toward the park where Lucy could play on the slides, swings and climbing frames. As she trotted next to Matt, clutching her sweets in a small paper bag, she frequently looked up at her father. His hand dwarfed hers and she felt the security of his strength. Every time she caught her shoes on the pavement, causing her to lose her balance, his strength would hold her up right and maintain their previous momentum until she was able to regain her balance.

The sound of the wheel, striking the curb caught Matt's attention. Instinctively he glanced over his right shoulder. The woman behind the wheel was struggling to control her vehicle as it careered towards him. With all the strength his shoulder muscles could muster, he flung his daughter into the driveway of the house they were passing before the car struck him.

Pain ripped through his body as the kinetic energy of the vehicle transferred from its steel body into the soft tissues of his body. Consciously he observed the rapid approach of the ornate garden wall until his head made violent contact with it. Blackness followed.

The lady driver did not stop her vehicle and drove off to some other destiny. Frightened and crying Lucy regained her feet and tottered towards the broken body of her father. She tugged at his jacket whilst she cried "Daddy, Daddy please get up" however, Matt did not move. The local residents came and so did the police. In turn, they attempted to comfort Lucy whilst they awaited the arrival of the ambulance. The Police asked her, what her name was and where she lived? All she could tell them was that her name was 'Lucy' and that she was frightened that her daddy was hurt.

With no identifying documents or local knowledge available, the Police were unable to identify where the child and casualty had come from. They had no alternative than to take the frightened child back to the Station where she could wait for a Social Services Agent who would take custody of her, until she could be identified and taken home. Lucy watched her father being prepared for transportation to hospital by the paramedics. She was settled into the rear seat of a Police car, a trembling, tearful child staring from the vantage more usually occupied by various miscreants. Her gaze was only broken when the Police Car turned a corner and drove her away from the scene.

Chapter 14

As she cleared away the plates and paraphernalia of their evening meal, Abdul watched her with a growing feeling of trepidation. He knew that he would have to tell her of the marriage proposition his uncle and father had suggested at the family party. The duty he felt towards Samira slowly overcame his dread of mentioning Al qasim's name to her. Slowly he stood from the table and walked across the kitchen to stand behind his wife. When she had placed the crockery into the dishwasher and closed the door he placed his hands gently on her shoulders spoke sullenly into her ear, "sit down darling I have something to tell you." She turned cautiously and stared into his face, she felt uneasy as he seldom spoke to her in that way and she could sense his reluctance to pass what was on his mind to her.

They sat together at the large table in their kitchen as Abdul relayed the details of the conversation he had shared with his uncle and father. Samira was shocked by the suggestion that Al qasim be married to Aesha. "No! Never! As long as there is breath in my body I shall never allow that aberration to happen," she shouted in an uncontrolled explosion of emotion. Abdul stood and held his wife close. They shared their pain and mutual revulsion at the idea naively proposed by Uncle Mohammed and Abdul's father. Comforting his wife Abdul spoke steadily and with all the conviction he could muster. "We will never let this come to pass, I vow to you my wife, our daughter will never be married to that pig." Taking comfort from her husband's resolve, she pulled away from him and began to make tea.

Sitting quietly Abdul considered his wife's back as she busied herself at the worktop. She was a beautiful lady. Long dark hair hung lightly down over her shoulders and most of her back. The olive skin of her arms shone almost imperceptivity in the bright light of the kitchen. The blue silk dress hung about her body emphasising the curves of her hips and buttocks. As he admired Samira's bottom he felt the familiar rush of sexual desire as his balls tightened and a strange tingling sensation spread across his groin. Averting his vision, he fought to exorcise the lust from his soul. There was no sin when a man found his wife attractive but he was keen to control his ardour for fear of the dark shadows that came with his desire. When the fire in his loins quenched, he felt the violation that always followed. A feeling as though someone had stolen a part of his very soul and that booty lost forever.

When Samira placed a mug of tea in front of him, Abdul spoke quietly to her without looking up from the table. "Do you ever think of him?" She placed her mug on the table and collapsed into the chair opposite her husband. Gazing at her hands as they lay in her lap, she spoke softly.

"No."

"Are you sure that you never revisit knowing him, when you lie in bed or when you are alone during the day when I am at work?"

Raising her head, she stared at him and stated coldly.

"You know I do not like it when you talk of it and that I want it buried with all the other horrors of the past."

Shrugging he left the table and went to the sanctuary of the front room to pray.

In preparation, Abdul sat quietly in the armchair by the flame effect fire and considered what he wanted to say to God. He was in need of forgiveness and guidance. For his wicked thoughts and behaviours, he required forgiveness and for his salvation, guidance to the path of strength and piety.

Logic dictated that the most effective approach to plotting his dialogue was, to recount the pertinent events in chronological order and matrix the results with his needs for forgiveness and guidance. Having decided on his approach Abdul cast his mind back to his student days at The London School of Economics.

As a young Asian student, he had felt great pride in securing his position at the prestigious university. He was full of ambition when he attended his first lecture. Within weeks, his desire to be like the other students had him drinking alcohol and by the Christmas break, he was freely fornicating with every woman that his privileged background could afford him to impress. The liberation of his libido roused a sleeping demon with in him and he began to experiment with homosexuality.

One cold winter's night in Soho, Abdul met John. He was from some dismal town in the North of England and had come to London to seek sanctuary from the dark spectre of his past. John introduced him to cocaine and love. The narcotic opened him up to sensations he had previously never considered and the emotion overwhelmed him. He became completely absorbed in the elements of his life that he shared with John, which was to the detriment of the remainder of his life. He had little contact with his family, ceased to attend the mosque, ceased to pray, frequently failed to attend lectures and alienated himself from his fellow students.

When eventually the extent of John's deception and his absolute commitment to his own self-interest was revealed to Abdul, he fell into a deep despair that pushed him further into the dark world of drug use and homosexual promiscuity. His self-destructive behaviour reigned unchecked for months; it became the only purpose in his life. Wrapped in the fetid cocoon of his debauched existence, Abdul had failed to consider the perception and strength of his father.

The first indication that his behaviour had not gone unnoticed was when his monthly allowance failed to arrive in his bank account. The second indication was a strongly worded summons to a meeting at his father's home. With great reluctance, Abdul caught the train that would take him to North London where he had hoped to persuade his father to reinstate his allowance.

Crunching his way up the gravel drive, Abdul was surprised by the number of vehicles parked in front of the house. He was bewildered when he stood in the foyer surrounded by nearly every male relative that he had known to be in England and a few from the old country. The atmosphere was cordial but cold and he felt every eye in the company following him as he walked with his father towards the study.

Sitting in his armchair, he burned with shame as he recalled the conversation that had taken place that day in his father's study. Initially he had tried to defend himself and to assure his father that there was nothing untoward. This initial approach had been a mistake; his father was no fool and was able to present the evidence that proved he was fully aware of every tawdry detail of Abdul's recent life. Mutual understanding assured, his father then went onto explain the extent of the shame that Abdul had brought on the family.

As he sat like a beaten child in the armchair before his father's desk, Abdul heard the door behind him open. Turning in the chair, he saw two of his uncles who had not been present in the foyer when he arrived, enter the room and move directly to his father's desk. They placed something onto the desk. Looking closer, he could see that they had brought his passport, which disturbed him. He had left the passport in his room at the flat he shared in Central London. His father looked up from the booklet before him and spoke directly to his brothers. "Is everything arranged?" They assured him that it was and left the room, leaving Abdul and his father alone again.

The intervention had been well arranged and it had become immediately apparent to Abdul that resistance to his father's will, would have been utterly futile. Escorted by an uncle and a cousin, Abdul was taken to the foothills of The Karakoma.

Abdul's correctional home sat amongst the rolling hills, high meadows and precipitous canyons of a savagely beautiful landscape. The foothills extended for many miles in all directions save for one, where the mighty snow-capped mountains majestically stood guard over their relatively diminutive geological siblings. The Madrassa consisted of several accommodation blocks and classrooms, all of which were centred about a mosque and enclosed by a compound wall. The fearsome winter weather had scoured much of the whitewash from the exterior walls of the buildings, giving the man-made structures a shabby appearance when set against their exquisite natural surroundings.

Standing in the early morning gloom, Abdul waved sullenly to his departing relatives. The world waited to burst into incandescent life, the rising sun breaking the horizon, fully illuminate the land. It had taken three weeks to journey from his father's home to the remote place of education that would serve as the facilitator of his rehabilitation. Communal living with shared chores, intense study of the Qur'an, little

94

sleep, meagre meals and all frequently punctuated by the call to prayer, was his routine for nearly four months.

Initially he had been resentful of his imposed religious retreat, frequently turning his thoughts to the life he had left in London, when he should have been considering the words of God. Eventually the teachings of the Imams opened his mind and the words of the Qur'an flooded into banish the darkness. The epiphany had been a glorious emotional experience for Abdul as he felt the weight of his sins being lifted from his shoulders. When the elders had been convinced of Abdul's return to the path of the righteous, word was sent to his family and he was collected and taken back to live with his relatives.

On his return to London Abdul's father re-instated his allowance and funded him to repeat his first year at university. Grateful and full of pious convictions, he dedicated his life to diligent study and a chaste observant Muslim lifestyle. This new approach had proved successful for Abdul and he duly graduated with a first class honours degree in Business Administration. After a brief return to the old country, his father secured him a position at the bank. With pious diligence, he applied himself to his new career. Rewarded with promotion and increased salary, his standing rose to a position where it was possible for him to support a wife.

The conclusion to the long-standing arrangement, for Abdul and Samira to marry, was planned; they were to be joined in a traditional ceremony in the old country. The dark shadow cast by his past had grown thin and Abdul viewed the forthcoming marriage as an opportunity to banish it forever with a faultless demonstration of Islamic family values. His father tacitly supported his ambitions and this had served greatly to strengthen his resolve.

On the eve of their wedding, as local tradition dictated, Samira and Abdul were separated. He spent the night feasting and carousing with his close friends and family, she remained in isolation with only her mother and sister as brief company. Her temporary prison was a large house outside of the village guarded by several of Abdul's cousins. Samira slept in the room that would serve as the wedding night conjugal bedroom, as her mother and sister slept in the room next door.

Outside the house, the cousins sat about a fire and chatted to each other long into the small hours.

When Orion plummeted towards the horizon, the cousins began to gather their blankets about them and one by one they fell asleep. Eventually Al qasim was the only cousin that remained awake. He stole from the fire into the house and made his way to where Samira slept. Abdul frequently imagined the scenario whenever he considered the terrible events of that night. He imagined Samira's shock as Al qasim climbed on top of her and forced himself into her virgin vagina. His fists would clench as he thought of her struggling under the heaving weight of his cousin and her sobbing as Al qasim spent his seed into her before tucking his, by then, flaccid penis away and walking silently from the room.

In his familiar armchair by the fire, Abdul fought back tears of rage and as he gained control of his emotions the demons came. Had she really resisted, had she sobbed, had she gained no pleasure from her first sexual experience? Fighting hard to stop hating his wife, Abdul cast his mind back to the time when she had confessed to him what had happened.

They had returned to his apartment on the banks of The Thames after a glorious honeymoon in The Seychelles. Sitting on the sofa, looking out over the river to the vista of the city skyline Samira turned to him and broke the news. He had stridden about the front room, venting his rage at the furnishings as she sat silently waiting for his attention to return to her. When Abdul moved towards the telephone she had sprung into action and held her husband long enough to bring him back to her.

Abdul's emotions had swung from outrage to hatred and crushing self-pity. Samira remained controlled throughout her husband's ranting, filling the occasional windows in his diatribe with balanced thoughts of reason. It had taken days and sleepless nights for her to persuade him that the greater good would be served best with their silent acceptance of what had happened and to live with the consequences. Her most powerful argument was that Al qasim had been the instrument of God doing his bidding in order to test their faith and love for each other. That argument alone had not been sufficient to convince Abdul however, even in his enraged state he could recognise the catastrophic consequences any alternative to silence and acceptance would have had on his family.

Swallowing his chagrin Abdul had agreed to remain silent and not to exact vengeance on his cousin. They had passed weeks barely speaking with each other and detached from the outside world. Samira clung desperately to the love she felt for Abdul and the sweet memories of their honeymoon. He had thrown himself into his work and faith and tried with all his moral fibre to repress his base instinct.

The chair had become uncomfortable and he stood up to remember the evening Samira had been waiting in their apartment for him to return from work. From the moment he had entered the room he knew something had changed. She looked up at him and without pre-amble broke the news that she was pregnant. "Is it his?" had been his first question. "I do not know" had come her simple reply.

Eventually Samira reached full term and Aesha was born. He had insisted on a paternity test. The test confirmed what he had suspected; she was not his child.

Drying the tears from his eyes, Abdul laid out his prayer mat and knelt on it to face in the direction of the holy city of Mecca. Before he began, he looked about the familiar room set to the front of their home, Tree Tops, nothing had changed and re-assured by this he began to pray. He prayed long and hard, relaying his fears, regrets and desires to God, he sought release from the darkness that threatened to swallow him forever.

God could not free him. Abdul had to be content with a re-ordering of his thoughts and with that, a divine logic to his life. Armed with the clarity his commune with God had given him, he felt confident to leave the front room and re-join Samira in the kitchen. After a brief apology for his earlier behaviour, he was back in her arms and love restored. They retired to bed.

Chapter 15

Pain is my ever-present companion. I feel It's company more acutely than is usual as I sit on the sarcophagus that has come to be my bed. My body aches with stabbing fuses of incandescent rage that burn from the numerous injuries I sustained from the beating and from the internal grinding of hunger, knotting and renting my vitals.

Shifting from my perch, I stumble in the darkness to retrieve my blanket from its usual cache. As I pull it over my shoulders and shamble back towards the open doorway, my intestines writhe as though some vindictive Haruspices sought the future from within me, having forgone the formality of prior evisceration. Accepting that this night would be no different from any other, in that I would not see her; I succumb to my body's demand for rest and slumped back onto the cold stone of my mattress.

The air hangs stagnant and heavy with moisture, wet stone and damp dust. The night shatters with the cry of a dog fox and repairs the silence with the gentle calling of an owl. Time passing brings increased noises of activity as the senses sharpen, silent screaming fine-tuned to hear the sounds of life. The dim night light through the door increasing in brightness as the eye adjusts.

As my senses sharpen, I become aware of the scratching, rustling, squeaking, barking, distant sirens, screeching, gnawing and hooting, the sounds of life in this place of the dead. I consider death as I begin to think of the woman murdered in my doorway. Who was she and why did someone take her to my theatre? Will she join me or will she pass straight to death. Caught in these thoughts I fail to hear her approach, until she is drawing to a halt in the long grass close to the doorway. My old friend had come to visit in the safe time prior to It issuing forth to hunt for victims.

Together we waited in each other's company, me on my stone bed and her standing in the long grass just beyond my door. The minutes passing in the warming glow of companionship. We had long since established a code of silence between us and as I sat in the darkness, I willed my thoughts to her. I told her how glad I was that she was back and how relieved I was that she continued to share my purgatory. No reply. I told her of my fear that she had finally passed over and left me all alone. No reply. I told her of the savaging It had given me. No reply. I told her of the beating the homosexual couple had given me. No reply. I told her about the lady who was murdered in my theatre. No Reply. I told her about the mission that The Willow Monks had revealed to me in their song. No reply. I told her about all of the dogs. No reply. I told her of my fear that inability to continue the mission would cause me to fail in my ambitions to shorten purgatory. No reply. Then I told her of how I had abandoned all hopes with the exception of one, the hope for death. No reply.

Sitting encased in damp stone, I broke our code and spoke directly to her.

"When we fall, will it simply end as we hit the ground or will we keep falling? Still falling through the darkness, faster and faster until we burst into flames. We would then be as a plume of fire, gloriously plummeting through the abyss only to burn out and leave nothing at all."

I wait for her response only to receive the expected silence. With that, I press this line of thinking.

"If the latter be the case, it would be as though we were never here and all our suffering in vain, save for the beauty of our eradication. What impossible consciousness could conceive such an abhorrent existence? I suppose mine, though I am not the creator of this painful travesty, I am only a spectator of this universal cruelty."
Silence.

"Alternatively the former hypothesis could be true and in which case there can be no colossus of consciousness. We would then be truly alone in an uncaring universe; where we serve only as the fodder of that ultimate of all predators; death."
Silence.

"There is a third possibility and that is: the monster that tortures us will reward us with an existence free from suffering and abounding in fulfilment once we have paid his price; the price being, blind obedience and unquestioning suffering, given with love and a smile. Counter intuitive behaviour required to gain the promised end. A promise with no guarantee or evidence that it will be honoured, given by a monster capable of the most fundamental cruelties. To trust this monster requires faith and faith is simply a form of non-thinking, stupidity in other words."

I heard her moving in the grass then I hear her speak, "goodbye" and with that, she walks away through the long grass and between the gravestones. I listen to her go, then lay my head down onto the cold stone and draw the blanket about me.

Cold as I am, I try to sleep. I long for sleep as it will allow me to avoid It when he comes to my door however, the realisation that I will never share her company again, keeps me awake. Again, my body has its way and I fall asleep to aid it in its pointless need to repair. Once asleep, the nightmares It gave me grasp and torture my mind.

Chapter 16

Once the car engine fell silent, the only sound was the recently energised generator, brought to life by the Scene of Crime Officers. They were establishing a preservation area on the path that ran alongside a railway that passed beneath the road where Detective Sergeant Gayle had parked the car. Car doors banged into place before Tommo Gayle pressed the 'blipper' key to lock the vehicle. A flourish of yellow flashing lights and an electronic 'bip bip' sound confirmed the successful execution of the radio command. He and Mac Gregor walked to the stairs, then nodding to the uniformed officer that stood guard, they ducked beneath the tape and descended to the path below.

Satisfied that he recognised the two CID Officers, the uniformed Officer returned his attention to the road. He had hoped for a quiet nightshift and was not prepared for the sight that greeted him when he first arrived at the bottom of the stairs. The shift worker, who had discovered them, was now being cared for at the local Accident and Emergency room where he was being treated for shock. No such respite for him, he had to remain at the scene hoping that relief would be sent to his location. His shift was due to finish in less than one hour. He was cold and longed for the familiarity of home, where he could drink to purge the terrible images from his mind.

A high security fence and the dense foliage beyond it separated the footpath from the railway lines. Across the path from the fence, dishevelled bushes and broken trees occupied the narrow verge between the path and a security wall. The wall protected the car park and service areas of a functional and banal hotel. From the base of the stairs, the path ran through sparse pools of yellow light, cast down from inadequate sodium lamps above. A ribbon of hard standing connecting the main road that passed over the railway lines and a quiet residential street where another uniformed Officer stood sentry.

101

Moisture condensed from the cold morning air onto the vegetation either side of the footpath. Mac Gregor, closely followed by his Sergeant, approached the white clad Officers who were busy assembling a large white tent over the path. The area about them lit up suddenly as the constant hum of the generator faltered before it adjusted to the energy drain required to power the arc lights. As the two newcomers approached, a Senior Scene of Crime Officer stepped away from the tent and moved to greet the Detectives. When he recognised Mac Gregor he spoke "good morning Sir" and mentally began to prepare his provisional briefing.

"What have you got here then," demanded Mac Gregor, of the officer in the white protective suit? After composing himself, with obvious thought, the man in white spoke in a measured tone.

"Two females, dead. There is a lot of blood and both have obvious head wounds. The scene is messy but that should provide plenty of evidence."

Mac Gregor and Tommo Gayle exchanged glances before the senior man gesticulated by raising his chin in the direction of the white tent. Without a word, both men walked past the Scene of Crime Officer towards the, now brightly lit, tent.

Taking care to follow the sanctioned route into the tent, the Detectives progressed through the morning mist, translucent in the incandescent light. They stood shoulder to shoulder holding the tent flaps apart whilst they absorbed the scene with their senses.

The women lay together the one on the right lay on her front with her legs apart, the one on the left lay on her side, tongue lolling from her gapping mouth and dead eyes looking at the corpse of her fellow victim. Crimson pools of blood surrounded their heads and merged. Their skirts pulled up about their waists, revealing sickly white flesh; neither woman wore underwear. Both had retained their high-heeled shoes.

"What is that smell?"

Tommo complained. Mac Gregor twitched his nose and replied.

"It's their bowels."

He nodded towards the victims to where excrement was smeared about their buttocks and dark pools of urine soaked the ground about them.

"Nice", quipped the sergeant.

"A reaction to blunt force trauma, especially to the skull."

Mac Gregor stated bluntly, as he turned and stepped from the tent, letting his flap fall across the aperture. Sergeant Gayle gazed on the carnage for a few seconds before letting his own flap fall and joining his Inspector.

Blowing a stream of smoke out into the morning mist, Mac Gregor turned briefly to confirm that it was Tommo that had stood at his side. After taking another draw of his freshly lit cigarette, he looked about the scene then spoke with his Sergeant.

"Well what do you make o' this then, linked tae the last one?"

Tommo pushed his hands deep into his pockets and answered his senior officer.

"Yeah I think there is more than a fair chance of that."

"Aye, ah would say that yer probably right aboot that Tommo, our Sean is now a serial killer."

Then he wandered about scanning the ground whilst he finished smoking his cigarette.

When they regained the road, Mac Gregor flicked his cigarette end into the darkness then waved to the bored looking uniformed Officer, as he and Sergeant Gayle walked to their car. Before they could climb into the car, another joined it. The silver Mercedes glided to a halt behind their vehicle and in one slick movement, the driver undid his seatbelt, killed the engine and climbed from behind the wheel.

"Mr Collins, good morning tae you."

Mac Gregor said as he walked around his car to greet the coroner.

"Morning Mac Gregor. Are you interested in this one too?"

The coroner replied as he shook the detective by his hand.

"Aye, looks like oor man has struck again, this time he killed twice."

Collins stood for a moment then asked

"The same M.O.?"

"Looks that way", said Mac Gregor with a shrug.

"Well I shall take a look and let you know Detective Inspector Mac Gregor."

Collins said in a friendly tone, then taking a bag from the boot of his Mercedes, he walked towards the stairs, where the uniformed Officer shifted his weight from one foot to the other and muttered to himself.

Lighting another cigarette, Mac Gregor leaned on the roof of their car and barked at Tommo.

"Where are you going?"

Startled by the suddenly harsh tone that his boss had adopted he snapped his attention from the car door handle and stared at Mac Gregor.

"Just getting in the car Guv."

"Well dinnae bother, I am having another smoke and since you object to me smoking in the car, we will wait here."

Conceding the Inspector's authority to give the order, Tommo relaxed and leaned on the roof opposite Mac Gregor.

"What's our next move Guv?"

"Let's get back tae the station and wait for the coroner's report and the evidence SOCO come up with, until then we will keep working on the first victim and this 'Sophistidates' web site. I want tae track that Sean character down, I've a strong feeling that he is in the middle of aw this."

Sergeant Gayle tried hard to think of something of profound value to offer his senior Officer but resigned himself to silence.

The familiar smells of the Incident Room filled his nostrils with the first inhalation he took on entering: musty paper, stale coffee, body odour and flatulence. Mac Gregor grunted a general salutation to the two young DCs that were already at their desks when he and his Sergeant arrived. He then demanded a coffee and marched to his office where he sat heavily on the chair behind his desk.

Sergeant Gayle loitered at the desk of one of the young DCs pretending to read his progress notes. He instructed the other DC to bring two coffees as he wanted a mug as well. Flicking through the notes the young man had made Tommo silently farted, then lingered only long enough to ensure he did not take the smell with him in his trousers to Mac Gregor's office.

As he walked towards the Inspector's office, leaving a gasping DC sat at his desk glaring after him, Sergeant Gayle was intercepted by another DC. Her short round frame hurried into the Incident Room and then accelerated to a bustle.

"Serge, wait. We have a positive hit on the website."
She called after him in order to slow his progress and allow her to catch up with him. Tommo stopped in his tracks and turned to face the fat DC.

"What have you got?"
She was slightly out of breath as she briefed the sergeant and then handed him a beige file.

"Thanks, I'll brief the Guv."
With those words, he dismissed her and resumed his progress to the office.

Tommo moved with deliberate purpose into MacGregors office.

"Guv we've made contact with Sean."
Mac Gregor looked away from his e-mails and focussed on his subordinate.

"What have you got?"

"He has approached one of our dummy profiles on that web-site, Sophistidates."
Mac Gregor held his hand out for Tommo to pass the file to him. Almost reluctantly, Tommo complied, handing over the file and leaving his boss in peace to read the contents.

Crazykatie was the screen name given to the dummy profile placed on Sophistidates. She was married with two children, thirty three years old and lived in St Albans. A photograph of a curvy brunette dressed in her underwear and her face obscured by her long hair had been used as the profile image. That morning a message was sent to the inbox of the profile. The message was from another profile under the screen name Loxtox. This in itself had not been remarkable as all of the dummy profiles attracted dozens of messages every day, what made this one interesting was that the sender had signed himself as Sean.

Loxtox's profile began with a photograph of a large erect penis that stood proud and dark against the lighter skin of his loins. The written profile detailed him as: thirty eight years old, married, no children and financially solvent. He had been married for fifteen years and whilst he had no desire to leave his wife, his sex life had become stale to the point that he only made love with his wife twice a year. He now wanted to meet a sexy woman who he could spoil with dinners and gifts. It was also an ambition of his that he find a woman that he could share his passion with. The message he had sent to Crazykatie read:

"Hi Katie,
Really love your profile and your picture is wonderful. I think that we would really get on, hope you might think the same way. If you are interested in getting to know each other better, please send me a message and we can take it from there.

Sean X"

Mac Gregor placed the file onto his desk and looked up at Tommo, who was still standing silently in his office.

"Well it has got to be worth a shot. Get on line and start flirting with this Sean, it might be the break we need."

"Yes Guv right away. Did you notice the time that the message was sent?"

"Yes Tommo I did, zero six fifteen this morning. If this is our Sean he will have had time to kill those two girls by the railway then get home, or wherever, to send that message." Nodding his agreement Sergeant Gayle took the file from Mac Gregor's desk and left the room.

Chapter 17

Mopping the beer, he had slopped, from the front of his shirt; Matt became aware of the presence of someone else in the room. He stared blankly at the stranger that stood just inside the doorway. She smiled at him and asked how he was feeling. His synapses re-routed the messages and within seconds, he recognised his wife, Lily.

"I am ok just spilt my beer Darling".
She looked disapprovingly at him.

"It is only ten AM, you should not be drinking at this time, especially as you are supposed to be sick."

He felt the chemistry change within his brain and with that, his mood changed instantly. Her constant disapproval and persistent criticism irritated him.

"I am not sick. I just needed some time away from work."
He snapped at her.

"I know darling I am just concerned that you are drinking too much."
She replied in a conciliatory manner.

"What has that got to do with you, are you my keeper or something?"

"No Dear, I know you have had a hard time of it since the accident and you deserve to relax."

"Accident! Accident you call it. That bitch tried to run me and our daughter down whilst we were on the pavement. You think that was an accident?"

"Well what else could it have been?"
She replied defensively. He stared at her and spoke in a cold threatening tone.

"What is that meant to mean?"
"Nothing."

Since regaining consciousness, Matt had changed. It had taken him weeks to regain his memories and once he approached normality, a number of subtle personality changes became apparent, not least of which was his increased truculence. Lily had learned to disengage with him when a

107

belligerent mood took him. Any attempt to reason with or to placate Matt, would inevitably result in an argument that would send him into a rage. He had never hit her, though she felt threatened when he was in that mood and in the darkest moments, she felt that it was only a matter of time before he lost control. Reluctantly she had concluded that he be left alone with his thoughts, hoping constantly that the effects of the brain damage he had sustained in the accident would repair and she could have her husband back.

After the accident Matt was taken to A&E and from there rushed to an operating theatre, where surgeons struggled to stop the bleeding on his brain. The operation had been successful though he had remained in hospital for a further three months before he was able to return home. Lucy had remained in care for nearly twenty four hours before she could be reunited with her mother. It was the most terrible time of Lily's life. Her husband and daughter had left the house to visit a local shop and did not return. She only learned of the accident after several telephone calls to the Police. Eventually information from different sources tied together and the connections were made that allowed the reunification of her family.

She had waited anxiously for the social worker to arrive with Lucy. Lucy had run from the car to her mother's arms. When the kindly lady had been packed off and Lily was re-united with her soft toy, Lambie, she loaded the car with her child and a bag for her husband then drove as fast as she dared to the hospital.

He had been unconscious, as he remained for nearly ten days, when Lily and Lucy came to his bedside. Matt's head was swathed in bandages, various machines monitoring his life signs with rhythmic and arrhythmic electronic tones. His daughter demanded answers to impossible questions from her mother. Lily stuttered platitudes and procrastinating answers as the electronic symphony accompanied their incomprehension and fear. They stayed at his bedside for as long as was possible. Clinical staff, who sought to reassure them, supportively interrupted their visits.

Slowly Matt recovered. His brain repaired itself to the point where consciousness became viable. Gradually his motor skills came back, as did his memories. It had taken nearly four weeks for him to recognise Lily and Lucy. The first time he called her name, when she had entered his hospital room was the first time she had dared to hope that everything would be all right.

When he learned to walk again and to care for himself, he was discharged and allowed to return home. Even by the time she helped him to the car to take him home, Lily had become wary of this new Matt. He frequently forgot where he was, who he was, who she was and what had happened to him. Her efforts to assist his memory were usually rebuffed with verbose insults and personal attacks. The husband that had cried when his affair with Vanya Byrd was revealed and had begged pitifully to save their marriage was now an intransigent ingrate, a changeling and propagator of oral violence.

Her attempts to re-introduce her altered husband to their circle of friends were disastrous. Historic fondness and pity could not compensate enough for the frequent onslaughts of insults, pedantry aggression and personal vitriolic attacks that Matt dispensed with evident glee. These events would end with Lily pouring out apologies and excuses to their departing guests before returning to the front room where she would find her husband, contently smug with his socially inept behaviour.

The woman, who had been driving the car that knocked him into the garden wall, could not be found. Matt could remember her face, looking dumbly at him over the steering wheel, just before the car she controlled hit him. He hated her, her dogged determination to evade justice, irked Matt more than he could bear within himself. This cardinal frustration made him a misanthrope. Until she was brought to account, he would make everyone else pay for her crime.

Eventually the patience of his employers wore thin and he was required to return to work or retire on medical grounds. For ten months, they had paid his full salary and the company health care plan had funded his private treatment. He knew that he had been fit enough to return to work months before he was required to however, he had resolved that he would make every person or organisation that he could, pay as dearly as he could. Grudgingly he allowed the doctor to pass him as fit for work and he returned to his old job, which had been kept open for him at great expense to his employers.

It took only weeks for him to conclude that he hated everyone that he worked with. Even those he had previously thought of as 'alright' and those that he had actually liked now grated on him. Their supercilious manners and utter conviction that their activity was of paramount importance, filled him with loathing. His resentment towards his employer only grew and he resolved that he would continue to make them pay. He would push it as far as he calculated that he could and feign relapses to excuse him from attending work.

Lily retreated to the kitchen where she began to make herself a cup of tea. The outburst from Matt was, by now, a typical event and would probably repeat itself later in the day. She had reluctantly grown accustomed to his behaviour, and was able to function around it. She needed to be strong for him, her child and herself. There was the housekeeping to be done and Lucy to be cared for. The money that Matt had received from the criminal injuries board had allowed her to give up work and concentrate on caring for her family: a beautiful young daughter and a brutal bugbear.

When she opened the fridge door to retrieve the milk for her tea she counted the tins of strong lager stacked on the top shelf, there were eight, last night after he had gone to bed, there had been twelve. Taking the milk from the shelf inside the fridge door, she walked back to where the kettle and mug waited for her attention, shaking her head.

As she crossed the kitchen to return the milk to the fridge, her attention was caught by something in the woods. She could see the trees clearly through her kitchen window. The edge of the woods was only yards away, across their front garden and the narrow road that ran before their bungalow. The trunks rose to form a great natural pillared hall, its ceiling a lush canopy of green. In the near distance the details of the woods could easily be discerned however, as the distance increased the less and less detail could be seen. In the darker recesses of the emerald hall something moved. It moved with regular anxiety, like an expectant father pacing a room. She could not form any shape for it in her mind, it was as if it were constantly changing like a chaotic cloud of shadow. It was black, blacker than the darkest corners of the wood and it was waiting.

Draining the last of the lager from his tin, he stood and walked deliberately to the hallway, which he followed to the kitchen. Having negotiated the 'L' shaped passage he turned into the kitchen. "What are you doing?" He demanded when he saw his wife standing motionless and staring out of the window. Snapping back to verisimilitude, Lily focussed on her husband, "nothing just looking out of the window". Matt opened the fridge door and muttered "fuck wit" then taking a fresh tin of lager from the top shelf he let the door swing shut and stomped out of the room.

She annoyed him. Always in his space and yet always so detached. Every time he felt that freedom was within his grasp, she would fuck it up. It was no wonder that he had fucked that fat black bitch for so long. At least she knew how to please him, unlike his frigid wife. Vitriol coursing through his mind as he sat on the sofa and opened his new tin of lager. Matt was angry, very angry, he had been dealt a significant injustice and no one seemed to care. He could not even rely on his wife to support him, all she did was criticise whatever action he took or did not take. Fuck her, he thought to himself as he took a long draught from his tin of beer, and then switched the TV on with the remote control, before casting the device onto the sofa next to him.

Vanya Byrd had been his mistress for a couple of years. Despite the subsequent hardship, his marriage endured after their affair was exposed, he had re-established contact with her. Matt had always enjoyed sex with Vanya. She performed oral sex with unbridled enthusiasm and enjoyed anal sex as much as she enjoyed vaginal penetration. These two aspects of her behaviour alone were sufficient to maintain his interest in her.

They met regularly, in hotels dotted along the M4 corridor, usually paid for by Matt's employer. Both would use the excuse of working away overnight to explain their absences from the respective marital beds. Those evenings were events that he looked forward to with great excitement. There would be a brief sex session in the room, sufficient to allow him to

111

reach climax, then they would move to the hotel bar for a drink before dinner.

After dinning together and sharing a bottle of wine, they would have a late drink in the bar and then retire to their room, for sex. He always admired the beautiful ebony of her skin, it emphasised the curves of her rounded body in the classically subdued lighting of the slightly above average hotel room. They wasted no time in removing their clothes and both would be naked within minutes of entering the room.

Their lovemaking always followed a routine yet maintained its newness and therefore its excitement throughout the affair. They began with oral sex; Matt would bury his face in her crotch, licking from anus to clitoris, where he would linger, gently biting and lapping with his tongue, then return to her backside. She would wantonly bob her head on his cock when it was her turn, saliva sloshing in her mouth as she nodded him towards orgasm. Cocking her leg to bring it across his body, she achieved her preferred position with her pussy and anus presented to Matt's face and his cock sitting neatly before her. When she climaxed in that position she would rub her vaginal fluids over his face with her labia and short, tightly curled pubic hair.

Matt especially enjoyed her habit of sucking his balls, which she always did just after orgasm in the 'sixty nine' position. Then from their oral lusts they would turn their attention, to fulfilling her need of penetration that she had for all of her orifices; that could reasonably accommodate his penis. She would sit straddling his groin as she took his manhood as deep as she could inside of her and rode him as hard as she could until her thighs were too sore to continue. Her capitulation to the lactic acid build up in her thighs was the moment that Matt waited for. This was his signal to manoeuvre her onto all fours and bugger her.

Though he lusted after her, and their evenings of sexual hedonism were keenly anticipated distractions, from the banality of his existence, the relationship he shared with Vanya could not escape the negative effects of his altered mental and social perspective. She had also begun to irritate him. Try as his libido forced him to, he could not disassociate

112

his mistress from the period of his life when the accident had happened.

Lying by her side, their congress complete, Matt peered at the ceiling. Having inspected the contours and cavities of the smoke alarm for nearly ten minutes he turned on his side to speak with Vanya. He had felt the endorphins from the recent sex diminish in his mind and for the darker emotions to return. It was as though he were outside of himself, observing his skin change colour with the chemical shadows passing across his brain, glowing through his translucent skull.

"Why did you call my house that morning?"

"What morning?"

She murmured to him through her relaxed and sexually fulfilled aura.

"Don't be so bloody obtuse, you know full well what morning I am asking about."

Matt shot back at her.

Shocked by his sudden change of mood, Vanya sat up on the bed and clutched a pillow to her chest.

"What are you being like this for?"

Her passive defence only served to exaggerate his foul mood and he unleashed a tirade of vitriol against her. She tried to reason, then to defend through attack and even seduction. All of her strategies failed and Matt became increasingly angry.

When he could not take her pathetic denials for another second, a flash of crimson red shot from his optical nerves and blinded his consciousness. The relief he felt was soft and warm, like being wrapped in a fleece blanket. Even the harsh pain from his right hand could not diminish the comfort of the satisfaction. Again, he felt detached as he watched himself punching, a weeping and bleeding Vanya, repeatedly in the face.

She had cut her tongue on the broken shard of a tooth. Tears and mucus flowed from her eyes and nose as she gasped rasping gulps of air between great sobs. Every time she focussed on recent events, her incredulity drove her back into stunned denial. It was impossible for her to believe that he had hit her, let alone beat her with such intensity. As she covered her face with her hands, she could feel the swelling on her face, so angry that it had almost closed her left eye.

His pleading had begun to annoy her. All she wanted was to feel better and for the pain to go away. Not content to have put her in that state he insisted on whining on about how he was sorry, how he was going to make it up to her and why she should not go to the Police. When he promised, for the second or third time, to give her anything if only she would not go to the Police, she recognised that this was her opportunity to gain the only thing that she wanted from him.

The image on the T.V. screen flicked from that of some imbecile sharing the intimated details of his life with the fifteen year old mother of his child, to a revolting American comedy with canned laughter. Matt swore to himself, "fuck" before finishing the beer from the tin he was holding in his left hand. He felt that life had not been kind to him of late and that it had just added insult to injury now that Vanya was expecting his child; the price of her silence.

Despite the assurances Vanya had given and the caveats that he had negotiated, Matt knew that the pregnancy and the resulting child could not be kept quiet. He expected that she would make it a project of hers to ensure that maximum impact be achieved from her successful impregnation. Did he want to lose his wife, did he care enough for her, would he be happier with Vanya or would he be happier on his own? These questions were, by now, constant companions of his and he could not decide on an answer. His thoughts would swing wildly between all four options throughout his waking hours. This made him vulnerable because he had to find the right answer. He needed to make the right decisions.

Chapter 18

With the unease of the previous night's 'condom' incident still fresh in her mind, Becky had risen early, taken Thomas over to her mother's and then returned to make breakfast. She hoped that waking up to a plate of food and the joyous peace that exists when a toddler is absent, would distract Brian from analysing the evidence available and the explanation that she had given. Now that she had slept on the matter, she was painfully aware of the flaws in her tale. It was an ambitious aim to distract him from the matter to the extent that it would never be mentioned again and she had to admit to herself that, he very probably would ask her again about the condoms he had found in her handbag.

The sausages were cooking in the oven as she beat the eggs with a whisk. Satisfied that she could achieve no more with her whisk she dropped it into the bowl and placed it on the work surface. Walking over to the cooker, she turned the grill on to allow it to heat up. Halving a couple of tomatoes, she arranged them on the grill pan with four rashers of back bacon then turned her attention to the toaster. She lifted the sliced bread from the side and fed two slices into the slots of the toaster, then depressed the leaver that activated the machines only function.

"Hey what yah doin'?"
Brian's voice came, in an affected American accent, from behind her. Startled, she turned rapidly to face her husband.

"Thought I would treat my fantastic husband with breakfast in bed."
He smiled at Becky and walked across the Kitchen to the coffee pot, where he filled a large mug to the brim and then carefully sipped at the hot liquid.

"I'll go back to bed then."
Brian said as he walked out of the room carrying his beverage.

Visibly relaxing, she returned her attention to the preparation of breakfast. Judging the sausages as sufficiently cooked, she placed the grill pan under the grill and then cut a large lump of butter from a block into a frying pan. She

115

checked the progress of the sausages again before firing the gas ring beneath the frying pan. Gradually the butter melted into a golden syrup pool in the pan. One of the many preferences that Brian had acquired through his younger years in America was scrambled eggs made in a frying pan. No milk or seasoning, other than a pinch of salt, the beaten eggs are simply turned into the melted butter and constantly agitated with the whisk until the desired consistency was achieved; he preferred them slightly on the firm side.

Bursting into the bedroom with a flourish, she presented the tray to Brian. He sat up and arranged the pillows behind him before he reached for the tray and settled it into his lap.

"Hey what are you doing all this for Darling, what have I done to deserve all this?"

"Oh nothing, just that I love you."

She bent over and kissed his cheek before retreating from the room to retrieve her own breakfast.

They sat side by side in the bed, each with a tray balanced on their lap. Cutlery scraped on the plates and smacking and slurping, they forked proteins, carbohydrates and fats into their mouths. Occasionally he would pause between mouthfuls to burp. She would also pause, drop her knife onto the tray and place her hand over her mouth prior to joining her husband in a burp. As they approached the conclusion of their fast breaking, Brian lifted his left buttock and forced a faecal bugle call to blast the miasma of his bowel contents into the fetid atmosphere confined beneath their duvet.

Cutlery clattered onto her plate when she had pushed the last of the scrambled egg on toast into her mouth. Brian had long since finished his breakfast with the last rasher of bacon, bent over three times and skewered onto the tines of his fork then forced into his wide mouth, set between the ample mounds of his ruddy cheeks. He enjoyed his food and his physique betrayed this personal fact with every bulge, ripple, overhang and additional chin.

Becky slipped from beneath the duvet, careful not to overturn the breakfast trays and moved like a cat to the bedroom door where her housecoat hung from a hook. She had always carried a few additional pounds on her frame but she wore it well, or so she had been told by her many admirers.

116

She doubted that anyone had said anything as flattering to her husband in many years. When she lifted his breakfast tray from his lap, she noted with mild revulsion his ample belly. It hung over the duvet in folds and nestled beneath his semi-pendulous breasts.

When she had left the room to deliver the dirty plates and cutlery to the kitchen, Brian sat thinking about the condoms he had found in Becky's handbag. He knew she was sleeping with someone else and her flimsy attempt at an excuse was proof positive that she took him for a fool. He despised himself for the absolute weakness that dwelt at the very core of his being. She should be faithful to her husband, she should have greater respect for the father of her child, she should count her blessings and above all, she should keep her infidelity hidden from all. For some time, he had resigned himself to his wife's weakness for congress with other men. Though knowledge of her activity had never stopped hurting, he had become used to the pain. What hurt him now was the new knowledge that she sought additional excitement with her beau, or beaus, by using ribbed condoms.

"Thank you for breakfast Darling, I love you."
Brian enthused when Becky returned to the bedroom. She felt uneasy and stood awkwardly at the end of the bed as she studied his face for signs of insincerity. Brian returned her studious look with a broad smile and a wink.

"Why don't you climb back into bed Darling?"
Reassured but still suspicious of his intentions she moved to her side of the bed and let her housecoat fall onto the floor. Pulling back the duvet, he implored her with his eyes to join him. After a brief, uncertain, pause she threw herself onto the mattress next to him.

She tried not to breathe, as he slobbered on her cheeks and neck, his breath stank stale food and sulphur. Podgy sweaty hands pawed at her still firm and ample breasts as his flabby thigh prised her legs apart. He replaced his thigh with a hand and groped at her vagina with his stumpy fingers. In order to free herself from his awful halitosis and the imminent vaginal penetration with his short, fat and dirty fingers she shifted her weight and reached down for his penis with her slender hand.

Wrapping her fingers about his stubby cock, she began to work her hand up and down the modest length and around his unimpressive girth. She worked enthusiastically on his erection in the hope that she could affect his climax before she would be required to perform any further sexual acts with him. Pretending to admire his penis, she kept her face pointing away from his and the revolting smelling gases he exhaled.

Resentment burned in him as he noted each ploy she used to avoid any of his terms in their intimacy. He first rested his hand on the top of her head and then gradually increased the downward pressure to push her face closer to his cock. Eventually he felt her take his manhood into her mouth. He held her head and thrust his groin towards her face, forcing his erection further into her mouth, when she gagged he relented and let her pull away a little then he thrust again. He knew that she tolerated his abuse to curry favour and avoid any further questions about the condoms. If that were the price she was willing to pay, he would collect every penny. Suck, gag, exhale and suck again.

To enhance his excitement he imagined his unfaithful wife sucking someone else's cock or moaning with pleasure as the stranger thrust his ribbed condom clad member into her. Revelling in his own patheticness and emasculated by his wife's clear preference to sleep with someone else, he found his sexual excitement enhanced. Her distress equally enhanced the sexual pleasure he drew from this intercourse and he felt almost triumphal when his climax exploded into her mouth as she gagged on his thrusting cock.

Relief washed over her as cum spurted into her mouth, 'at last' she thought to herself. The whole act had taken only a minute or so yet, it seemed to her to have lasted far too long. She had pretended to gag on his diminutive penis throughout, in the hope of avoiding the need to allow the rancid, stubby little thing into her pussy. She preferred to reserve that coupling for those special men, the ones she could be herself with, the ones with whom she enjoyed sex. Swallowing his sperm, she let his flaccid penis, which was even smaller than his woeful erection; flop sadly from her mouth onto one of his abdominal folds. It lay there, almost lost amongst the vast undulations of flesh surrounding it. 'Pathetic' she thought to herself as she gazed down at his manhood, now barely the size of a chipolata.

Rolling off the bed, Brian made his way to the bathroom where he urinated and farted before shaking his cock and returning to the bedroom. When he re-entered the room Becky had already dressed herself in a pair of jeans and a yellow T-shirt. She slipped her feet into a pair of pink fluffy slippers and went to the kitchen to make tea. He sighed as he considered his lot in life then returned to the bathroom to shower, shave and perhaps to empty his bowels.

He joined her in the kitchen as she was finishing her second mug of tea.

"I am going down to the canal for a bit, what are your plans for today?"

He asked nonchalantly. She stared at him with disbelief etched on her face.

"I'll do some housework then go get our son from Mother's."

Un-phased by the look on her face, Brian continued.

"Yeah I wondered where he was."

'Bloody typical' she thought to herself, he had the opportunity to spend the day with her and no distraction from their child but instead he would rather go fishing. She slapped the kettle on again and began making herself another mug of tea whilst he rummaged in the cupboard under the stairs for his fishing equipment.

Becky thought he looked like 'a real fucking prat' as he walked off down the road carrying his tackle box, landing net and two fishing rods. On his back, he carried the most ridiculous backpack arrangement, its frame could fold out to form an armchair and the cup holder inserts of the arms were clearly visible as he strode down the pavement. He wore a smock and trousers made of a disruptive pattern materiel with a matching floppy hat, on his feet he wore knee high rubber boots that, from a distance, could be mistaken for Jackboots. His rotund figure and distinctive costume, gave him the appearance of a Third World Military Commander.

Turning from the window through which she had been watching her ridiculous husband's progress, she walked to the front room where she lifted the top on her computer and pressed the 'ON' button. If he were not willing to spend time with her, she would find those that desired her company 'on-line'.

The cheaper or free websites had nothing to offer her beyond the usual collection of shadowy profiled players, some of whom could possibly be genuine, most of whom would be fishing for on-line fantasies. She hurriedly replied to those that held the slimmest of possibilities for sophisticated adult fun with short and flirty messages then logged out. Her nature was always to save the best to last and true to form; she typed her favourite site's address into the address bar then initiated the connection. To her delight, she had seven messages in her 'inbox'. The first three were from characters she would consider as 'possibles', the fourth and fifth 'red hot' and the last two were from men she had already had sex with; Dave from Watford who had screwed her on a canal boat and Steve from Barnet who had been so big she had difficulty walking for days after their liaison.

Dave had one of the smallest penises she had ever put inside of herself and she did not intend to re-live the ten minutes of boredom, staring at a chipped plywood ceiling from a damp mattress as his flabby body heaved away on her. Steve she would have definitely considered seeing again but for her general rule of 'no return'. Becky toyed with the 'possibles' by replying with questions of: how naughty would they like to be, what would they like her to wear and where would they like to cum in or on her. The two 'red hot' characters received greater attention.

'Muffdivingman' had a picture of a very cute naked bottom as his main profile picture and a series of shots of an average yet attractive erect penis. The text of his profile stated that he was married and was looking for 'no strings' sexy fun. She liked what he had to say and what he was looking for in the partner that he sought. His message explained that he found her photographs sexy and that he really liked her profile. Her reply was deeply suggestive and opened the door for them to meet.

'Loxtox' had only one photograph on his profile, which was an image of a large erect penis. She squirmed in her seat as she felt the dampness that spread from her pussy soaking

120

her knickers. Images of some cocks did nothing for her and the image of others turned her on. The effect this member had on her was all the motivation she needed to desire sex with that stranger. His message detailed how he wanted to have sex with her in a risqué location and in what positions he would like to take her in. Unusually he signed the message. Most men did not. Her reply read:

'*Hi Sean,*

Thanks for your message. Your profile is hot, love your cock would love to have it in my mouth. Like the idea of a nice meal then a dirty fuck from behind in an alleyway. Would love to wear my stockings for you, what would you prefer sheer or fishnet?

Bex
XX'

In order to inspire action from others there must be a mutual, albeit proportional, gain. If there is no material benefit, action will only be achieved through the effective application of violence or charm. Violence can materialise as a slightly raised voice or any assault up to and including murder. Charm will range from a smile through to sex. Matt understood this philosophy and had always applied it in his professional, and on occasion his personal, life.

As he perceived the issue, his employers did not provide sufficient material gain to the functionaries of the company to inspire the intensity of activity that they demanded of them. This in turn asked unreasonable outputs from the supervisory and junior managerial levels of the operation. This presented a paradox: Matt would demand of his middle managers the results dictated, ultimately by the shareholders, through his employers by the agreed budgets for the business.

For proportional gain to be available, the price for the provided service would have to go up. This could not happen for two reasons: firstly, the competitive tender market would not stand for it, each competitor was willing to push exploitation to, and beyond, the absolute limit, and secondly if the price could be increased, the shareholders would want the additional benefit regardless of the needs of others. The essence of Capitalism is usury.

Shareholders, like customers, believed that they had divine authority. Ownership of a company or payment for a product or service gave them license to act as the Gods of Olympus, to demand the unreasonable and to punish, with petulant impunity, any failure to comply. Employment law existed to protect the rights of the employee, however outsourcing and slyly constructed industrial relations agreements ensured that the Gods always won the war, even if the occasional battle was lost.

Matt sat at the small meeting table in Ann's office. Before him, he had several business reports that detailed the budgeted targets for her area and the results to date. The results fell short of expectation and Matt had decided to visit her operation to discuss the shortfall with her.

Ann returned with two mugs of instant coffee and sat opposite Matt, placing one mug patterned with the company logo in front of him and nursing the other in her hands. The office was a rundown tatty affair in comparison to the salubrious environ of his office, situated in the UK Head Quarters. Paint peeled from the walls of her office, which were festooned with graphs displaying data of dubious value. Her desk was tiny and broken, the laminate curled up at all of the edges giving it the appearance of the poor relation to the shabby meeting table across which they now faced each other.

Pausing only to thank her for the coffee, Matt addressed the subject of her region's non-performance directly. He wanted her to furnish him with tangible local business issues that had caused the shortfall and her plan to correct the matter. Ann could only give him excuses for why the business was not working as planned. She supported her position with tacit posturing about the impossibility of the budget that, she believed, she had been browbeaten into agreeing. He smiled at her and delivered the 'we are all in this together' speech. This was to no avail, as she did not move her position one iota. He then explained that this was a business absolute and that she was expected to produce the results that other managers, in her position, were achieving. Ann met that approach with the same excuses that she had presented in her defence originally, only now couched in defiant terms.

Matt reiterated the manifest shortfall, the negative comparison to other business units and the need for each budget to be achieved. Ann accepted the facts without moving her position. He asked if he could help, either directly or by the provision of greater resources, she appeared dejected and resigned to failure. This frustrated Matt to the extent that he raised his voice when he explained that, she was expected to manage that area and if she were incapable of doing so, he would find another Manager to replace her. She began to cry.

It was an impossible position for Matt. He knew the impracticalities of their operation and the unreasonableness of the company's demands however, he also knew that his job was to get the results. He could feel the chemistry in his brain changing and he fought hard to suppress the outburst that was rising within him.

A few deep breaths later, he stood up and moved to Ann's side of the desk. Placing a hand on her shoulder, he spoke softly.

"Hey its ok we can work this out."

Matt rubbed her sobbing shoulder gently and leaned down to rest his head against hers,

"come on" he said encouragingly.

Then slipping his hand from her shoulder, he slowly rubbed her back, all the time pressing his head against hers whilst he spoke platitudes. Perceiving that she moved her body closer to his, he pushed his arm across her back and under her arm where his hand came to rest, cupping her breast.

With a start, she pulled away and looked up directly into Matt's face. Misinterpreting her actions, he moved in for a kiss.

"What are you doing?"

She exclaimed as she pushed fully away from him and stumbled to her feet. Ann stood in astonishment glaring at her boss.

"What!?"

He demanded as the chagrin rose within.

"What the hell do you think you are doing, you cannot do this it's, it's sick."

She protested.

As the anger grew in him, he advanced on his subordinate Manager with an, ever increasing, posture of menace. Staring into her face, he remembered the face of the stranger driving onto the kerb directly at him and his child. Matt grabbed Ann's shoulders roughly, as he screamed into her face.

"What the fuck do you think you are saying, we need to sort this out and I am only trying to help you!"

She cringed in his grip and began to repeat the word 'please' over and over again. Losing his temper, he threw her onto the floor and stood over her prone body.

"You better get a grip of yourself and stop fucking about or you will be out of a job!"

Ann's Administrator looked surprised, when Matt barged past her and out of the office when she had come to the door to ask 'if everything was ok'. He stormed through the building and out into the car park where he climbed into his car and sped away from the scene. He drove the car hard, breaking only at the very last minute and shouting his frustrations at any driver that impeded his progress. Opting not to return to his own office, he switched off his mobile 'phone and drove to his local pub.

The Dog and Dyke had the atmosphere of a post-party clean up. Lunchtime clientele had deserted the establishment in a procession of vehicles from the pub car park. Already the smell of cooking was growing stale in the air, individual chips or peas scattered on the carpet or corner tables marked the feasting that had taken place. A young girl moved with no air of urgency between the tables, clearing and cleaning them. Matt waited at the bar while Steve, the Landlord, concluded his business with a Sales Representative.

Steve the Landlord had never taken to Matt. He found his manor arrogant and on occasion robust to the point of rudeness. He was surprised to see Matt in the bar on a mid-week afternoon. He usually came in with his wife and latterly daughter for a meal in the evening. Almost resenting his presence, having grown used to an empty village pub on the weekday afternoons, Steve greeted Matt and asked him, 'what he wanted'?

He usually drank red wine, on this occasion however, he wanted a large drink, a pint of something strong, something that would calm his thoughts and chemically alter his mind quickly. He considered and rejected the real ale pumps, arranged along the central area of the bar. Matt found it curious that a one-time 'working man's' drink, ale, should become the preserve of the modern middle-classes, in their middle-class country pubs, in their middle-class villages and towns. Lager was now the drink of the 'working man', the stronger the better. That observation brought him to a decision. He forwent any courtesies and stated bluntly, "Stella. Pint." Smarting from Matt's bluntness Steve retrieved a pint glass from beneath the bar and filled it with the golden liquid. Grudgingly he took the note, offered by Matt and returned his change, without a word passing between the two men.

Taking his pint from the bar, Matt sought the sanctuary of an alcove table, where he sat glaring across the room over the top of the frothing white head in his glass. The room was typical of a 'Home Counties' village pub. Dark wood, yellow walls, heavy duty patterned red carpet, horse brasses and assorted rural tat, scattered across all horizontal surfaces without utility. Each table adorned with a large green ashtray bearing the name of the owning brewery. A loud clatter from the kitchen caught his attention and he watched as Steve swung the door behind the bar open and groaned as he walked through it. Matt left alone in the pub, with his thoughts, already calmer and more ordered.

His anger remained with him though he could feel the edges blunting as the strong lager took its effect. 'Why do all those bastards not just accept that life is not fair and that we all have to push, cut corners and drive the unreasonable in order to achieve what is required of us', he raged to himself. He knew beyond question that, if his people stopped whinging and just did what they were expected to do, there would be no issues and his life would be far simpler.

When he noticed Steve return to his post behind the bar, Matt took his empty glass to the bar and ordered a refill. With no greater ceremony than before, his glass was re-charged and the transaction completed. Passing the afternoon sat at the alcove table, angry thoughts and vague accusations tumbling about inside his head, Matt drank eight pints. Eventually, some of the early evening drinkers joined him in the room and he became conscious of the effect that the beer had on him.

He stumbled back to his car, feeling shaky on his feet when the cooler outdoor air hit him. Taking several deep breaths before he slid behind the wheel he started the engine and pulled out of the parking space that his car occupied. He drove the half-mile home, at the speed limit, with the side window down and the stereo turned off. Over-thinking every manoeuvre and driving action, it was an anxious journey for Matt and it was with tangible relief that he pulled his car to a halt outside of his home. Jumping from the vehicle, he thought smugly to himself, 'another risk taken and another reckoning cheated'.

Lily lifted her head when she heard Matt's key in the lock of the front door whilst Lucy continued to giggle and play with a brightly coloured plastic toy, which she splashed into her bathwater with repeated glee. "We're in here", she called to him when she heard the front door close. No response. She listened to his familiar home routine, shoes removed, jacket pockets emptied onto the kitchen table and then his progress to their bedroom. Her attention returned fully to her daughter. She had learned to leave him alone if he did not reply. Since the accident, he had become an increasingly volatile man and silence was a significant warning; his mood was not good.

Eyes opening and closing in a slow motion blink, Lucy placidly observed her father who sat on the sofa wearing a grey tracksuit. He stared with overt disinterest at the early evening news on television. "Matt" she snapped with irritated incredulity. Slowly his head rolled away from the direction of the TV and lolled on his shoulder as he slowly slurred "what" in response.

"Your daughter is going to bed now; do you want to say good night?"

"Yes of course" he stated affectedly and yet with conviction.

Matt held his arms out and Lily delivered their daughter to him then retreated a few paces to stand nervously by. He held the baby girl to him, kissed her cheek and wished her sweet dreams. Cold words summonsed the child's mother to gather her from a dangling position at the end of his outstretched arms. His daughter looked bewildered when taken from the room, and her father's attention returned to the 'picture box' in the corner of the room.

When Lucy settled in her cot, Lily went to the kitchen, where she fished a boxed pie from the middle shelf of the freezer then plastic bags of frozen vegetable from the bottom drawer. Clunking them onto the work surface, she turned the oven on and clattered about in one of the cupboards until she had found the metal trays she desired. The timpani of her supper preparation continued when she slapped the metal trays onto the work surface and delivered the frozen chips onto one of them, with a harsh metallic series of reports followed by the bass thump of the pie dropping from its box onto the other tray. Staccato concussions of the peas, as they flowed from the plastic bag into the dry pan, pushed the sound intensity of the operation to a new high, followed closely by the torrent noise as the pan filled with water to cover the frozen peas. The symphony of percussion continued until the larger items were thawing rapidly in the oven and the frozen spheres of green lay, submerged, in water thawing gently and awaiting the fire that would be lit under them.

He smelled strongly of drink, she had smelt it from the moment she had left the bathroom with her washed baby, wrapped in a soft towel, in her arms and walked the short distance to the nursery. It hung in the air of the hallway like the residual vapours of putrid flatulence. Lily sat in the armchair and silently observed her husband motionlessly staring at the images of weather patterns over the landmass of The British Isles.

It irritated him when people would look at him and not say anything. As he watched the weather report on television, he could feel her eyes peering at him from just beyond the field of his peripheral vision. If she had something to say to him, she should just come out and say it. Why sit there staring at the back of his head, what did she hope to achieve? Matt knew her real motivation was to shame him for drinking too much or for drinking and driving. Turning to face her rapidly he yelled "what"! Jumping visibly in her seat Lily's jaw dropped and she gaped at him whilst she struggled for the words she could employ to structure a response to his sudden outburst of aggression.

"Just what the bloody hell is it that you want?"

"Nothing I was, errr, just thinking."

"No you weren't you were staring at me."

"I was looking at you, not staring."

"Same difference. So what is it that you want?"

She sighed before she spoke.

"You've been drinking?"

"Yes so what of it?"

"You know I have never minded you drinking but I don't like it when you drink and drive."

"So I fancied a couple of pints after work and you want to make a big issue about it."

"No I just…"

"Fuck off."

She sat silently, studiously averting her gaze from Matt. The pretence of watching TV lasted for several minutes before she returned to the kitchen in order to resume her supper making duties. The percussive symphony re-started with the kettle drumming of the oven door and the cymbal clash of a smashing plate.

Pie, chips and peas constituted a modest supper. It had been one of their joint favourite meals since the very early days of the relationship and she was glad that she had decided to prepare it that evening. Once plated, she served the two meals on the kitchen table and went to fetch her husband.

Matt was in the same position, location and temperament that she had left him previously. Not wishing to be accused of staring at him again, she spoke immediately as she entered the front room, to inform him that supper was ready. He moved as though it pained him. With deliberately hesitant progress, he made his way to the kitchen, where he poured himself a large glass of red wine before he sat at the table and began to eat. Raising his glass, he added a fair sized swallow of wine to the large forkful of food he had pressed into his mouth. Lily joined him at the table and began to eat.

They ate together in silence, she not daring to aggravate her husband and he not interested in anything she might have to say. Matt was most of the way through his meal when he reached across the table to his mobile telephone, which he had left there since emptying his jacket pockets. Casually he pressed the small button to bring his 'phone back to life. The telephone's display told him that he had twenty six missed calls. 'Bollocks' he thought to himself as he cast the mobile back down on the table and poured another large glass of red wine.

That night it was a full two hours after she had retired, that Matt joined her in bed. She had stayed with him in the front room for as long as she dared. Lucy would wake early in the morning and Lily would be required to rise and deal with her infant's needs. He had sat quietly all evening, drinking red wine at an alarmingly fast rate of consumption and occasionally moving restlessly. His mental health worried her, primarily because she did not know if the belligerent, self-absorbed bully he could occasionally become was the real him; released as a result of the brain damage or if it were some odious stranger that occasionally occupied her husband's mind. Either way she knew that unless there was some fundamental improvement their relationship was doomed. It teetered on the edge of an abyss. One more loathsome outburst, negative aspect of his personality revealed or a further step down the road of abuse and their relationship would tip beyond recovery, and be lost forever.

When he climbed into bed with her, he had taken no trouble to reduce the noise he made in the room. He let his belt buckle drop with his trousers noisily onto the bare floorboards of the bedroom. He then grumbled loudly, cursing to himself about other people and other situations. Pretending to be asleep, she moved with the undulations of the mattress that his thoughtless thrashing inaugurated as he bundled himself into bed. Wishing to dream of happier times, she pushed her face into the pillow as she sought the sanctuary of her memories. He breathed as though he were wearing an aqualung then with depressing predictability the rasping hacking of his snoring began. Lily pressed her face further into the pillow whilst she waited for the temporary release that sleep would bring.

Dawn broke and the birds sang their spring chorus to greet Helios' rise. The electronic screaming tore through his slumbering and injured mind. A mouth like a putty tub and tonsils that ached from the trauma of night-long snoring, laboured painfully to groan in protest, at the unpleasant sensation inducing noise that Matt's mobile promulgated. Cursing as his hand slapped about the bedside table, he eventually found his 'phone and fumbled with his numb unresponsive hands to hold the luminous screen in front of his bleared, unfocussed eyes. As he struggled to remember which button would kill the alarm, Matt's eyes focussed and his memory began to function as it frantically searched for recognition. With eventual clarity, he read the screen and recognised the electronic tone, his telephone was alerting him to an incoming call and not to his morning alarm as he had assumed.

Pressing the 'reject' button, he dropped the 'phone onto the dressing table and cursed "fuck it" before continuing to the bathroom. He had set the alarm to rouse him later as he had anticipated a hangover. He had not anticipated that his Managing Director would be trying to contact him before even the alarm activated. If he were honest with himself, he had not expected to hear from his boss until the management meeting at the end of the following week. As he sat on the toilet, he heard the alarm sounding from his telephone. 'Not much to do about it' he thought to himself and left it for Lily to deal with, then returned to his considerations of the possible motivations that his MD might have to call him that early in the morning.

His hands tingled uncomfortably, submerged in the hot water. Matt prepared for his morning shave. Leaning into the basin of water, he looked up at his face, reflected in the bathroom mirror. Deep dark bags hung above the tracks of broken veins that spread across his cheekbones and over his nose. Piggy eyes peered back at him, whites yellowed and rims reddened. "Christ! I look rough", he said to himself before he filled his left hand with a meringue of shaving foam from and aerosol canister. With his right hand, he splashed water onto his face before plastering the foam over the lower half of his face and began to shave with a shaking hand.

When he emerged from the shower, he could hear the trilling of the mobile 'phone in the bedroom. Ignoring it again, he padded from the bathroom to the kitchen where he made himself a cup of strong instant coffee. By the time he had dressed in a suit and consumed most of the coffee, he was feeling better. His recovery was obviously fragile as any sudden movement or bright light immediately initiated a hazing nausea. It felt as though a goblin was kicking his eyeballs from inside his skull.

Lily had been up for some time, tending to Lucy's needs. Matt kissed them both quickly then shouted, "must dash" before disappearing with a brief wave over his shoulder. As he climbed into his car, he draped his jacket onto the passenger seat and fitted his 'phone into the hands-free cradle. With the initiation of his car's engine the music began and he was on his way to work, though he had not crossed the boundaries of his village before the 'phone rang.

Jabbing his finger forward, he accepted the call and the music cut to the sound of the caller. Matt recognised The Managing Director's voice.

"Matt, is that you?"

"Yeah it is Trevor, what can I do for you?"

"Are you on the way into the office?"

"Yeah, I am. Running a bit late but should be there in about thirty."

"Ok, listen we have an issue. I need you to come directly to my office when you get here."

"Why what's the matter?"

"We'll discuss it when you get here."

"Ok Trevor I'll be there as soon as I can."

"See you soon."

The line went dead and Matt tried to put the implications of the telephone conversation to the back of his mind whilst he concentrated on his driving.

Distractedly he navigated his executive saloon through the morning traffic of South London to his parking space in front of the Company's Head Office. He was nervous by the time he left his vehicle and walked the short distance to the main entrance. The sun shone brightly and had his mood been more relaxed, Matt might well have been reasonably happy however, the conversation that he had with his boss unsettled him. Angst gnawed at his natural confidence as he strode into the entrance and greeted the Receptionist with an overly loud "Morning", proclaimed with faux jocularity.

When Matt reached the staircase, he resolved to go directly to The MD's office and confront whatever issue he wanted to discuss with him. Taking the stairs two at a time he soon reaches the first floor and made his way through carpet-tiled corridors to the desk of his boss's Personal Assistant, Lisa. "Boss wants to see me" he stated with deliberate casual charm. Lisa looked up at him with her practiced, 'I know nothing' look, "he is expecting you and told me to ask you to go directly in." Unsettled by the ease with which he achieved instant access to Trevor, Matt hesitated before moving to the dark wooden door and tapping on it with his knuckles. "Come in" came the immediate response. Matt opened the door and entered, steeling himself with a deep breath.

Trevor stood up from behind his desk and moved rapidly around it and the meeting table that stood before it, to greet Matt with a short handshake. Then indicating a seat at the meeting table, he took a seat opposite. Matt sat down where his boss expected him to sit and moved uneasily in his seat.

"Thanks for coming straight here Matt."

"No problem Trevor, what's this issue we need to discuss?"

"There has been a very serious complaint made against you."

Matt slouched in his chair forced a wry smile onto his face and drawled in a tired voice.

"Not that stupid cow Ann?"

"Where were you yesterday afternoon?"

"I went up to our Thetford Office to review the performance of the Manager, Ann."

"I tried to call you all afternoon and your 'phone seemed to be off."

"Ah yeah, I felt one of my headaches coming on when I was driving home so I switched my 'phone off so I could concentrate on driving and when I got home I went straight to bed."

Trevor nodded without giving any impression that he believed Matt, then taking a brief breath he looked down and up before continuing.

"The nature of her complaint is very serious…"

"Come on Trevor, it's all shit, she just doesn't want to do her job and she will say anything to take the spotlight off her."

"Matt! I have to take this seriously and so I shall, from the end of this meeting, be suspending you."

"What!? You must be kidding, what have I done?"

"I think you know that I am not kidding. A very serious allegation has been made against you and I shall have no choice but suspend you with full pay until we have had an opportunity to investigate the matter."

"Who's made the complaint and what am I supposed to have done? Let me guess; it was that cow Ann and she has probably said something ridiculous like I tried to shag her? Am I right?"

"The allegation has been made by Ann and it is an allegation of inappropriate behaviour. We need to get to the bottom of this, statements will be taken then we will consider the evidence then meet to discuss the way forward. Until then you are officially suspended. You will be paid. You may have full use of the company car. Keep your 'phone in case I need to reach you, please do not speak with anyone else from the business."

"Trevor you do not believe any of this do you?"

"Matt you know what we have to do, now please help us do it and maintain your professionalism."

He was eager to leave the car park but did not know where to go. If he returned home, he would have to explain himself to Lily and he did not feel ready for that challenge. He started the engine and pulled away with no destination and a head full of shock and consequence.

Chapter 20

The BMW drew to a halt on the gravel drive. Abdul turned off the engine and sat contemplating the meeting ahead. He loved and respected his father; however, he rarely looked forward to seeing him and today was no exception. It was late afternoon and the sun was starting to set, the cooling air driving an evening breeze to caress the treetops and draw forth a broad sigh from the foliage. There was no way back now, his father was expecting him and he would no doubt be aware of his son's car parked on the drive. Briefly, he offered up a prayer and then opened the car door.

A breeze forced the back of Abdul's shirt, wet with perspiration, against his skin, causing him to shiver slightly in the cool spring breeze as he swung his jacket over his shoulders and slid his arms into the sleeves. The car door closed with a quality affirming 'clunk' as he walked slowly towards his father's front door. Birdsong hung tangibly in the air like a thousand chimes moving in the wind. In the distance, he could hear the low hiss of the traffic on the nearby trunk road.

As fresh virgin snow that rarely blanketed these lands in the colder months, the gravel crunched under each footfall. The collective fluid function of the aggregate underfoot served to hinder Abdul's progress to the portal of his Parent's home. Each grinding step robbed of two inches by the submissive material beneath. Sun shining and gentle breeze carrying the scents of herbs and flowers with it as it ambled about the surface of the ample gardens, belying the intensity of the dark and demanding matter that had brought him. The sound of insects on the wing would rise rapidly only to diminish with equal suddenness, like feigned jabs from a superior opponent. Obligingly fulfilling the role of cautious challenger he hunched over, as though shouldering a great weight or diminishing the target area his upper body presented as he ascended. The marble steps, flanked by two guardian steles, house number emblazoned in gold on each, carried him upward towards the portal of his dread.

The heavy green door swung open only a fraction of a second after Abdul had pressed the doorbell. His mother embraced him warmly and ushered him inside to the large entrance hall. He accepted his mother's offer of a glass of lemonade and smiled warmly at her as she retreated to the kitchen, leaving him standing in the hallway.

"Abdul my Son" his father's voice boomed from the staircase where he stood. Abdul was not sure how long his father had been standing there and his greeting had made him jump. Then climbing the stairs to his father's embrace, he regained his inner composure. The older man asked for news of his health and Abdul dutifully assured him of his wellbeing before returning the customary compliment.

"So Son what is this grave matter that you must discuss with me so urgently, can we cover it in the comfort of the sitting room or will we have to use my office?"

Abdul's father spoke with relaxed authority and obvious affection for his son. Abdul could not bring himself to return his father's smile before he asked if they could use the office. Concerned by his son's solemnity the patriarch's smile straightened, moving to one side he indicated the way with his left hand and waited for Abdul to ascend the remainder of the stairs to the first floor.

Childhood memories of mystic awe re-surfaced into his consciousness when the unique smells of the office filled his nose. The room seemed ageless, ostentation in every respect with furniture of the darkest woods or gaudiest gilts. Heavy velvet drapes drawn uniformly to either sides of the three large windows that allowed the bright afternoon sunlight to penetrate this strangely styled 'East meets West' collision of decors. Whilst he associated the room's atmosphere with all things masculine, Abdul noticed for the first time that the scent of the air was almost wholly feminine. Musk, rose and jasmine combined to remind him of fine perfumes, the smell Samira would leave in a room after she had passed through. Her scent would fade after a second however, the air hung heavily with it in his father's office.

When both men settled on the large leather sofa, his father sighed loudly, linked his finger in front of himself and rested his hands in his lap. "What's this all about Abdul?" Abdul was

136

about to answer when there was a gentle knocking on the office door. Before either man could respond, the door opened slowly and his mother entered carrying a tray. A large jug and two glasses balanced on the tray, "I've brought you some lemonade." They sat patiently whilst she placed the tray on the table before them and poured two glasses before retiring from the room.

The glasses of lemonade presented a welcome distraction. Neither of them was eager to address a matter so awkward that it could create such an atmosphere between father and son. When both had taken deep draughts from their glasses, returned them to the table surface and sat back on the sofa, Abdul's father broke the silence.

"Now Son what is this about?"

"Aesha."

"What about your daughter, she is well I trust?"

"Yes father she is very well and we intend to keep her that way."

The bluntness of Abdul's answers solicited rigidity in his father's disposition, as though his persona were made of quick-drying cement and the sun's rays through the window, set it.

"Then what is it you wish to discuss with me?"

"We cannot allow a marriage between her and Al qasim to take place."

"Son, your Uncle and I only presented the suggestion to you at the family party for your consideration. It is of course a decision that only her parents can make and I hoped only for you and Samira to give it fair attention."

"Well we have father and we cannot countenance such a proposition."

"May I ask why?"

Abdul felt uneasy lying to his father but the truth would blow the family apart.

"We feel that they are too close in family for it to be a good union."

"Nonsense, He is your Cousin not hers. Such a union is permitted in The Qu'ran and in the law of this land."

"Also we feel that the age gap is too great between them."

"For her to have an older husband is not a bad thing. He will be mature and established by the time she is of age. A girl can do much worse than to take a husband who will care for her earthly being as well as her spiritual being and an older man is far better placed to do this than a man of her years."

"I hear what you are saying father however our minds are made up and I would ask you to relay this to Uncle Mohammed."

The older man stood up from the sofa and walked slowly behind his desk where he leaned on the flat top with his palms spread wide. With a sigh he let his head fall forward, revealing the bare circle of scalp at the top of his pate, surrounded with the grey of his remaining hair. Abdul studied his father, standing motionless for over a minute in the rays of warm light from the windows. The sweet feminine smell of the office intensified as the tension in the air grew.

In the distance, a lawnmower spluttered into life and settled into a rattling drone as some unknown gardener cut a neighbouring lawn. Like a sentry protecting man's rights to dominance over nature, he would be marching behind a petrol-driven harvester as it groomed the grass into two-toned strips of green. Abdul recalled the natural beauty of the high meadows amongst the foothills beneath the Karakoma in the sure knowledge that his father's mind currently occupied the same temporal zone.

Barely audible groans that accompany the movement of an old man brought his attention back to the office as he followed his father with his eyes. The old man moved deliberately to the centre window where he stood momentarily with his hands clasped behind his back, studying the garden beyond. He spoke as if addressing the distant gardener.

"There is much that has been wrong and I have done all that I could to make that right and to build a good family in the eyes of Allah. From the works of the Devil I have rescued you and with you I have pulled us all back from the brink."

"I know father and not a day passes that I do not thank Allah for you."

Slowly the older man turned to look at his son.

"I did not want to involve the family as I had no desire to make your sins known to them but I had no choice.

You gave me no choice. I did not possess all that I needed to save you and so I called on them for support, support they gave willingly."

"What has this to do with Aesha?"

"Your sins may not be spoken of openly now but they are not forgotten. To save you we needed to call on the wider community, the price of their support was the common knowledge of how far you had fallen. Your sins hang like a plague warning over your house, you may find that suitable husbands for Aesha are not so easily come by as you imagine."

"How can that be, no objections were raised when I married Samira?"

"All things have a cost, Samira came without a dowry."

"How have I not been made aware of this before?"

"I felt that it was better that you never knew so that you could concentrate on repairing yourself and building a good life."

"We shall find a husband for Aesha. The whole world cannot know of my failings."

"As I said Son, all things have a cost. Even family do not give so generously without an expectation of recompense."

"What are you trying to say father?"

"To gain Mohammed's full support I had to promise him that, should it become necessary and possible our side of the family will provide wives."

"You promised Aesha before she was even born?"

"What choice did I have? You had fallen so far that I needed to intervene. I could not do that without my brother's help. Besides it is not wrong for Mohammed to want to see his line continue and he and I want to make this family stronger."

Abdul could feel the dampness in his armpits and the beaded moisture on his forehead as he began to perspire again. His mind raced as he tried to reason with the information and case his father had presented to him. His mouth opened and closed with every thought he could conjure to counter his father's perception however, no thoughts of his, when examined, proved viable enough to survive to oratory.

Sensing that he had made his case strongly enough for the moment, Abdul's father relaxed and re-joined his son on the sofa. His father's presence was strangely re-assuring and he found it difficult to despise the man that had saved him, though he found the price of that salvation difficult to swallow.

The lawnmower coughed and fell silent, leaving a blanket silence over the gardens as Abdul walked slowly towards his car. Only when he stopped by the driver's door and sought his keys from his jacket pockets did he begin to think again. With sentience came awareness of the birdsong, distant traffic noises and the awful realisation of what he had promised his father he would do.

Chapter 21

Amy Roland and Zoe Clark had been friends since school, now both in their late twenties they remained close friends. They both worked for Insurance Companies but not the same one. They both married in their early twenties though Amy was divorced two years ago. They both had children, Amy a boy now aged five, Zoe a boy aged five and a girl aged three. According to their friends, they shared a reputation for being 'a bit wild' and 'a bit mad' when they were out together. Those reputations were now posthumous as they were dead. Sculls crushed by heavy blows from a blunt object, their corpses found by a railway line, knickers around their ankles and covered in blood, faeces and urine.

Their night out may have been madly wild but it was also fatal. They had been seen drinking together in several bars and were last seen in 'The Feathers', a bar well known to be the place to end a night in, if you were open to sexual liaisons with fellow strangers. The Doorman remembered the two women leaving with a man who was probably in his early thirties. He could recall little of the man they left with but could describe what the two women were wearing with an accuracy that made Mac Gregor uneasy.

Tommo Gayle took notes whilst his boss interviewed the staff of The Feathers. Apparently, the man with Amy and Zoe had bought them several, expensive, drinks and they had reciprocated by flirting heavily with him as a pair. Their behaviour had become so bawdy at one point, that the Bar Manager had asked them to tone down their conversation and actions. The Glass Collector confirmed that as he cleared the tables about them, he could see that one of the women was rubbing the man's crotch whilst he was plunging his tongue into the mouth of the other. They talked loudly about a threesome and the man declared that he wanted 'to fuck two slags from behind', it had been that declaration that prompted the couple at the adjacent table to complain to the Manager.

The forensic report confirmed that not only was the murder's Modus Operandi (M.O.) identical to that of Shirley

Babcock's murderer but that the same blunt instrument, probably a hammer, had been used to kill Zoe and Amy. As part of their investigations into the Babcock case, Mac Gregor and his team established a 'Glove Puppet' account on a website called Sophistidates where they had identified a major suspect, Sean. Given that the same murder weapon and M.O. was used, Mac Gregor and his Sergeant had to assume that their suspect could be the key to solving the mystery of all three murders.

Both incidents had taken place within days of each other and press reports were now verging on the hysterical. The last thing Mac Gregor needed was another incident to fan the flames of panic. It was his experience, that when panic spreads people listen to idiots and things are not done well, when cognisance is taken of what idiots may say.

Having digested all the new evidence available on the double murder by the railway, Mac Gregor checked on the progress of their internet investigation. He was pleased to hear that the virtual flirtation with Loxtox (aka Sean) was going well. Satisfied that he would have achieved some progress within a couple of days He decided to be at home that evening in time to dine with his wife. Mary Mac Gregor had begun to complain of, never seeing her husband and he had learned, many years previously, that it was wise to invest a little effort to placate his wife before the matter ballooned into a relationship threatening issue.

When he had finished briefing his Chief Inspector on the telephone Mac Gregor hung up, pulled the jacket from the back of the chair that he had been sitting on, and made for the outer office. With a rapid general farewell, he bade his team a goodnight and made directly for the exit. The relief he felt when he managed to reach his car, without interruption or re-call to the investigation room, demonstrated by the unusual sight of a smile on his face. He climbed enthusiastically into his vehicle and set off for home.

An evening of rare family time at home was a welcome relief from the investigation. When he woke, he felt fully rested and even to his own surprise, looking forward to the day ahead.

Mac Gregor was driving through the city street in the bright morning sunshine on his way to the station when his mobile 'phone trilled an alert. Answering his mobile with some irritation Mac Gregor barked a salutation into the handset and continued to drive through the thickening traffic.

"Hi Boss it's me, Tommo."

"Aye Tommo what can Ah dae for you?"

"There's been another one."

Detective Inspector Mac Gregor made it to the station in record time, thanks to the assistance of a patrol car and its associated blues and twos. Sergeant Gayle was waiting for him in the car park.

"Over here Guv." Tommo called to Mac Gregor.

"Got cha' Tommo, what wheels we got?"

"Special treatment Guv, we got the SAAB."

They climbed into the green car that Tommo had indicated and set off for the latest, potentially related, crime scene. Both men were anxious as they made their way through the morning traffic. They knew that the pressure exerted on them from senior officers for a result would increase exponentially with this latest development.

"When was the body found?"

Mac Gregor asked blandly as he gazed out of the car window.

"Six thirty this morning Guv. Old lady walking her mutt found the body in the park."

"Does it sound like the work o' oor man?"

"Yes, arse in the air and no knickers etc."

"Bloody hell the Chief's gonna be all oo'er us like a fat bird oan a buffet."

"He's already left word at the investigation room for you to brief him when you have finished at the crime scene."

"And so the circus begins."

Leaving the car parked on a residential street leading to the park gates, the detectives walked into the park and set a definite course across the grass towards a taped off area, diagonally opposite, where white-suited personnel busied themselves, guarded by two uniformed Officers. A small crowd of on-lookers gathered on the grass facing the white tent construction covering the immediate area of the scene of crime, all hoping that inside they might come across information that would establish them as a local expert on the extraordinary event. Police vehicles clustered by the thick bushes and occasional trees that occupied the far corner of the park.

"Lazy bastards, look at the mess they've made here." Mac Gregor grumbled as he pointed to the tyre tracks pressed deeply into the soft turf of the park.

"You're right there Guv. If we walk it, they can do the same."

"Aye a' would say some o' oor collegues would spend an entire shift in the car if thae could."

Both men jumped at the sound of the car horn. The large Mercedes passed them silently as its rear wheels slithered slightly over the grass. They recognised the driver when he parked his vehicle by the Police cars and climbed out from behind the wheel.

"Looks like the Coroner's got himself a new car." Observed Sergeant Gayle, dryly.

"Aye business must be good what wae aw them deed bodies we keep caa'n him oot fir."

Approaching the crowd of spectators gathered ghoulishly by the tape that marked the scene boundaries, Mac Gregor instructed them to move on. He then detailed the two uniformed officers to complete the crowd dispersal and gather his sergeant to his side and moved to the white tent.

Poking their heads in through the entrance flaps of the tent Mac Gregor and Tommo gained their first sight of the crime scene together. The Chlorophyll-gorged monster consumed the upper half of her body. A consumption prompted by pure spite. Organic nutrients and energy from the sun providing all the sustenance required for its existence, thus rendering the ingestion of the human redundant. Two tubes of flesh emerged from the flora feeding on the fauna. Bulbous buttocks at the leaved orifice tapered, with diminishing oscillation, down to the feet that barely touched the meagre earth.

Her blue skirt surrounded her upper abdomen where it entered the thick bush. Lumps of excrement adorned her buttock cleft and thighs, which rested against the foliage. Most of her weight appeared to be supported by the shrubbery she had fallen, face first, into. A small pair of red knickers hung limply from her right ankle and a pair of green strappy shoes abandoned her feet at curious angles. Partially concealed by the lower reaches of the leaves a patent green handbag laid on its side.

Looking down Mac Gregor noticed the evidence marker cone just inside of the tent.

"Hey, what's this doin' aw the way oo'er here?"
The Inspector demanded of the Scene of Crime Officers working in the tent.

"We need to test it, Sir."

" Dae ye think she fired that aw the way oo'er here?"

"Probably not Sir, my guess is that it belonged to the old lady's dog. Chances are she only noticed the body because her mutt pulled her in here so it could take a dump."

"You foond any good bits fir me?"

"Just what you see Sir. I can ask one of the lads to get you a spoon if you would like."

"Very funny noo shut yer smart mooth and tell me the good news."

"Well Sir the soft earth has given us some prints, which is more than we got at the other scenes."

"What can you tell me fea that?"

"Just the two of them in here, our victim and a male with feet about size nine, I'd say. At one point she stood facing the bush and he stood behind her. Make of that what you will."

"Thanks, anything else."

"Nothing obvious Sir."

Mr Collins the Coroner interrupted and began to perform his initial examination of the body. Mac Gregor and his Sergeant stepped outside and surveyed the park.

"My guess Tommo is that Collins is going to tell us that she died o' heid injuries in the wee hours."

"I happen to think you are right there Guv."

"Another romantic liaison, gone wrang."

"Think we had better find that Sean character."

"Aye Tommo we better find him soon. He's killing them faster than we can keep up. Come on let's get back tae the Incident Room and get cracking."

They took their leave of the attending officers and Mac Gregor asked Collins the Coroner to telephone him when he had finished at the scene. Together the two detectives set off across the grass, both deep in thought and weighed down by the demands the case was now going to make of them.

From the passenger door of the stationary Saab Mac Gregor scanned the windows rowed either side of the suburban street. Double ranks of netted portals to the secret lives of the souls beyond. Milky eyes, crusted with splitting varnished wood gazed impassively on the two instruments of justice standing by the green car, imploring them to find a killer.

Fingers like wizened parsnips opened the pupil of a glazed eye, pulling the net curtain to one side, allowing the ancient face to peer across an over-grown tiny garden at the Detectives. Holding her attention by locking his keen brown eyes to her ruined vacant orbs, Sergeant Gayle called his senior officer's attention to the window with a sharp nod. Mac Gregor turned to follow his Sergeant's gaze. "Let's hae a word." He stated blandly as he released the car door and approached the frosted glass of the old lady's front door.

She appeared startled when the two Detectives walked the short distance up her garden path and knocked on the door. After an unreasonably long wait a thin voice called from within.

"Who is it?"

"We're Police Officers, can we have a word?"

Tommo spoke with reassuring authority.

"What about?"

"We are investigating a very serious incident and I would like to ask you some questions."

"I don't know anything, please go away."

"It would be very helpful if you were to open the door and answer some questions."

"I don't know anything, go away."

Tommo held his warrant card to the frosted glass and persisted.

"It really is very important."

"I told you I don't know anything."

146

Mac Gregor finally lost his patients with the occupant and barked.

"Open the door, noo!"

There was a brief silence before the sound of a chain drawn and the key rotating in a lock. Slowly the door opened and a face like a walnut stared out at them from the same height as Tommo's waist. Thrusting their warrant cards at the old woman, the two men exchanged glances before Tommo spoke in his kindest voice.

"Can we come in Dear?"

Her time-ravaged face gazed uncomprehendingly through the fissure she had opened on the World.

"Come on Dear we are Police Officers and we need to talk with you."

Eyes like a terrified heifer's, locked onto the block of Mac Gregor's being and her jaw hung slackly.

"Let us in, noo."

Mac Gregor spoke with his customary gruffness.

With obvious reluctance, she shuffled backwards, drawing the door open as she went. The stench from inside flooded outward into the wind-freshened daylight. Tommo caught his breath and began to regret their decision to speak with the random nosey parker. She stood silently with her body mostly immersed in a thick curtain of old coats that hung from the hallway wall and waited for he uninvited guests to enter. Looking to his boss, Tommo received the instruction to enter when Mac Gregor flicked his head in the direction of the open door.

The Detectives filed into the hallway and waited for further instructions from their host. Leaning on the door lock, she painfully tottered the door closed then performed a laborious 'about turn' on the spot to face them and then inched forward to pass. When she gained the internal doorway, she spoke in a voice, fragile as sugarglass. "In here." Dutifully they followed her into the front room.

The room was as dark as the hallway had been. The filthy net curtains acting as overly effective filters for the invasive light of the outside. There was barely space on the threadbare carpet for the men to stand. Stacks of old newspapers and magazines stood like unmoving occupants, their rectangular forms reaching the height of a small person, taller than the resident if she unfolded her aberrant spine. Anaglypta, stained brown, peeled from the walls and hung like bats around the ceiling. Centrepiece to the room was a light bulb, dust glued to its surface by an unspeakable resin.

Dressed in a thick stained overcoat and burst slippers, she hobbled about to point her backside at a moth-eaten armchair. She dropped into the cushioned hollow worn by years of labour under her ever-disintegrating body. Cast about her throne were opened tins, long since emptied of their consumable contents. One tin stood erect with a shaft of an eating utensil protruding from its hacked open top, ravioli, her most recent meal. In the bay of the window sat a bucket surrounded by sheets of newspaper, stained brown and yellow.

Struggling to control his gag reflex Mac Gregor drew air through his mouth and fixed the grey, yellow and white bag of skin hanging in the chair with a firm gaze.

"There was a very serious incident in the park last night."

Head hanging as though on a rope, strung from the ceiling, she did not respond.

"Did you see anything?"

"No. I don't go to the park."

"Did you see anyone from your window last night?"

He motioned with his head to the aperture over his shoulder.

"I saw them walking together."

"Who? Who did you see and what time was this?"

"Late, I saw them late."

"Who did you see late?"

"Him and a girl."

"Do you ken him?"

"I know of him. He is a devil."

"Whae's a devil?"

"Him."

"Whae's he?"

"I don't know."

"Look, try to remember. What time was this?"

"Late."

"You said it was late, what 'am askin' is how late?"

"Dark."

148

"Help me out here, I need to know who you saw and what time you saw them."

"The foxes were barking and he took her up the road to the park but he did not bring her back down."

"Do you ken either o' them?"

"He is a devil."

"You ken him?"

"I know of him."

"Could you describe him?"

"Yes."

"What did he look like?"

"Dark."

Mac Gregor turned to his Sergeant in frustration and flapped his hands to his sides. Tommo held his palm up to the Inspector then turned to face her throne.

"Can you help us? We really do need to know everything you can tell us about last night and what you saw."

"I was pissing in my toilet when I saw them pass. He held her and she kept kissing him. They kissed by my garden whilst I was pissing."

"You saw them from your bathroom window?"

"Yes."

She held her crippled hand out to indicate the bucket by the window. Subconsciously Tommo and McGregor shuffled some inches away from the bay window.

"Then what did they do?"

"They walked into the park."

"How do you know they went to the park?"

"The road doesn't go anywhere else."

"How do you know they didn't go into one of the other houses?"

"I know everyone who lives here."

"And they don't?"

"No."

"You said he was a devil, why?"

"I know these things."

"How do you know them?"

"The closer to death you are the more secrets you learn."

"What do you mean?"

149

"You will learn when you have earned."

Almost instantly, he regretted snorting air in through his nose. That proclamation of indignation and impatiens carried the stench of the old woman's home into the recesses of Mac Gregor's nose. His stomach heaved and the years of stalwart self-control, tested to the absolute as he fought his body's demands to retch. The other Detective took a moment to re-assess his line of questioning before he pressed on with his possible witness.

"Listen to me carefully Ma'am and try to help us. It is very important and you could help us put a 'devil' away for a long time. Do you know the man you called a devil?"

"We all know devils."

Tommo could feel the tension in Mac Gregor's bearing give way. Like caustic thunder, The Inspector's brogue filled the room.

"For Christ's sake, will you listen and stop talking shite!"

"Easy Guv."

Tommo cautioned the senior officer.

"Fuck it Tommo, av had enough o this auld Gobshite."

"Guv."

"Right listen tae me. Dae ye ken the man ye saw?"

She sat dumbly staring at Mac Gregor, head still hanging from the invisible ceiling rope.

"Whit time did ye see them?"

"Guv, let me try again."

Mac Gregor threw a glance at the ceiling and gestured with both hands to his Sergeant.

"Could you point the man out if you saw him again?"

"No. The devils change shapes."

"Have you seen him since?"

"Yes he walked back down the road later on."

"You mean after you saw him the first time?"

"Yes."

"Tell me what happened."

"I was at toilet again."

"In the bucket?"

Tommo gestured with an inclination of his head towards the bucket.

"No I was shitting."

"Excuse me?"

"I shit on paper by the window or where your friend is standing, then put it in the bucket, can't squat that long you see, so I kneel."

Mac Gregor looked down to his feet in disgust. His only escape from his current position was to move closer to the bucket, he decided against that option and stood his ground.

"So you were kneeling by the window then when you saw him come back down the road."

"Yes I was. It was a big one and I was farting and straining for near fifteen minutes before I was done."

"Ahem, well yes I erm ahem. Was the woman with him?"

"No he was on his own and he was running."

"And you are sure it was the same man?"

"Yes. I had just finished and was standing up to wrap up my doings when I saw him running like Gabriel was chasing him from The Pearly Gates."

"How much later was this after you saw him and the lady walking up the road?"

"Well I finished my piss and got all the way back to my chair and I sat for a bit and then needed to shit. I must have been at the shit for fifteen minutes but I wasn't long in my chairs so I would say twenty minutes in all."

"Ok well thank you for that Dear. One last question, what time do the foxes bark?"

"They never start before midnight."

"Thank you."

Sergeant Gayle looked pleased with his work when he looked over at his boss. Mac Gregor held Tommo's gaze then rolled his eyes to the ceiling. Placing his feet shoulder width apart and crossing his arms in front of his chest the older Detective fixed the old woman with a hard look.

"What's yer name?"

"You do speak English then."

The old woman demonstrated her bright sarcasm.

"I – asked – what – your – name - was."

Mac Gregor pronounced each word violently, an axe thrown at her each time.

"The nice Policeman said that was the end of the questions."

"That's as maybe but I still have a few questions."

Her hands were claws, knuckles swollen grotesquely with arthritis. She slowly began to pull at the large buttons on her ragged coat. With audible effort, she released the top button and began struggling with the second.

"Are you going to tell me your name?"

She held Mac Gregor's gaze and her silence as the second button released and she began on the third.

"Do you live here alone or does someone look after you?"

There was the hint of a smile on her face as the third button released and Mac Gregor realised she was naked beneath the coat. Empty bags of skin hung where her breasts had once been, tiny darkened nipples pulling them to points. She looked like a skeleton in a suit that was several sizes too big for it. When she released the final button, she flung the coat open and spread her legs as far as she could to reveal her vagina to Mac Gregor. It grimaced at him like an angry wound. Only the faintest whisps of platinum pubic hair remained to frame the entrance to her withered womb. Her rusted oesophagus rattled as she expressed the pleasure she drew from the situation through enthusiastic guffaws.

Cursing beneath his breath, Mac Gregor gently pushed Tommo towards the door, both men initially unable to take their eyes from her crotch where she rubbed a deformed digit between the mottled flaps of her labia.

"C'mon let's get the fuck oot o' here."

"I'm with you Guv."

Stumbling into open retreat, both men clattered at the front door until the latch activated and they released themselves into the relative purity of the late spring morning. Behind them, the old woman's cackles degenerated to the primal noises of animal carnality as her pleasure source changed from situational to onanistic.

Their pace slowed as they reached the pavement. Both men changing their demeanour with affected casualness. He could

152

smell the stinking interior on his clothing. Filth, carrion, bodily waste, rotted food and physical deterioration all furred inside Mac Gregor's nose and mouth. Seeking relief from the fetid stench, he fumbled a cigarette from a pack in his jacket pocket and flicked a lighter into function. The tangy smoke felt welcome in his mouth as he sucked it down into his lungs then pushed it up and out through his nostrils.

"Well what the fuck did you make o' that then Tommo?"

"I think she saw our man last night."

"Really? I am not sure she knows what planet she is on."

"She's a weirdo, that's for sure, but I do think she saw him. Unfortunately I think we have got all the useful information that we are going to get out of her."

"So what has she told us? Oor man walked up here wi' the victim sometime after midnight, then came back doon at the run twenty minutes later."

"Yeah I would say that's about it."

"Well I do not think that was worth the smell and the sight o' her minging auld fanny."

"Probably not Guv."

"Come on let's get back to the Incident Room and leave the 'door to door' to uniform."

Simultaneously they swung the car doors open and climbed into the vehicle. Briefest of scraping whines sounded, before the engine caught. Tommo selected a gear and they pulled away. With indicator ticking at the end of the road, Mac Gregor pulled his mobile telephone from his pocket and selected the call option for the Incident Room.

"Hello. Whae's that?"

Tommo could hear the distant chirping of a female voice at the other end of Mac Gregor's connection, but could not discern any of the words it spoke.

"Right Clare, I want you tae get hold o' Social Services and tell them I know someone whae needs their help."

Chapter 22

Pain shone from her disbelieving eyes. Had she not been so radiantly beautiful, she would have looked like an imbecile sat on the sofa; mouth hanging open, shoulders slumped, defeated by life. Balanced on the edge of the armchair and possibly rationality itself, he breathed the room's air, thick with jasmine and lavender. His heart raced, bird-like in the clutches of a cat, breathing rapid and shallow. Their eyes locked together, invisible bonds impossible to break from within.

In the background, the sentient communication of a talk show host suffers incessantly from the static of some vacuous celebrity's gibbering and the moronic approval of those sufficiently idiotic to desire inclusion. Monkey house noises accompany a wave of applause flowing from the television set in the corner of the room. The flickering images cause the subdued lighting of the large room to strobe, giving them a surreal appearance, like two manikins perched on soft furnishings and facing each other in the shop window of human tragedy. Storm fast approaching, TV lightening and idiot hand-slapping thunder, both preambles to the down pouring of her tears.

Gulping great mouthfuls of air, Abdul fought for composure. His heart refused to quit its frantic beating, war drums of the mountain tribes. When he was able to hold air in his chest for longer than one second he deliberately spoke one word to his wife, "sorry", then rejoined his battle for self-control. With the jaunty signature tune and rapturous applause, the storm broke and her tears came in floods, which broke the invisible bond between their eyes.

Frustrated by his inability to consol his wife and the unfair demands of fate, which his weakness had conspired to make of him, Abdul stood and spoke coldly to Samira. "I am leaving now." She did not look up, keeping her down-turned face cradled in her hands as her tears flowed. Without another word, he left the house and walked to his car where he sat briefly behind the wheel looking back at his home. It sat peacefully and largely in darkness at the centre of its beautiful garden. Inside the children slept and his wife wept. With a resigned sigh, he pressed the button to wake the engine and drove off into the night.

A worldly face of wrinkled concern for the state of humanity filled the TV screen, before Samira pressed the 'standby' button to banish the image and its associated noise. The deafening silence that followed filled every corner of the house and forced a distant whistling to occupy the inevitable void in her ears. A clicking hum broke the silence and reminded her of the passing months. With the rapid onset of summer, it took longer everyday for the thermostat to activate the central heating system.

Released from the crippling embrace of silence, she stirred from her seat and went to the children's rooms. In each bedroom, she paused to watch her sleeping daughters and listen to the gentle symphony of their slumbered breathing. Then satisfied that her angels were safe and well, she returned to the front room to sit with her thoughts, fears, regrets and desires. Alone in her private prison, shackled to its fabric by the two things she loved the most, Aesha and Zaynab.

The band of gold rotated with ease on her slender finger as she rolled it between her forefinger and thumb. Untarnished heavy metal, the antipathy of the union it signified. Hopes and desires carried forward from her years of innocence, broken, broken before they had even begun to be realised. It seemed intolerably unfair that her charms could drive one man to force himself upon her and yet not powerful enough to command the loyalty of the man she had given herself to. She had sacrificed herself to truth before and embraced deceit to protect the family's future, foregoing any chance of just retribution. Such sacrifice and still Abdul's fall from grace could continue to weigh so heavily. What magnitude of transgression had he been guilty of for them to consider it just that her daughter be bound to a rapist, a rapist and her own father? Al qasim was guilty of his own misdeeds and they, her husband and herself, were guilty of deceit, deceit that allowed the family's ignorance of his crimes.

She knew that Abdul had led a less than pious life whilst in his first year of University however, she had been told by her father that he was redeemed and brought back to the path of the righteous. So what now could force this consideration on them, how far had her husband fallen? Abdul would only say that he was not pure, The Devil had taken him and he was lost until his family had brought him back to Allah. In all other matters, he was the perfect husband, caring, supportive and loving. He worked hard to provide for them, harder than ever now that this cloud had settled over their family. Abdul had even taken to working late into the night on his computer and spending nights out socialising to increase his portfolio of customers and brokers.

It had seemed so simple when he explained it to her. His father had made him promise to re-consider the proposed arrangement for Aesha's marriage as his salvation meant he owed a great deal to his extended family. Abdul had not agreed to the arrangement and that he and Samira had the right to refuse, after further consideration, if they so desired. Words are simple, they construct statements that are, for the educated, easy to understand. Implications are complex, they pervade every statement; linking the agendas of others with the histories and ambitions of all that make them. Only proclamations on the truly banal are without ambition and ambiguity.

Those that brokered the power within 'The Family' knew the details of Abdul's lost months. Samira felt cheated that she was not privy to the knowledge of that group of Patriarchs, yet until now, she had accepted that it was not the role of women to interfere directly in those matters. Women were to content themselves with gossip and conjecture, neither of which she concerned herself with when related to her husband as it was never flattering.

Growling in frustration, she rose from her seat and walked to the kitchen. Convincing herself that, peppermint tea was what she needed she set about fulfilling that lie. The truth was she needed to do something as the angst of her fears threatened to overwhelm her if she had continued to sit still.

Overhead fluorescent tubes initiated, flooding the kitchen with impersonal brightness. Tea made, she opted to sit at the breakfast bar to drink it. Testing the rim of the mug on her bottom lip, she blew to cool the liquid before sipping. The tea felt clean and refreshing as it spread over her tongue and charmed her senses with its flavour and fragrance. Before she could spoil her senses with too much of the herbal pleasure, she placed the mug down on the bar surface and stared at her reflection in the black mirror of the kitchen window. The distant reflection of herself implored her to face the conclusions of her analysis. She had deciphered all that she was going to from the circumstance and content of Abdul's statement. Uncle Mohammed clearly felt confident of the advantage he held with the rest of his family. The significance of that advantage was acknowledged by Abdul's father's willingness to push the betrothal matter beyond the boundaries that were usual for him. The only possible source of such effective leverage was the support rendered by Mohammed's branch of the family to save Abdul, support that must have been of an extraordinary magnitude. The extent of their assistance would have been directly proportional to the sins Abdul was guilty of and the depth to which he had immersed himself in their malignancy. In order for him to provide the required support, Mohammed would have had to be in possession of every detail; complete knowledge of his Nephew's malfeasance.

Abdul himself must be cognisant of the extremity of his sins and willing to pay almost any price to maintain the silent balance of their rectification. Willing to countenance the sanction of incest, a sin he would ordinarily reject out-of-hand. Willing to consider giving a child, he had raised as his own, to a rapist. Willing to open his heart to such darkness in order to keep his wife from the truth, the man he had once been and the demon he was. Samira had only conjecture to estimate the depravities her husband had practiced whilst with The Devil. Sins so great that perhaps his cousin, Al qasim, felt it his sacred duty to ensure a righteous man took her flower before a wretched vassal of Satan, an abomination to Allah, lay with her.

Plunging the house into darkness by degrees as she extinguished the lights, she retired to bed. Sleep would not come to her or her to it. She would lie, surrounded by benign darkness to await the return of her husband. Tomorrow the daystar would return and in its warmth, she would re-join the battle.

Chapter 23

The Investigation Team gathered for a briefing given by Detective Inspector Mac Gregor. They sat, waiting for the Inspector, on every available surface whilst a young Detective Constable shared a story he had heard from the Uniformed Branch over lunch. He relayed the tale with obvious relish as he detailed the unpleasant experience of two uniformed Officers who were assisting the investigation with door to door inquiries. His eyes widened and his voice stumbled over evident mirth as he described how a 'stinking old bag' had answered her front door and then proceeded to remove her overcoat, when they began to question her. She had not been wearing any clothes beneath the coat and the Police Officers had not known where to look as they stood on her doorstep. Then calming his audience with a 'Nazi style' salute that he slowly waved across the room, he continued in conspiratorial tone. He told his colleagues that she had explained to the Officers that her 'Police boyfriends', he motioned the quotation marks in the air before him, had already been round to 'help her play with her fanny and squirt juices all down her legs', again he punctuated in the air. The group burst into whoops of laughter and mock banter, designed to identify who amongst them were the old woman's boyfriends.

Mac Gregor's forceful brogue silenced their jocularity like a fire blanket on a chip pan fire.

"Claire! Ah thought Ah telt yae tae get Social Services round tae that auld lady."

Detective Constable Claire Aldridge looked shocked and indignant at the Inspector's aggressive interjection.

"Sorry Sir, I did pass your concerns onto them and they said that they would get around to her when their case-load allowed."

"Not good enough lassie, get back on tae them an tell them Ah think that auld bag is a danger tae hersel and others."

She stared back at the senior officer with trembling resentment.

"Do it Noo!"

With that barked command, she scurried off to a desk in the corner of the room and snatched the receiver from the telephone that sat there.

Mac Gregor 'eyeballed' any Detective that was not already moving to a perch from which they could pay attention to his briefing. Every loiterer withered under his stare and moved quickly to join their colleagues.

"For your information that old lady was, thanks to the excellent Policing skills of Detective Sergeant Gayle here, the source of some very interesting information."

Mac Gregor indicated Tommo with a nod of his head. One of the Detectives gave a knowing look to his neighbours on hearing the news. His smiling face froze when he turned his face to the front again and found himself facing into Mac Gregor's stern glare.

"Take that stupit look af yer ugly pus noo, afore Ah come oer there and slap it af fir yea."

With his dominance re-affirmed, Mac Gregor returned to his softer, more gentile, accent and continued with the briefing.

"Right here's the situation. In the space o' one week we have four deid. Aw female and aw murdered. The M.O. employed in a' four murders, strongly suggests that we have a serial murderer on oor hands.

Shirley Babcock, thirty two years old, scull smashed wi' a blunt instrument, probably a hammer, and her body left in a fire escape doorway. Her skirt was hitched up aboot her waist and her undergarment pulled doon tae her ankles. She was married wi' a wee child. Her penchant for extramarital affairs led us tae the 'Sophistidates' website where we are pursuing a strong line of inquiry. The unusual element tae this murder is that the body seems to have been arranged into a pose, post mortem. A' the subsequent ones appear tae have been left where they fell.

Amy Roland, thirty years old, found wi' her friend Zoe Clark, thirty years old, lying on a path next tae a railway. They had both had their sculls smashed in a similar fashion to Shirley Babcock's. They both had their skirts hitched up and their knickers aboot their ankles. Whilst these two appear tae have shared a reputation for wild antics and there is more than a suggestion of promiscuity aboot them, neither were using

159

'Sophistidates' or even appear tae hae been 'on-line'. Amy wiz married wi' sma' children, Zoe divorced with one wee one. It would appear that they met their murderer in a bar whilst on a night oot. They were seen with a good looking man in his late thirties. He has been described as Caucasian wi' dark colouring. They were flirting together as a threesome when they left The Feathers Bar and neither girl was seen alive again. There are differences, however the cause of death would suggest that we have the same perpetrator fir a' three murders.

This morning's victim, Melanie Hughes, thirty six years old, scull smashed in an identical manner tae the others, bringing the head count for our, likely, serial killer tae four. Her body wiz left where it fell in a public park wi' her skirt up and her kecks doon. She wiz married wi' two young children. Early indications are that she is an avid user o' the internet and she does appear to have been a customer o' 'Sophistidates'. We may also hae a witness whea says she saw Melanie and an unidentified male walking up towards the park sometime after midnight and then the male running back from the park approximately twenty minutes later.

Aw four victims were killed in the same way, struck repeatedly on the heid from behind wi' a hammer. They appear tae have been facing away from their attacker with their skirts hitched up and their knickers aboot their ankles. Two of our victims appear to use the same website to trawl for extra-marital liaisons, the other two seem to enjoy a reputation for promiscuity. There has been no evidence of rape or sexual assault and all seem to have gone willingly to their place of murder.

Ladies and Gentlemen, your thoughts please?"
Mac Gregor surveyed the assembled Detectives for the first person to proffer a theory or suggested line of inquiry. Blank faces stared back at him until, frustrated, he spun to look at his Sergeant.

"Come on Tommo, you must hae something tae share."

"Sorry Guv you covered it all."
Desperate to break the atmosphere Mac Gregor swung back to his team and implored them to do themselves credit by

160

demonstrating their collective abilities as Detectives. Tommo slid from his position, standing behind Mac Gregor's right shoulder, to take a relaxed perch on the corner of one of the desks.

Exasperated, Mac Gregor proclaimed that they would continue to interview all possible witnesses, he would get onto the press to launch a reconstruction and appeal to the public. That morning's crime scene had yielded some footprints and possibly more evidence and they should crosscheck for matches on the database. Then as though he were playing his trump card, he fixed the two Detectives that he had detailed to work the 'sock puppets' on the web, with his piercing eyes.

"You two, how's your on-line love affair going?"

"Yeah well Sir, he seems to have taken the bait and we are exchanging flirtatious messages."

"Any pattern tae when he makes contact?"

"We have two 'sock puppets' in contact with him at the moment, one more advanced than the other. He always contacts either late evening or early morning."

"Whit dae ye ken aboot your virtual boyfriend."

"To be honest we have only really confirmed that he appears to be a kinky bastard and he uses the same background story with us as he did with Shirley Babcock."

"So when are we going tae get tae meet this paramour of yours then."

"We have tried to set up a meeting through one of our 'puppets' but he is being coy. I guess he is busy murdering other people at the moment and we shall probably have to wait our turn."

"Come on! Use your charms I want tae meet this bastard."

"At the moment I think the best we can hope for is a meet sometime next week."

"Well dae yer best. Try for a cancellation or something. See if we need tae get to him before he kills again."

With that, Mac Gregor dismissed his team, they returned to their duties and he to his office. Detective Sergeant Gayle watched the team disperse then returned to his desk where he held a statement file in front of him. He scanned the activity in the Incident Room over the file. Observing the hunters, locked into their task of trapping an entity as elusive as a wraith and vicious as a wolverine, Tommo enjoyed the inner thrill he felt when his superiority was proven through small victories. He was happy to assist where he could but he sought different prey, his target was less wolverine more the weakling of a herd.

Re-focussing his gaze Tommo began to study the statements he had collected in his folder. He would keep these under lock and key until he could use them to maximum effect. Confident in his cunning, he relaxed into his chair and casually perused the statements whilst always alert to opportunities to stay one-step ahead of those about him.

Chapter 24

Daisies penetrated the blanket of green grass and moss, a random scattering of alternatively ordered matter cast across the firmament from which they had sprung. Like hundreds of distant suns shining against an omni-coloured background, a patch of night sky on a different scale, seemingly following the same laws. Buzzing craft travelled between the points of focus, the centres of gravity or a different force that pulls them with inexorable attraction to serve one or the other's function, or perhaps the function of a higher order.

The canopy of the day, from artificial horizon to artificial horizon, azure fabric seamed with white vapour trails and hung from a ball of blazing fusion. Despite the rapid approach of aphelion, the planet's axial bias increasingly gave solar advantage to the Northern Hemisphere with every day that passed. The patches of manicured flora attached to the domiciles that constitute parts of the greater organism of the city, were rousing from seasonally imposed dormancy to push volume and colour into the environs.

A patch of checked pattern spread on the grass, meaningless counterfeit of some design by an ancient unconquered people. A child of man sat on this raft of symmetric pattern. He occupied himself in the shade cast by a brightly coloured construct of unnatural fabric, held aloft on sprung poles anchored in opposite corners to form a shelter.

Becky sat on her haunches to peer into the brightly coloured tent pitched at the end of a tartan travel rug. Her son threw soft toys, fashioned to resemble stylised animals, to the rear of his shelter where they tumbled together, forming a mound of straight stumpy legs, muzzles and flopping ears. When the last of his toys flew onto the fluffy pile, he held his arm out with exclamation and looked to his mother to retrieve them from the lightweight nylon igloo.

Pressing her knuckles into the woollen blanket, she leaned forward, kissed the infant on his head, and cooed her submission to his demand. Then on all fours, she crawled forward to position her upper body inside the tent. Flicking the toys between her legs, she re-established the child's soft arsenal. Turning to sit she smiled warmly at him and shuffled from the nylon confines.

Thomas clutched a doglike toy to him and giggled at his mother's curious movements. He wore a T-shirt, some monstrous mechanical humanoid blasting bright rays of destruction from its eyes emblazoned across the front. His red shorts surrounded his white thighs loosely and white shoes, held with Velcro straps, made his feet look disproportionably large. Joining her son's mirth, Becky began to laugh. Only he had the power to invoke that most innocent of reactions she possessed, like a lost memory of childhood she laughed for no other reason, than that of joy.

To indulge the wave of love she felt within, Becky leaned over her son and kissed his prominent red cheeks then cupped his face in her lily fingers and searched his features. Greedily her eyes ate up every image; every detail they could strip from Thomas' little face. Elfin eyes shone with gaiety above his button nose and chortling mouth, delicate pegs of white rimming the tiny chasm framed by thin lips of deep pink. Leaning forward again, she kissed his nose and sat back onto her heels to watch her child resume his game.

The oscillating hums and grates of electrical garden machinery sounded at various distances. Only the local fauna could make themselves heard above the horticultural noise pollution. Through this resonating battle, an electronic scream told Becky that the washing machine had completed the task she had earlier given it, a mechanical slave, using the most basic of languages to command its master's attention. Employing soft reassurances Becky excused herself from her son's audience to attend the most recent summons.

As she stood to leave Thomas's little hand grasped at the thin cotton of her shorts, catching a good handful when she was halfway to erect. Completing the movement she left one side of her shorts behind, the elastic waist sliding downwards over her hips to reveal her bottom. Rounded peach-like cheeks separated by the thin cord of her knickers and framed above by their lacy upper half. "Thomas" she chided her child. Then half turning to reassure him with a smile, she pulled her shorts from his grasp and back into position.

Adolescence predominant on his gradually maturing face, he stared in open wonder over the hedge that he had been trimming. When their eyes met he stood transfixed, rabbit in the headlights, until his father's voice sounded, "Why have you stopped?" Looking down to the hedge trimmer in his hands the callow youth broke eye contact with the woman next door. He stood awkwardly as his father joined him at the hedge. Recognition spread across the older man's face when he noticed his neighbour and her son standing on their side of the domestic boundary.

"Oh hi there Becky, lovely day isn't it?"

"Hi Tim. Yes it is. How's Kate?"

"She's well, visiting her mother today but should be back by tea time."

"Well do tell her I was asking after her when she gets home."

"I will and how's Brian?"

"Fishing again, at least it's a day trip today. Sometimes he is out all night bloody fishing."

"He must like fish."

"Drinking beer and talking rubbish with his mates more like."

Drawn by the inactivity of the others and sounds of the conversation a younger face joined father and son looking over the hedge at Becky.

"Hello there, Colin isn't it?"

"Yes this is my youngest Colin and I think you already know my eldest David."

"And how old are you two strapping lads then?"

Becky looked from one boy to the other as she asked the question. The younger males kept their silence long enough for the patriarch to banish the gathering awkwardness by answering on behalf of his sons.

"Little Colin here was eight last week and this big lump will be fourteen next month."

David wriggled uncomfortably when his father wrapped him up in his arms as he detailed his age to the woman next door.

"They seem to be a big help to you there in the garden."

165

"They are good boys, David does the hedges and borders, I do the grass and Colin pulls out all the weeds. Don't you son?"

Both boys looked outwardly shy but inwardly proud.

"I need to get Brian to cut my hedge when he is not fishing."

"David will do that for you, won't you son?"

"Oh no, I couldn't possibly ask him to do that."

"He won't mind, will you son?"

David's face reddened as he shifted his weight nervously from foot to foot, studiously avoiding eye contact.

"Well if you're sure he doesn't mind that would be a great help."

"Great, I'll send him round in an hour or so."

The matter decided, they said their polite farewells and both sides of the hedge returned to the tasks with which they had previously been occupied. Becky recovered the soft toys from the tent for Thomas to re-start his game before she answered the machine's call.

From the stainless steel belly of the white box, fitted into the kitchen units, she pulled a loose rope of wet clothing. Deceptively it moved with sentient eagerness to the white plastic basket into which Becky birthed it.

The irrational concerns of a mother quelled, when she noted with relief that Thomas continued to play by the doorway to his tent. She had returned to the garden with driven urgency and now felt slightly foolish. She turned and bent her back to place the basket of washing onto the grass. Looking ahead of herself, she saw David staring at her from over the hedge. He had progressed two feet in the cutting of the foliage. Dropping her head, she could look down between her breasts, which hung full and rounded into the white cotton of her vest top.

In a flourish, her hair spread through the warm air to settle full and wispy about her shoulders after a practiced flick of her head. She fixed David's stare with the adhesive power of her rich brown eyes. Slowly she straightened up, weight on one leg with her forward hip pushed towards the adolescent. Hands resting lightly on her hips, she smiled a mystery at him. Unsure of Becky's intent, David stood transfixed, the garden implement clattering in his hands. Eyes bright, smile wide and inviting, she swung her weight onto the other hip and cocked her head slightly to one side and then turning away, spoke softly with her child who continued to play on the rug, unaware of his mother's obvious charms.

Released from her eyes he began to move the hedge trimmer in slow progressive arcs across the bushes, bringing neat order to their overgrown faces. The regular outcome of his activity allowed him to function whilst dedicating most of his visual perception to the image of his neighbour. She moved from her child to the plastic basket of laundry on the grass beneath her washing line. The red shorts she wore emphasised the wonderful curvature of her bottom, hips and slight paunch. Moving deliberately in her sandals on the uneven surface of the lawn she drew a bag of pegs, hung on the washing line, towards the basket. Each step causing her breasts to swing slightly in the short white vest top that rose above her naval, revealing the jewellery hanging from the pierced hole in her stomach. Inexplicably he sensed that she was watching him, even though she never looked directly at him.

Standing with her back to him she bent over, legs straight, to push her backside high in the air as she selected an item of laundry from the basket. With the seams of a shirt held in each hand, she straightened her back to push her hips forward as she pegged the wet garment onto the line. The shorts, partially consumed by her buttocks as her back arched, revealed the lower curvature of her buttocks. Hedge trimmer static again he studied the colourful pixie tattoo emblazoned on her left cheek.

He followed the red and green pixie, frozen in the act of some jovial mischief, with his eyes as she bent to retrieve another item of laundry. Briefly she walked in his direction before tuning to hang a dripping T-shirt from the line, her breasts moving almost independently to her body. His progress along the hedge slowed considerably as she worked her way down the line towards him. "Hello" she said when at the closest point to their dividing boundary. Dry mouthed; struck dumb he struggled to grasp a reply from the maelstrom in his mind. She hung the item and returned to the basket, his eyes never leaving her backside as she went.

Reversing the process, she bent to retrieve further items from the basket, this time allowing David a clear view down her vest. She worked her way away from him, hanging laundry with each stoop, stand and pace. His concentration shattered constantly by the seductive glimpses of forbidden flesh and the swelling in his own shorts. Unfailingly however, the machine in his hands clattered to proclaim his productivity to the members of his own household as they pursued their own garden tasks.

With the placement of her last peg, Becky lifted Thomas in one arm then collected the basket with the other. Walking towards her back door, bum swinging from side to side, she turned to cast over her shoulder a broad smile from beneath sparkling brown eyes, to the young man pretending to cut a hedge.

All distractions gone from view, David set about his task with renewed vigour. His mind worked hard to store every erotic image, so that they could be retrieved, when he was alone in bed that night. Slowly his erection faded leaving only a wet satin stain of pre-cum in his pants.

Thomas climbed onto the sofa and demanded, with broken sentences and gesticulations, that his mother switch on the television set. He sat uncomplainingly watching the animated figures, which sprang into life, dance about the screen. His eyelids were heavy, they slowly closed than sprang open again as he fought the need to sleep. Becky brought him a beaker of diluted blackcurrant cordial, which he eagerly slurped with relish, each long draft terminated with a loud gasp of satisfaction. When he had finished his drink, he held the beaker up for his mother to re-fill. Taking the container from him Becky denied his implied request and suggested that he sleep for a bit. Without a word Thomas flopped onto his side and rested his head on a cushion, he continued to watch the television until sleep closed his eyes.

When she was sure her son had drifted off to sleep, she went to the kitchen to make a cup of tea for herself. She returned to the front room with a steaming mug and chocolate biscuit. Gratefully she sat in the armchair and used the remote control to change the television to a channel showing adult programmes. Mother and son shared the room in silence, only the noise of a show exposing the car crash lives of the poorly educated filled the room. Sipping her tea and munching on her biscuit, Becky watched intently as a fat, teenage girl threw punches at a mentally sub-normal youth. He shouted censored profanities at his obese assailant whilst two large men in matching T-shirts, hauled her flabby carcass back to the chair she had previously lumbered from. When her ample bottom squeezed into the confines of her seat, the host regained control and began to provoke his dancing monkeys again. Simian boy, bottom lip protruding as his mouth hung loosely open and his gargantuan ex-lover exchanged glance of hatred whilst the polished TV host suggested that either or both were a waste of flesh.

The cheerful chiming of the doorbell interrupted the host's closing oratory. Becky pulled the corners of her mouth back to form a sly smile and placed the, now nearly empty, mug onto the occasional table by her armchair. Rising from her comfort, she briefly checked her son's continued slumber and walked to the hallway. Adjusting her hair with subtle flicks of her hands and standing for a short while in front of the hallway mirror, she confirmed her beauty.

David stood on the doorstep, hedge trimmer in hand. He felt awkward about his unfamiliar anticipation and hoped that she would remember that his father had volunteered his gardening assistance. It seemed to him an eternity before he saw softly deformed images, moving against the static shadows of the interior through the rippling glass of the front door. His heart rate doubled when the curiously distinct patches of moving light coalesced in the glass and the mechanism of a lock sounded.

He caught his breath as the sweetness of her scent flooded out to caress him. She stood in the doorway, his familiar neighbour who had smiled at him since he was a small boy. She continued to smile at him, though now her smile held many promises and secrets, his heart felt like it was melting and flowing through his temporal lobes into her eyes. With feigned surprise, she exclaimed his name, and then with equal insincerity she remembered and composed herself.

169

"Thank you for coming round."

She moved her head slightly to one side and softened her voice.

"Are you here to trim my hedge?"

"Errr yes, my Dad sent me round."

"Well come in then."

Standing to one side, she made him press past her into the hallway and closed the door behind him.

"Come through to the kitchen and I shall make us a cup of tea, or would you prefer lemonade?"

"Lemonade please, Mrs Owens."

"Please call me Becky, you're old enough now."

Flush with her flattery David carried the trimmer through to the kitchen. She followed him and indicated the back door.

"Put that thing out there and I shall fix our drinks."

Dutifully he did as he was told, then stood shyly leaning on the kitchen work surface, watching her. She filled two glasses with lemonade from a large plastic bottle and dropped two ice cubes from the freezer into both.

"Come on through."

She commanded and led the way to the front room carrying the drinks.

He froze when he entered the room and noticed the infant sleeping on the sofa. She smiled when she saw his wide questioning eyes looking at her son.

"Don't worry about him, he won't wake up until he's ready and he has only just gone to sleep."

Relaxing a little, he looked about for a place to sit. Becky indicated the armchair that she had previously been sitting in.

"Sit here David. We can relax for a bit before you have to do my hedge."

Tentatively he crossed the room, his trainers squeaking slightly on the laminate flooring. She stood away from the chair to allow him to sit down then bending over she dragged a large footstool across the floor towards him. The pixie smiled at him from the soft flesh of her bottom as it advanced to within two feet of his face. Releasing the stool, she turned abruptly, catching him averting his gaze, and sat down to face him.

She placed a hand on his thigh and leaned forward to retrieve her drink from the table by the chair where she had left them. Her touch made David freeze; terrified of doing anything, which would be interpreted as inappropriate in the adult world. He held his breath until she had settled her bottom back onto the stool and terminated the contact with two brief pats of his bare leg. He admired the slow motion of her elegant neck as she swallowed some lemonade then taking the remaining glass he gulped clumsily at its contents.

They made small talk about the health of his family, what subjects he was taking at school and what his ambitions were for the future. With the customary in-articulation of adolescents, he stumbled through his reports as she hummed and nodded encouragingly. He began to feel the reassuring sensation of being a child in an adult's company again and began to relax. With almost maternal concern, she cautioned him about his course choices and approach to achieving his ambitions. Grateful for her concern he smiled and tried to exercise his schoolboy charm that his female relatives always appreciated.

Leaning back, Becky pushed her hips and stomach forward, hands braced on the two rear corners of the footstool.

"Stand up."

"Sorry Mrs Owe…, Becky?"

"I said stand up David, let's have a look at you?"

Like a faltering geriatric, he eased himself out of the armchair with maximum assistance from his arms and the arms of the chair. Upright, he stood with his arms hanging like lengths of rope at his sides. He looked down at the lady who lived next door to him and his family. A low whistle came from his slightly open mouth as his chest convulsed great draws of breath between his lips. Without breaking eye contact with the boy, she ran her tongue slowly across her top lip, then leaning slightly to the left she rolled herself into a sitting position.

Looking up at him with brown eyes from crotch height, she placed her hand on the front of his shorts. The only acknowledgment of a boundary breached was the strangled gag of his faltered breath. Gently she began to rub the organs she could feel beneath the fabric of his shorts and pants, smile growing correspondingly with the stiffness of his penis. He

171

the bottom of the bed whilst she stripped off her vest. She stood proudly displaying her breast to him before she kicked off her sandals and let her shorts drop to the floor. After a brief pirouette, she jumped onto the bed and held her hand out for him to join her. With wide-eyed enthusiasm, he struggled out of his shorts and pants, which still held the glistening 'snail-trail' of his earlier excitement in the garden. He sat on the side of the bed forcing each trainer from his feet whist she rested her hand on his narrow shoulder. When he had freed himself from his footwear, he cast off his T-shirt and knelt, naked, before her. His youthful exuberance had made his penis erect again and Becky wasted no time in kicking her knickers off and drawing her juvenile beau between her legs.

He fumbled at her breasts and then at his cock and her crotch. Calming him with her hands on his shoulders and a whispered "Ssssssh", she took control. With calm, practiced ease, she took hold of his urgent penis and guided it between her labia, and then with the gentle persuasion of her hands on his smooth buttocks she drew him fully inside her. She let him slap inexperienced kisses all over her face and neck whilst she maintained a comfortable rhythm to the coitus with her hold on his backside and the movement of her hips.

Groaning he froze inside her and the trembling of his body told her he was ejaculating inside her. She held him lightly until he was finished.

"Mmmmm you certainly did trim my hedge."

"What?"

"Nothing David."

"Was I alright?"

"You were fine, nothing to be ashamed of there Dear."

She patted his shoulder and he rolled off her to lie on his back, mouth open and gazing at the ceiling. As Becky sat forward to begin dressing she felt his cum trickling out of her onto the duvet cover, 'better change the bedding before Brian gets back' she thought to herself. The post coitus tranquillity was broke by the cries of Thomas from the room below. She quickly pulled on her shorts, leaving the knickers on the floor by the bed and made her way to the door as she pulled her vest

173

over her head. "Get dressed and you can really trim my hedge." She snapped at him as she rushed from the room.

When David joined her in the front room, she was sitting with Thomas on her lap watching children's programmes on television. She smiled at him benignly and returned her attention to her child. After pausing awkwardly in the front room he made his way to the garden and began the task, he had been sent to complete. Becky smiled to herself when she heard the clatter of the hedge trimmers from the back garden.

It took him only thirty minutes to complete the hedge. Standing in the front doorway as they said goodbye and Becky thanked him once again for his assistance, David looked anxious.

"Can I see you again?"

"Of course we shall see each other. We are neighbours after all."

"No I mean see each other, like earlier I mean."

She laughed a little with her own amusement then patted his flat chest.

"We'll see. Bye for now."

Numb and confused by the rules of the grown up world, David moped back to his own house. His mother would be back soon and he hoped there would be something nice to eat for dinner.

Becky took Thomas upstairs so that she could keep an eye on him whilst she changed the bedding. "Cheeky little bastard." She exclaimed when she noticed that her knickers were no longer on the bedroom floor where she had left them.

Chapter 25

The route of a disused railway line, now a cycle path, provides me with a functional access route to the hunting grounds. The sun rising in an azure sky warmed the early morning chill from my aching body as I perambulate my access route in reverse; now my egress route. Orion returning from the hunt, bloodied tool now sheathed in the pocket of my overcoat pulling it lop-sided, gravity clawing at the sticky metal of the hammer's head.

Dawn patrol of the uniformed streets, where the living abide, had provided me with a target rich environment. Eight pointless canines destroyed before the occupants of the surrounding houses had eaten breakfast or made for the front door to begin their ritualistic commute to work. A harvest such as this will contribute significantly to the reduction of my purgatory and pleased with my efforts, I have decided to reward myself.

There is a place where the two worlds combine, the living touch those of us who are alive yet without life. From within their life they reach out to ease our suffering at this place and it is there I am bound. I have given my body no sustenance for five days and the familiar agonies of starvation are gnawing at me. Today I shall allow myself the luxury of eating.

Passing beneath a bridge, a high arch of stone blocks supporting the road that runs above, I cut right to ascend the bank. Thick bushes tear at my clothes and uncovered flesh as I push upwards, clinging to the bridge stone on my right for balance and reassurance. Metal smells of exhaust poisoned vegetation and soil waft up in thick invisible clouds as I force my body onwards up the dusty bank. Gaining the summit, I appear troll-like between old railings and the parapet wall of the bridge, to challenge all who cross.

Breaking like a wave about a dark rock, igneous and unyielding, commuters part to avoid the bridge troll. I stand defiantly for a moment or two before I continue my progress and further challenge the unseeing senses of the living. With no sign of acknowledgment, they skilfully avoid all contact with me.

I patrol the busy shopping streets until it is time to go to the place. When I sense the time is right I steer a course that takes me from the pedestrianised thoroughfares to the more conventional streets of the city. Ahead of me, two fat women push buggies along the pavement, each with a child on-board. A small child stumbles along between the matriarchs and drops an empty plastic bottle that once contained a beverage, long since consumed by the child, onto the paving slabs. Complaining he draws his mother's attention to his loss with a plea to halt their progress and return to collect the vessel. His mother conducts a rapid appraisal of the situation, and then explained with sharp commands that the lost item was not worth the effort of recovery. Proving his cognitive and reasoning ability the child learns and applies. Turning he ran several paces back towards the empty bottle and threw the blue plastic top after its functional partner and then returned to his role model and educator.

Small shops line the road, each with goods for sale from a different ethnic origin. Exotic smells fill the air as the living pass into and dash out of the dark doorways beyond which, constantly vigilant vendors lurk behind tills. Boxes of battered fruit and vegetables push forward from the shop fronts to encroach on the pavement area. Decrepit souls pick carefully through the damaged produce in the hope of collecting the pick of the crop, sufficient for their needs.

Between the shops, stand restaurants bearing names from an old country. Empty for now, they await the evening and late night trade to revive them. Family enterprises, growing empires built on the gradual accumulation of capital and the ever-willing cheap labour of distant relatives, eager for the opportunity to build a new life in the homeland of the erstwhile imperious masters of trade.

Already black bin bags full of rubbish have begun to appear in piles by the pavement's edge. The ever-warming air draws the sickly smell of organic matter rotting from the shops and their discarded bags of waste, to mix with the rich aromas of herbs and spices. Though the air is thick with scents the occasional child holds its nose and passes some comment, quickly silenced by their accompanying guardian, about the odour my being exudes.

No evidence of my fellow dead clustered about the doorway to a Victorian hall tells me immediately that the place is open. To enter, I pass beneath the words: 'The Salvation Army'. Inside, smells of boiling vegetables and heating pastry. I take a plastic tray from a stack and slide it along the metal rails that run before the servery until I reach a pile of warm plates. Taking a plate, I place it on my tray and continue my progress through this simple process.

Middle-aged ladies with kind voices serve me a meat pie, boiled potatoes, carrots and peas. A bowl containing a cube of sponge, covered with anaemic custard, then a mug of tea, which I shall lace with sugar. When I reach the end of the metal rails, a kind lady asks if I can afford to contribute, blankly I stare back at her until she gestures with a flick of her head that I was dismissed.

Those of my fellow diners, closer to life than I, clustered together near the centre of the hall. Those further from life, like me, sat alone, scattered towards the outer reaches of the hall. I select a table and sit diagonally opposite the only other occupant. Without a word and in perfect isolation I begin to feed. The food makes the hinges of my jaw ache as I hold it in my mouth, eager enzymes dissolving its substance. Swallowing the savoury paste, I feed another forkful into my ragged mouth, then another and another until the plate is clear. With minimum delay, I start on the pudding, its sweetness contrasting wonderfully on my palate with the first course.

Continuing my dining experience, I sweeten the tea to my taste and sip it with considered relish. Sitting back in my seat, I look directly, for the first time, at the other diner sharing the table with me. He is as dead as I am. His plates are also empty and he sits staring at the table surface with dead eyes, his life long gone, all he knows is purgatory and its grinding cruelty. For this moment his stomach is full, he is safe and the chair bears his weight, relieving wasted lower limbs from the burden of his body. He is not in a hurry to plough the unfriendly streets and so he sits waiting for death in relative comfort whilst he considers God's dark plan.

Leaving my distant dining companion to his unspoken soliloquy, I take my tray to the wheeled racking and slide it into the middle bracket then walk silently from the building. The streets are as I had left them, busy with the passage of lives. Wrapped in my cloak of invisibility, I set a course for one of the larger parks and navigate the rivers of the unseeing living to my objective.

Spring is growing old, flowers heavy with blooms brighten the beds of the park and insects float between the competing floral displays. Those with everything to live for gather in groups on the wide expanding areas of grass sharing jokes and cigarettes. Mothers indulge their children with ice creams, swings and slides. I sit amongst the roots of an old oak tree. These vessels were sent forth to delve the earth for water and succour during the reign of King Charles II, restoration and rebirth, new hopes and old sins.

The dogs have been barking and yapping at: each other, passing mutts and the breeze in the trees. My soul aches to silence them. The hammer feels heavy in my coat pocket and in my mind's eye; I see their sculls shattering beneath its uncaring head. Afternoon sunshine, ice cream in the park, too many eyes to witness canine slaughter, too many eager drones willing to protect, detain and vex my ambition.

Hounds of excrement, brought forth by a tribe of miscreants now gathered about a wooden picnic table in an area set aside for that purpose. They separate: two remain with the loathsome pets and three take their young beyond the wooden staved pail to purchase ice creams from the vendor there.

In the blue sky above, I follow with my eyes space hardware traversing the firmament. A spot of silvering white, moving at great speed, its metallic body reflecting the Earthshine back to us. The satellite's light blinked out thirty degrees above the distant horizon, I resolve to remain in this place to await its return.

The incessant cacophony made by the shit machines, is punctuated by the heart-rending scream of a frightened child. Whilst returning with his ice cream one of the tribe's young had pushed the staved gate open to pass. It had closed quicker than he had anticipated on its spring and knocked him, from behind, to the ground. Lying face down and prone, ice cream splattered onto the dirt before him, the lower staves of the gate had trapped is ankle. He wailed for rescue and reassurance.

Idiot dog-keepers treated each other to a running commentary on the misfortunes of the child as they slowly gathered about him. One adult crouched and tried to pull the child's foot free long enough to establish that it would not come free and that the action inflicted pain on the boy. Another suggested that they remove the child's shoe and bent to the task, bending and twisting the trapped limb causing further distress to the child. The remainder of the feeble-minded stood holding dogs on straining leads as they answered the need to be as close as possible to the centre of the drama.

When I arrive I do not hesitate, taking hold of the upper horizontal bar of the gate I tear it from its hinges and cast it to the side. Sensing his freedom the boy scrabbled into a sitting position and continued to sob as he recounted his hurts and fears. The dog idiots stare at me with open mistrust. Unable to disguise my disgust, now being visible, I storm off to the sanctuary of my tree roots where I disappear.

Those people are the personification of poor humanity and putrid society. They thought nothing of inconveniencing decent people with the abhorrent din of their foul pets, and to litter areas of recreation and industry with canine scat, juxtaposition to this inconsideration sat the consideration of, not damaging the gate, even if that were to prolong the fear and pain of a child. Scum, barely human scum, antipathetic to all around them save hidden authority. At times like these, I am nearly pleased that my life ended and I departed from humanity.

Wrapped in the veil that protects and separates me, I settle into the roots to await the return of the satellite. In the background, I can hear the protestations of adults, wailing children and barking dogs. It is a remarkable day by my standards.

For the remainder of the day I sat amongst the roots until the evening breeze became chill. From the park, I trawled the streets back to the central precinct where I watched the drinkers go about their reverie then I watched a young couple copulating near the underground tube station. After that, I drifted for home.

In darkness, I return to the garden of the dead. The dark monoliths and steles rise from the deep grass to point at the stars. Familiar stone shapes loom from the thick night as I progress to my shelter. There is emptiness here since she left. I am glad she has crossed over but I do miss her. It continues to stalk the garden. I do not dawdle as I near my byre. Once safely inside the mausoleum I fish out the blanket and make my bed up.

The ceiling I stare up at as I lie on my stone cot has disappeared. I stare into a black tunnel pulling me irresistibly upward into the night sky. So strong is its force, the light from the stars cannot escape its singular attraction. I can feel myself falling upward through my frontal lobs and into a vortex of darkness, an invisible maelstrom.

Outside in the garden I can hear something moving. At first, I assumed It was abroad, skulking in the shadows and oozing venom. Idly I listen to the movement until I realise that this is something new. Visitors are rare in the darkest corner of this cemetery. Curiosity pulls me upright and I shuffle, blanket about my shoulders, to the doorway. Looking out into the gloom, I see them moving some distance from my abode.

The small boy led the retard amongst the monuments to the fortunate dead. I see him watching them with lustful malevolence from behind one of the stone buttresses of the church. Fear and divine restriction paralyse me into impotence when I attempt to call a warning to them. With diligence and compassion, the boy led his imbecile charge by the hand. His feet stepped lightly as he went, dirty burst trainers picking the way through the undergrowth. Dried mud adorned the knees and backside of his trousers, the red pullover that he wore allowed flashes of his yellow shirt to shine through numerous holes, worn by necessary fatigue, fulfilling its function of warmth retention. His brain-damaged companion stumbled on stiff legs, feet pointing inwards and arms hanging loosely from his slumped shoulders. Though his neck is stooped, his face looks vacantly ahead, mouth hanging open adding to the dullness of his appearance. He wears a tracksuit so white that it appeared translucent against the ebony night.

It struck with lethal ferocity. Frozen with fear and by the terms of the covenant I hold in purgatory, I am bound to witness the attack. Claws cut deep into the simpleton's chest. Only brief, pointless protestations issued from his lips before the massive blood loss took what brain function he had from him. The boy, who had been knocked to the ground by the irresistible concussion of It's attack on the retard, realised almost instantly that his ward was dead. Regaining his feet, the boy took his last step. Snapping his head rapidly towards the fleeing child, It severed his hamstring with a single snap of his powerful jaws. Immobilised, the boy sat weeping in the grass, watching It as he began to feed on the corpse of the idiot. It became apparent that It found the taste of the fool's flesh distasteful. He vomited the soft tissue that he had swallowed. Then burying his jaws in the long grass cleaned the unviable flesh from them. The boys screams reached a hysterical pitch when It's terrible eyes appeared above the grass, staring malevolently at him. Slowly he closed on the boy, greedy relish burning in his eyes as he contemplated the meal to come.

Scrabbling at the dirt and grasses, he tries, unsuccessfully, to maintain the distance between them. Gradually It closes on the boy, then suddenly It is on him. Awful screams accompany his meal as It feeds on the boy. His legs, then abdomen are consumed. Shock, arriving at last, begins to close the boy's body down and gradually the screams falter then stop as unconsciousness takes him. The child died only minutes before It raised his head from the meal, having taken his fill.

Prowling about his two kills, It snarled into the darkness, with a vicious look deep in his eyes, scanning the garden for further targets. There being none to be found, It turned and slipped into the night, where he will defecate innocence corrupted to filth.

From their gallery, hidden in the darkest corner of our garden, The Willow Monks chant a strange requiem for the boy and his charge. Weakened by the event It had made me witness, I stumble backwards until the cool stone of my bed presses against the backs of my legs. I sit then lie on my crib, listening all the while to the complex sounds made by the invisible choristers. Gradually their song changes and I hear the references to me. Cruelly they recount my history, every error, every pain, everything I have lost. Usually they are not so vicious, preferring to sooth me not to torture me. The Monks carry their song from my past to my present. After crediting my progress on my mission, they sing of my future. Not long now and I shall be released, my mission nearing completion. Tantalisingly they state that, someone from my past will play a part in my passing. I dare not dream of who that may be, a rare warmth to a bleak and pre-determined future.

As the Monks conclude their song, they deliver the news. My mission is to change and I must complete it in order to pass. It has broken the covenant and now hunts beyond the pale of the Garden of The Dead. The terrible events I have just witnessed were a facsimile of his carnage. To be delivered I must hunt him and destroy him.

Before I sleep, I dwell on hope, a rare luxury in times like these. I hope that the one who will assist my passing will be someone that once loved me. I take a glimmering hope, terrible images and a dreadful fear to sleep with me.

Chapter 26

The compromise agreement was generous enough: six months salary, a lump sum compensating for the loss of the use of a company car and fuel card for six months and a payment to cover half a year's holiday entitlement. All funds were payable tax-free. Subsequent to token legal advice, paid for by his employer, Matt waived his employment rights in order to comply with the terms of the agreement and benefit from his employer's offer.

He maintained his position that he had not done a thing that would warrant the termination of his employment contract. His employer however, was adamant that he leave the business. The choice presented to him was stark: leave with a reference and a large lump sum or be dismissed and try to fight for his rights in an employment tribunal. Matt's confidence in his blamelessness was not sufficient for him to risk the latter option.

Dark grey clouds moved ominously across the sky. There was a chill to the wind and a definite sense to the day, that summer was over and that autumn had seized the world. He stood outside the Solicitor's office. Inside the office he had signed the compromise agreement, now outside, he had telephoned his ex-employer's Human Resources Department to confirm that the payment would be in his account by the end of the week and that his company car be collected, from his home, the following morning.

Standing on the pavement as he looked at the darkening sky, he felt a cold spark that cut through to his heart and shadows pass over his soul. There was nothing else to do at that moment in time but to get drunk. With purpose, he set off down the road in the direction of a large popular bar.

The pub was one of a chain across the country, each the same as the next. It was surprisingly busy for a mid-week afternoon. The clientele were exclusively male, each patron sitting alone at a table with a pint of beer and his own thoughts. The absence of television or piped music gave the place the atmosphere of a reading room, Matt's fellow sallow drinkers sat motionless and silently.

When he approached the bar, a Barmaid who appeared barely old enough to be behind the bar, sauntered from her position of rest, to meet Matt and take his order. Fidgeting on the spot, he felt conspicuous in his business suit as he waited for her to deliver the pint of strong lager he had ordered. When his beverage arrived, he paid for it with a twenty pound note and turned to look for a place to sit. He found a seat at a raised island table, where he perched on a high stool, scanned the room with the eyes of a raptor and began to reflect on recent events.

When he first explained to Lily that he had been suspended, she stood bouncing Lucy in her arms with a look of loathing on her face. She appeared so disappointed, he was moved to follow her about, reassuring her as he went that everything would be all right. Not for the first time in recent years, he felt that he had broken the sacred covenant of marriage. He was the husband, the one who provides and protects. Now he had failed once again, leaving his family to face an uncertain future.

In retrospect, from the point of his suspension the outcome of the investigation was a fait-a-complete. His conduct had given his employer the opportunity to remove him from the business, an opportunity, of which, they were very glad to take advantage. His persistent absenteeism through claimed illness and his petulant tardiness had made him unpopular with most of his colleagues. The only consolation he could draw from the situation was that his removal from the company had cost them a significant amount of money, money he could use to relax for a while before finding another, better, job.

Fingering the dried rings embossed onto the table's veneer from the numerous glasses that had rested there before, Matt absorbed his surroundings. An all-pervasive smell of stale beer and body odour hung heavily in the air. The other drinkers animated only to shuffle outside for a smoke, attend the bar for a refill or to delve further into the bowels of the establishment to find the urinals. He appeared to be beyond the common synchronicity that governed the other's drinking habits. His glass was nearly empty and the others had at least half a pint sitting in their glasses, growing warm and sticky.

Matt poured the remainder of his drink into his mouth and was on the way to the bar for a re-fill before he had swallowed it. The Barmaid saw him coming and was there to ask if he wanted, 'the same again'? With a nod of his head, he confirmed his desire and began to count through the changed he had fished from his trouser pocket. Satisfied with the efficiency of the transaction and feeling the welcome effects of the alcohol, tingling in his brain, he returned to his seat.

After satisfying himself that his surrounding had not altered in anyway and that no significant change was imminent, he took a long draft from his glass and began to count his misfortunes. Looking beyond the linear and circular patterns on the tabletop, his eyes focus on some distant place. A shell-shocked sentry; at his post but only dimly aware of his duties. Walking wounded filling a non-critical gap in the roster, battling his demons and not the enemies of his regiment. Several times, he broke cover. Moving swiftly from his hide to rendezvous with the agent behind the bar, he replenished his glass. Then with considered stealth, he navigated the archipelago of tables, each with its lonely occupant, to regain the sanctuary of his stool. The numerous successful sojourns ensured that he had achieved an altered state of being and the conclusion of his thoughts was that, it was not his fault. He did not expose the affair; Vanya was to blame for that. It was not his choice that Vanya became pregnant; again, that was her fault. He had not lost his job, that lying cow Ann had used innocent and effective, if eccentric, management to mis-represent the situation and deceive the company into getting rid of him. His marriage had never fully recovered from the affair, that was the biggest fault of all, and the blame lay entirely with the bitch that had driven her car into him.

A dimming of the lights informed the clientele that the bar was now entering the evening phase of that day's trade. Matt was surprised how quickly the afternoon had passed. He had told Lily that he would be home for dinner however; he had no desire to stop drinking. She would make him feel uncomfortable if he were to continue drinking at home. Uncomfortable in his own home, that would make it her fault if he were to feel so uncomfortable that he opted to stay in the bar drinking for another hour or so.

Her voice disturbed his plotting, glorious reverie of his enemies abducted and tortured to death, future successes to place him well beyond any previous position, all to be known to those that he wished to hurt. She was in an eclectic company of scruffy idiots and Saxon wide-boys all shaved heads, tattoos and fat folds. They occupied one of the larger tables beneath Matt's island perch, where they competed with each other to substitute reason and informed logical thought with crass verbosity.

The Bar had become significantly busier as local workers spewed forth from their places of servitude to drink with colleagues before returning to their other lives. For the first time that day, the place began to develop an atmosphere more conducive with that of a public house. The gathering host consisted of people that Matt would not ordinarily associate. She was no exception to that social observation. In her Scots accent, she fired a constant staccato of reports at her company, which resounded throughout the premises. Age and gender differentiating her from her companions, she comfortably adopted a matriarchal role in her group, holding forth with judgements and advice relating to others absent from that coven.

Surreptitiously Matt studied his neighbours and their self-appointed matriarch. Her hair was shoulder length auburn with grey roots. Her clothes were for a woman twenty years her junior and at least one dress size smaller than her deteriorating body required. Despite her obvious shortcomings, he found himself attracted to her. With a sideways gaze, he admired her bottom through the nylon trousers she wore, when she stood and reached across her table to accept a home-rolled cigarette from a boasting buffoon.

With the majority of her fellows, she left the table to smoke outside in the designated area. They left a two-man rearguard to hold the territory and protect personal items cached at their base. Together the 'Stay Behind Party' discussed their mutual incomprehension of how the others could afford to smoke when they existed on state benefits. They agreed that neither of them could manage to afford the luxury that their companions concurrently were enjoying.

When the smokers returned, Matt managed to achieve eye contact with her. Holding the contact, he risked a smile, rewarded with a broad smile and a 'look away and back again' routine from his Celtic fancy. She sat in a different seat, allowing Matt and her to exchange furtive glances and secret smiles as the raconteurs of her group held forth with practiced ignorance.

They dispersed in groups of two or three. When the last group departed Suzy, assured them that would be 'ok' and that she intended to stay a little longer because she had seen an old friend. Accepting her lie, the last of her companions left her alone. After she waved her final farewell, she turned in her seat and looked at Matt through her false eyelashes and crow's feet. Returning her smile Matt picked up his glass and moved to join the Scots woman at the next table.

"Can I buy you a drink?"

"We haven't been introduced."

"Well allow me. I am Matt, how do you do?"

"I am Suzy, how are you?"

"I am well thank you. Now may I buy you a drink?"

"You may, I would like a glass of wine."

"Any particular type of wine?"

"White. The Pinot Grigio if they have it still."

"Give me one moment and I'll be right back. Don't go away."

Smiling at her, he turned and marched to the bar. Much to his annoyance the Barmaid was no longer on duty and many more customers were occupying the staff with their orders. It was the longest that he had had to wait at the bar all day to replenish his own drink and acquire Suzy's large glass of Pinot Grigio. With clear relief, he sat opposite her and having placed the wine before her lifted his glass with a brief salutation. Retuning the salutation she lifted her glass to join his with a barely audible 'clink'. They both drank then began to exchange information about themselves.

When they had established that neither of them had eaten that day, they moved to a nearby Indian Restaurant. Suzy drank a bottle of white wine with her meal and Matt continued

187

with large bottles of Indian Lager. When he had paid the bill, Matt had to assist Suzy from her chair, through the restaurant and out into the chilly autumn night air.

"Where to now?" Suzy demanded as she swayed against his arm, both moving like a handicapped three-legged race team as they headed into the night. Though he was not sober himself, Matt managed to steer a reeling Suzy towards the taxi rank, saving her from diving onto the pavement several times.

"Where are we going?"

She demanded as she swayed and struggled to focus on Matt.

"Where would you like to go?"

"Back to yours," She stated bluntly.

"No we can't go there."

"Why are you married?"

"Yes I am."

"I don't care. You can come back to mine but I warn you it is not very nice. I only have a room in a shared house."

"Do you share with friends?"

"I wouldn't say that, the guy that owns the house will let a room to anyone, just now I share with a Pole, a Romanian and two Lithuanians, I'm the only one who speaks English properly there."

"How cosmopolitan," Matt jibed with an affected accent.

"I wouldn't say that, they are pissed every night, very loud and all much younger than me."

"How old are you if I may ask?"

Matt had a cheeky look on his face whilst she gave him a sideways look of distain, then relenting she answered.

"My last birthday was a big one, my fiftieth. How old are you?"

"Thirty nine."

They climbed into a minicab and she slurred her address at the driver. Once progress towards her abode was established, she sought reassurance from Matt that she did not look her age. She bolstered her fragile confidence by informing him, several times, that her previous boyfriend had been a toy boy. Tired of reciting platitudes, Matt decided to ignore her until they reached the end of the journey. En route, they had the driver pull over at a late night off license, where Matt jumped from the taxi to purchase two bottles of cheap wine.

Eventually the cab pulled up outside a rundown semi-detached house in the body of a huge housing estate. Matt settled the, larger than expected, fare and they stepped gingerly from the taxi and through the unkempt garden to the front door. A rococo fanlight in the door had every pane of glass replaced by various coloured panels of chipboard. When she opened the door a stale air of dampness and overfilled bins rushed out to envelope them.

It was a house of dysfunction, occupied by a collection of itinerant Greater European Union citizens. Shouts in various Eastern European languages, indecipherable yet threatening by intonation, rang out regularly and for no apparent reason. The hallway was filthy and Matt tried not to touch any surfaces as they climbed the stairs and made their way to her room. They both looked as though they had navigated a difficult journey to sanctuary as she closed the bedroom door behind them, the lock giving a mechanical 'clunk' as the door settled into its frame.

"Well here it is, home sweet home," she slurred.

"Nice, I love what you have done with the place," he lied.

She opened the first of the bottles of wine as Matt sat awkwardly on her bed. The room, furnished with a broken down collection of furniture, the sort that could be easily acquired from second-hand shops, had the appearance of a grotty pub's storeroom. Yellowed woodchip wallpaper peeled from the corners, both upward and downwards. The thin carpet wore a complex design of stains, spills and holes, displaying a history of many occupants and their fetid lives. Suzy passed him a glass of wine and sat beside him with her own glass held lightly in her hand as she balanced it on the topmost knee of her crossed legs.

Slurring inanities in her faux educated Edinburgh accent, Suzy attempted to play hostess to her 'Gentleman Caller'. Her performance appeared to be unhindered by the obvious incongruity of the setting. His discomfort increased when she pulled a cigarette from the pack of ten, fished from the bowels of her handbag. The brand of the cigarette was a cheap one and the room already stank of stale smoke before she lit it. Placing her drink amongst grubby personal possessions on the dishevelled fridge that served as a bedside cabinet, she levered herself up by placing her hand on Matt's knee, to grasp an overflowing ashtray from the floor, presenting him with her bony backside as she lent over.

Her bed was a single and felt uncomfortably soft. It moved with exaggerated undulations whenever she shifted her body weight on it. Blowing a long stream of smoke from her mouth, she stubbed the cigarette out into the ashtray, lifted her bottom and sat again onto the mattress, this time more fully facing Matt.

"Let's get into bed for a cuddle."

She stated her suggestion without preamble or affection. Matt agreed with a nod of his head and began to unbutton his shirt.

Rapidly she removed her make-up with a pad of cotton wool and some lotion from a pink bottle.

"Now you see me naked," she smiled at him from her now clean face, "hope it doesn't put you off."

Without the benefit of cosmetics, she appeared closer to sixty than fifty. Years of hard drinking and constant smoking ensured that she rarely had money or the appetite for food. She switched the light, a single naked energy-saver bulb, off to protect her modesty as she undressed. In the strange orange light of the extraneous street lamps, he watched her undress. Although not fat, her figure was not attractive. Her legs were skinny and shapeless, her bottom was flat, her breasts hung like pointless monuments to her long lost fertility and her stomach some how retained a paunch.

Matt stood awkwardly by the bed, dressed only in his boxer shorts. She stood next him and pushed her black knickers away from her crotch. Bending over her breasts hung perpendicular to the horizontal as though her nipples were unnaturally attracted to Earth and that the glands within had shrivelled to negligible volume, pointed empty bags. They remained in that position no matter what angle her torso occupied. When she stepped out of her underwear, she turned to admire the man she had brought home. Smiling at him, she seized the waistband of his shorts and pulling towards her and downwards revealed his penis.

The windows of the room covered by filthy net curtains, allowed the sodium glow of the streetlights to filter through the chintz and lace to illuminate their naked bodies. Despite the filth and dilapidation of the environment and the repugnancy of the company, Matt's manhood stood proud. Pushing him onto the bed Suzy cupped his balls in her right hand and sucked greedily on the head of his cock. Her thick mane of dyed hair fell forward over her face and draped his loins. Burying his hands deep into her hair, he massaged her scalp as she worked on his cock.

Feeling his balls tighten he encouraged her upward away from his penis. Crawling upwards, she pressed her aging body against his until her labia rested against his cock. With some adjustments by hand, he was able to slide his erection into her moistening pussy. She pressed her sagging tits into his chest hair as she kissed his mouth passionately. The strong smell of burning on her breath was testament to the rapid oxidisation of her body, borne of her unhealthy lifestyle.

Rotating their bodies awkwardly they achieved the traditional mating position. He lifted his upper body on fully extended arms and turned his hip upward to achieve fullest penetration. Matt pushed in with measured force then withdrew gently. Their hips moved in opposite and complimentary ways.

Through the sepia light of the darkened room, he glimpsed her former beauty, limited light, masking the ravages of age and lifestyle to turn back time. Through the grotty illusion, he saw the face of a blossoming young girl, smiling through her burgeoning womanhood, looking up at him. This is how she had looked when she first discovered love, when the world held boundless promise and when her angels fought with her demons. Her current situation was absolute proof that, despite her embellished memories, the demons had won.

The illusion being significantly more attractive than the reality of his situation, Matt clung to it, greatly enhancing the coitus he practiced with the old woman beneath him. Thrusting to climax with the young woman, he collapsed onto his back and waited for the old woman to speak. She held him tightly as a mother would hold a frightened child and kissed his head repeatedly. Eventually releasing her grip, she moved

191

her hips and grasped at his now flaccid penis in the hope of resurrecting his ardour.

With liberation from the captivity of lust, the truth of his situation flooded in. He should have caught the train home hours ago, he was in a hovel with an ugly old woman, miles from where he should have been or wanted to be. Freeing himself from the hags clutches, he stood and began to dress.

"Where are you going lover?"

"I've got to go, should have been home hours ago."

"Wifey waiting for you?"

"Yes and the rest of my life."

She shifted from her back to prop herself up on an elbow.

"What's that supposed to mean?"

"It means that I can't be here anymore."

"Am I going to see you again lover?"

"No."

Pulling his jacket on, he left the room letting the door swing closed behind him with an unintended 'bang'. By the top of the stairs a door opened and an alcohol glazed imbecile leered out at him, muttering an incomprehensible phrase repeatedly. Matt ignored him and descended past another of the house's occupants who ascended the stairs. The climbing man turned and demanded something of Matt in an Eastern European language. The demand repeated in a louder voice as he fumbled the front door open and plunged out into the night. Leaving the detritus of the new European dream behind, he struck out into the liberty of darkness.

When he was beyond the boundary of the garden, he chose to turn right only to find that direction led to a cul-de-sac. Retracing his route past the scene of his earlier passions, he struck out into the darkness seeking a way home. In the anonymous distance dogs barked and the hissing of traffic rose and fell in sporadic patterns as he hurried along roads lined with sleeping households. With no knowledge of his exact whereabouts, Matt walked towards the brighter lights of the more significant thoroughfares, which he followed until he identified a railway line. He shadowed the course of the steel rails until the signage indicated a station. It was far too late to hope that the trains would be running so when he arrived at the station he moved directly to the lit shack from which a minicab firm operated.

There were no cabs parked up outside of the shack and Matt could only just see the top of someone's head behind the control desk. The door creaked loudly as he yanked it open and stepped inside. Rough wooden benches lined three of the four walls within, their surfaces long since shined by the backsides of the previous night's revellers who had waited for their ride home. A skinny woman with a ponytail and bad skin observed him with bemused incredulity from the control desk beyond a Perspex screen. Her eyes widened with even greater incredulity when he told her his desired destination.

Ponytail canvassed the few drivers that she had on duty over the airwaves to identify a willing candidate to drive Matt home. It was a long way and few wished to embark on a fare of that magnitude. One driver did eventually accept the business and Matt settled on the wooden bench to wait for the arrival of his ride home. He shivered and wished he had worn an overcoat as he pulled his, long since muted, 'phone from his jacket and checked the screen. Many missed calls, all from his wife and a string of increasing angry then concerned voicemail messages. With a sigh, he returned the 'phone to his pocket and began to concoct his excuses.

Chapter 27

It was nearly four thirty in the morning when the cab pulled up outside Matt's home. He had asked the driver to stop at an ATM on the way home so that he could withdraw sufficient cash to settle the exorbitant fare. Counting the twenties from one hand to another he handed the driver the wad and told him to 'keep the change' before climbing from the front passenger seat to face the music.

He had fallen asleep in the cab and was feeling drowsy, sick and disgusted by his own behaviour as he crunched up the path to his front door. Concentrating hard, he tried to slip his key into the lock and turn the mechanism as silently as possible. With a soft click, he closed the door behind him and crept along the hallway passing the nursery where Lucy slept and onto the bedroom, he and Lily shared. The familiar scents of home welcomed him and the hearth fire environment eased his soul, a soul come home, a soul returned to its people from darkness.

He slipped out of his shoes by the bedroom door and then moved silently into the room, removing his jacket and tie as he went. Easing himself onto the bed, he removed his trousers and socks before whipping his shirt off and sliding beneath the duvet.

"Where, the bloody hell, have you been?"

"Ah not now darling it's been a hell of a day."

"And night, I've been worried sick. You haven't been answering your 'phone."

"Yeah I know I had a bit of a disaster there."

"Really? I'll bet."

"It has been manic babe. I'm knackered can we talk about it in the morning?"

"Not until you tell me where the hell you have been all night."

"I said it's been mad. I bumped into Mike in the Pub and we had one or two too many then he invited me back to his place for a game of cards."

194

"You never play cards and you stink of cheap perfume."

"I know that's why I ended up losing so much money. The perfume must have been Mike's Missus, she must have bathed in it."

"You really expect me to believe that load of old shit?"

"Yes. I do, because it is the truth."

Lily settled back into her pillow and pulled the duvet about her neck. Behind her, she could feel the mattress and bedding moving as Matt made himself comfortable in preparation for sleep. She waited until he had stopped moving and his breathing became slower and deeper before she spoke.

"Bollocks."

Despite his attempts to convince her or to amend or enhance his story, she ignored him and pretended to be sleeping until her ruse became reality.

As the chemistry of his brain altered Matt's bearing changed from that of desperate contrition to barbed resentment. With two clumsy oral swipes delivered, his head, the pillow and all consciousness deserted him for several hours.

Bedding damp with his sweat, clung to his skin as he woke and shifted position to ease stiff joints and tingling digits. Through the bedroom window, Matt could see the branches of an apple tree. The last of that year's fruit hanging amongst the thinning foliage, rustic colouring against the battleship grey of the sky. Heavy clouds scudded through the atmosphere, soaking the land below as they released their burdens. Burdens carried from the ocean, bonded molecules of volatile oxygen and Hydrogen almost as old as the universe itself.

The timpani of rain on the roof began again and startled Matt from his silent thoughts into action. He rolled onto his opposite side and focussed on the alarm clock by the bed. Both hands pointed to the ceiling, telling him that it was time to rise.

Lily sat in the front room with their daughter. They played together, Lucy waved a doll in the clothing of a prostitute about before her mother's face and Lily swung another doll, wearing only a bikini, from a hiding place to meet and greet

195

the tart doll. Shrieks of utter delight came from his child every time Lily presented one figurine to the other. Matt stood in the doorway watching them for a moment, enjoying the normality of the scene.

"Morning you two."

"Afternoon."

"Look eh I am sorry about last night."

"I don't care."

He shifted his weight as he formulated his next step.

"I am going into town."

"You need to catch the bus then. They have taken your car away this morning."

"Bloody hell they didn't hang about did they?"

"I am sure they told you they were taking it back."

"Yeah they did. Fair enough I suppose a company car for a company that I am no longer part of."

"You will no longer be part of many more things unless you start to think of others."

"What's that supposed to mean?"

She drew her attention from the game she played with her daughter and stared directly at him.

"You know full well what I mean."

As he glared back at her he became convinced of her resolve on the matter and chose not to push it to the limit.

"Can I borrow your car?"

"Depends."

"Depends on what?"

"Well if I lend you my car will I see it again today?"

"Yes I promise I will only be a couple of hours."

"Keys are on the kitchen table."

"Thanks."

With a loose wave of his hand, Matt turned in the doorway and walked towards the kitchen. Her felt angry because she persisted in her bad mood and appeared to take pleasure from his misfortune in losing his company car.

True to his word, Matt returned later that afternoon. In his hand, he clutched a receipt for the holiday that he had just purchased in town. An early season, ten day, break in Barbados for him and Lily. His wife was astounded, it had never occurred to her that Matt could have been on a mission

196

that would favour them mutually. She had been on the verge of surrendering all hope that their marriage would be saved when, that one act of kindness and consideration re-established the fire of hope within her heart.

Lucy was delivered to her Grandmother for safekeeping whilst Matt and Lily sought emotional salvation in The Caribbean. The anticipation of this holiday had made the four weeks, they had to wait from the booking to embarkation, bearable together and an atmosphere of comfortable normality returned to their home. Lily felt the thrill, she thought lost to her many years previously as she settled into her seat on the plane.

Within hours of arriving at their luxury beach resort Matt and Lily had resumed sexual relations. They made love on the king size bed, this was the first time in months and both of them felt a closeness that had become almost alien to them. As they unpacked and nested in the apartment, that would be their home for the duration of the holiday, they re-assured each other of with mutual attention and consideration.

That night they dined together by the beach, listening to the gentle crash of surf on sand and the incessant squeaking of the hidden tree frogs. To any who witnessed their meal they would appear as a successful couple who were deeply in love with each other. Both Matt and Lily knew neither of those observations to be accurate; however, they both hoped that that they could be.

Within days they had settled into a routine of late rising, lying in the sun reading, drinking at the poolside bar, dining out in a different restaurant each night and love making under the slowly revolving fan over their bed. Suspending reality, they accepted the leisurely lifestyle as normality. Matt felt good, very good, his mood remained constant and he felt a confidence in his own brain function that he had lost some time before. His mental confidence allowed him to relax and with that casualness, the charm that Lily loved so much returned. Forgetting their troubles, they absorbed the local zeitgeist and let the days flow by.

The rapid decent of the sun to hide behind the gradual topography of sedimentary geology of the island marked the end of the last day of their holiday. Kicking his heels in the pool and drinking a rum punch, Matt watched Lily swim towards him. Illuminated from beneath by the lights on the pool bottom she looked like an aquatic angel on a mission from Poseidon, long torpedo of soft flesh hunting her target. With a loud tearing, she forced her body upwards from the pool, shards of water propelled into the air, then to crash back to the aqueous body of their kindred molecules. The liquid veil fell from her body as she stood before Matt.

"Order me one of those."

"Rum punch? Sure."

"Before you go."

"Yes?"

"I love you."

"I love you too."

Matt climbed to his feet and with a smile at Lily, stepped carefully on the wet poolside to the bar. She checked the arrangement of her bikini before ascending the fanned marble steps to ground level. When she had dried herself with a towel, pulled from one of the sun-beds, she pushed her arms into a light robe and tied it about her waist. They sat together at one of the glass tables set to the side of the pool and shared their enthusiastic observations of the holiday and their regret that it was their final night on the Island that lay before them.

"Where shall we eat tonight?"

"Let's push the boat out and eat at that green restaurant, down by the other beach?"

"Shall we?"

"Yeah."

"Ok Darling I am going to take this drink in with me and start to get ready. Are you coming?"

"No Babes, I'm going stay out here for a bit and finish my drink then I'll be right with you."

"Ok, don't take too long I am getting hungry."

"I won't, promise."

Bending she kissed Matt on the lips and then carried her drink into their apartment through the double garden doors that opened onto the small poolside garden. He watched her go, admiring her figure until she disappeared into the obscured recesses of the holiday apartment. Alone, his thoughts returned to the ugly possibility that had presented itself that morning in the bathroom.

The vague feeling of discomfort had given way to an unidentifiable pain whilst urinating, then a discharge from his urethra came and that morning he could see that the end of his urethra was swollen and discoloured. On close inspection, Matt saw that the end of his penis was now a weeping sore. Throughout the day, he had re-affirmed the horrific revelation by checking his penis in the toilets nearly every thirty minutes. Last night of their holiday it was, however they would not be following the established routine. If he had been lucky enough not to contaminate Lily, he was not going to push his luck now. He needed to formulate a plan that would allow him to gain treatment for his condition and to keep it hidden from his wife. If Lily were contaminated he would have a very difficult problem on his hands. The only solution he could think of was to find some way to treat his wife's sexually transferred infection without her knowing she was being treated or even that she was infected.

In the peripheries of his mind, Matt felt the beating wings of his Despair Angels. He had enjoyed the mental clarity that had come with the change of scenery. It was even more depressing that the darkness had returned on his last day in the Caribbean. The change was clearly systemic, he felt like a drowning man exhausted to the point of capitulation. Tempting as the dark abyss was, he could not afford the luxury of surrender, the appearance of normality was required, if he was to have any chance of repairing his family.

After pouring the last of his drink into his mouth, Matt stood and walked towards their apartment through the warm air, scented by numerous exotic blossoms and neighbouring kitchens where hundreds of dinners were being prepared. With deep controlled breathes he forced the dark spectre of his sins behind the mask that Lily would face and joined her to dress for the evening.

He was almost disappointed to see her looking so beautiful. Standing with her back to him whilst she brushed her hair, she smiled at him in the mirror. As she moved, her lace thong could occasionally be seen above the rounding of her bottom, through the light fabric of the white culottes she wore. A tight spaghetti top covered her breasts and her shoulders carried a short, see-through, patterned blouse, tied just below her chest. The challenge of the chasten night grew exponentially when she bent over to fit her gold sandals, bottom held high beyond the bed. That evening would present only one believable escape route from the obvious progress towards congress, intoxication. Matt would have to consume enough alcohol to convince Lily that he was sufficiently intoxicated that he would be unable to perform sexually. Typical of his life, he now faced the prospect of having to deceive in order to counter his own intuition and deny himself pleasure.

Chapter 28

When a cancer or an infection gains control of a limb, it is necessary to amputate the limb in order to assure life. Evil is the moral equivalent of cancer or infection and the same draconian natural laws apply, amputate or die. The demon came to him and he had let it lead him into debauchery. Bacchanalian nights led him beyond all decency and into the dark places of this forest through which we live. Those that cared defied the demon to delve into the darkness and recover Abdul to the path of light. To survive the moral cancer, amputation is necessary. However, with this form of oncologistic dismemberment, the limb must be metaphoric, a limb of a family perhaps.

It is true that often what we initially believe to be appropriate penance is erroneous. Given time all things change, or is it because things change that we perceive the passing of time? Be change a function of time or time a function of change, both are inevitable and we must wait to see what will be. Tock will always follow tick. Man made noises of time, a constant since those twins of Cronos were born from the belly of their mother, a golem created by the first horologists, then refined by the likes of Harrison and other disciples of Saturn. Cronos was eventually silenced, his twins began to pass us without a sound, electronic pulses or atomic decay mark the changing world. We must remember to monitor our temporal location, as the silent assassin carries us inexorably to our graves.

When fixing our location in the fourth dimension, we predominantly do so in a casual manner to establish what time of day it is or how long it is until the weekend. Very occasionally we use a chronological sextant to identify the progress of our ailments, for then we shall know how and when to act.

Nature has a habit of creating a cure close to any pathogen or malignant cyto-activity. The cancer began when Abdul had been led astray in London, Saturn passed or changed then the potential cure was created. The more Abdul considered the possibility, the greater the beauty he perceived in the design. Aesha was the cure, sent to him by God. It had not been a demon that possessed Al qasim when he forced himself on Samira, it had been an angel. When at an earlier location, he had been convinced that the actions of his cousin were entirely unconnected with his own actions at university. Now that his position relative to Saturn had altered, he was fully aware of the interconnection of all things and in particular the direct relationship between his malfeasance and that of his cousin's.

God, in his infinite kindness, had sent Abdul the means with which to cure his cancer. Initially he had believed prayer and observance was sufficient however, only with progression did he realise the magnitude of his cancer's malignance. Greater sacrifice was required to achieve full moral wellbeing. Truth would have to be amputated and Aesha sacrificed.

It had taken the efforts of Abdul's extended family to save him from the poisonous intent of the demon, it therefore made sense that in order for the healing cycle to be complete the family should benefit. There could be no doubt that, a union between the two major branches, before they grew too far removed from each other would strengthen his family. As the proposition of an arrangement for marriage between Aesha and Al qasim was not superficially unreasonable they would have to have a sound and obvious reason to object. There was, of course, a very good reason why they should not marry however, that reason he and Samira had buried for years and they could not undo their original deceit. The die was cast and God's will shall be done, for his will it undoubtedly was. Only he had the power to create a scenario with such an absolute outcome and with no effective latitude for its players.

Abdul had to consider the very nature of truth. Could man really determine, absolutely, what truth was or did that knowledge remain the prerogative of God? It is possible that God determined what truth is to meet his purposes. There was certainly a reason why it had been determined that, what befell them had and in such a way guided them to the place they were now. Without faith the circumstances seemed intolerable and without solution. With faith, the answer to the quandary was simple and straightforward.

His sins had been part of the grand design they initiated a family intervention that mobilised every branch and sept. It was God's will that Abdul's family grow stronger and to that end, he sent Aesha in the full and certain knowledge that her union with her father could not be stopped by man, as those that would object have been silenced by their own lies. They were of the same blood to strengthen the family bond. God had even sent an earthquake to undo the previous arrangements made for Al qasim's marriage. There was intelligence behind this design that mortal men could never hope to comprehend.

All that remained for him to do now was to convince Samira of the wisdom he now perceived. It had been a reflective journey home, Abdul's expensive education had provided him with a good knowledge of The Classics, facilitating analysis of any situation in terms of any mythology or religion. Many refused to make the distinction between the two however, Abdul did.

He felt much happier when he stepped from his BMW and walked towards the front door of their home. The late spring evening held the promise of a warm summer, casual afternoons reclining in the back garden with cool drinks and the joyous sounds of the girls playing on the lawn. A strong smell of rosemary from the herb garden filled the air by the door as he pushed his key into the lock and entered to find his girls waiting there for him. They would be pleased, there was no need for him to leave the house tonight and he had not brought any pressing matters home with him, his attention was all theirs.

Zaynab and Aesha's parents kept their inner thoughts and fears from them. The Girls knew nothing of Abdul's epiphany or Samira's mortal dread. They played happily in the bath, Abdul 'dive-bombed' the surface suds with a Goofy doll whilst Samira washed their raven hair. When the bathing was complete, they stabbed their little feet rapidly at the tiled floor, giving the image of some curious folk dance from the indigenous tribes of North America, whilst their parents rubbed them dry with huge thick towels.

When presented, by their mother, to Abdul in the front room they shone. Two perfect little girls, hair so dark it reflected light like the velvet coat of a black cat, eyes deep pools of mahogany and skin of olive perfection. Both stood in their nightdresses, each clutching a teddy of choice to them. He felt a tingling burning behind his eyeballs, then the hot moisture of his tears, gathering in the corners of his eyes. Their beauty was absolute. He had been taught that perfection cannot exist in an imperfect world, yet here they were. Perhaps the other side of that equation must move; the world was perfect or God had rewarded Abdul Hadi with this vision for his efforts to make the world perfect.

With tears stinging his eyes, he embraced the children and kissed their foreheads before staring, through red rimmed, hot blurring eyes, into each of their faces. Assuring them both of his love, he released them to the custody of their mother. As they climbed the stairs to bed he could hear her reassuring the girls that, 'there was nothing wrong with Daddy'. Abdul allowed himself a brief moment of reverie before he began to prepare for the return of his wife to the front room.

She bore an air of incandescent rage when she returned to the room. Without a word, she threw herself into one of the large armchairs that flanked the impressive fireplace and pierced his aura with the black fire that flared from her eyes. He remained calm as he felt her fire break about the cool shield of his reason and righteousness. Then with, well chosen, words of praise for the girls and their mother, he sought to ease the atmosphere. The words of praise brought no response so Abdul employed small talk. Samira demonstrated her distain for the subject of London traffic flow by turning her crossed knees from him and throwing her gaze at the rug before the fireplace.

"Where the hell were you last night?"

"I told you I had dinner with a potential client, his account is very valuable to the bank."

"You did not get back here until two thirty and then you were away again this morning at six."

"I am sorry Darling, I am busy at work and I am doing this for us."

"You must keep me informed, otherwise I worry."

"Yes Dear I know and I am sorry I shall if I am late again."

Samira shifted in her seat and relaxed her posture sufficiently for Abdul to feel more at ease with the situation.

"Have you told your father that we have no intention of betrothing Aesha to that pig Al qasim?"

"I need to talk with you about that."

Abdul's face shone with a new found enthusiasm and his eyes began to sparkle at the prospect of enlightening Samira.

"What is there to talk about?"

"As you know I was just as shocked by the prospect of Aesha's betrothal to Al qasim as you were. However, I have now had an opportunity to really think about the situation and then it came to me."

"What the hell are you talking about?"

"I can now see it all clearly and I have the answer."

"As long as the answer is you telling your father 'no'."

"Well when you look at it from another, higher, angle."

"I do not believe I am hearing this. You had better not be about to agree with your father."

Abdul explained, in laborious detail, the epiphany he had received whilst driving home. His wife sat perfectly still as she listened and glared at him over her, agape, mouth. When he finished with a lengthy assurance that, it was God's will, Samira stood up and left the room without a word. He called after her and followed as far as the front room door where he stopped and watched her ascend the staircase, one delicate hand resting on the dark wood banister and her head held high in defiance. Unbowed, unbeaten, uncowed she felt the resolve of a mother, set in her heart as her rage carried her upwards and to bed.

Echoing thudding marked the closure of the bedroom portal and the announcement of her intended solitary rest. He slumped in the doorway and sighed. It was an anathema to him that she had failed to agree with him, the revelation he gave her was obvious, logical and right. Her obtuseness was typical of women and it was for that reason that God had placed men above them. It was for that reason Abdul had to take control, women cannot be trusted to do the right thing and it fell to men to take positive action, for if they did not, God's will would not be done and The World would never improve.

Darkness snapped in each of the ground floor rooms as Abdul followed the night-time closure routine, general scan of the room, switching off any item left in action then extinguishing the light before moving to the next. He crept up the staircase and to his office where he closed the door and sat at the desk. Admiring his features, reflected in the darkness of the window, he thanked God for his handsome face. After a moment of reflection, he pulled the laptop to himself, opened the lid and pressed the 'On' button. As the screen threw its sickly light onto his face, Abdul prepared to continue his work towards Utopia.

There are no absolutes in human misery and things can always, and usually do, get worse. For evil to drag us all into putrid degeneration, we need do only one thing, nothing. Mankind needed people like Abdul. It was the actions of the morally courageous that kept Satan at bay and vexed his insidious plans, plans that would corrupt us all if they were not effectively opposed. He was, in his own mind, a crusader for truth, piety and humanity. God will reward him.

The most effective of all angels have spent time in the company of Satan, that way knowing the true enemy and knowing his weaknesses. Abdul had served his time under the Morning Star, Lucifer, and he was convinced of his newfound piety. He was now an angel, made by God for a divine purpose: Light in the darkness, clarity in confusion, rock in a storm and reaper of the malignant.

Chapter 29

A group of ugly fat boors dominate one end of the room, unfit bloated bodies denying territory or passage to any other patron, their verbose profanities and idiotic humour filling the entire pub. Mac Gregor glared with undisguised loathing at the ignoramuses, bobbling and swaying at the opposite end of the bar in their football shirts and baseball caps, sporting paraphernalia, incongruous garments for a collective of slobs. He held his pint up to the light, checking its clarity before pulling a long swallow from the glass and placing it back on the bar.

Between the bottles of rarely ordered liqueurs in the browned mirror backing of the tatty Victorian gantry, he saw Willox arriving trough the chipped swing-doors. Mac Gregor observed the Detective Sergeant scanning the bar for him and waited until he locked on to his position and walked towards him before turning to greet him.

"Bruce, whit are ye fir?"

"Evening Guv. I'll have a pint of Bitter."

"Aye, any particular flavour or variety?"

Detective Sergeant Bruce Willox swung his gaze across the pump handles arrayed along the bar and the gang of bellowing buffoons.

"Pint of London and a machine gun."

"Aye a' ken whit ye mean. They could dae wi' a volume control."

The two detectives laughed and Mac Gregor ordered Bruce's pint from the Barmaid.

Taking his change from the girl behind the bar Mac Gregor turned and motioned towards an empty table in the corner of the room. Willox took the lead and they picked their way through the threadbare furnishings to the relative sanctuary of their table.

"So how are ye dain' withoot me?"

"Got that last job wrapped up. It should get to court in a month or so."

"Whit are ye workin' on noo?"

"I've got a murder in the traveller community."

"Is that the one where they're going aboot blamin' everyone fir the

 disappearance o' that wee toe-rag?"

"That's the one."

"Whit are yer thoughts oan it?"

"I know who did it."

"Oh aye, that wiz quick work."

"The lad who disappeared, we haven't recovered a body yet, he was a poof. His boyfriend, also a traveller, did it and had his uncle crush the body in a car."

"Why are aw the Tinkers still runnin' aboot fir then?"

"One last bit of the puzzle to go and I will charge the poofy Gypo with murder and that will give the whole travelling community a bit of a red face. No bad thing eh?"

"Aye tidy Bruce, tidy."

The two Detectives sat in quiet reflection as they enjoyed their beer and each other's company. Bruce Willox cleared his thought and leaned forward.

"How is your serial murder case progressing?"

"Aye tough one, could use you oan this one."

"Got any good leads?"

"Nah just the internet connection but even that's no consistent."

"I understand that he has been using a hammer."

"Aye that's right. Sick bastard."

"Weird one. Some idiot is running about killing dogs, the Titheads have been looking for him."

"Aye a' heard aboot that, how's it goin'?"

"Hard one to get a beat on, they've been taking statements but the culprit seems to be invisible, comes out of nowhere kills the dog brutally then disappears. The only description they get is: scruffy male of indeterminable age. Sometimes he kicks the mutt to death, others he uses a hammer."

"Hammer ye say?"

"Yes, must be quite a heavy one, crushes the scull like an egg shell."

"Interesting, wonder if there's any connection wi ma case?"

"Could be. A serial killer of dogs and women. I hear there is a link with the internet and your case, this man doesn't sound like the computer literate type."

"Maybe he is using a disguise?"

"Could be Guv, he certainly appears to be cunning enough."

"Worth haein' a closer look. I'll get Tommo tae hae a word wi Uniform"

"Good idea Guv. How are you getting on with Tommo?"

"Aye no bad, a' think he's getting' used tae ma ways."

Bruce Willox moved uncomfortably in his seat and took a drink from the pint before him.

"Look Guv I wanted to warn you."

"Warn me aboot whit?"

"Tommo."

"Tommo? Whit are ye sayin' Bruce?"

"Guv we go back a long way and you know you can trust me don't you?"

"Aye Bruce we've done a bit taegether."

"Don't trust him Guv, he's a slippery one. Fancies himself as the next Chief Constable."

"Nowt wrang wi a wee bit o' ambition."

"True Guv but this one doesn't mind who he steps on to get on."

"Whits been said like?"

"Nothing directly but you're not his only boss."

"Whits that supposed tae mean?"

"He spends more time in the station than you do and I don't think it is all spent trying to find your killer. When you are not about he seems to spend a lot of time on the fourth floor."

"Oh aye whaes door is he sniffin' roond?"

"Forester's."

They sat together in silence whilst Mac Gregor considered the implications of the Willox's warning. Chief Inspector Forester was not an admirer of Mac Gregor's work or his methods. They had started in the Force together, Forester had always been a more political animal than Mac Gregor and that had helped him to rise faster. They mutually, though silently, accepted that Mac Gregor was the better copper but Forester was slicker and knew how to ingratiate himself with Senior Officers. It was widely accepted that Forester did not like Mac Gregor and would rather he was not on the same Force.

Leaving Mac Gregor to his thoughts Willox returned to the bar for a second round of drinks. The oafs had moved from their corner of the bar to congregate by the pool table where two of their number played a game as though there was nothing more important than the outcome. The others clustered nearer the bar and continued their odious rhetoric. They made an eclectic gathering with regard to size and body shape, thought their interests and dress sense were clearly much of a mind. He had to shout for the Barmaid to hear his order over their mindless hubbub.

Willox thanked the Barmaid as he received his change and picked up two pints from the bar. When he turned to return to the table he shared with Mac Gregor one of the oafs placed a heavy podgy hand onto his shoulder.

"Oi that's ma pint." The dullard spoke as if he struggled to form each word.

"Oh I am terribly sorry, must have picked the wrong one up."

Willox returned both pints to the bar and began to look for his second. Within seconds, it became obvious that there was no second pint and the oaf was trying it on. Willox picked up the original two glasses and turned to go.

"Oi ah said that was ma pint."

"I don't think so, sorry."

"Fack off, you aint gonna steal ma beer. Put it back."

"Look I don't know what you think you are playing at but I can assure you, both of these drinks are mine and that I have just paid for them at the bar."

"Fack off you cant, just 'cause you wearin' a suit, don't make you right. So give me ma fackin' pint back and fack off back to your boyfriend over there, you fackin' suit wearing cant!"

The dispute attracted a great deal of attention from the collected miscreants. They began to hover closer to their comrade, adding grammatically aberrant statements in support of his attempted beer banditry. It was clear to Willox that he was expected to give up one or both of the pints and if he were brave enough to order and pay for another brace. The detectives resolve was greater than the troop of petty brigands had anticipated and he pressed past them to return to his seat. Concentrating on the glasses, one in each hand, Willox swung his left leg beyond the barstool that partially blocked his way. As his weight shifted from his right leg to his left, the leg snagged and he stumbled, dropping both pints onto the floor. The rambunctious guffaw that followed, confirmed to him that he had been tripped.

Regaining his balance and composure, he turned to confront his tormentors. The fat would-be beer bandit, squared up to him with a mocking smile on his bloated, misshapen face.

"Excuse me, what do you think you are doing?" said Willox.

"Don't know nuffin about what you're on about."

"Yes you bloody well do, you tripped me up so I would drop my drinks."

"And you can fackin' prove that can you?"

"I don't need to, we both know full well what you did."

"So fackin' what, you want me to buy you anover drink do you?"

"Yes as a matter of fact I believe that would be the very least you could do."

"Aw fack off you cant."

With that, the fat man threw a flabby arm forward to push Willox over or away. His reactions surprised all of the louts, in one movement he grasped the fat man's thumb and twisted it into a painful lock that brought the blubbery bully to his knees, wailing for relief from the pain.

The first person to react was one of the smaller oafs who looked like a shaved monkey decorated with tattoos. He swung a vicious punch aimed at his temple from behind Willox. In the very last split second, Bruce Willox detected the incoming blow in his peripheral vision and began to duck. He did not have sufficient time to avoid the blow altogether, however instinctual movement ensured that the shaved monkey's blow struck a hard scull plate and not the soft tissues clustered at his temple. The blow was sufficient to distract Willox and allow the fat beer bandit to struggle free from his grip and push him to the floor. He lay on his back looking up at the circle of ugly faces peering down at him. As a body of men the dullards were about to begin kicking him and they would probably continue until he lost consciousness. Willox prepared to curl into the foetal position on the first impact from a boot.

The shaved monkey was the first to fall. He dropped to his knees then with an uncomprehending look on his face he toppled onto his side and lay there with his eyes open. A tall fat man, with a contorted nose, lifted the peak of his baseball cap to look beyond his fallen comrade in time to register the fist that ploughed into his head, smashing his nose and rendering him unconscious on the floor next to his simian colleague. Willox rolled to one side as Mac Gregor swung his right foot hard into the crotch of one of the fat halfwits, quickly followed by driving his knee up into the buffoon's face.

A particularly obese specimen of imbecile brought his pint glass hard down onto the bar, only for it to shatter into tiny shards, leaving his hand empty. Deprived of the weapon he hoped to hold, the rotund idiot stood, vacantly looking at his bleeding hand. He remained transfixed by his misfortune, when Willox swept his feet from under him. The bleeding fat man landed hard on his back, stunning him from his vacancy. His attention focussed in time to stare at Willox's fist as it drove down into his face.

When Willox regained his feet, the melee was quickly over. The oafs had the stomach to bully but not fight. The last openly offensive action by any of the apish curs was when a small member of their number threw down his baseball cap and strode towards Mac Gregor stating that, 'he would deal with the old cunt'. He fell to his knees screaming when, with the movement of an uppercut, Mac Gregor drove his index and middle fingers into his left eyeball. The Detectives could feel the warmth, admiration and gratitude of the bars other patrons, when the remaining chavs made it clear they had no wish to continue the conflict.

MacGregors adjusted the cuffs of his suit and the shirt then suggested that he and his colleague go somewhere else as there was 'shite' all over the floor of that bar. With a smile, Willox clapped a hand onto his senior officer's shoulder and guided him to the door. The fat boors, those that were conscious, followed the detectives with their eyes as they wondered how they could alter the accounts of what had just happened, in order to make it less humiliating for them.

The two Police Officers agreed that a meal in an Indian Restaurant was a good idea and they walked the short distance to a place that they both used frequently. The owner greeted both of them by name and showed them to a table away from the door. When the waiter arrived with the menus, they waived him away and told him that they were ready to order, returning with a pad he wrote down their choices and left them to their conversation.

When the two beers arrived at their table, they were already deep in conversation about the possible machinations of Tommo Gayle. Mac Gregor consistently stated that his position was apolitical and that he had no desire to pursue a political career and that had been the reason he chose the Police Force when he had left The Army. Sergeant Gayle counselled his colleague and mentor that 'like it or not, the whole world was now political'. Tearing a lump from the nan bread, Mac Gregor dropped it onto the side plate and wiped his greasy hands on the red napkin in his lap.

"Just why the fuck would a scrote like Tommo want tae set me up?"

"Forester does not like you. He does not like you because you are a better Copper than him. You are one of those doers that make him uncomfortable. If your style can be criticised and discredited he will be vindicated."

"Whit has that goat tae dae wi Tommo?"

"Tommo is a twisted little bastard that will follow any arsehole that promises to shine light."

"And he thinks that Forester's gonna shine a light oan him?"

"Shit on him more like, but he doesn't see it like that, yet."

"How much dae ye think I a cannae trust him?"

"He has no bravery; he will simply stab you in the back. The old fashioned term for him is a toady."

"Aye ah see whit you mean."

"He would have run away from that altercation we had earlier."

"Aye no doubt."

They tucked into their curries and talked of times past. Though neither man admitted to it, they did miss each other. Mac Gregor trusted Willox as he had always found him to be loyal, courageous and conscientious. Willox liked Mac Gregor because he was straight, he said it as it was and genuinely cared for everyone he met. Mac Gregor would kick your teeth in, nick you and throw you in gaol; but within the hour, he would have also made sure your family had enough to eat. They both shared the view that the likes of Forester and Tommo were fundamentally egregious examples of humanity. They would consistently place their own ambitions before the needs of those they served.

Chapter 30

Within forty-eight hours of returning to the UK Matt attended a Genitourinary Medicine Clinic. After sitting in a sterile waiting room with his fellow infected for nearly thirty minutes, he was taken to a treatment room where a nurse examined his penis. She wore latex gloves but managed to avoid actually touching him preferring instead to ask Matt to manipulate his manhood to afford her the clinically required vantage. She took a swab from his penis and a file of blood from his arm. When he had pulled up his pants and trousers, he was dismissed with the assurance that they would telephone him with the results of the tests.

Five days later, he received a call on his mobile telephone. The detached clinical voice informed him that he had Gonorrhoea and Chlamydia. Matt had dared to hope that his self-diagnosis was wrong, a foolish approach as it served only to multiply his devastation on hearing the truth. Frantically, he accepted the first available appointment they had to offer for treatment.

The treatment was simple, one dose of a strong antibiotic and he would be clear of Gonorrhoea within five days, ten to be on the safe side. To resolve the Chlamydia infection he had to take a five-day course of lesser antibiotics. The nurse gave him the standard lecture about the importance of contacting all his previous sexual partners and the need for the responsible use of condoms.

After sitting patiently through the nurse's oratory, Matt asked if he could take the means with which to treat his wife with him. She was unwilling at first but when Matt had explained: that it had been his wife that infected him and that she was too shy to seek treatment, the nurse sought the opinion of the resident medical practitioner. On advice, she relented and handed Matt a bottle containing one pill and a bottle containing five pills, to treat his wife's likely ailments and an extensive list of possible complications and symptoms that should initiate the immediate seeking of professional medical treatment.

He felt rather smug as he hurried back to the second-hand Audi A4 that he had bought to replace his company car. For the first time in over a week, he felt that he had a realistic opportunity to avoid the terrifying prospect of Lily discovering that he had infected her with a sexually transmitted infection. To achieve his ambition he required three outputs: avoidance of sexual intercourse for a further ten days, administer the medication to Lily without her noticing and that she did not notice any of the symptoms in herself. The first two he was confident of achieving however, he doubted that he would risk administering the Chlamydia treatment. Too many pills, too many chances of being discovered; besides he would treat himself and take the chance that she had not caught it, as an infection it had no symptoms and nobody really cared if the Invisible Man comes to dinner. The third was beyond his direct influence and all he could do was hope.

Lily was just putting Lucy down for her afternoon nap when Matt returned from his appointment at the clinic. 'No time like the present' he thought to himself and offered to make her a cup of tea. Gratefully she accepted the offer and sat heavily onto the sofa. Adding slightly more sugar than usual to mask the taste of the antibiotic tablet, he took the mug from the kitchen and gently handed it to Lucy. He sat in his armchair pretending to read a newspaper. Surreptitiously he watched as she tested the rim of the mug for temperature with her bottom lip before starting to sip the tea. As the tea cooled, lily began to take deeper drafts from her mug. Matt felt comfortable that he had cheated consequence once again and began to read the newspaper for real. Predictably enough, the press was full of articles about the war in Iraq. Simple scare stories, presented for the digestion of the moronic masses in order to assure their democratic support for invasion and subsequent regime change. A regime change that, regardless of expense, legality or collateral damage, would be affected. Unfortunately, for the Iraqis, they were a sovereign nation that did not recognise the rules that the USA would impose on all in the guise of freedom; for that reason, their country was attacked.

Shattering the grey silence of the autumnal afternoon, the telephone rang. Clarion electronic tones, incongruous and

216

unwelcome in the peace that had descended on the room. Lily shifted her weight on the sofa and gently raised the handset from the cradle.

"Hello?"

………

"Speaking."

………

"Yes, yes I am."

………

"Oh right what do they say?"

………

"I see."

………

"Yes I can make that."

………

"Ok I'll be there."

Lily pressed the red button to sever the connection and toyed with the handset for a short time before turning to Matt.

"Bastard!"

He started in his chair and let the newspaper fall into his lap.

"What? Why do you…"

"You fucking bastard, did you think that I wouldn't have noticed?"

"What are you talking about? I have no idea what you are talking about."

"Yes you bloody well do."

"No I bloody well do not."

"You have given me the clap you dirty bastard."

Shaking violently and sweating profusely, he mouthed words that would not come until he regained some control of the situation by standing up to mitigate the vulnerability, he felt.

"What makes you say that?"

"That was the doctor's surgery on the 'phone. I have Gonorrhoca and Chlamydia and there is only one place I could have got them."

"But darling I don't know…"

"Look, just stop fucking lying, will you. I felt uncomfortable and painful when we got back from holiday so I went to the doctors. I thought it might be the clap but I hoped it wasn't, serves me right for trusting you, you utter bastard.

217

You've been shagging about again and now you've managed to give me the clap, which you have clearly caught from one of your whores."

She burst into tears and fled from the room, leaving Matt standing like a mute witness to some civil atrocity.

Dark wings of fear beat about his mind. Desperately Matt sought the lucidity required to formulate an effective response to the situation. He began to pace the room, unsure of the optimum action required to avoid the gaping chasm of despair and dark consequence that threatened to swallow him. He would not capitulate to the forces that conspired to ruin him, he was confident that despite their malevolent exuberance he could find, in his mind, a scenario that would vindicate him and return them to the peace and security that had previously reigned.

As he paced, muttering to himself, he became aware of a presence in the doorway. Lily stood with Lucy in her arms, watching her pacing husband. Her demeanour was that of utter dispassion, gazing with eyes of blue ice as she held a bewildered child close. Stopping he looked at her with an expression of complete wretchedness.

"Darling I…"

"Get out."

"But Darling I just…"

"Get out."

"Please Baby, don't make me leave."

"I want you to go please."

"Don't make me leave my home, we can work this out."

"I said that I want you to leave. Please will you just go?"

"Come on Darling we can…"

"If you don't go, then I will."

"But where will I go?"

"You can go to hell for all I care. I just want you out of my sight."

There was silence in the room, save for the gentle whimpering of their daughter.

The hopelessness of Matt's situation took him almost a minute to comprehend. Whichever way he played his options in his head he drew the conclusion that he must leave. Raising his hands in defeat, Matt walked towards Lily. She stood to one side, allowing him to pass into the hallway. As he walked towards the bedroom, he heard the weak thin voice behind him call out "Daddy".

Packing some clothes into a leather holdall as quickly as he could, Matt sensed his brain chemistry altering to facilitate the emergence of his Mr Hyde. Bag in hand, he returned to the front room where Lily was consoling Lucy, she was sitting on her mother's lap complaining that she did not want her Daddy to leave.

"Proud of yourself, are you?"

"Just get out Matt."

"Happy just to break this family up and to destroy our home?"

"Me break this family up!? I think you managed to do that all by yourself.

Don't make this harder than it needs to be, just get out Matt."

"So you are just going to throw everything away, just like that?"

"Get out. You sicken me. You…"

Lily stopped herself before the words she wanted to say broke the dam that was holding back her rage. Matt stared at her then softening his expression he looked at his daughter.

"Don't worry Lucy Darling; Daddy will be back very soon."

"Daddy, don't go," whimpered the child.

"Daddy has to Lucy. Mummy is making him go away."

Lily pulled her wailing child close to her chest.

"That's enough, get out now!"

Mechanical arms worked furiously to beat the torrential rain from the screen. Oncoming lights glared at him through prisms of water as each passing vehicle hissed by with Doppler affected pitch. He needed shelter from the storm, time to compose his thoughts, somewhere to rest his head, somewhere to take stock.

Green strobing light from the dash gave his face a sickly dark appearance as he flicked the indicator and turned the wheel. The Audi decelerated as it turned into the car park of the roadside hotel. Choosing a space near to the entrance Matt parked the car and switched off the engine. The rain crashed on the shell of the vehicle as he sat peering through the windshield, rain cascading over the glass, at the cold light of the reception area. With no obvious initiating stimulus, he grabbed the bag from the passenger seat and made a run for it.

In the cream light of the foyer, he surveyed the corporate décor, claret carpet, worn to a darker shade, by the reception desk and at the entranceway, a rigid settee that looked as though no one had ever sat on it, pressed hard against the wall opposite, beneath a non-descript print hanging from the beige wall. The air smelled of furniture polish and a distant memory of smouldering dust. Reception was unattended. Distant voices murmured in some office, hidden from view by a paper-thin partition wall.

The 'ting' from the brass bell on the reception desk cut the silence to conclude the murmured conversation and summons a young woman in a burgundy suit. When she emerged from the functional space behind reception, she had a face like thunder. With perceivable effort, she smiled and approached the traveller waiting at the desk.

"Good evening Sir, how may I help you?"

"Do you have a room?"

"Just for this evening, Sir?"

"Yes I think so."

"I'll just check for you."

She tapped the keyboard hidden beneath the counter and consulted the monitor that protruded above. The badge on her jacket informed Matt that her name was Michelle.

He took the first room she offered him and with obvious disinterest, he answered her questions and handed over his credit card. Suffering the arrival protocol, Matt cased the layout of the establishment by reading the faux brass plaques that pointed towards the available facilities until she handed him the key card and he was free to go to his allocated room.

He threw the leather bag onto the bed where it bounced to the edge, toppled and fell to the floor. Matt sat heavily on the bed and plunged his head into his hands. The enormity of his situation had not fully sunk in and he was painfully aware of the fact that he would have to face it with cold realism, a realism that would not protect him from the genuine bleakness of his world and the terrifying potential consequences. Traditionally people in his position would seek solace in a friend's guest bedroom, offering company and shelter. Since the accident however, Matt had systematically alienated all of his friends with inappropriate misanthropic attitudes and argumentative drunkenness. Lily had been the last of his friends and now he had done an emphatic job of losing her.

As he reflected on his situation, Matt drew a preliminary conclusion that without his home and his family he had very little. The house that he called home was rented, Lily's Porsche was leased, he had no job, savings or investments; what he did have was debts and plenty of them. The money his previous employer had paid him to leave was rapidly evaporating, spent on their recent holiday in The Caribbean and his Audi. In addition, it serviced his debts and paid their living expenses. Not only did he have the immediate emotional trauma of a potential marriage breaking down, he also faced homelessness and bankruptcy.

Vulnerability was not a condition that Matt was familiar with, natural arrogance, a good salary and a supportive wife had always protected him from such insecurities. If he were to avoid the ominous prospect, suggested by his initial appraisal of the situation, he would require the support of at least two of the triumvirate of crutches that had sustained him thus far. The job was gone and could not be recovered overnight, his natural arrogance would sustain him for some time however, it would eventually diminish. Lily was not yet lost and if he were to work quickly and cleverly, he might just secure her continued support.

With a lingering groan guttering in his throat, he raised his head and focussed on the TV screen where a welcome message displayed. The message invited him to browse information on the facilities of the hotel and information on local amenities and sites, available through the interactive television services. Rising from the bed, Matt lifted the remote control from the top of the TV and pressed the stand-bye button to turn the screen to black, then recovered his bag from the floor and fished through its contents for a clean shirt.

Before he donned the shirt, he sprayed deodorant liberally over his body and into his armpits.

Whilst he adjusted the collar and cuffs of his shirt in the mirror, he reasoned that, whilst he had much to think about, there could be some attractive women travelling on business present in the bar and there was no reason that he should not seek solace for that night in the arms of a fellow stranger. His sexual health would necessitate the use of a condom and he hoped the toilets would have a vending machine.

Slipping the key card into the top pocket of his jacket, Matt patted himself down to confirm that the inner pockets contained his wallet and his mobile telephone. Then with a final inspection in the mirror, he left the room for the hotel bar where he would formulate his recovery strategy or find some company.

Chapter 31

The fatiguing banality of her daily routine was ending as she placed the plate of food onto the dining table in front of Brian. Without a word, he picked up the cutlery before him and proceeded to eat. Returning to the table with a second plate Becky joined him. They ate in silence, occasionally exchanging meaningless glances. She watched his ample jowls working on the food he shovelled into his mouth and felt the ever-present resentment that she carried rise from the pit of her stomach to quell her modest appetite.

He pushed the empty plate away from him before half-heartedly complementing her on the meal. As she picked at the food on her plate, he stared, un-sated hunger in his beady eyes. Inwardly sighing with resignation, she stood and replaced his empty plate with her half-eaten supper. Brian glanced up at her briefly with the closest she had seen to affection from him in a long time.

When she returned from the kitchen, Brian had emptied her plate and was sitting in his armchair. Clearing the table, Becky felt a thrill in her crotch as she recalled the fun she had had with the neighbour before Brian's chair. What a contrast she thought to herself, a proud eager young cock standing before her and a big fat slob loafing before her. There could be no reasonable condemnation of her extramarital activities.

Bringing Brian a mug of sweet tea, she joined him in front of the television. He struggled in his armchair to sit up and sip from the patterned mug and then turning his attention to his wife, he spoke.

"How was Thomas today?"

"He was fine. You only just missed him. I got him off to sleep just before you got home."

"That's a shame, I had work late again."

"I just don't know why you do that. It's not as if they pay you overtime."

"These days it's just good to have a job."

"Things still not good?"

"I heard they are going to lay some guys off up in Manchester."

"Let's hope they don't start that nonsense down here then."

"Yeah well you see why I gotta keep em sweet."

She sat in anticipation of further dialogue but soon realised that his attention was now, fully occupied by the television.

Settling back into her own seat she sipped her tea and began to flick through a magazine. Glossy images of celebrities leading lives of glamour and unimaginable luxury occupied her mind as she waited for him to go. As time slowly slipped by, she became increasing impatient for his departure. Becky's persistently jogging leg caught Brian's attention.

"What's the matter with you?"

"Nothing."

"Yes there is. What's the matter?"

Becky pretended to be engrossed in her magazine.

"Come on Jack quit the stone-walling, what's up?"

"Look I don't know what you mean. There is nothing up."

"Then why is your leg going like that?"

"Like what?"

"Ten to the dozen like that."

Brian pointed to her leg, agitatedly bouncing up and down. Acknowledging his observation with a look of irritation, she returned her outward attention to the magazine.

"Come on what is it?"

"Nothing. I thought you were going out."

"I will be shortly. Is that why you are bouncing your leg like that?"

With gasp of exasperation, she slapped the magazine down into her lap and stared directly at him.

"No, I don't mind you going out. Now will you leave me in peace to read?"

"Woaah take it easy tiger I was only asking."

"Well don't and get out from under my feet."

Obeying his wife's command, he pulled his trainers on and stood. Then with a smile of sarcastic submission, he went to the hallway and donned his grubby baseball jacket. Brian bellowed 'farewell' as he pulled the front door open and slammed it behind him as he set off down the garden path.

"At last" she said out loud when she heard the garden gate clang shut. The rest of the night was hers, free from any distraction. Throughout the day, she had longed for that period of the night when she would be left to her own devises, no child to demand her attention and no husband to annoy her. Reaching down by the side of the sofa, she drew up her laptop, switched it on, and began to log in.

The inbox of her e-mail account contained several alerts informing her that she had received personal messages on the numerous dating websites where she was a member. There were also two e-mails from long standing on-line admirers. Opening these first, she scanned the images attached. They were the usual photographs of penises in varying states of arousal and a video segment showing a man masturbating. She replied to each of these messages with words of compliment and encouragement to keep the visual material coming.

Pulling down the history bar on the screen she selected the 'Sophistidates' option and fidgeted with suppressed excitement as the 'log in' screen loaded. Entering her user name and password, she waited until the page had fully loaded before she selected the 'inbox' option. With a broad smile, she noted the user name she was hoping to find, listed amongst those that had sent her a message. Loxtox was the user name of Sean, the on line prospective sexual partner that she currently desired the most.

Sean's message explained how much he was 'turned on' by her accounts of previous sexual encounters. Becky found it exciting that he found the details of her sexual conquests arousing. In her previous message she had detailed a few of her 'one night stands' and how much she wanted to feel his impressive cock inside her. The content of his message was encouraging and full of graphic detail about the sex he had planned for them.

Giggling excitedly Becky skipped to the kitchen where she filled a large glass with white wine. She sipped the wine as she returned to the sofa and then placed the glass to one side before pulling her pc onto her lap. After re-reading Sean's message, Becky sat considering which of her sexual experiences she would detail for him next and how she could encourage him to organise a meeting between the two of them. Smiling and occasionally chuckling to herself, she replayed some of her favourite encounters in her head. Then with a huge smile, she settled on one particular memory that she would communicate to him in her reply.

Debbie was a good friend of hers who she would frequently visit when she could find someone to look after Thomas overnight. In Debbie's local pub, she had met Tyron, a married man who she had sex with every time they met. On one particular occasion, she and Debbie had returned to Debbie's flat with Tyron and his friend Zac. On that night, she had made her attraction to Zac clear and Tyron had settled for Debbie.

Becky had cajoled Zac into the kitchen whilst Debbie and Tyron kissed and groped each other on the sofa in the front room. It had not taken her long to get Zac's cock out of his trousers and to have him frantically pulling her jeans and knickers down to her ankles. Crouching before her, he lapped clumsily at her pussy as she sat wide legged, on the worktop. He was not good at cunnilingus but she had enjoyed the attention and the hedonistic nature of the evening.

With marked urgency he had stood up and pulled her from the worktop, she kissed him passionately as she enjoyed the taste of herself on his face. Turning her about he pushed his hard cock into her from behind and pumped her hard for nearly ten minutes before his grip on her hips tightened and his muffled gasps announced the twitching of his cock, which was by then buried as deep as it would go in her. His climax complete Zac pulled out of her and steadied himself against the worktop. Becky had just pulled her knickers and jeans back into place before Debbie appeared in the kitchen to inform them that she was going to bed.

When Debbie had left the kitchen, an embarrassed Zac re-dressed and explained that he too had to leave. Hurriedly he kissed her on the mouth and scurried out of the room. Left alone, she could hear Zac and Tyron talking in the sitting room before the front door thumped shut heralding his departure.

Becky returned to the front room where she found Tyron sitting on the sofa. Joining him, they began to kiss. They kissed passionately as they rolled from the sofa onto the carpet. Debbie had clearly decided not to satisfy him before retiring to bed as his manhood pressed hard against the front of his trousers. Luckily, for Tyron, she decided to suck him off before he too departed to return to his wife. It had been a glorious feeling she experienced as she sat alone on the sofa: Zac's cum running out of her pussy soaking the gusset of her knickers and the salty taste of Tyron's spunk in her mouth. The entire apartment had reeked of sex as indeed had Becky.

As she reviewed what she had written, Becky felt very aroused. Placing the laptop to one side, she undid her trousers and pushed her hand down the front to play with herself. Pleasure spread throughout her from her firm clitoris until she felt the minor rapture of a clitoral orgasm. Still in a state of high sexual arousal, she returned to the keyboard and treated Sean to a detailed account of how she had seduced the boy next door, taking his virginity. She concluded the message with a warning that he would receive no more accounts from her until they had met, then with a satisfied smile she sent the message.

Standing up she pulled her trousers and knickers down before sprawling over the large footstool. Masturbating intensely with both hands, she brought herself to a deep orgasm before re-dressing and returning to the messages in her inbox.

It did not take her long to process the remaining messages. She rejected only one and sent encouraging messages to the others. Becky needed to maintain a pipeline of suitable candidates for her sexual encounters. When her messaging was complete, she logged off and placed the laptop at the side of the sofa. She then settled down to watch television and await the return of her husband.

227

It had been a wonderful evening. The meal was excellent and the company, as charming as she had ever experienced. She had been nervous earlier that evening, nagging doubts heightening her anxiety. Primary of all her misgivings was the fear that her date would not keep their appointment. Disappointment can be seductive and she had nearly fallen for its charms when her mobile telephone 'beeped' to inform her that it had received a text message, just as she waved off her taxi. Groaning in resignation, she examined the screen, anticipating a grovelling apology and some feeble excuse why he could not keep their engagement. As expected, the message was from her date but to her excited relief it was not cancelling their arrangements, just changing the point of rendezvous from the original restaurant to another a short distance from where she had alighted the taxi.

They had come to the exciting point of the night, the purpose of the entire relationship. As they had planned in vivid detail on the internet, she stood in the doorway, feet wide apart, then pulled her knickers from beneath her pink mini-skirt down as far as she could stretch them about her parted thighs. Hitching her skirt up to her waist, she bent over and rested her hands on her knees. Quickly she pushed one hand between her legs to test the dampness of her vagina, satisfied with her findings she returned the hand to her knee. With excitement squirming inside her, Sarah tossed her head upwards, causing her hair to float through the air and come to rest on her back, then she waited for Sean.

Bright searing white incandescence, exploded from the centre of her visual range, expanding to leave only a dark murky corona at the periphery as she heard a crackling thud. Pressure built rapidly behind her sinuses as she gasped and her head began to spin. Core muscles clenched involuntarily and her senses faded, only her sense of smell remained and increased to an unfamiliar acuteness. She could smell the stale urine in the doorway and the rotting restaurant detritus.

The second blow struck, she smelt her own bowel contents then she felt the cold ground as she fell heavily. Pain spread like wildfire through her head and the incandescence faded to darkness. The taste of metal filled her mouth, the warm pool that grew about her prone body tried feebly to replace the heat that rapidly abandoned her. Nothingness came in clearly defined stages, devoid of sentimentality.

Outside Mac Gregor's bungalow, the blue Saab pulled to a gradual halt. Detective Sergeant Tommo Gayle pulled the handbrake on and sat looking out at the gradually lightening grey sky as the dawn glow on the Eastern horizon steadily grew. It irked him that Mac Gregor insisted that he pick him up from his home, he had better things to do than act as an Inspector's driver. 'Dinosaurs' like Mac Gregor irritated him. They clogged up the promotional paths and vexed the brighter and younger officer's ambitions.

Slightly startled by the opening of the passenger-side door, Tommo flinched and shifted in his seat to look at the embarking passenger. Mac Gregor sat heavily in the passenger seat and fidgeted for a seeming age before he settled and closed the door.

"Morning Tommo."

"Morning Guv, how are you?"

"No bad Tommo lad, no bad."

"Well sounds as if our man has struck again."

"Aye, sounds like it. Let's get going then and have a wee look."

After inspecting the scene of crime, there could be little or no doubt that the crime had been the work of the man that they were hunting. The victim was a forty year old married woman with two children. They removed a laptop from her home after interviewing her husband. Both detectives were convinced that the pc would reveal that the victim was a customer of Sophistidates.

When they returned to the Incident Room, the excitement in the air was tangible. The suspect had agreed on-line to meet with one of the sock-puppet characters that they had invented on Sophistidates. Mac Gregor and his Sergeant sat together in his office as the young DC briefed them on the details. The suspect, Sean, had responded to one of the more sexually graphic messages, suggesting that he meet with the invented character. He asked that they meet in a restaurant, The Rosa, at twenty hundred hours on Saturday. His reply had also detailed, an overview of how he foresaw the date progressing from a meal with wine to sexual intercourse in a secluded part of the local environment. Attached to the message were several explicit images, none of which afforded a view of his face.

The DC completed her briefing and Mac Gregor relaxed into his chair and looked at Tommo.

"Well he's no shy is he?"

"True Guv he's a card and that's for sure."

"Today's Monday so let's agree tae the meet and see whit mare details we can draw frame him."

"Agreed Guv, seems like the best move."

Mac Gregor held Sergeant Gayle's gaze just long enough to make his subordinate feel uncomfortable.

With a sudden burst of movement, Mac Gregor turned to the young DC still sitting across the desk from him.

"Right, git back oan the computer and agree tae the meet."

"Yes Sir."

She appeared to glow as she enthusiastically confirmed her intended compliance.

"And whilst yer at it tell him yer up fir his kinky ideas and want tae ken mare aboot them, gee him a phane number and draw a service phane, mind tae keep it manned."

"Yes Sir."

"Dae yer best tae persuade him tae gee you his mobile number, maybe we can get a fix oan him that way."

"Yes Sir."

"Let him think he's in control, let him set the stage an' you jist play alang."

"Yes Sir."

He turned deliberately to look at Gayle.

"Agreed?"

Tommo Gayle looked suspicious as he considered his reply.

"Agreed Guv."

Mac Gregor's manner became almost jocular as he jumped to his feet, clapping his hands together and peering at the DC.

"Right, let's git tae it."

"Yes Sir."

Once the DC had left the office, the two senior detectives faced each other in an awkward silence for a seeming age before Mac Gregor broke the silence.

"Ah hear you've been puttin' the oors in Tommo."

"Yes Guv, I am taking this one seriously."

"Dae ye think am no?"

"I didn't say that Guv."

"Maybe no, but mind if yeav goat anything' tae say, say it."

"What's that supposed to mean."

Mac Gregor placed his hands onto the desk and leaned over towards Gayle.

"Ah ken yer type Son, Av dealt wi' yer kind since afore you were oan thae beat. Dinnae think am daft, am no."

"I have no idea what you are on about Guv."

"Aye yea dae."

"No Guv, I do not. If you have something to say to me say it."

"Ah jist have. Noo tak it oan board and jist dae yer job, that bein' ma Sergeant oan this case, nothin' else."

"If you want to make a complaint about me, I suggest that you make it formal."

"Dinnae talk wet Son. Ah wisnae born yesterday."

"I am sorry Guv, I do not know what your problem is."

A wry smile grew across Mac Gregor's face as he stood up to his full height.

"Aye play it yer way, jist remember am oan tae you."

"Well I still have no idea what your problem is but I can promise you that I will do my job."

"See that ye dae, now get doon tae the lab and see how they're getting on wi the victim's laptop."

Smirking with implied insubordination, Sergeant Gayle stood up abruptly and without a word, strode from the office. Mac Gregor moved back to his chair and sat down. He knew that he could have handled the matter better however; he had never enjoyed playing games and felt much better having confronted his temporary Sergeant. They would never work together as well as he and Bruce Willox did but he was confident enough that, he could keep Tommo in check long enough to close the case.

It was over an hour before Tommo returned to Mac Gregor's office, clutching a beige folder under his left arm. Knocking briefly on the door, Tommo burst into the office.

"As suspected Guv our victim was a member of Sophistidates."

"Aye well we'd guessed as much."

Sergeant Gayle continued as though nothing untoward had passed between them.

"Ah but this time they have made all the arrangement over the internet, so we have a much better picture of what's going on."

"Oh Aye do tell, whit have we goat?"

Pulling a chair up to the desk Tommo slapped the file down, opened it and sat.

"They arranged to meet at nineteen hundred in 'The World's End on Robson Street."

"Aye ah ken it. That's wan o them Gastropubs."

"That's the one and he detailed exactly what he wanted her to do for him after dinner."

"Go on."

"Well, after dinner they were to leave the pub together and when they got to an undisclosed location she was to walk ahead of him into a doorway and prepare herself. She was to pull her knickers down and bend over for him to then join her and to penetrate her from behind."

"And she agreed tae that?"

"Obviously she did Guv."

"Aye ah guess."

"Unfortunately we have not found a 'phone on the body or we could find out if she caught a taxi and if so which firm she used."

"It's a fair guess that she did so git wan o' the DCs tae phone roond local cab firms and see if any o' thame had a pick up at her hame address last night."

"That sounds like a plan."

"Good. Right come oan, me and ye are going tae hae a chat wi the staff."

Grabbing his jacket from the back of the chair, Mac Gregor made for the door, quickly followed by Sergeant Gayle. They stopped briefly to detail one of the younger detectives to telephone all of the local taxi companies before they made for the car park.

After several circumnavigations of the block, Tommo found a space to park the Saab. As they climbed from the vehicle, it began to rain. It being late spring, none of the passing pedestrians were prepared for precipitation, they ran with improvised umbrellas made of plastic bags, newspapers or briefcases from shelter to shelter. The Detectives walked slowly through the rain and scurrying passers-by to the pub.

The Victorian exterior gave no hint of the modern interior. Spaced about the high ceiling were slowly rotating fans, moving against the sterile whiteness that contrasted vigorously with the wood flooring. There was limited standing room, much of the floor space occupied by large dark-wood tables, surrounded with matching chairs. Local office workers occupied some of the tables having escaped early from their desks or loitered on extended lunch breaks.

They waited patiently whilst a young woman struggled with the complexities of one of the tills behind the bar. Eventually she gave them her attention.

"Good afternoon can I help you?"

"Aye. A am Detective Inspector Mac Gregor and this is DS Gayle, we would like tae speak wi anyone whae wis working here last night."

"Well I was here. I am Nicki the Duty Manager and I was on duty all last night."

"Is there anywhere we could have a wee chat?"

Nicki called one of the prowling Waitresses over and told her watch the bar, and then led the Detectives to a table in the empty quarter of the restaurant. Mac Gregor showed her a photograph of the victim and asked if she had seen the woman on the previous night. With an annoying chattering voice, she over-used the expression "oh my God" and the words 'literally' and 'like' to explain that she had not seen the victim before and that the place had been relatively quiet that evening. On Mac Gregor's insistence she took the photograph over to the other Waitresses then returned shaking her head. Nicki then checked the previous night's table reservations and confirmed that none had been booked for seven thirty. She was also confident that none of the previous night's customers matched the woman in the photograph.

When they left the building, it had stopped raining. Mac Gregor pulled a cigarette from his jacket pocket, pushed it into his mouth and hunched to click a lighter into life. Tommo waited for Mac Gregor to light his cigarette before he spoke.

"Well that was a waste of time."

"Aye, but we ken she met him so whit happened?"

"Maybe they met outside and decided to go somewhere else?"

"Aye. Plenty o' choice roond here."

"Shall I get a couple of DCs to pound the rounds?"

"Aye, that's the best we can dae just noo."

They walked together towards the car. When he had finished his smoke, Mac Gregor flicked the butt into the gutter then waited for Gayle to unlock the car doors.

On their return to the Station, there was some good news. A taxi firm had one of its Drivers pick a woman up from the victims address and drive her too 'The World's End'. The Detective Constable who made the call had visited the cab office and spoken with the Driver. He confirmed that he had picked the victim up at nineteen hundred hours at her address and taken her to the pub on Robson Street. He had not seen her enter the pub or speak with anyone else.

Nodding eagerly, Mac Gregor absorbed the information about the Taxi Driver proffered by the DC. After commending him for good work, Mac Gregor left the DC and walked briskly across the Incident Room to his office. After a brief visit to the 'Gents' Sergeant Gayle joined him in the office.

"Well Guv what do you make of that then?"

"We ken she made the rendezvous, on time, so oor man's still in the frame."

"Do you think they were actually in 'The World's End'?"

234

"We'll hae someone trawl the CCTV but I doubt it, yon Bubbleheid o' a Manager seemed adamant that she had not seen her and that kind dinnae forget faces."

"So what happened to her after she got out the taxi?"

"Dinnae ken Tommo, maybe she met Sean on the pavement."

"I didn't notice any CCTV on the street, which is a shame."

"Aye, av checked there isnae any."

"Hopefully the two we've put on checking restaurants will turn something up."

"Aye ah hope so. The best shot we hae at thae moment is the internet and as it stands that gees him time tae kill again."

Mac Gregor began to pull sheets of paper from the top drawer of his desk and fished about in his jacket for a pen. Sergeant Gayle sat quietly for a minute before standing.

"I am going to check on our guys doing the rounds of the hostelries this evening."

"Good fir you Tommo, am gonna dae ma expenses."

He began to empty receipts out of his wallet and arranging them in chronological order. Before Tommo left the office, Mac Gregor spoke without taking his attention away from his paperwork.

"Dinnae forget whit ah telt ye."

"What's that Guv?"

"Am oan tae ye."

Smiling broadly, Tommo slowly turned on his heels and walked casually from the office, taking care to close the door behind him as gently as he could. Then with a quickening pace he made his way through the office and out to the stairwell in the main corridor.

Chapter 33

Cool Egyptian cotton caressed her smooth light brown body. She felt its fresh weave stroking her firm buttocks as she turned over and pressed her face into the soft down pillow. It was very unusual for her to sleep naked. Occasionally she had fallen asleep after Abdul had undressed her and made love with her, but rarely had she elected to go to bed without some form of nightdress. This night it was hot, surprisingly hot as it was barely summer, she also felt her internal temperature rise whenever her mind turned to consider her rage.

Unable to settle, she wriggled beneath the light summer duvet and rolled onto her back where she lay motionless with her raven hair across her face. Drawing a delicate hand through the silken strands, Samira uncovered her face and opened her eyes to stare at the dark ceiling above. She had lain in bed for nearly three hours, sleep evading her throughout. Her mind could not find the peace required for sleep, and she was not sufficiently exhausted that her consciousness would surrender involuntarily to the arms of Morpheus.

Familiar shadows silhouetted against the lighter shades of the bedroom walls, loitered with inexplicable expectation as though they had some unfathomable plan to execute whilst she slept. The silence of the house, broken with the nocturnal cracks and thumps that any house will make, covered all save the occasional sounds of Abdul moving about his study or the rattle of the keyboard as he composed messages, reports or proposals. She listened for the distant breathing of her children but those gentle noises could not penetrate the soft blanket of silence.

She had no expectation of being disturbed. Abdul had taken to sleeping in one of the spare bedrooms. Initially she had been grateful of the arrangement, as she had no desire to be intimate with her husband. After several nights alone in their marital bed, it became apparent that he was punishing her for not agreeing with him. Samira was not sure which annoyed her the most: the fact that he felt that she should be punished or that he believed that his absence from her bed was a punishment. It increased the base level of the rage she felt when she considered the required extent of his arrogance to facilitate his outrageous perspective. Abdul had decided that their daughter be sacrificed to a rapist, her biological father, as penance for his own sins. The egregiousness of his position was entirely lost on him as he sought to justify it with ever more bizarre and esoteric logic. Increasingly she felt it to be the logic of a mad man.

Nausea ached in her empty stomach. She had been unable to eat for days. The overwhelming revulsion she felt at the prospect of Al qasim laying his soiled hands on her beautiful daughter, precluded any natural function. The anger she felt towards her deluded husband fuelled her hatred and rage. Now she was a creature with a sole purpose, to protect her child.

Driving her heels down onto the mattress, she bounced her bottom upwards and flipped onto her side where she drew up into the foetal position and remembered. The room dark, full of the scent of jasmine, warm air from the plains slowly being chased from the building by the colder air falling from the mountains in a thick blanket over the land, as the night intensified. A sudden crack and creek heralding his arrival, petrified she stared from beneath the covers as he entered. Standing silently with a broad smile on his face, he pulled his robe up and over his head then allowed it to fall casually onto the floor. He stood naked before her. That was the first time she had ever seen a mature male naked.

Al qasim was aroused, his member urgent and erect. It appeared darker than the rest of him, the tip reaching almost to his navel and the full scrotum hanging like a tennis ball from the base of the shaft. Menace purveyed from his every movement as he approached her bedside. In a rude manner, he pulled the bedclothes from her and cast them on the floor. Then he was on her, kissing her face roughly and pawing at her body through the soft cloth of her nightdress. Gasping and struggling she tried to fight him off as he forced his hand between her legs, his long fingernails scratching at the entrance to her vagina. Prising her thighs apart with his knee, he manoeuvred himself between her legs, drew away from her face as he held her wrists, and smiled down at her. "Don't fight. It is God's will that you should know a real man." he

237

spoke gently as he consolidated his entry position. Pain entered her groin as his penis pressed hard against her dry vulva. Frustrated by the lack of penetration he pulled back and spat twice intro his hand then rubbed his saliva over his manhood and between her lips.

Labouring to breathe under his body weight pressed onto her chest, Samira felt herself torn apart from the crotch, his cock filling her gradually and relentlessly. Begging for the pain and the increasing violation to stop, she thrashed weakly as he slobbered over her face. It came as almost a relief when his progress into her came eventually to a halt and he slowly began to withdraw. Briefly, she had hoped that he would withdraw completely but he did not. The process continued, increasingly rapid and accompanied by his rasping breaths, with each stroke he seemed to grow larger inside her. She could feel his saliva drying on her face and his perspiration soaking her nightdress. He began to grunt, and then he forced his penis as deep as he could into her and with a low wail, he spent himself.

In what could have been his attempt at an apology, Al qasim kissed her and slipped from her bed. Samira lay frozen; terrified to move for fear that any action from her would draw further attention from him. Without a word, he dressed and left, he did not hesitate to look back just closed the bedroom door as quietly as he could.

She could not be certain that the events of that night were exactly as she remembered them to be but that was how they were now recorded in her memory. Samira had only known two men, her limited experience allowed her only one comparison; Al qasim was much larger than Abdul. Her husband had never filled her in the complete and agonising way that his cousin had. It had been a secret disappointment when Abdul had first bedded her and she saw for the first time his erection. It was far from the impressive member that she had been raped with, and the sensations her husband had invoked with it, far from what she had hoped them to be.

To her it was an act of pseudo violence, she perpetrated on the men that she had known, to compare their relative endowments. They could never know of her mental assault on them but to her it was a catharsis, a violation of their cardinal egos. Cerebral retribution, taken from those that would hurt her or her children. Vengeance she would visit on the man that raped her and the man that had unilaterally decided to sacrifice her daughter, to appease his nagging conscience.

If Aesha were given to Al qasim, Samira wondered if her first night with her husband would be as it was when she had lain with him. Would she receive what she had not, compassion, or would he just take what would rightfully be his? She shuddered as she considered what her daughter might feel when his ample appendage was introduced to her virgin flower. It remained utterly inconceivable to her that this, abomination of a union, be condoned and facilitated by the family.

Though she had refused to capitulate to his twisted strategy, Abdul had forced the matter by simply agreeing to the arranged marriage, proposed by his father and Uncle. Leaving their marital negotiations unfinished, he had visited his father and given their consent to the union then returned home to inform Samira of what he had done. That news had been shocking enough, and then to compound her revulsion he informed her that there was to be a family party on Thursday at his father's home, where they intended to announce the betrothal of Aesha to Al qasim.

Delivering the fait a complete, he stood casually in the front room as though he were explaining the details of some financial arrangement or the mechanical workings of an internal combustion engine. It was his cool absolute conviction that galled her the most, his utter inability to empathise with his wife's point of view. If he had cognisance of her position on the matter, his face did not betray it. When he had said all that he wanted to, he had wandered off to the kitchen to make himself a cup of tea, leaving Samira in a state of emotional shock.

Men were physically stronger than women were but they were morally and socially weaker. They could rape, use and blame the opposite sex but they could never crush the fire a woman carries within and that fire will burn to eternity, an eternal flame, burning the fuel of their weakness in the oxygen of a woman's rage. No, she would never allow this thing to happen. Regardless of the machinations of men, she will protect her children.

Taking strength from her enhanced resolve, Samira allowed her mind to drift back to the present. It was an undeniable truth that, others could do as they pleased to you without ever touching your inner thoughts. The mind was a sanctuary where the soul dwelt in complete freedom. She was free in her mind to consider anything that she could perceive. Apart from the physical world, her being could soar on wings of liberty, plunging through the restorative breakers on the surface of an ocean of hopes and dreams. To rise on thermals of reverie, then to experience the exhilaration of plunging back to the ocean, only to rise once again.

Her heart beat strongly and steadily as she became aware of her hand, pushed into her crotch. Feeling the warm wetness that spread from inside her, she moved it slowly in whichever way gave her pleasure. In her mind, she was free to enjoy the forbidden fruit, only this time she would imbue it with a far sweeter taste.

Chapter 34

Her hands trembled with excitement as they tapped the keyboard of her laptop. Sean's message outlined how much he had enjoyed the accounts of her sexual exploits, which she had detailed in her previous message to him. He embellished the declaration of his enjoyment with a detailed account of how he had masturbated after reading the message. Though gratified by his confirmation of titillation, what really excited her was his accession to a meeting.

The closing sentence of his message asked that they meet in a restaurant, 'The Bird Pie', at seven thirty on Friday evening. Becky would have to concoct an explanation for her absence from the family home on Friday night and though she was skilled in deceit, this was rather short notice. She was visiting her friend Debbie later that evening and to take another night that week to go out without him would increase Brian's suspicions. Regardless she immediately began to type a response that assured Sean she would be at 'The Bird Pie' for their meeting, then after briefly re-reading the message she had written, clicked the 'send' option.

Becky was happy that Sean had eventually arranged a meeting and was especially pleased that he now seemed to be very keen, if not impatient, to meet. The only disappointing note she had drawn from his message was that he had not returned her earlier compliment and listed his mobile telephone number as she had done. She would have welcomed the facility to flirt by text message with Sean over the intervening period before they would meet on Friday. Nevertheless, she did intend to have as much sexy fun with him as she could.

Thomas, who was playing contentedly on the front room carpet before his mother, turned his attention to the pc on her lap. As he careered towards her, Becky snapped "No Thomas. Leave Mummy's computer alone." Looking rather peeved with his mother's implied reprimand; Thomas pulled up short and holding his right hand up, displayed the toy he had been playing with to Becky. Feeling remorse for her harshness, she

241

softened her posture and using gentle tones encouraged her son to tell her about the toy he held. As Thomas told the tale of the amazing talents the small plastic figurine in his hand possessed, Becky began the process of logging out and closing down her laptop. It was late in the afternoon and she would have to start to prepare supper if it was going to be ready in time for Brian's return from work. That evening the family would dine together as Becky had demanded that her husband be home early enough to allow her to go to see her friend, Debbie.

When the shutdown procedure was complete, Becky closed the lid and slid it down to the side of the sofa. Seizing his opportunity Thomas clambered onto the sofa and struggled onto her lap. For fifteen minutes, she indulged her son with close cuddles and butterfly kisses. He giggled almost constantly as he wriggled in his mother's arms and Becky felt content. She had a wonderful loving child, a good home, a hot date for Friday night, a stupid husband and the prospect of an evening away from home with her best friend, a night ripe with the possibility of sexual impropriety.

Unusually Brian returned home on time. Becky had laid the table and plated the evening meal by the time he had removed his jacket, washed his hands and wandered towards the table, rolling up the sleeves of his shirt as he came. Once Thomas settled into his seat at the table, Becky brought the supper through from the kitchen and placed the plates with appropriate portions of food in front of her son and husband.

By the time Becky joined her family at the dinner table Brian was using his fork to spoon food into his mouth. Throughout the meal, she concentrated on Thomas as he played with each morsel before he could be encouraged to eat it. When Thomas engaged with the ingestion of his dinner, Becky could rapidly eat some of her own meal. There was no conversation beyond her stilted and frequently frustrated dialogue with her son. Brian did not speak, preferring to keep his face above his plate and relentlessly push forkfuls of food into his loose smacking mouth. When he had finished what was on his plate, Becky offered him the remains of her own supper, which he accepted.

The meal complete, Becky returned Thomas to the garishly coloured space station on the front room carpet where he resumed his earlier play. She then gathered empty plates, associated paraphernalia from the dinner table, and took them to the kitchen. Storing the condiments and loading the dishwasher with cutlery and plates, she turned her attention to the kitchen sink and the pans she had used to prepare the meal. With brush and sponge she scoured the pots until she was satisfied that all the residual food was removed, then with resigned patience, she began to dry the containers with a tea towel.

She hated the banality of domestic chores and sometimes she hated her home life. Staring out of the kitchen window she allowed herself to dream of a different life, a life free from responsibility, free from drudgery and most of all, free from Brian. The only thing she had to be grateful for was his support when she had lost control of her car and hit the man with the child in Kent. She often wondered if she ever left him, would he report her misdemeanour to The Police. His need for vengeance would probably take priority over his self-preservation instinct and regardless of his role in covering up the accident, he would tell all, despite the possible consequences.

Grudgingly Brian agreed to bath Thomas whilst Becky prepared for her night out. She felt herself coming to life as she showered and washed her hair, then escaping from the bathroom to allow her husband to fill the bath and undress their child. In the bedroom, she sat looking into the mirror of her dressing table as the hairdryer blew hot air into the brush, with which she styled her hair. It would not be long and she would free again for a whole night. Once content with the appearance of her hair she began to apply her make-up, not too heavy to rouse any interest from Brian, just a base layer she would enhance once she had made the sanctuary of Debbie's flat.

Hair styled and face painted she applied a body spray and waited for Brian to take Thomas downstairs before she selected her underwear, she had no desire for him to know that she would wear sexy lingerie that night. After she had squeezed the lower part of her body into a pair of pattered

243

jeans and carefully pulled on a light gypsy-style top with an embroidered floral design, she sprayed her favourite perfume onto her neck and wrists. She selected a short leather jacket from her wardrobe, checked the contents of her hand and overnight bags then descended to the front room.

Thomas shone in his pyjamas. He had returned to the space station and was acting out some repetitive scenario with two of the small plastic spacemen. Brian had returned to his armchair and was watching the evening news on television. The Newsreader sat grim-faced as she addressed the camera with the latest developments. The serial killer now known as 'The Hammer' had struck again, another unfortunate bludgeoned to death in one of the darker corners of the city. Becky placed her bags on the sofa and bent to pick her son up.

After he had said 'Goodnight' to his father and received a kiss, his mother carried Thomas upstairs to bed. Under his duvet, he lay peacefully listening to his mother's gentle voice as she read to him from a book. It was a story about a rabbit and its Mummy, Thomas liked the story as it made him feel worried then as the story resolved the angst, he felt warm inside and reassured. When the story ended Thomas snuggled further under his duvet as his mother held his hand and sang the song about a star.

When she completed the final verse, Thomas sighed contentedly and curled up. Becky lent over her child and softly kissed his head before smoothing the duvet with her hand. Quietly she left the room and went back downstairs. Although she had left her bags in the front room with Brian, she was not concerned. There was no contraband or incriminating items in her luggage so even if he had searched her bags there would be no need for a confrontation.

Pulling on her jacket, she stood in front of the television and informed her husband of her imminent departure. Brian focussed briefly on Becky before smiling as he looked away, "Have a nice time and don't be late tomorrow morning." Shifting her weight from one leg to the other, she turned on the spot and moved to the sofa where she gathered up her bags. With a bland assurance that she would not be late, she left the house, pausing only to pick up her car keys.

Debbie opened the door and greeted her friend with a broad smile and a loud 'Hey' before they kissed each other's cheeks and she ushered Becky into the flat. She was drinking a glass of wine whilst adding the finishing touches to her make-up in the bedroom mirror. Becky poured herself a glass of wine and joined her friend and taking the opportunity to enhance her own gilding.

They chatted, non-stop, each taking their cue from the other, as one approached the mirror to apply make-up the other talked. Becky complained about Brian and Debbie complained about the man who took her on a date, spent the night with her and never called again. When they had exhausted the subject of their immediate male partners, they asked each other questions about any recent contact with previous sexual conquests. They reminisced about historic antics that they had shared and laughed at the many absurd situations in which they had found themselves.

Satisfied with their appearance and confirming each other's attractiveness, they finished their drinks and left the flat. It was a short walk to the local pub, arm in arm with heels clicking; they perambulated the two hundred yards. They laughed together and speculated who they might meet that night.

The Oak was a grotty little bar, frequented predominately by old men and young manual labourers. Both Becky and Debbie were well known in the pub and as a result, they never felt intimidated by the clientele; on the contrary, they were warmly welcomed. They chose to drink there for several reasons: it was convenient, cheap, they drew significant attention, rarely had to buy their own drinks, some of the young manual labourers, though stupid, were attractive and Tyron drank there.

Tyron was a married man who drank too much and used cocaine at every opportunity. The excessive amounts of alcohol and narcotic caused him to sweat very heavily in bed, even with the lightest of exertion. Regardless Becky considered him to be a good 'shag' and she had used him as her 'fallback' if she did not find a more suitable candidate for her sexual cravings.

245

Clustered furniture filled the grim interior, the chipped dark veneer of the tables revealed the light, cheep, wood beneath. An old dartboard hung from the yellowed wall, plumes of horsehair billowing from the more severe wounds it had received throughout its loyal service. The dark red vinyl covering the benches split on the seats to expose foam, picked at thousands of times by the locals to create festering chasms where compounds of spilt drink, dropped snacks and sweat fermented, adding to the repugnant perfume of the establishment.

Two old men, tired of life, sat at opposite ends of the room. Lost in their own thoughts, they gloomily reflected on the futility of all that had gone before. Their lives effectively over, they contented themselves with the empty pleasure of drink and waited out the remainder of their time, alone in front of a television set or alone in The Oak.

The combination of their scents and the noise of their heels on the cracked flooring drew the immediate attention of Barny, The Landlord. With unusual eagerness, he moved to face Debbie over the bar.

"Good evening girls, what can I get you?"

"Hi Barny, Two glasses of dry white wine."

He pulled two glasses from a shelf beneath the bar and began to fill them from a screw-top wine bottle.

"How've you been keepin'?"

"Good Barny, you remember my friend Becky?"

"How could I forget the beautiful Becky?"

Barny leered at them across the bar. Debbie paid for the drinks and they retired to the smoking area outside, Becky flashed a flirty look over her shoulder at the old fat man behind the bar as they passed through the door.

It was a glorious evening. The smoking area, filled with the excited bellowing of the unintelligent, contained the majority of the customers. All male and all under the age of thirty, they chided each other and recounted the poorly considered activities of their absent fellows.

Debbie led her friend to a corner of the outside area and began to fish in her handbag for her cigarettes. The young men immediately noticed their arrival and continued their previous conversations with frequent glances towards the two women

246

in the corner. Becky recognised at least one of them as she had previously slept with him, but she could not remember his name.

Without looking over at the men, Becky and Debbie gossiped about them. Debbie had slept with two of them, one of which was the one Becky had bedded. Debbie tried to compare notes on his performance with her friend but Becky could not remember much about the congress only that he had fucked her on Debbie's sofa. They mutually agreed that they hoped that the choice of men would improve over the course of the evening.

Two of the bolder lads sauntered over to their corner and asked if they could by them a drink. Becky readily agreed and asked for a further two glasses of wine. The one that stood closest to Debbie went to the bar whilst the other, the taller of the two, tried to entertain both ladies with his puerile banter. His jeans stained and torn at the knees, his t-shirt splattered with paint, on his shaven head he wore baseball cap adorned with a brand name. Every second or third word he uttered was a profanity, delivered no doubt to enhance his masculinity and confirm his self-ideal as a simple man.

When the shorter of the two returned with the drinks, the company paired up. Both Becky and Debbie shared no sexual history with either of their, would be suitors and had they been consulted they would not have been able to choose between the young men the only discerning feature being their height. One tall and scruffy; one shorter and scruffy; both passably attractive, though their obvious lack of substance gave them an unattractive air. The males decided and Becky found her personal space invaded by the shorter of the two.

After introducing himself, Dave began to regale Becky with heroic tales of his prowess on the field of play when representing the local football club. Embellishing the story of his sporting life, he invented tales of a terrible injury that ended a career that would have certainly led to him turning professional. She nodded and tried to feign interest whilst avoiding his rank breath.

When the taller of the two went to the bar to buy them another drink and Dave excused himself to visit the toilet, Becky and Debbie stood closer together to discuss the men.

By the time they returned, the women had established that neither of them fancied either of them.

Unaware of the decision that the objects of their desires had come to, the young men returned to their original positions and proceeded with their futile attempts at wooing. Increasingly the shorter one touched Becky's shoulder as he forced his idiotic lies on her and filled the air about her head with his halitosis. Deciding enough was enough Becky told him to stop touching her.

"Why what's the matter?" he complained.

"Look stop it, I'm married."

"So, he's not here is he?"

"I just don't want you touching me."

"Why not?"

"I told you, I am married."

"Never stopped you before."

"What's that supposed to mean?"

"Stuart over there said he's fucked you and your mate there."

He swung his head about loosely to indicate the subjects of his comment.

"What!"

"Stuart says…"

"I heard what you said."

"So how about it, want to fuck me?"

"No I do not."

"Come on don't be like that."

He leaned in towards her trying to make contact between their lips. She pressed her hand firmly against his chest and tried to push him away.

"I've told you I'm married and I'm not interested."

The change in her tone drew Debbie's attention. Despite the taller one's best efforts, she ignored him and stood next to her friend.

"She's told you she's not interested so just do one."

Dave clearly did not welcome Debbie's intervention and he stared with blatant hatred at her. His taller friend stood menacingly behind his left shoulder as he formulated a response to the situation. Becky felt very uneasy and began to fear that the situation was about to turn ugly. When she glanced about the smoking area, she recognised Tyron coming out from the bar, pint in hand.

Tyron was older, closer to Becky's age, than the aggressive youngsters were and enjoyed a local reputation as a bit of a hard man. Becky broke the tense standoff by calling to Tyron, who immediately walked over to them deliberately ignoring the two younger men.

"Hey Becks how's it going?"

"Hi Tyron, was hoping we would see you tonight."

"Well here I am."

They leaned in and kissed each other on the cheek. Tyron then turned to Debbie and nodded, "Debs, you alright?" When she returned his nod, he turned to the youngsters.

"You still here?"

"Eh hi Tyron how's it going?"

"I said; are you still here?"

"Well we were just chattin' and I was telling her about my football."

"Right boys last time, you still here?"

Without another word, the youngsters skulked off to re-join their mates and Tyron returned his attention to Becky and Debbie. Glad to be relieved of the difficult situation they had found themselves in, both women smiled and relaxed in his company. They started chatting and laughing as though nothing had happened, both women flirting with him. He placed his pint next to them and returned to the bar to buy both of them another drink. Now clearly under Tyron's protection, none of the youngsters bothered them in his absence.

The remainder of the evening was fun, Tyron flirted outrageously with both women and they reciprocated. All three drank copiously and by the time the bar closed they were drunk, Becky more so than her companions. Debbie suggested that they return to her flat and continue the evening. Even in her inebriated state, Becky knew that the evening would end with her fucking Tyron.

Linking arms they staggered the short distance to Debbie's flat, laughing loudly and making lewd comments to each other. Tyron hushed them as they passed his home, for fear of them drawing his wife's attention to the window. Giggling and shushing each other, they hurried passed and on to the sanctuary of their destination.

They burst through the front door in fits of giggles, falling over each other as they went. Becky and Tyron stumbled to the sofa in the sitting room and collapsed together, arms about each other punctuating their laughter with stolen kisses. Debbie went directly to the kitchen where she opened a bottle of wine and took three glasses from the cupboard. When she entered the front room Becky and Tyron un-entwined and bounced into an upright position. Placing the glasses and wine bottle on the table before them she sat next to Tyron as he filled all three glasses and handed them in turn to his companions.

Debbie and Tyron both lit cigarettes and sat back to relax. Becky moved forward on the sofa and regarded her companions with fondness as she sipped rapidly from her glass. Enjoying his position between two women he suggested that he was a lucky man and raised his glass to each in turn then took a long draft nearly emptying the glass in one gulp. Becky leaned forward and clutching the bottle, refilled his glass before re-charging her own.

"Cheers Darling." Tyron chirped at her with a big smile.

"You're welcome Tyron boy."

"What about me?" Debbie interjected.

"I'll do you." said Tyron as he leaned forward to extinguish his cigarette.

They all laughed as he filled Debbie's glass and lay back with his arms about both of them, pulling Becky back into a posture that matched his and Debbie's. The women drank from their glasses as he alternatively nuzzled into each of them, kissing them lightly and making whispered suggestive comments.

Leaning forward Becky placed her glass on the table and moving onto her hip leaned over and kissed Tyron passionately. When he could reasonably break from the kiss Tyron did and turned his head to Debbie, she moved immediately to press her mouth against his. Without taking her eyes off her companions, Becky began to rub Tyron's erection through his jeans. The caresses of his genitalia drew him from Debbie to kiss Becky again and sliding his hand down the other's back, he held her bottom firmly.

All glasses returned to the table, the three of them exchanged passionate kisses and sexual caresses. Within minutes and with significant fumbling and awkward manoeuvring, both women had lost their tops and bras, Tyron's trousers and pants were about his ankles. Debbie and Becky held his shaft, moving in unison to increase his arousal. "Let's go to bed," whispered Debbie and the others readily agreed.

The women lead the way, Debbie clutching the wine bottle and glasses, Becky gathering their clothes from the floor and following her to the bedroom. Tyron struggled to untie his bootlaces as quickly as he could, then kicking off his footwear, jeans, pants and socks he followed the objects of his carnal lust.

They lay on either side of the bed, both with a glass of wine and naked.

"Hey there sexy come join us."

"Well there is a wonderful sight."

Tyron pulled his shirt off and clambered between them, like an eager puppy invited onto its owners bed. Becky handed him a glass of wine from the bedside cabinet and they all 'clinked' glasses before drinking. Having filled her mouth with wine Becky slid down Tyron's body and pushed his penis into her mouth where she swilled the wine about it as she gently bobbed her head up and down. With a moan of pleasure, he surrendered to his seducers.

Debbie took a drink of wine and placed her glass to the side, then with a speed that surprised Tyron, knelt up, swung her leg across his chest and pressed her pussy down onto his mouth. Eager to please, he worked rapidly with his tongue to pleasure the woman he stared up at over her pelvic mound and pert breasts. She had an almost benign expression on her face as she looked down on him. She moved her hips gently to maximise the pleasure she drew and gasping lightly through open lips.

With all the wine in her still full mouth swallowed, Becky looked up and chose to seize the moment. Straddling his groin, she held his penis vertical and eased herself onto it. Feeling the rhythm of her mount changing, Debbie looked over her shoulder and smiled at her friend. With some awkwardness, she turned around so that her bum rested on Tyron's face and she faced Becky. Leaning forward she pressed her crotch into his face and began to suck on Becky's breasts. Together the women rode Tyron, selfishly seeking every ounce of pleasure they could draw from his engorged member and flicking tongue.

Her ample breast fell from Debbie's mouth with a loud sucking noise. Returning briefly to kiss her nipple Debbie sat up onto Tyron's face and mouthed 'let's swap' to her friend. He was surprised by a flurry of activity as the women clambered from him and squeezed past each other with caressing hands to reverse their previous positions. The newly introduced pussy tasted gloriously of sex and musk and the tight pussy that forced its way onto his cock felt quite different from the one that had, until moments ago, occupied that position. It was Becky's turn to fondle and kiss Debbie's tits.

When his cock began to twitch inside of her, Debbie clambered off him and away from Becky's mouth and hands to grab the base of his shaft and cover the remainder of his manhood with her mouth. Hot spurts of cum hit the back of her throat and slid easily down her gullet. Tyron, almost in spasm, clutched desperately at Becky's thighs and moaned into her pussy. Sensing his lost interest in her vagina, Becky climbed down to join her friend by his spent cock. Selflessly Debbie pulled his manhood from her mouth and offered it to Becky who licked its length seeking any of his seed that her friend may have missed.

With a coy smugness, Debbie sat back on her haunches and smiled at a contented Tyron. His penis began to lose all rigidity rapidly. In an effort to reverse his decline Becky sucked the flaccid member into her mouth and worked as hard as she knew how with her oral facets.

"No, please, I need to pee." complained Tyron.
Becky raised her eyes too him and refused to remove his cock from her mouth.

"No seriously, I need to pee."
Holding his desperate stare, she refused to budge. The meaning of her gaze became apparent to him, and with a

252

resigned smile, he relaxed his bladder. Gradually at first, his urine began flow through his urethra into Becky's mouth. Aiming his, ever increasing, flow to the back of her mouth she swallowed frantically, determined not to spill a drop. Debbie looked on with a look of absolute disbelief on her face.

"Is she…?"

Tyron confirmed her suspicion with a wry, knowing smile, and then he lay back, relaxing and emptying his bladder.

When he had finished, Becky sat up and smiled with a pleased expression on her face.

"Bet you never had anyone do that to you before."

"For sure." he replied as he smiled from one woman to the other.

"What now," demanded Debbie?

"Sorry ladies I have to get home."

"What? You cannot go just yet. What about us?"

"What about you?"

"We haven't cum yet."

"Sorry girls gotta go, Wifie will be waiting."

"Go on then piss off." they both said in unison.

Struggling off the bed, he grabbed his shirt from the floor and moved to the sitting room. Sitting together, they could hear him frantically pulling his clothes on and then the silence as he laced his boots. After a moment, Tyron re-appeared in the bedroom doorway with a cheeky smile on his face.

"Thanks girls it's been a pleasure."

"Don't mention it." Debbie replied in a bitter tone.

"We must do it again sometime."

"Not likely and close the door behind you when you go."

With a shrug, Tyron disappeared into the darkness of the hallway and left the building.

"Cheeky bastard, he could have made us cum."

"Yeah selfish twat."

"What are we going to do now?"

Both women looked at each other and laughed, then falling backwards on the bed began to kiss and caress each other.

Through mutual masturbation and cunnilingus, they brought each other to climax several times before they relented. Their ardour sated, the friends lay holding each other as they waited for sleep to come. Debbie thought briefly of her friend's remarkable sexual behaviour before her fatigue and the comfort of the soft breathing beside her soothed her to sleep. Becky lay awake longer than the friend she cradled in her arms and thought of the date she had arranged with Sean, she had only three days to wait before she could reveal her passionate side again.

Chapter 35

From behind the shield of the net curtains, he watched her walking confidently to her car. He had both hands pushed into the pockets of his trousers and he rocked from the balls of his feet to his heels and back again. Tunelessly he blew a dry whistle through his teeth, some song he had heard on the radio that day at work. As she climbed into her car and started the engine, he could feel the discomfort of his stomach, as usual, he had eaten far too much and as usual, he was now beginning to regret his greed.

Her car pulled away and was soon lost from view. Brian remained in his position, staring out at the unremarkable suburban street. It was then he noticed the teenager next-door standing in his front garden, staring in the direction Becky's car had gone. Slowly the boy turned and went inside. He envied and resented him, his young life still full of hopes and possibilities. A life yet to be lived and yet to ruined, all men are born free and everywhere they are in chains. Could it be that, when the last vestiges of childhood innocence are lost and the inescapable awfulness of life becomes apparent, that this forms the epiphany that accounts for the relatively high instances of Teenage suicide? It would explain much, as very many more boys kill themselves than girls.

Although past seven, it remained broad daylight outside, a beautiful early summer evening. He could see the moon in the azure sky. Sunshine to Earthshine to Moonshine. Silently he contemplated light bouncing about the Galaxy and beyond. Light spewed out from countless stars across the Universe, the crucibles in which all commonplace matter was forged. The matter used to build the Earth, its life and humanity. What made sin, was it born as a dark concept in mankind's nascent conscious or was it given to us? Brian did not know the answer. He only knew the pain it gave him.

Sighing loudly he turned from the window and shambled through to the kitchen. Everything stowed neatly in its place, the work surfaces immaculate and the gentle murmur of the dishwasher executing its task. She knew how to keep a home, if not a family. He tugged on the refrigerator door, a large American type, a luxury he considered essential since his days living in The USA. From the bottom shelf, he pulled a tin of beer and cracked it open. The first mouthful of chill beer, exciting and refreshing, a once a day experience, with each subsequent mouthful that sensation would diminish, replaced by the mind's increasing demand for the soporific and altering effects of alcohol.

Letting the door swing closed behind him, he returned to the sitting room and his armchair. The television kept him company as his parental vigil began. Sounds and moving images entertained the two most dominant of his senses as his mind travelled further than the space he occupied.

He was not as stupid as she thought him to be. Her obvious arrogance irked him and he was tired of suppressing his natural instincts. In his mind's eye, he could visualise the sight that had greeted him when he had returned home early from work to surprise and care for his heavily pregnant wife. The look on her face when she had looked up from the floor and seen him standing there etched into his mind forever. The almost comical awkwardness of her lover, kneeling behind her with his cock buried deep inside her, vying for position with Brian's unborn son. He had reacted, as all men would have in that situation, gaining him nothing but a fat lip. After that, he resolved to build a family and play a longer game, a game where he lost many battles but continued to conspire towards overall victory.

Her advantages were her charm and promiscuity. His advantages were his cunning and patience. He knew far more about her nefarious activities that she could possibly contemplate. Victory and vengeance would be facilitated through the imbalance of knowledge. Betrayal such as hers, he would punish.

Men are naturally competitive and territorial and it was their instinct to fight for what they believed to be theirs. Becky was his; he provided for her, kept a roof over her head and supported her through the most difficult parts of her life to date. Brian knew where she was and what she would probably do that night. Her regular visits to her friend Debbie's, was a means by which she could escape him and their home to

256

indulge her passion for infidelity. They would almost certainly be in the grotty little pub down the road from Debbie's flat, getting drunk and chatting up the young men. He was under no illusion. He knew that she would probably have sex with one of the pub's clientele. Then in the morning, she would return with fabricated tales of how they sat chatting and drinking wine in front of the television yet beneath the fresh smell of shampoo and deodorant she would stink of sex.

Instinctually he wanted to drive to the 'The Oak' or Debbie's place and catch her in the act. He could then indulge his base desire for violence. In the dark corners of his mind, he imagined her lying on her back with some youngster between her legs when he burst in and confronted them. He would make them suffer a slow and painful death as he recounted all her betrayals. Although satisfying, he knew that thought to be no more than a cathartic daydream. He needed to be cleverer than that and besides he could not leave Thomas alone. The game was afoot and he was now fully committed to his strategy.

Brian finished his beer and took the empty tin to the kitchen where he disposed of it in the correct re-cycling bin. He pulled the wash basket from the alcove next to the washing machine and searched it for items of Becky's underwear. The source of much of his knowledge was his methodical observation. He made a mental catalogue of her underwear awaiting washing then searched the contents of the tumble dryer drum and the ironing basket adding any relevant items to the list. It was then possible to compile that information with what remained in her lingerie drawers to deduce what she wore that night.

Satisfied with his diligence, Brian went upstairs to their bedroom and began to search through Becky's drawers. It had been a painstaking process, cataloguing her underwear but he had managed it and now had a detailed knowledge of every item she possessed, knowledge he up dated every time she returned from a shopping trip. When he completed his search he concluded that a rather bland pair of blue knickers was missing and a cream coloured bra, equally unexciting, however a matching set of red lace was also missing. Whoever screwed his wife that night would be in for a treat, Brian thought to himself.

Feeling an incongruous combination of nausea and sexual excitement, Brian's heart began to race. His knees felt weak as he descended the stairs to the sitting room where he paused for a moment before continuing to the Kitchen. When he pulled another tin of beer from the fridge, he noticed that his hands were shaking. Struggling to control his involuntary movements, he opened the tin and returned to his armchair on unsteady legs. He tried hard not to think of Becky with other men but that proved impossible and he surrendered to the erotic images his mind forced on him. Staring unseeingly at the TV he slowly sipped his beer until the tin was dry whilst a storm raged in his head.

By the time he cracked his third tin, he was back in control. Coldly he contemplated his next action. Becky's friendship with Debbie and the freedom she demanded to enjoy regular nights out with her friends were not the only portals she had to her promiscuous life. There was also her addiction to the internet. She believed that it was only her that, knew how to, or care to, use the internet in their household. She was wrong.

Brian hauled his bulk out of the armchair and carried his beer to the sofa. When he had made himself comfortable on the unfamiliar cushioning, he reached down the side of the armrest and pulled the laptop up and onto his ample thighs. With practiced ease he lifted the lid and switched it on and waited for the 'log in' screen. When Becky had first been given the pc, by Brian for her birthday, it had not taken him long to work out her username and password. The extent of her blind arrogance was such that she used the same codes to gain entry to every site she accessed, making Brian's task very much easier.

He trawled through all of the sites he knew she used regularly. As he followed her activity, reading the messages she sent and received, his hands began to shake again and a terrible nausea gnawed at his innards. All was revealed and the end game forced unavoidably on him. He stored all the new relevant data in his head and logged out of her account and into his own. He had work to do in order to prepare for the final stage.

That night he lay in bed, his head fogged by the alcohol and his heart racing with stress-induced adrenalin. He had always known this moment would come and he had prepared himself well, yet somehow the finality of the moment scared him. The prospect of the end, had sustained him all this time but now that it was imminent, he doubted his own conviction to conclude matters.

Chapter 36

The flat stank of stale dampness, reminiscent of a public lavatory. It smelled that way when he had first entered several months prior. Nevertheless, he paid the modest deposit and advanced rent there and then to the agent. He had been desperate for a permanent base, an address to be his home, a building to shelter him, a destination at the end of every day or activity.

Waking, he was happy. He had been dreaming, all was well, the sun shone, she loved him and their closeness was absolute, nothing could come between them. Leaving the dream, he first became aware of the smell, then the cold and then gradually his realisation increased to bring him back to his wretched reality. He had no job, no family, no money, no hope, no love and no home; he merely sheltered in that hovel.

Clouds materialised over his face and dispersed quickly into the bitterly cold air above the duvet. He studied the filthy net curtain hanging across the window, the desiccated corpses of bluebottles and wasps hanging from the intricate lace patterns, the work of a truly gifted spider, a fastidious arachnid. The months of his occupation had been the cold months of winter; he therefore concluded that the insects had been hanging there when he moved in. He often regretted his decision to rent the place, it was a shit hole, uncharacteristically he had put the limitation of his resources above his own desires and taste when he handed over the money and received the keys.

When it became painfully apparent to him that there was to be no rapid reconciliation with Lily, Matt had contacted several letting agents hoping to find a reasonably priced flat close to his estranged home. There were none to be found in the rural environs that he had previously occupied and he had to content himself with a one-bedroom hole in the suburbs of London. His landlord, Mr Patel, had originally promised to repair a few item and even to fit a cooker in the kitchen. In the event however, he did nothing to the property. In retrospect, he should have seen that coming, due to his woeful credit rating and his lack of a job he had to part with six months' rent in advance, significantly depleting his rapidly diminishing resources and giving Mr Patel no incentive to fulfil his promises.

As events transpired, the proximity of his abode to his broken family home became irrelevant. Shortly after he moved into the dump, Lily moved all of their furniture out of their home, handed the keys back to the letting agent and moved her and Lucy to an address they would not disclose to him. It was true that he had made a bit of a pest of himself around the old house and had frequently turned up at the front door asking to stay the night or to see his daughter. Now his only connection with them was a mobile telephone number.

Since the bitter break up, Matt had made it perfectly clear that he would do anything to regain his family, his home and Lily's love. Unfortunately, for Matt, Lily had made it equally clear that he would not realise any of his ambitions that involved her or their daughter. Such intransigence frustrated him so much, he could never keep any promise he made to remain reasonable and to abide by the terms that Lily would demand before agreeing to any meeting. His resulting behaviour convinced Lucy's mother that her estranged husband was mentally unstable and a potential danger to them both. Several times the Police were called to his home and Matt was driven away in disgrace, on the back seat of a panda car.

Fully aware of his behavioural difficulties, Matt frequently wondered how better equipped to deal with the demands of the circumstances he would have been if he had not been forced, head first, into a garden wall by some idiot of a female driver. It was true that since the accident he functioned differently, his thoughts and actions did not line up as well as they once did. It had been an insidious process and for much of the time since, he had not been aware of the changes. The trauma of the breakup had served to focus his remembered emotions and subsequent actions into an awareness that he had not previously possessed. An awareness that shed no light on his reasoning, it served only to provide him with a painful understanding of his mind's dysfunction and the aching knowledge that he was no longer the high-functioning individual that he once had been. He could not be sure how much the accident had diminished his emotional intelligence and to that end, how much it was responsible for the disintegration of his life.

It was a frustrating sensation, trapped inside an irrational brain. Matt could consciously observe from his inner self as his frontal lobes ran amok. Often silently screaming for it to stop and cease the damaging process, frequently cringing at his own social behaviour, he could only watch as he smashed his own life onto the rocks of society. All along, he knew there would be a reckoning and that the price would be paid by his inner self and not by the mad man that had taken possession of him.

During the increasingly rare moments of sanity, he vowed to keep control then repair his life. Invariably he broke those vows whenever his doppelganger came to call in his myriad of guises: anger, lust, resentment, jealousy et al and Matt, relegated to the ineffective role of observer, could only watch as another carriage careered into and derailed in the train smash of his life.

There could be only one person on Earth responsible for his misery, though he did not know her name, the sound of her voice or the colour of her eyes, Matt hated the woman that had driven the car into him. She had ruined everything; her wrathful legacy with him for the remainder of his life, constantly gnawing at his sanity and pulling him further from survival. Her vicious selfishness would chase him to his grave, the sins he accumulated en route, paid for when he got there. Matt concluded that the only purpose of his destruction and pain was for the entertainment of a dark God, a sick twisted God of cardinal darkness, an Old Testament God.

Ignoring his aching loins, Matt rolled onto his side and tried to return to the place from which he had woken. He knew that there would be no return but to try, was infinitely preferable than to brave the cold air of the revolting little flat or to dwell on his real condition. He tried to absorb all the warmth his duvet held as he pulled it close about himself and forced his thoughts to remember a life now lost. Failing, he reluctantly struggled from the bed and stumbled briskly to the bathroom to empty his bulging bladder.

The thin jogging bottoms and cotton T-shirt provided little protection from the clinging wet air that hung like numbing spectres in a crowded room. Shivering, he aimed his urine at the stained under-rim of the toilet bowl, occasionally washing away gelatinous slithers of opaque brown. The bathroom did not smell, though Matt was confident that was because the temperature inside the flat had never been above three degrees centigrade since he had taken up residence. Frequently he would dress and go for a walk to warm himself in the relatively tepid air of the streets.

He considered returning to the sparse comfort of the duvet before deciding to brave the shower. Matt switched both bars of the electric fire on in the front room and the solitary bar of the bedroom fire, prior to dragging the towel from his bed where he had placed it the night before, to warm and dry in preparation for his morning shower. The taps rattled as he turned them full on, jumping backward he avoided the weak splattering of bitterly cold water and stood waiting for the warm water to achieve dominance. He shaved in the shower to maintain his core temperature at a bearable level, judging the execution of his depilation more by touch than by sight, the image of his face reflected in the small lime scale stained mirror, hanging from the soap dish, revealing little detail.

In a frenzy of activity, he recovered from the shower to dry himself in front of the electric fire by the bedroom wall. Like a victim of the ravages of St Vitus Dance, he paddled, swung, dragged and rubbed the towel about his body as he hopped, skipped and boogied. He dropped the towel and began, without delay, to don his clothing as quickly as he could, a frantic activity to conserve every last fraction of a degree of heat.

The dank air permeated every corner of his flat and so did the smell. Sniffing his pullover, he tried to discern the damp odour but was unable to, over the background stench that he had breathed all night. With resignation, he struggled into the garment with the full knowledge, because others had told him, that all of his clothes smelled of the rancid hovel. Today was an important day to him and he resented the fact that he had to experience it smelling like a public lavatory in winter.

Dully creaking, the door to the front room gave as he pushed on it. The air smelled of burning dust and mould, two strips of red trying in vain to push the cold air from the electric fire. Radiated energy dissipated rapidly into the clinging fug of the room. He pulled the orange nylon drapes back, damp strips of fabric reluctantly moving along the plastic rail to reveal the grey day outside, familiar vista of cheap housing and a corner shop, revealed beyond the filthy nets, no solace or joy there. The interior formed in the cold light, admitted by his actions: a blue two-seater sofa, a non-descript cabinet that supported a small portable TV and a pile of paperbacks, stacked neatly by the yellow stained wall.

Grabbing his wallet from next to the TV, he flopped onto the sofa. The clawing fabric seemed to dampen his clothing and draw more heat from his body than the surrounding atmosphere. He had not thought of or even remembered any part of his childhood in a very long time. Slouched like an unstrung marionette, Matt closed his eyes and probed his memory for the oldest data stored there. Only vague disjointed situations emerged from the foggy past, though strong remembered emotions accompanied them. He recalled the concern and love he felt for the world, the disappointed ambition for a beautiful world crushed by the actions of grown-ups that he could not understand. Those compassionate sentiments his father beat from him and the clawing sickly love, his mother would lavish on him when they were alone, the insincerity of which indisputably demonstrated when her husband's abuses directed at him, ignored by her, became manifest. Rare kindnesses, smuggled to him by his Maternal Grandmother, softened his memories and he could enjoy those very distant and obscured occasions when he had been happy as a child.

The safety net of a family had been denied him early in his life. By the time he had found any form of independence, he severed all contact with his family and they in turn made no effort to recover their estranged son. He had tried to build his own family but that was taken from him by his own demons. He was alone in the world with no one to help. Should he trip and fall, he found himself severed from both antecedents and posterity alike.

Banging on the front door sent waves of concussive noise throughout the flat. Matt sat still listening to the efforts of his caller to attract his attention. The banging repeated several times before he heard the squeaking of the letterbox opening.

"I know you're in there. Answer the door."

Silence.

"Come on open up, the rent's overdue."

Silence.

"Open the bloody door I want to talk to you."

Silence.

"You owe me two months' rent now and I want it today."

Silence.

"I know you are claiming housing benefit and you haven't paid me anything since you moved in."

Silence.

"Come on for fuck's sake you said you would pay six monthly in advance and you've been in there for eight months."

Silence.

"I am being reasonable. I'm not asking for the full six months just the two you owe me."

Silence.

"Don't make me an enemy. I can make life hard for you."

Silence.

"Right, have it your own way. I'll be back."

Matt listened to the receding footsteps, echo down the landing and descend the stairwell. Then with casual resignation, he opened the wallet, it contained two ten pound notes, a photograph of his daughter, his driving license and the bankcard for his basic account. Placing the wallet by his side, he dug into his pockets and fished out the change they contained. Four pounds and seventy-two pence, enhancing his means to twenty-four pounds and seventy-two pence, given his current position, a reasonable amount. This would have to sustain him for a further week, he needed to top up his electric key, take his daughter out later that day and to feed himself, then there was the matter of the rent. It was true that he had been claiming housing benefit from the local council however, he had not been able to afford to live and travel to see Lucy on his Jobseekers allowance and so he had used the housing money to fill the shortfall.

It was painfully obvious that his current financial situation was not viable. He would have to address the issue of his overdue rent or he would find himself homeless, a prospect that he dreaded. If he could find a job, he could come to an agreement with his landlord and begin to save for a decent place of his own, where his child could come and stay with him. He was trying, Monday to Friday he visited the library and used the internet to, amongst other things, search for job vacancies. Over the previous months, he had applied for nearly sixty jobs, received many polite refusals, one invitation to interview and heard only silence from the majority of his applications. He had not progressed past the first stage with the interview, Matt knew that the interview had not gone well, he was on edge and self-conscious of the fact that his suit smelled of the dump that he lived in. Hope was a solid crutch onto which he could lean all of his worries. Despite the mounting evidence to the contrary, he continued to hope that things would get better.

Initially he was reluctant to move for fear of introducing his body to air or fabric that had not already been warmed by his own energy however, baser needs drove him from the front room to the coldest room in the flat; the kitchen. He whistled a dry tune through his teeth as he prepared a breakfast, then carrying a mug of tea and a plate of buttered toast he returned to the discomfort of the sofa and the front room. He watched the tiny screen of his television set as he munched on the toast, soft with molten butter it deteriorated to a pasty pulp in his mouth almost instantly. When his meal was finished, he laid the crockery next to his wallet on the sofa and returned his attention to the little electronic portal on the world.

When the time came, he roused himself from the sofa, pulled his leather jacket on and collected the polythene bag that contained a present for Lucy. After checking that he had his door key and his wallet, he left the flat, pulling the chipped and ill-fitting door to behind him. He descended the stairs rapidly and then plunged through the external door out of the building. The doorway had the familiar smell of stale urine and rotting bin bags.

Out in the street occasional cars drove along between their parked counterparts, tyres hissing in the surface water left from an early morning heavy shower. Matt crossed the road and walked past the corner shop, barely edible fruit and vegetables stacked, rotting, in crates on the pavement in front of the windows that allowed no view of the interior, boxes of practical items filling every available inch of the glass. He wore his Chelsea boots and the sock on his right foot was already feeling wet. All of his shoes had holes in their soles as he did not have the means to pay for repairs. There was an uncomfortable squelching sensation in his right boot by the time he reached the bus stop.

He did not have long to wait before the bus rounded the corner and progressed to the stop. Patiently Matt waited whilst three old ladies maximised the social intercourse they could muster from the simple transaction of displaying a pass to the driver. When it was his turn, he purchased a return ticket into town, reducing his means to marginally below twenty pounds. The bus pulled away and he lurched down the central aisle considering the occupants of each seat as potential neighbours for the journey. Eventually he swung himself into an unoccupied seat near the rear and peered out of the window at the passing damp grey streets, streets that could have been in any urban sprawl in the country. Manifestly anonymous and ubiquitous the decaying Victorian architecture rolled by as though on a relatively short loop.

Once the older buildings gave way to the hideous concrete blockhouses of the nineteen seventies, Matt knew he was approaching his stop. He pressed the red button and waited for the bus to come to a complete halt. When the doors issued their high-pitched wailing vibrations as they opened, he stood immediately and strode to the exit. Thanking the driver, he jumped down onto the pavement and began to navigate his route through the Saturday afternoon throng towards the rendezvous.

They stood together in the department store doorway like two complete strangers. His wife, his daughter, his family, rent from his life and now, as though it had never been so, they

267

waited for the stranger, her father, her husband. Lucy held her mother's hand as she followed individual passers-by with her eyes, wide with innocence and anticipation. Lily looked tired, drawn by the demands of her new life without him. She wore clothes he had never seen before and she had changed her hair, long blonde locks replaced by a styled bob. He wanted to hold both of them close, to let his life force flow into them and repair all the damage that he had done.

With curt recognition, she acknowledged his approach and crouched to her child, saying words of information and comfort. Only when she had finished her dialogue with Lucy did she stand upright and engage with him.

"You're late."

"Yeah sorry about that, the bus was running late; heavy traffic."

"Whatever. Don't be late when you bring her back."

"I won't, promise."

He wanted to hug her, to feel the warmth of the woman he loved, to feed the aching hollow of loss that filled him. Opening his arms, he stepped towards her. Her extended arm, palm held open in a halt gesture, she stopped him.

"Matt don't."

Sighing he dropped his arms to his sides and bent down to Lucy. There was no hesitation there; she immediately threw her arms up for a cuddle from her father. Lifting her up in a close embrace, he whispered into her small ear how much he loved and missed her. Lily interrupted the moment with a cold matter-of-fact voice.

"What are you going to do?"

"I thought we could go to the pictures and to McDonalds."

"I thought you wanted to spend time with your daughter?"

"I do that's why I'm here."

"You won't get much quality time if you are sat in a cinema."

"Well what else would you suggest?"

"I don't know, not my problem."

"Ok look would you like to come with us?"

"No thanks. I have things to do."

"Would you like to join us for something to eat after?"

"No thanks."

Matt looked dejectedly at the pavement and struggled for words to say.

"When you get to McDonalds, send me a text and I will pick Lucy up there when you have finished eating."

"Ok. I'll do that. It's errr well you know erm nice to see you."

"Whatever Matt, have a nice time and I'll see you later."

She leaned forward, kissed her daughter and told her to be good for Daddy, and then as if she had never been there, she turned and was gone.

The film had been a big budget Hollywood animation. There was some humour for the adults and almost non-stop sentimental bungling and slapstick to entertain its target audience of children. Lucy scampered ahead of him into the foyer once they had negotiated the still darkened steps out of the theatre, credits rolling down the screen. When he asked her if she had enjoyed the film, she explained, with her limited vocabulary, that she had and especially liked the donkey character, as he was funny. She then bombarded Matt with questions about the intricacies of the plot that she had failed to grasp. Looking down into her glowing face and feeling the terrible pit of emptiness within, he thought that it was good that God kept the truth of life from children, for if he did not, they would not have the heart to start at all.

In the fast-food restaurant, Matt held a plastic tray, on which their meal, arranged in brightly coloured Styrofoam containers and cardboard cups balanced, in one hand and held onto Lucy with the other. They sat opposite each other eating the reconstituted potato and bread products that surrounded the centrepiece of strangely sweet meat. She had emptied four sachets of ketchup onto the tray and was liberally covering everything she put in her mouth with it. Between mouthfuls, they chatted about the film. Lucy, who would insist on recounting her favourite scenes with exaggerated enthusiasm, ignored every attempt Matt made to change the subject to more personal matters. It did not take long for either of them to become bored and silence fell as he sipped his black coffee and she slurped the last of her drink from the bottom of the cup through a straw.

Inexplicably he felt a surge of happiness when Lily entered the restaurant. Waving his arm above his head, he captured her attention and she made straight for their table. Standing up, he offered her a seat.

"No thanks must get going. Hello Darling did you have a nice time with Daddy?"

Lucy nodded to indicate that she had enjoyed herself.

"Right well thanks for that Matt, text me when you know when you can see her again."

With that, she gathered up her child and left without another word.

Alone, he sat contemplating his position. The day's activities had reduced his cash situation to less than ten pounds. He would have to make the most of the fast-food meal he had just consumed, as it looked likely that food would not be very plentiful over the coming week. A clawing depression filled his heart when he remembered that he needed to put money on his electric key or his hovel would be even more uncomfortable without heating and lighting.

Lightly grasping the, half-empty, cardboard cup, he sipped the lukewarm coffee and gazed at the empty seat opposite which had, until moments before, been occupied by Lucy. When they had departed, a hollow emptiness gripped his core being. His time with Lucy is now and that is now time squandered or denied. The awful magnitude of this loss glided into focus when he considered that one day she would, as we all shall, die. Matt understood beyond question; knew, she would go to heaven and he would not.

He could still smell her in the air and he fancied he could hear her little voice prattling on about the movie. With an audible sigh, he looked away from the red plastic chair and gazed about the restaurant.

A newly arrived group of diners caught his attention. They passed along the nave of the fast-food cathedral. He proceeded with slightly more decorum than his children, who could not disguise their obvious excitement at the prospect of eating processed chicken and reconstituted faux chips. The children made constant suggestions of what they might order, their mother rejecting most on the grounds of cost.

Leading his family towards the tills, he gave undue deference to his fellow customers. He wore his only shoes, a pair of white trainers. His sporting footwear complimented his tracksuit bottoms but were incongruous when considered with the checked nylon pullover that he wore. There was a fresh green grass stain on his trousers and an unidentifiable brown stain on both knees.

As children are, and these were no exception, they understood little of poverty; they knew only the sensations of its depravities. Other children would eat in a restaurant such as this regularly and think nothing of it; they would enjoy the experience only once every fortnight. The dining event always limited by the strict budget that was available to their parents.

The role of a wife and mother was to hold a family together her mother had always taught her. She had grown up with that purpose etched into her being. It was her only ambition in life, to be in the position where she could employ her mother's advice.

Checking the notes and coins in her purse for the fourth time, she confirmed her budget to feed the family. It hurt her that she had to deny her children things because they did not have the money. She felt sick when she remembered her children crying because they were cold and she did not have sufficient money to top up the electric key and heat their home. Her eyes would fill with stinging tears when she recalled the time that she had to feed her children mouldy bread because they had nothing else.

When they assembled at the gauche counter, she checked her appearance in the mirror between the vending appliances that fronted the kitchen whilst her husband placed their order. He checked every item he ordered with a glance to her, which he would hold until she nodded confirmation that no cost boundary had been crossed. Her reflected image confirmed that she looked awful. Her hair hung like rats' tails over her head, face like a stepped-on tomato and a figure like a sack of potatoes. She was no longer the cute fourteen year old that had let him have his way with her.

271

Her son and daughter pushed each other as they vied for their parent's attention. Their father leaned on the counter waiting for the food that he had ordered. His wife stood awkwardly clutching her purse whilst her daughter pulled incessantly at her clothing to keep her focus on the child's need for the ordered milkshake. Their son fidgeted and clearly felt uncomfortable in the nappy he wore. Ordinarily he would be far too old for a nappy but his obvious mental deficiencies made it clear why he might need such protection.

Staring over his, now cold coffee, Matt could see the child's nappy protruding from the waistband of his trousers. At first, it struck him as appropriate that the youngest child of this obviously dysfunctional family be a retard, and then as they gathered their food from the counter and meandered their way to a table, he felt a strange loss. It occurred to him that, the emotion he had felt was not pity or distain it was jealousy. For all their obvious disadvantages, they had each other; each other and love, each other and a sense of belonging, each other and security, each other and a home.

Chapter 37

When the sound of the footsteps receded down the stairwell and the outside door made its familiar banging sound as it closed behind his recent, unwelcome and ignored visitor, he began to rouse from beneath the protective barrier of the duvet. He had been lying, tightly wrapped in insulation, daydreaming of his old life when the persistent banging on the front door broke the silence. After he had failed to open the door to his Landlord, the letterbox flap squeaked open and Mr Patel ran through his, now familiar, repartee beginning with chiding then moving through reason to threats.

Matt completed his morning ablutions with the customary haste then moving to the kitchen he switched the kettle on and began to trim mould from two slices of bread, which he placed into the toaster and depressed the initiator. His breakfast preparations were brought to an immediate halt when the electricity cut out. He opened the dusty dark cupboard by the kitchen door and pressed the small button on the electricity meter that gave the flat an emergency supply of electricity. A supply that he hoped would last for a further three days until his Jobseeker's allowance was paid and he could afford to top up his utility key.

After buttering the toast Matt sat by the front room window, glumly chewing on his breakfast, washing each mouthful down with a large swallow of tea. He had no enthusiasm for the remainder of the day, the one day every fortnight that he was required to attend the Job Centre in order to sign on, which assured he was in receipt of on-going benefits. The experience had been soul-destroying from the outset. Over all the years of his working life, he contributed significantly more money through his National Insurance than he had, or was ever likely to, receive in state benefits. He had performed the calculation several times and each time the result angered him, especially when he considered how the odious individuals, who managed his claim at the Jobcentre, treated him. To him it seemed unfair that he should be punished and humiliated at every turn for his sins. The loss of his family and home should be sufficient punishment for all his misdemeanours, yet the Universe was intent on destroying him. Human misery knows no boundary; when a person considers that 'things could not get any worse', they invariably do.

Outside in the street below, Matt could see people hurrying by, coats buttoned closed, hats pulled down and hands firmly thrust into pockets. Heavy clouds darkened the day to little more than the half-light of evening. Greying residue from the last snowfall lay in the unpopular corners of the street, slowly honeycombing to nothing. He sensed a collective resignation to the inevitability of further snow from the hunched shoulders and straight legged shuffling of the pedestrians.

Matt stood, moved away from the battered drop-leaf table by the window and sat on the dank sofa to watch television until it was time to leave for the Jobcentre. The usual mind numbing rubbish, punctuated with adverts targeting the retired and the underclass, filled the TV screen. Matt felt increasingly isolated. With every passing day, he felt his place in the world slipping away. These days only Raj in the corner shop, the woman at the Library and the bastards in the Jobcentre seemed to acknowledge him. As the real world seemed to recede, he drew no closer to empathy with the daytime TV world that he scrutinised day in, day out.

Beyond the television, in the corner of the room, there were patterns on the wall. When he had first noticed them they held no significance for him, slowly and with gradual penetration, the symmetry of the patterns became apparent. With every step forward in understanding, truths were revealed, truths that opened a portal through to a new place. During the early months, when he thought about them, he would doubt the learning he perceived as he lay in his bed. On rising and after an hour of further study of the patterns he became a devout acolyte, with each new epiphany came greater understanding of the truth. A truth never revealed to him before. A truth, he came to believe that could have saved him, had it been available when he was self-destructing.

He sat motionless, staring at the corner of the room for over an hour. With a simple blink, he once again became animated. Checking his watch, Matt stood up, pulled on his overcoat, and checked the contents of his pockets. The meagre collection of coins he dug out would not purchase a ticket for the bus. With a resigned sigh, he buttoned his coat, set off into the street and walked the four and half miles to the Jobcentre.

The room looked as it always did. Bright fluorescent light, tinged with a slight orange, illuminated the grey brown carpet tiles and rows of identical grey-topped desks. The central area, spined with back-to-back rows of orange soft seating, on which, the numerous unfortunate clients of the Department of Work and Pensions sat, awaiting their fortnightly support session.

Matt dropped a clear plastic envelope into the yellow basket, sitting on the appropriate desk and retreated to one of the orange seats from where he could view the miserable looking old woman who was due to conduct his support session. She sat behind her desk tapping occasionally on her keyboard and refusing to look up. Suddenly she moved with great purpose, a look of determination on her face, to a desk that sat three behind her. She engaged the younger woman, sitting at the desk, with meaningful statements and powerful head gestures.

The time of his appointment came and went as he sat upright in his seat staring across the empty desks at his adviser and the younger colleague with whom she discussed the arrangements for breaks. Eventually and with overt reluctance, she slid her ample and misshapen backside off the desk and ambled to her own duty station. She fidgeted for an unnecessarily long time before she settled and with belligerent idleness, reached into the small yellow basket. Taking the plastic envelope out of the basket, she screwed up her face to read the details, and then with a look of disgust she dropped it on the desk and began to tap on her keyboard again.

He made her call him twice before he rose from his seat and approached her desk. Looking up from her computer screen with a puzzled expression, she struggled to grasp the situation before eventually realising Matt was standing before her desk because she had not invited him to sit down. When she indicated the chair with her open palm, he sat down and waited for proceedings to begin. She mouthed some words silently as she read from her screen then cleared her throat and continued to read. Her breathing was loud enough to hear above the general murmur of numerous conversations taking place in the room. He hated her; she was everything he despised in a stereotypical Civil Servant.

Without looking at him, she spoke.

"How's your job search going?"

"Not well."

"Why not?"

"Because I have not got a job."

She stopped looking at her screen, turning her attention instead to him then to the small plastic envelope on the desk before her. She pulled out the contents and began looking through the folded sheets of paper.

"Is this your job search?"

"I beg your pardon?"

"Is this your job search?"

She held up a sheet of paper.

"I heard you and obviously it is my job search as it states that at the top of the form."

"Well there's not a great deal of activity recorded on this."

"In your opinion, I reserve the right to differ."

"We require that you actively seek employment when you're claiming Jobseekers allowance."

"I am fully aware of that and I have recorded all significant actions that I've taken."

"Well it's not acceptable, we require greater detail."

"Why do you need more information, all pertinent information is there, I am looking for a job?"

"Look Sir, I'm not sure I like your attitude."

"What attitude? You're the one making unreasonable demands."

"There's nothing unreasonable about our requirements and I suggest you comply."

"What makes you think you have the authority to make me comply."

"Sir, if you don't comply I will be forced to sanction you and you will lose your benefits."

"For Christ's sake are you enjoying this, do you like the power your paltry little position gives you?"

276

"There's no need to take that attitude Sir, you are living off the state and in return we demand details of your job search."

"Living off the state! Living? This is not living; this is dying."

Matt could feel his brain chemistry altering and the belligerent demons manifesting themselves across his consciousness. His synapses snapped connections through his frontal lobes and adrenalin spiced resolve, set in his mind. He could not understand the monotone drone issuing from her ugly fat face as he stood up but was aware of the nervous Security Officers slowly moving towards his position.

"Fuck you, I have paid for my sins! Why do you have to punish me further?"

Staring ahead of himself, he stormed out of the building ignoring the half-hearted attempts of the Security Officers as they tried to detain him.

The rain, flecked with occasional flakes of snow, grew heavier as he turned for home. By the two-mile mark, it was snowing heavily and by the three-mile mark, he was bitterly regretting his action at the Jobcentre.

His outburst would cost him dearly. The old bag will certainly sanction his benefit payment. Matt was not sure if the sanction would effect his Housing Benefit but he was certain to loose his Jobseeker Allowance for an extended period and this would compound his financial difficulties. With stunned incredulity, he reflected on his earlier actions. He could not fathom what had possessed him to act like that, what demon had taken his rational and drove his mind through fire to attack. It felt as though he had been chained to a lunatic; a lunatic for whose actions, he would be held fully responsible.

Terrifyingly he was able to control his emotions and thoughts less with every passing day. Increasingly Matt began to feel his personality changing. Even as he walked the familiar route home from the Job Centre, he seemed to view the world from a constantly shifting and invariably unfavourable perspective.

Snow was melting through the holes in his shoes and his right sock gave a curious squelching sensation every time he placed that foot in the snow. When he turned into his road and set eyes on the flat, he was immediately reminded of his rent arrears and the seemingly unsolvable issues surrounding his tenancy. It was now becoming painfully obvious to Matt that others were now guiding his destiny and that those others sought constantly to disadvantage him. He was being bullied by the world and he was scared where it would lead. He was sick of it. At every turn, his ambitions had been thwarted. The worst of all possible scenarios had been the outcome of every decisive juncture in his recent life.

Many years before he had watched a TV programme that focussed on the nature of courage. Matt remembered how soldiers decorated for bravery had explained that they had never intended to be heroes and at the onset of a difficult situation, they had been terrified, then when they realised that another person was creating the circumstance in which they found themselves they became angry. They explained that no man likes to be pushed around, so when they believed that the enemy were pushing them about that revelation created anger and that anger created courage. In anger, all valour was born and so it should be for him. Matt would start to fight back. The world was full of people who would push him around and it was now that he would make his stand.

Pushing the tatty external door open Matt stepped through the piss stained doorway into the stairwell of his block of flats. Wearily he placed his left hand on the banister and began to climb with slow, flat-footed, ascending paces. The regular scuffing report of his steps echoed off the rundown Victorian plasterwork and battered doors of the individual flats. He stared at each step before him, plotting his revenge as he heaved on the banister to assist his progress. When he reached his landing, he paused for a moment whilst he drew a couple of breaths and then shuffled on to his front door.

Fumbling in his trouser pockets, Matt found his door key and tried to fit it in the lock. Frustrated, he adjusted his hold on the key and re-doubled his efforts. They key scrabbled at the metal housing of the lock whilst he muttered curses into the stale cold air.

The door suddenly swung open suddenly and two brown arms grabbed the sleeves of his coat. They dragged Matt into his flat with eager force and propelled him into the hallway

278

wall. He managed marginally to break the impact by extending his hands at the very last moment. Two hard blows, delivered in quick succession to his kidneys caused his innards to explode in disabling pain.

When the searing disorientating pain subsided to the point where he was able to sense something else he realised that he was again travelling at speed down the hallway towards the front room. Just prior to passing through the portal, he became airborne and flew into the fading light, which illuminated the room through the filthy nets hanging across the window. He landed heavily on the damp and stinking carpet where he lay in stunned incomprehension. With an audible groan, Matt drew his hands under his chest and pushed his head and shoulders upward. A blurred image of brown leather heralded the kick that violently exploded in his face. Hot angry sensations raged and his eyes filled with burning tears. Cupping his hands in front of his nose and mouth, he waited for the pain to subside.

Slowly he parted his fingers and peered through to gain an understanding of his situation. From where he lay, he could make out two pairs of feet in close proximity to his upper body. They wore cheap leather shoes with soles of synthetic fabric and nylon socks. In the air, he could vaguely smell sickly cologne over the ever-present stench of dampness and stale decay. The inaction of the feet encouraged him to attempt to move again. Pushing with his arms, he began to raise his face from the carpet. Sharp pain stabbed between his shoulder blades, inducing such agony that he felt the need to vomit.

The hands that grabbed him belonged to people who ignored his pleas to be 'left alone'. They dragged him over then upwards onto a hard backed chair. He tried to lean forward to ease the pain in his body but viciously he was pushed back into the sitting position. Screwing his eyes shut in the hope of controlling the stabbing discomforts that ravaged his body, Matt gasped through the involuntary retching his misery demanded.

"What the fuck do you want?"

"Shut up."

Matt recognised the voice that replied and struggled to open his eyes.

When he was able to look around, he saw his Landlord, Mr Patel, standing by a younger Asian man. He could also sense someone standing behind him; he was uncomfortably close and stood with an air of menace. Matt gulped air to control his breathing and subdue the constant need to vomit.

"What do you want?"

"My rent, what else would I want from you?"

"Look I haven't got it."

"I guessed as much. So what are we going to do about that?"

"I'm sure I will get a job soon and when I am paid I will pay everything I owe you."

"So you are asking me to wait for my money?"

"Yeah, yeah I am."

"What kind of interest do you think you should pay on these outstanding monies?"

"You what?"

"Well if I am going to lend you the rent until you can pay it, I expect interest."

"Ok what would you suggest?"

Mr Patel made a point of breathing deeply and examining his own fingernails whilst he shuffled his feet. The room seemed to be waiting for him to talk then slowly he raised his face to meet Matt's gaze.

"Fuck off you deadbeat, I'll never see my money from you. Here's what we are going to do. My nephews will go through all your belongings and select everything they can sell on, then they will throw what is worthless, that includes you, out of the flat. You might have noticed also, when you were trying to open the door that I have already changed the locks."

Matt tried to get to his feet but a hand, slapped down hard on his shoulder, caught him before he could fully extend his legs and forced him back into the chair.

A cold sweat was forming on his brow and down his spine as he gained a full understanding of the intransigence of his circumstance. He felt panic rising inside as he contemplated the possible consequences of his situation. Mr Patel had the confidence of a person fully in control. It occurred to Matt that this was clearly not the first time that his Landlord had found himself in the position of captor, tormentor and avenger. Mouth hanging open in despair and eyes pleadingly wide, he gasped at the owner of the hovel.

"I have nothing. I don't want to be like this but I am."

"You fucked with the wrong man when you stole my rent."

"I didn't steal it. I just needed it to see my little girl."

"Two months' rent money! That is an expensive bus ticket."

"No I needed to buy her a gift and to have money to take her out and I saw her more than once."

"It's just tough shit that her 'Daddy' is a waste of flesh."

"It's not my fault."

"It's never your types fault, is it? Well you fucked with the wrong Packie when you fucked with me arsehole."

"I don't want to fuck with you. I am just asking for you to show some compassion."

Mr Patel stared at him with a look of amusement on his face.

"Empty your pockets."

"What?"

The Goon behind him cuffed the back of his head viciously and with that, Matt fully understood his Landlord's command. Cautiously he trawled through the pockets of his coat, jacket and trousers whilst he tried to balance the contents that he found in his lap. The Henchman standing beside Patel stepped forward and kicked his legs apart, causing his belongings to spill onto the floor between them. Matt looked askant at his assailant who motioned with a jabbing index finger that he should continue to empty his pockets.

Slapping his hands on his hips, Matt indicated that his pockets were empty and then with two open hands he gestured to the pitiful pile of belongings lying on the floor before him. Patel stepped forward and crouched to inspect his Tenant's belongings, immediately he seized the mobile 'phone lying on the floor and held it up before his face.

"Not so poor that you can't afford a mobile telephone, eh?"

"It's 'Pay as You Go' and I've no credit at the moment."

"Still the 'phone itself will be worth something."

"Please don't take that, it's the only way I have of contacting my Ex and our daughter?"

Patel gazed impassively as he casually put the 'phone into his own pocket and another vicious cuff to back of the head, silenced Matt's protestations.

Picking up the wallet, he flicked through the dividing leaves and explored the pockets with an extended finger until he triumphantly pulled out the small plastic card.

"Ah ha, a bank card."

"There is nothing in the account."

"We'll need your PIN to check that for ourselves, thank you."

"I'm not going to give you my PIN."

Mr Patel held up his hand in a halting manner to stay the hand of his Henchman and then returned his attention to Matt.

"Are you sure about that?"

"Yes, yes I am."

"Ok we will see about that."

With a barely audible groan, the Landlord got to his feet and with a sweep of his head issued his orders to the Henchmen.

When the Henchman moved towards him, Matt instinctually pressed his back against the chair in a vain attempt to maintain the distance between them. In an instance, the arms behind the chair wrapped both him and the chair back in a bear hug. The advancing man pulled a handkerchief from his trouser pocket, balled it in his left hand, and stood menacingly before Matt. Patel moved to the side of the curious formation and spoke softly.

"What is your PIN?"

When Matt tried to reply, the balled handkerchief was thrust forward, filling his mouth and gagging him. With an unpleasant smile on his face, the man in front of Matt pulled a gas cigarette lighter from his jacket pocket and sparked the flame into life. Slowly he pushed the flame towards Matt's face. He could feel the end of his nose getting warmer. With a final flourish, the Goon applied the flame to Matt's septum. The pain was excruciating. It felt as though his entire face was on fire. He gagged on the handkerchief as he tried to scream and writhed in the arms of the man restraining him. Twitching as in a fit and moaning a deep woeful lament, Matt could only suffer until his tormentor seen fit to cease the violation.

Suddenly, with rapid precision, the torturer let the lighter extinguish and pulled the handkerchief from Matt's mouth. The Landlord crouched down by his victim and leaned in.

"What is your PIN?"

Gasping and sweating profusely, Matt shook in the arms that embraced him, holding him close in his suffering. With obvious effort, he allowed his head to loll over to face Mr Patel.

"Three, zero, seven, four."

Triumphantly, Patel stood upright and clapped his hands together.

"Good. Thank you for not making us have to continue with such Barbaric measures. We shall see how much of my money we can recover from your account later."

With a wave of his hand, the Landlord dismissed his men and they left the room. Matt and Patel stared at each other but neither spoke a word.

Eventually the Goons returned with black bin-liners bulging with what Matt could only guess was the better items of his clothing, bedding and towels. They dumped the bags on the floor and left the room again for a short period prior to returning with all of Matt's baggage, all but one of which were clearly full. One of Patel's apes carried the briefcase that he used to store all of his personal documents. His Landlord grabbed the briefcase and opened it. Passport, birth certificate, driver's license were all slipped into Mr Patel's inside pocket.

"I will always find a market for these, Thank you Matt."

Curiously, Matt noted that this was the first time his tormentor used his name. It had not been a formal address, it had sounded almost friendly, adding to the perceived unreality of his situation. The only real thing he could be certain of was the throbbing pain in centre of his face.

His portable television was un-plugged and packed into the semi-empty holdall the Goons had brought back from the bedroom. Matt felt a lurch of panic when he saw that one of the enforcers had collected all of the photographs he had placed around the flat of Lily and Lucy. The ape pulled all of the photos from their frames and dropped the empty frames into the bag with the TV. Patel leant down to where his assistant had let the photos drop on the floor and gathered them into a pile, which he held in his hand. Matt almost reached out to receive the photos but thought better of it when he realised that they were not being offered to him.

"All of the stuff you see before you is now my property."

Matt stared blankly back at him and did not confirm or deny.

"Do you understand?"

Again, he maintained his silence. He was angry again and wanted to fight back. His rising belligerence was not lost on Patel who, snapping his fingers and held his hand out to one of his men. The Henchman rummaged in his jacket pocket as the Landlord spoke to Matt in a cold voice.

"I see you feel that I am unjust in my business dealings."

Then taking the lighter his Goon proffered, Patel lit the corner of one of Matt's photographs. Matt lurched forward in an attempt to rescue the image of his wife and daughter from the flame. The sudden movement caught the attention of the other two men who reacted instantly, they caught Matt as he moved and restrained him, howling and kicking. Patel burned every photograph Matt possessed of his family.

He wept with rage, pain and loss. Prone on the stinking carpet, he fondled the blackened ashes of his photographs that shattered silently with the slightest pressure from his fingers. Patel and his men enjoyed Matt's suffering and misery for a moment before the Landlord gave orders for him to be removed.

The fingers pushed into his hair and then locked onto a great handful. His hair pulled him forward on his hands and knees. Frantically he swung a couple of haymakers at the thug's shins. He walked backwards, dragging Matt with him. Flopping out of the front door onto the landing, a boot helping him on his way, Matt landed heavily and lay for a moment whilst he listed to the door slamming behind him.

After rolling into the sitting position, Matt struggled to his feet and began pounding on the door.

"Let me in you bastards! Give me my stuff back!"

The door swung open again and a clenched fist rammed into his face, causing pain to explode from his damaged nose and Matt to fall backwards onto his backside. Cautiously cradling his wounded nose, Matt peered through his tear-filled eyes at the front door of his old abode.

It appeared to float through the air as it advanced on his position. The black bin liner's velocity increased in the final stages of its approach, catching Matt unawares as it ballooned into his face. Slapping the bin liner aside, he swung his head back to face the door. Mr Patel stood in the doorway with his Henchmen behind him.

"Now fuck off or I shall have my nephews kick you down every stair."
The door slammed shut again and Matt could hear raucous laughter from inside the hovel. Tears running down his cheeks, he pulled the bin liner to him and lurched to his feet then moved, brokenly, down the stairwell.

The unmanaged woodland on the opposite bank of the canal formed in the rising dawn light. Black veins of lignum bearing caps and epaulettes of translucent snow, all gilded with the silver of extreme cold. As he scanned the far bank, the dense air magnified every detail of the frozen vista. He moved only his eyeballs, as he dare not disturb any other part of his ice-covered body. Four wheels on sticks sat on the surface of the frozen water, like the amputated limbs of a shopping trolley, deceiving the onlooker, as the trolley was intact beneath the ice. It had been a very cold night, surprisingly cold as it was now early April. The dawn had arrived at the earlier springtime but winter continued to exert its influence.

The black bin liner contained some clothes, mostly with holes in, and a pair of tennis shoes. Trying to protect against the hellish cold of the night, Matt had dressed in as many of the garments as he could. He lay on the bench gazing, unfocussed, across the canal at the sharp mono-chromed vista, born of the morning's grey. His corpse-like stillness belied the tempest within his head.

When he had stumbled from the external door into the easing snow of the previous evening, he had intended to make directly for the Police Station. He had hoped to gain justice and retribution for the misdeeds done to him.

With the bin liner slung over his shoulder, he shambled through the darkened streets on pavements of snow, like some Father Christmas from an anti-matter universe. He stopped when the Police Station came into view and considered his next action, it was then that it struck him, perhaps there was more at play than he had previously considered. Then with flashing visions and thoughts, exploding in his mind Matt had turned and wandered back into the night to consider, more fully, his next course of action.

His reflective wanderings had eventually taken him to the canal where he found the bench that served as his bed for the night. Sleep would not come. Every time he approached the point of slumber, his body would shiver so violently, that he was denied the only state of being that might have relieved his pain.

Matt had been, unwittingly, a bad person. He fought against the divine plan and bemoaned his misfortune at every turn. It was time to embrace some truths and a new way. Matt was convinced that it was the cardinal truth of his existence and that he be with Lily and Lucy. That was his purpose in the World and the role that he had in the great plan. He had defied the plan by having the affair with Vanya, and for that, he had been punished.

Angels and Demons walk amongst us, their roles contrary to each other's. Angels wish to keep us in line with the great plan and Demons try to draw us from the planned path. The previously unseen truth flooded into his head as each part fell into place. The woman he had always hated, the woman who ran him over and damaged his brain was actually an Angel. The damage she did to his mind was to ensure that, if he should drift from the path, he would destroy himself, as he had indeed done. The women he had slept with or treated inappropriately were Demons always trying to pull him from the plan.

When Lily had thrown him out of his home, he had felt that his life had fallen apart. He now knew that he had been wrong. That windy wet night back at the very death of summer, when he had driven to the hotel, his life had ended but it was then that his journey out of the world, in which he had previously dwelt, began. On numerous occasions when he had been in the World of the living, he had wandered far from the planned path and so now, he must serve in purgatory until he had paid in pain and suffering, the debt he owed.

Matt lay, unfocussed, on the bench contemplating purgatory and those that might exist there. Then staring out across the canal, all he could feel was loneliness and loss. He was scared; he was a non-person, all memories of him erased, every trace dissolved and all lines of communication cut. He was now as utterly alone as any being could possibly be. Looked for but never seen, listened for and never heard, felt for, never touched.

Chapter 38

When working on a major case he missed the morning routine that he and Mirren had established over many years of marriage. There was much to do and pressure was building for Mac Gregor to be replaced as the lead Detective on the serial killer case. He should have been at the Station early that morning but he had decided he would treat himself to his wife's company for breakfast.

Gazing across the table, he thought to himself, how wonderful she was. When he was in the shower, she had risen and prepared their breakfast. She now sat at the table in her dressing gown, the morning sun shining on her brushed hair. Like most woman of her age, she coloured her hair. Though grey roots betrayed her advancing years, he continued to see her as the pretty girl he had met in the village pub back home in Scotland. Radiant complexion contrasting with her raven hair and eyes that shone with a joyous life force that could have been the very essence of love, imprinted on his mind and he had loved her from that moment. She could have chosen any of the eligible young men that lived in the village or the glens surrounding, however, she had chosen him.

He loved the way she had decided that they would be together for the rest of their lives and having made that decision, she demonstrated her formidable resolve by working in every way she could to make it happen. The day they had married, they became one. Their strength was as a family unit and never as individual. She was the lady of his hearth fire, always there to support him, selflessly caring for him and their daughters and he was her man, providing, protecting and comforting.

When he had transferred from the Tayside Constabulary to the Metropolitan Police Force, Mirren had been pregnant with their eldest daughter. Together they had faced the challenge of a new family in a new country. He knew that he would never have done it without her, without her support, he would have given up on London and returned home months after arriving in the English Capital.

His had been a steady career. He had gradually advanced through the ranks until he achieved Detective Inspector, he would go no further and did not care, he was happy that he had done his best and had always done the right thing by people. There was only a few years remaining before he could retire and take his pension and wife back home to Scotland. Their daughters would probably remain in England and he looked forward to them visiting, hopefully with grandchildren.

Mary Mac Gregor looked up from her breakfast and met his gaze. Initially she looked a little puzzled then smiling, she told him that she loved him. Mac Gregor returned the compliment and drank the last of the coffee in his cup. Reluctantly he stood up from the table.

"Mirren, Darling, I have to get going."

"Ok Dear, have a nice day and look after yourself."

"I always do. See you later."

"Love you."

"I love you too."

Swinging his jacket about his shoulders, he thrust his arms into the sleeves and shrugged it to settle. Patting his pockets to confirm the required contents, he picked up his keys, kissed his wife and left.

Predictably, traffic was heavy as he drove to the station. It was a warm morning and the day threatened to become uncomfortably hot. Mac Gregor adjusted the air conditioning as he pulled away from the give-way line onto a roundabout. Negotiating the lanes, he exited onto the dual carriageway that took him the final distance to the Station.

The car park was busy and he had to park on the row furthest from the Station entrance. Stepping from the cool interior of the car, Mac Gregor arched his neck to look up at the cloudless sky, pastel blue. He used the car key to blip the lock and walked slowly through the parked vehicles to the entrance.

When he entered the incident room, Mac Gregor could sense a peculiar atmosphere. All the detectives present were studiously peering at papers on their desks, the usual chatter punctuated with laughter, absent. There was a subdued greeting from detectives as he passed their desks en route to his office. Stopping, he turned and asked, to no one in particular.

"Has anyone seen Sergeant Gayle?"

"He is in your office Guv, with Superintendent Forester."

He wanted to ask more but realised he had not noticed who had answered him and he did not want to interrogate his entire team.

He stood to the side of the office door and looked through the open blind that covered the internal window. Forester looked comfortable, sat at Mac Gregor's desk, nodding intently with a grave look on his face. Tommo Gayle sat the other side of the desk with his back to the door, gesticulating as he talked. He pondered on what they were discussing for a moment until Forester noticed him and stood, gesticulating for him to join them. When the Superintendent stood up from the desk, Tommo glance furtively over his shoulder at Mac Gregor.

The office was very warm and smelled as though both men had been in occupancy for a considerable period. Forester held his hand out to indicate that Mac Gregor should take the vacant seat next to Tommo.

"Ah Mac Gregor, nice of you to join us. Sergeant Gayle here has been filling me in on your investigation."

"Good tae see ye too Sir. Tae whit dae we owe the honour?"

"Just thought that I needed to acquaint myself with the details of your case."

"Have ye no been getting' ma briefings Sir?"

"I have Mac Gregor and thank you for that, but I just felt that I needed a face to face briefing and as you were not here, your sergeant stepped into the breach. I hope you do not mind?"

"Not at all Sir. Ah hope he's telt you everything."

"He has been most helpful. Now I just have a few questions that perhaps you can help me with."

"Ah will dae ma best Sir."

Holding Tommo with a challenging glare, Mac Gregor settled into the chair then returned his attention to Forester.

"Whit can ah tell ye Sir,"

"I believe that you have a press conference this afternoon."

"That's right Sir."

"You also have a 'sting' operation planned for Saturday to catch the killer."

"Absolutely correct Sir."

"Do you plan to release the internet aspect of this case to the press?"

"No Sir, Ah do not."

"Why not?"

"It could alert oor murderer and blow Saturday's op."

"It could also save another potential victim's life."

"There is that tae, bit ah think we need tae be bold so that we can get this character. This is oor best shot."

"And if he kills again before Saturday?"

"That would be unfortunate bit I really believe if we dinnae get him wi this op it could be months before we get this close again, how many could he kill in that time?"

"So you are willing to run the risk that the killer is able to stalk his victims via a specific media, that we are fully aware of, and not warn the public?"

"Aye Sir ah am."

"Bold move Mac Gregor, I hope for your sake you are right."

"So dae ah Sir."

"Well good luck, both of you, keep me informed."

"Sir."

They both stood when the senior officer rose to leave the room. They remained standing for an awkward moment after Forester had left until Mac Gregor reclaimed his seat behind his desk. Sergeant Gayle remained standing, expectantly waiting for the Inspector to speak. After checking for messages on his desk, Mac Gregor raised his head and held Tommos gaze.

"Well suppose ye sit doon and brief me noo."

"Yes Guv."

"Ah ken most o' it so jist tell me the latest oan the internet developments."

"Sean has taken the bait, hook line and sinker Guv. We have not managed to gain a telephone number from him

291

yet but we are trying. He is well educated or at least his grammar and spelling are excellent. "

"Aye well we guessed as much. Whit has he been askin fir?"

"He's been asking a lot about previous sexual activities and we have sent him a few juicy tales. Last night he detailed what he wanted to happen on the date."

"Oh Aye, whit has he in mind fir this romantic liaison?"

"After their meal he wants our character to lead the way to a dark corner, lift her skirt, drop her knickers and bend over to wait for him."

"Aye he's a kinky one and that pose would fit wi the positions that all oor victims were found in. So that is how he does it, they think it is aw part o' a kinky game, until he batters them oan the back o' the heid wi a hammer. We've goat a right nasty bastard here Tommo and a very manipulative individual. A sociopath."

"How are we going to approach this then Guv?"

Mac Gregor stood and began to pace the office floor then stopped by the external window and stared out over the car park.

"Right Tommo, we hae a time, date and location. Pick a volunteer whey could pass fir the images we pit oan line and make sure she is dressed like Sean wants her tae be. We shall drop her in a taxi at The Rosa where she can wait for him. When he approaches her and she confirms its Sean we will move in. I want uniform back-up, well oot o sight, the tables nearest the door tae the restaurant occupied wi officers and the rest in a vehicle parked ootside. We can expect him tae be cautious but he is also likely tae be arrogant and that might make him careless."

"Sounds like a good plan to me Guv."

He considered his plan for a second then sat back behind his desk and considered his Sergeant. Tommo was clearly uncomfortable with his Inspectors close attention and began to fidget in his seat.

"Whit dae ye think Tommo?"

"About what Guv?"

"Aboot the press conference."

"What about it?"

"Dae ye think that Forester is right?"

"About what?"

"Telling the press aboot the internet link."

"He never said that Guv."

"He didnae need tae."

"Well I'm with you Guv."

"Are ye, are ye really?"

Mac Gregor sat deadpan as he looked across the desk at Tommo.

"I am Guv. Come on let's get this bastard."

"We'll dae oor best. Noo off yae go and start gettin the teams organised fir Saturday."

"Roger Guv."

Sergeant Gayle looked almost relieved to be dismissed from the office as he closed the door behind him and walked briskly across the incident room. Mac Gregor watched him intently as he semi-swaggered between the desks and flat-handed the exit open. It irritated him that he had given Tommo a direct order that he could only obey by working in the incident room yet he had walked directly out of the exit towards an unknown destination. He maintained a vigil on the portal long enough to establish that his Sergeant had not left simply to use the bathroom. 'Slimy little twat' Mac Gregor thought to himself as he pulled his main case-file from the drawer and opened it on his desk.

Flicking through the statements, photos of the victims and the crime scene reports, his mind became numb to the tragic contents of the file. With his mental detachment came the broad thoughts of injustice. He felt angry, very angry, that someone could move about the precincts with seeming impunity, corrupting and murdering. Mac Gregor was fully cognisant of the victims' iniquities; nevertheless, he felt a deep-seated guilt on behalf of society. Those women should have been protected from the predatory lusus naturae that he hunted, yet they were not and now they were dead. The many years he spent in the force had hardened his exterior persona, inside however, he remained as vulnerable as he had been as a schoolboy. Every time a person lost their life, a victim abandoned in fear and innocence lost too soon, he felt pain in his soul.

As a boy in his village, he had learned to hate injustice. He had listened to tales that the old people of his community told of the Highland Clearances, Fuadach nan Gàidheal as they would say in their native tongue. That disgraceful period of human history, where greed drove absent landlords, most of whom were of the indigenous patriarchal stock, to destroy the lives of others with their repugnant avarice. The Countess of Sutherland and her English husband being amongst the worst of the rapists but by no means alone as they were joined by many, not least of which: Gordon, MacDonell and MacLeod on the roll of shame. Tales of their vile bullying usury and indifference to their fellow man, infuriated young Mac Gregor. It was then that he vowed to do something with his life and fight against the animals that would harm others for their own pleasure or gain.

Injustice was not unique to his native land. When he had made the move south of the border, he was conscious of equal, albeit not as devastating, social injustices visited upon the English. The Enclosures Act of 1809, again, the pursuit off profit and progress for the benefit of the few at the expense of the common rights of man. The theft of common land from the many so that the favoured select would flourish. Filthy dogs feeding on the corpse of a Nation, slain by the shepherds; shepherds elected by those that stood to gain. The granting of pseudo-power in exchange for the freedom to exploit, to rape, to harm, to re-seize the divine rights of Kings borne not of birthright but of connection.

He was convinced that his inability to comprehend how a human being could treat another in a cruel or conscienceless manner had been a limiting factor in his career as a Detective. The ability to empathise with the criminal has frequently assisted his colleagues to second-guess the bad guys, he however, had never been able to do that. Mac Gregor was a good man and he would not change that for anything but his inherent goodness was a hindrance that he had only become aware of within the recent years. Tired of the evil that men do, the Machiavellian backbiting of the law enforcement agencies, the poisonous self-serving duplicity of their political masters and the moral feebleness of the ill-educated masses, he felt that it was time to go; time to retire from the urban world, time to have little contact with his fellow man and time to find his own peace.

In his mind, he could vividly imagine the scene when those foolishly licentious women would offer their backsides to a stranger, waiting for illicit carnal pleasure that never occurred. Instead, they would be brutally killed by a cold, calculating monster with motivations all of his own. Closing in on them as they waited submissively posed, then at the heightening moment of anticipation he would strike, only pain, death and mourning resulted from his callous acts. Orphans and widowers left with the harsh intimate knowledge of deceit and no way to seek closure for the remainder of their lives. This case reeked of evil, more so than any other he had dealt with. If Mac Gregor were to find any form of peace, he would have to find this man; Sean as he styled himself, The Hammer as the press now referred to him.

The malevolence of these crimes sickened him to the pit of his stomach. In his heart, he wanted to take his daughters with him when eventually he and Mary returned to the relative sanctum of the Highlands. Middle-age pragmatism gave him the sure knowledge that there was no argument he could use that would convince his children to follow them. They would insist on finding their own way home. On a daily basis, he fought the primal urge to lecture those he loved on the dangers that surrounded them. In deference to their happiness, he chose every time to keep the darkness he saw from them. Assuring their ignorant happiness increased his own sense of responsibility, adding significantly to his desire to find The Hammer and by that action to leave London, the Sodom and Gomorrah of this land, a safer place for his girls.

It frustrated him that he had an internal battle to fight whilst he sought the killer. Tommo Gayle, for his own reasons, was trying to undermine him. Over the years, Mac Gregor had made enemies within the force and now one of his most vehement, and senior, enemies was using his Sergeant against him. When he was handed this case, he had not considered it unusual or sinister that his usual partner, Bruce Willox had been replaced and he was allocated a Sergeant

Tommo Gayle. In retrospect, there did seem to be some agenda or intent, driving the incidents surrounding the case and he was unable to define them. It could be that Forester was prosecuting a vendetta against him in order to discredit him and have him removed to some 'backwater' to wait out his remaining years. It could be that Gayle had ingratiated himself somehow with Forester and was working hard to destroy Mac Gregor's career and by that action, assure his own promotion. Either way he would have to watch his own back. Willox was a good man and he knew that he could trust him, but they were separated, leaving him exposed.

When he checked his watch, he realised that nearly an hour had passed since he had dismissed Sergeant Gayle. A brief scan of the incident room established that Tommo was not tending to the duties he had given him. Mac Gregor considered his options briefly before he sprang to his feet and marched out of the office and through the incident room, ignoring the curious faces that lifted from the work before them as he passed.

The stairwell had the ubiquitous odour of disinfectant and dirty water that pervaded the uncarpeted parts of the building. He climbed the stairs two at a time until reached the fourth floor. Mac Gregor's proximity pass would not gain him access through the door to the carpeted hallway and the offices beyond, so he loitered three steps from the top. When a figure appeared in the narrow wired glass window in the door, he resumed his assent. When the magnetic lock de-activated with a clunking click, he pulled the door open and stood back to allow the civilian administrator to pass. She returned his chirpy "Good afternoon" and descended the stairs with echoing clacks of her heels on the bare steps.

With renewed urgency, he pressed on through the corridor to Forester's office. Glancing in through the door window as he passed Mac Gregor confirmed his suspicions. Tommo Gayle sat before Forester's desk and the Superintendent sat facing him with the same look of studied concentration on his face that he had worn earlier. He checked over his shoulder that the corridor was empty before he swung round and returned to the office door.

Giving two loud raps on the door, he opened it, without waiting for a summons, and entered.

"Sorry tae disturb you Sir but a need a word wi Sergeant Gayle."

"What the bloody hell are you doing up here Mac Gregor?"

Superintendent Forester's usual air of indifferent superiority was briefly lost when the troublesome Detective Inspector burst through his office door.

"As ah said Sir, my apologies for the intrusion bit ah dae need tae speak wi Sargent Gayle here."

"Sergeant Gayle and I are in a meeting."

"As a said Sir…"

"I heard what you said Detective Inspector but you have no business being on this floor unless you have been invited and you have not been invited."

"Maybe you should review yer security Sir 'cause ah jist walked in here."

"Don't be flippant with me Mac Gregor and get out."

"Bit as a said Sir a need tae speak…"

Forester's practiced restraint failed him and he snapped to his feet.

"Get out of my office now or I shall have you on report!"

"Bit Sir it's important, it's aboot the case."

"Get out!"

The senior officer stood with his straight arm and index finger pointing to the door. He was shaking and his face was growing an evermore-deeper shade of scarlet. Tommo Gayle sat quietly, trying to make himself as invisible as he could.

"Sorry Sir a'll leave right away."

Backing out of the office, Mac Gregor closed the door as quietly as he could and stood peering through the door window at Forester. When he was sure that the Superintendent was about to explode, he disappeared from his view and retraced his steps to the stairwell and down to his own office.

He sat down softly into his chair and considered his own actions. It was not yet fully apparent what his appearance on the fourth floor would ultimately lead to but he had the satisfaction of irritating Forester, making Tommo feel very uncomfortable and letting both of them know that he knew that there was something going on. His immediate hope was that his interruption would flush them out and force them to show their hands sooner rather than later.

The feeling of short-term triumph faded rapidly and Mac Gregor began to feel isolated and vulnerable. Reaching across his desk, he lifted the handset from the telephone and dialled. The reassuringly familiar voice of Bruce Willox answered.

"DS Willox, CID."

"Bruce, you fancy a coffee?"

"You buying Guv."

"Aye."

"See you in the canteen in ten then."

"See you then."

Hanging and standing up, he glanced about his office then wandered out to the incident room, where he chatted briefly with a few of his team before leaving for the canteen.

Cheap pine tables and chairs lined either side of the canteen, prints of lakes and landscapes hung at regular intervals on the walls above the tables. It was lunchtime and the place was busy with uniformed and plain clothed Police Officers. At one table the civilian support staff had congregated to wait out the entirety of their one hour lunch break, fat ladies munching on salads, stodgy puddings and packets of crisps then washing their meals down with tins of diet coke. The air was thick with the smells of economically prepared foodstuffs and the noise of eclectic conversations.

Bruce Willox was already standing in the queue. Mac Gregor joined him in the slow but gradual progress towards the till.

"Just in time Guv, I thought I was going to have to pay for these."

He indicated the two coffees that sat on the tray that he pushed along the metal guide rails.

"Aye and that would hiv broke the bank eh?"

"Well we are not all on Inspector's salary you know."

"Only a matter o' time Bruce lad, ye ken that."

"Well I do hope so; my kids just keep getting more expensive."

Reaching the end of the guide rail, Bruce stepped back to allow Mac Gregor to pay the peculiar lady that manned the till. He rummaged in his trouser pockets until he was able to draw all of his change out in a cupped hand and picked through it until he had selected the exact amount. Dropping the change into the extended expectant hand, they turned and searched for two vacant seats.

Spotting two Detective Constables sat at one of the round smaller tables by the entrance, Mac Gregor made a bee-line for them.

"Should youz two no be upstairs pull taegether the family report oan the last victim?"

The DCs looked up from their conversation in mild surprised before they recognised who had spoken, they then began to move rapidly, finishing their drinks and vacating the table.

"Yes Sir, just having a short break. We're off now."

"Guid and if ye see Sergeant Gayle tell him tae wait fir me in the incident room."

"Yes Sir."

Briskly the junior Detectives left the room, dropping the empty tins into the recycle bin as they went.

Mac Gregor watched them go before he sat down to join Willox at the table.

"What's on your mind Guv?"

"Whit makes ye say that?"

"You rarely invite me for coffee unless there is something bothering you and you want to talk with me about it."

"Aye Bruce ye ken me well."

"Well what is it Guv?"

"What dae ye really ken aboot Gayle?"

"I was right then?"

"Right aboot whit?"

"Hc's up to something."

"Aye a guess ye were."

"All I know is that he is an ambitious smart ass. I've been on a few courses with him and can't say that I like the man."

"In whit way?"

"He thinks he knows it all and that us older Coppers can't teach him anything. He resents the fact that he is not fast-tracked to greater things and blames the likes of us for that."

"Aye you said as much thae other night. Whit's he like as a man?"

"Cowardly smart ass, smiling snake."

"Whit dae ye mean?"

"I was on a course with him six months ago and he spent the first three days smart mouthing Baz Williams. Now you know Baz, nicer guy, you could not meet; bit thick at times but fundamentally a good Copper. Well you know it takes a lot rile him but once he's riled best not be the one to have upset him. Anyway Tommo kept at him for three days then that evening we were all in the club having a drink and he starts on Baz again but this time Baz has had enough and asked Tommo outside."

"Whit did the wee snake dae at that?"

"Shit himself. Wouldn't go outside with Baz. Just sat there, quoting standards of behaviour expected of a Police Officer."

"How did Baz take that?"

"Not well, he stood over Tommo for nearly ten minutes shouting at him that he was a weasely little cunt and that he was going to get his head kicked in if he didn't shut his mouth."

"So did Tommo dae anything?"

"Not that night, he just sat there staring at his pint and reciting standards. The following morning he reported the incident and had Baz kicked off the course."

"Wee shite."

"You said it Guv. After that even the other smart arses on the course would have nothing to do with him."

They paused as both men reflected on what had been said and what they wanted to say. The clattering of crockery when their cups were returned to their saucers broke the silence and Mac Gregor leaned forward.

"Whit connection does Gayle hae wi' Forester?"

"They used to work together in C Division."

"Is there any smell aboot them?"

"Sorry Guv, not that I am aware of, pure as the driven snow."

"So whit can it be that those two are so paly aw o a sudden?"

"Are you sure of that Guv?"

"Aye."

Mac Gregor relayed the details of recent events to Bruce Willox, who sat quietly listening to the detail and waited for his Inspector to finish.

"Sounds to me Guv, like you've been given a viper."

"Aye it does."

"I'll do my best to watch your back but I'm not so close to you now so you will have to do a good job of that yourself."

"Aye cheers fir that Bruce, I'll see you later. Maybe we can go for a pint again when things quieten down?"

"That'll be good Guv, just no more fighting this time."

"Aye look wheas talkin'."

With that, he stood up and walked to the door, leaving his cup and saucer on the table.

Bruce Willox watched him go. He liked Mac Gregor, he was a good man and a loyal man. He had learnt much from working with him but sorely wished that Mac Gregor had learnt from working with him. Mac Gregor biggest problem was that he was not a political creature. He hated the politics of the job and had always avoided playing games, preferring instead to concentrate on doing what he saw the job to be, protecting the public.

They were clearly setting Mac Gregor up for a fall and no doubt Forester was behind it with that little turd Gayle feeding him all the ammunition he needed to destroy the old boy. He wished that he could help his old boss more, as he knew Mac Gregor was not up to this internal challenge. He would probably blunder in to confront any threat head on and those toadies would have predicted his behaviour so there would be a perfectly set ambush waiting for him. To Bruce Willox it was a great shame; he had enjoyed working with the cantankerous Scots git and would miss him.

301

Dawn rapidly lit the day. The curtains on the bedroom window, incandescent with the backlight of the Day Star, moved almost imperceptivity in the gentle warm morning breeze. Brian had followed the brisk illumination from the onset of the day to full daylight. He had not slept well, dozing for spells of half an hour or so throughout the night. Lying in his bed he waited for the first sounds of Thomas stirring, he would then wait for Becky to return and then he would wait until it was time to go to work. After that, he would continue to wait.

With a deep groan, he rolled onto his back, planted his feet flat on the mattress, bent his knees, opened his legs and broke wind. Arching the small of his back up, he maximised the satisfaction of the gaseous birthing experience. When he had squeezed the last of the backlogged fart through his sphincter, he relaxed his pose to lie with his legs apart and flat on the mattress. Sliding his right hand to his crotch Brian began to rub his hardening penis through the lacy satin of Becky's black thong. Her underwear was tight on him and he could feel the loose flesh of his scrotum puckering through the holes in the lace pattern.

He imagined Becky cavorting with various faceless men. In his imagination she gave herself away with abandon, howled, and moaned in an ecstasy that she never demonstrated when she was with him. Jealousy and erotic reverie flooded his mind as he pressed the emotional torment that delinquently brought him pleasure of an inexplicable primal nature.

His own, significantly more modest than Becky's imagined lover's, penis was now fully erect. Sliding it out of the side of the thong, he began to masturbate. Slowly at first as he imagined her sucking hungrily on an ample tool, then steadily faster as his fantasies jumped through a plethora of erotic scenarios until with the image in his imagination of her face and tits sprayed with copious quantities of cum, he emptied his own load over his bulging stomach.

Brian let out a low mournful moan as he rubbed his seed into the hairs on his belly then opened his eyes. He had no way of knowing how long Thomas had stood silently at the bottom of the bed, clutching his teddy and staring at his Daddy. Struggling onto his elbows and taking care to ensure that the quilt covered everything below his chest, he forced a smile to his son.

"Hey, morning big guy. How are you?"

"Mummy?"

"Mummy's not here just now Son. She will be home soon."

"Daddy crying?"

"No Son I just had a funny dream, that's all."

"Hungry."

"Ok Son you go and choose the clothes you want to wear today and

Daddy will be with you in a minute. Then we'll have breakfast."

Thomas paused uncertainly for a moment before he slowly turned and scampered off to his room.

"Bollocks" Brian muttered to himself as he struggled out of the thong beneath the covers and balled it into his hand. With obvious effort, he pulled his flabby body from beneath the duvet and stood naked before the mirror, the rapidly drying sperm pulling his stomach hair into dark spirals over the taught bag of fat that hung from his front. Donning his housecoat and dropping the soiled lingerie into the wash basket, he tied the cord about his waist and followed his son to the nursery.

Thomas had selected a T-shirt with a super hero motif and a pair of grey shorts. Brian helped his son to dress and they both went down to the kitchen for breakfast. With the top removed, Thomas set about devouring his boiled egg and soldiers with obvious relish. His father watched contentedly and sipped coffee from his mug as he listened to music from the radio.

The peace they shared shattered when Becky arrived home. Banging through the front door, keys rattling and bags bumping each other and the hallway furnishings, she announced her return with a loud "hi", the vowel sounding in an elongated upward turning inflection. Immediately distracted, Thomas fidgeted in his seat and forgot all about his breakfast as he swivelled back and forth to gain a vantage of his mother. Brian groaned inwardly when he acknowledged that a special moment he and his son were sharing was lost forever, trampled underfoot by the slut that had just burst through the door.

She swept her child off the chair and up into a close embrace, smothered him in loud kisses then carried him to his father where she bent and kissed Brian on the cheek.

"How's my two favourite boys?"

"He was eating his breakfast."

"Ok ok I have just missed my special little boy."

"He was doing really well, no playing with his food or anything."

"Ok Mr Grumpy."

Then turning Thomas to look directly into her face, she spoke in an affected voice somewhere between an imbecile and a children's TV presenter.

"Daddy's a grumpy old man isn't he? Oh yes he is."

Thomas giggled at his mother's idiotic behaviour until she placed him before his breakfast and turned her back on him.

When Brian caught her eye, she froze in incomprehension. He was smiling at her, his eyes fixed on her face. She was unused to close attention from her husband; detached disinterest was his natural demeanour when in proximity to his wife. Disinterest that extended to every aspect of her life, with the exception of her body. He would focus unwanted attention on her body when he became sexually aroused. Becky had no idea what would arouse him and had no way of predicting when she would be required to suck on his penis or open her legs and allow him to pump her with his unimpressive member.

Composing herself, Becky returned Brian's smile and cocked a hip in a coquettish gesture. He remained motionless, smiling and staring. The unease she felt grew rapidly with every passing moment. She moved her weight from one foot to the other then dropped her arms to her sides and sighed as she pretended to look around the room before returning her gaze to meet his.

"What?"

"Nothing."

She felt reassured when he answered her and her confidence began to return.

"Why are you staring at me with that stupid look on your face?"

"You think I am stupid?"

"I didn't mean that and you know it."

"No, regardless of the look on my face, do you think I am stupid?"

"Why? What has brought this on?"

"I just want to know what you think of me."

"I think you are the most wonderful, sexy man in the world and I love you."

"Do you think I'm stupid?"

"No I do not think you are stupid, silly."

"Do you think I'm silly then?"

"No. Now stop it, will you?"

Becky swayed round to his side of the table, stole a triangular slice of toast from the plate before him, and walked away, with a pronounced wiggle of her bottom. Brian followed her with cold set eyes, the smile fell from his face the moment she had turned around and eye contact was lost. His lips worked on unarticulated words and his empty hands worked on unknown tasks.

A low solitary tone broke Brian's reflection and drew his attention towards his son, sitting across the table from him watching intently, close to tears. Immediately softening his expression and adopting a smile, he reassured Thomas that all was well and sealed their relationship with a conspiratorial wink. When the boy smiled and returned his attention to his cold egg Brian stood up from the table and moved to stand directly behind Becky.

"Did you have fun last night?"

"You startled me. What are you doing sneaking up on me like that?"

"Well, did you have fun last night?"

"Yeah it was great. We had some wine and good girlie catch up."

"Catch up, what did you catch up?"

"What do you mean? You know catch up, gossip etc."

"Did you go out?"

"We did think about going down to the local but chose instead to stay in with wine."

"Just the two of you then?"

"Of course. Who else do you think would be there?"

"I don't know. Maybe you and Debbie had a stud round for an orgy."

"Don't be ridiculous, you know I would never do anything like that and I would never be unfaithful to you."

He stood allowing her previous statement to hang. Realising he had dropped the subject abruptly she resigned to the silence and returned her attention to gathering the used crockery onto the worktop by the sink.

When she eventually turned round Brian was standing exactly the same place and pose looking at her intently. In the background, Thomas was asking to leave the table. After giving her child the permission he sought, she leaned against the worktop and folded her arms.

"What is the matter with you today?"

"What do you mean?"

"This behaviour, you're acting weird. And before you say it, I don't think you're weird."

"I only asked if you had a nice time last night."

"Whatever Brian."

"Have I upset you?"

"No but you are getting on my wick acting like this."

"Sorry."

"Ok but stop being a lunatic."

"I'll try. When are you seeing her next?"

"Who?"

"Debbie."

"Oh yeah I meant to ask you, is it ok if I go out with Debbie on Friday night? It's her sister's birthday and Debs has organised a meal in town for her."

"Sorry Darling I'll be working late on Friday."

"Are you? You never mentioned it."

"We have a shipment that will clear customs late Friday Afternoon and I will have to co-ordinate the trucks to distribute it. Don't know when I'll get finished."

"Oh bugger."

"Why not ask your mother to look after Thomas?"

"That's a good idea. Would you mind if I went out?"

"No not at all. Go have a good time."

"Thank you Darling."

Leaping forward she placed her hands on his shoulders and kissed him on the cheek.

"Well I better get ready for work then."

"Ok darling."

She pulled away from Brian. He wandered out of the room and up the stairs to the bedroom.

It had surprised Becky that Brian suggested asking her mother to baby-sit. He was usually uncooperative when it came to helping her out in these situations. She was suspicious at first but a result is a result and it had been a lot easier than she had anticipated it to be. Smiling to herself, she imagined the fun she would experience on Friday.

Sean was a kinky one. Becky had been with many men, some were rubbish and some were fantastic. She always enjoyed herself with the kinky ones. It excited her when men asked her to do something for them or for her to indulge them in some kink or perversion. Men dressed in women's clothing and men in rubber masks had both thrashed about between her thighs. She had worn a large strap-on dildo and fucked several men hard from behind. She always found it curious that most men actually enjoyed being buggered. Becky was indifferent to anal sex, she would oblige if her partner wanted to stretch her ring but she would not initiate that coitus.

Over the weeks they had been communicating, Sean had asked for details of her previous sexual encounters and shared some of his experiences with her. Boasting about her nefarious activities was a big turn on for her. She also enjoyed the detailed description he had sent her of his plans and wishes for their date on Friday. With an inward thrill, she imagined bending over with her bare arse in the air and the throbbing pleasure of a big cock forcing its way into her. She did hope he was big, the photos looked like it was a big one but she

307

could never be too sure until she actually got her hands on it, so to speak. He had requested, and received, explicit pictures of Becky, the best of which showed her sucking on a huge penis. Only she knew to whom the penis belonged and she always refused to reveal its owner when she was asked by the few who had seen the image. The man behind the impressive tool was in fact her mother's ex-boyfriend. He had been living with Becky's mother when he asked her to suck him off and for him to photograph the event. He was much older than her, probably in his late sixties, and it had taken some effort to rouse his manhood to its fullest glory. Serendipity, it had been the most enjoyable blowjob she had ever given, big tool and copious amounts of cum when eventually he climaxed. She had only agreed to the act when he offered to pay her one hundred pounds. She sucked him dry and took the money; they never mentioned it again.

Men could not help getting competitive over penis size. Even Sean had remarked on the size of the old man's cock when he had seen the photograph and asked 'who it belonged to'. She supposed that men with small penises would always have an inferiority complex. It was an absolute truth, size did matter, she would never settle for a small one. Brian's little member was probably one of the major factors that kept her searching for sexual fulfilment elsewhere.

A bellowed farewell from Brian at the front door brought her back to the immediate banality of her life. Sighing she went to the front room and engaged with Thomas. Later that day she would encourage him to nap in the afternoon, she could then recount last night's activities in her mind whilst she masturbated or perhaps she could toy with her most recent fantasy where she has the youngster, David, from next door bring his friends round in the afternoon and she would service them all. She may yet make that fantasy a reality.

Chapter 40

Even the children were silent as the Mercedes cruised through the relatively light traffic. Sunlight enhanced the otherwise drab and dishevelled architecture, a myriad of Victorian, eighties and every period between. Town houses now converted to bed-sits, municipal buildings designed with the finesse of Stalin, shopping malls incongruous and impersonal, all interspersed with streets of rotting domiciles. Gradually the City's twilight zone gave way to the more affluent suburbs where the houses became increasingly detached and grandiose.

She gazed out of the passenger-side window, barely registering the passing vista, her smouldering resentment assuring sultry muteness. Abdul drove carefully, his face contorted with an inane grin that gave him the appearance of an American evangelist, confident and elated that his half-baked assertions would not be challenged by his deficient flock. Zaynab slept in her car seat and Aesha occupied herself with a small doll she had brought for that purpose. Outwardly, they appeared to be a nuclear family, travelling on a shared mission of cordial intent. Each individual in the motorcar however, had a vastly differing anticipation of the forthcoming event, none darker than Samira's.

Slowing the vehicle to a stop, Abdul lifted the indicator lever and sat tapping the steering wheel whilst he waited for the oncoming traffic to pass before manoeuvring right onto his father's driveway. The quiet roar of the gravel under the large tyres heralded their arrival and a familiar face appeared at a window by the front door. By the time the Mercedes had drawn fully to a halt, the door opened and numerous relatives issued forth to greet them.

As though startled from a dream Samira, struggled with the lever and flung the car door open. She moved quickly to the rear doors and began to retrieve her daughters only giving half-hearted responses to the numerous greetings cast her way from the gathering relatives. Carrying Zaynab in her left arm and clutching Aesha by the hand on her right, she moved through the mobbing relatives towards the front door, nodding and smiling as she went; her head full of silent screams.

Embracing his father then his mother, Abdul was gregariously returning all of the greetings and congratulations that his extended family showered on him. He moved amongst them like a conquering hero or a returning athlete with some remarkable prize, his arms extended in all directions to acknowledge the adoration he perceived to be on offer. Resplendent in his dark grey Armani suit with a red open collar silk shirt, he looked as he felt he should look. Successful, pious, family man full of virtue and benevolent to all about him, Abdul was now as he had always wished to be, respectable and loved. Slowly the dynamic of the crowd changed as Abdul reached the thinning rear of it, his progress pulling them in a rough arrowhead towards the door.

Ahead Al qasim stood in the pillared doorway with his arms folded across his chest and a tight smile etched onto his face. He felt an irrational resentment, his cousin's arrival having taken the focus away from him and Abdul's obviously expensive attire diminishing by comparison his own, more modest, costume of slacks and pullover. Irrational only in so much as he had no reason to envy this effete son of his Uncle. He was a half-man, an abomination in the eyes of God, weak in every aspect of being a man. Al qasim had had his woman and in the not-so-distant future, he would have his daughter. Sex was a powerful weapon and he would use it to conquer all that Abdul had.

They embraced warmly, kissing each other on the cheeks and slapping each other's shoulders like long parted comrades. Turning to face the gathered relatives, Abdul and Al qasim held hands and waved to the crowd before walking together into the large hallway beyond the front door.

In the reception area, hired staff stood neatly to attention bearing silver trays of fruit juice and iced tea, their pristine white coats effulgent in the relative gloom of the indoors. As the guests followed the cousins into the building, the serving staff, brought to life on a silent command, advanced to distribute refreshments. The air filled with babbling voices, numerous conversations only two subjects: the weather or the impending announcement that Aesha was to be betrothed to Al qasim. White coated automatons, having no interest in either subject and no invite beyond their functionary roles withdrew momentarily, then returned with trays of canopies.

The relatives fed differently on the trays of food, some would pick one item, which they balanced delicately on a napkin that covered one hand and others would construct small towers of food on their napkins possibly fearing that they would not see the serving staff again for the remainder of that afternoon. Samira allowed her daughters to select one samosa each then waved the attentive server away. Unlike the other guests, she had no appetite large or small for the fare or the celebration. She was a tigress; warily she watched those that, wittingly or unwittingly, threatened one of her cubs. Never leaving them, she stood guard engaging with others only to return polite greetings or passing pleasantries.

In the large reception room, she found a quiet corner where she sat with her children on big comfortable floor cushions. In that relative sanctuary, she was able to escape the constant pestering attentions of the other guests and to concentrate her attention onto Aesha and Zaynab. The room was a triumph of gaudy over decoration. Two walls lined with vividly coloured settees, luxuriously upholstered to the point that the coverings appeared to be at bursting point. Heavy drapes in red and gold hung either side of the large French windows that led to the expansive back garden. There were numerous hard backed chairs scattered about the room that despite their gouache expensiveness would not have looked out of place in an Indian restaurant. The wallpaper assaulted the eye with its brightly coloured velour stripes, clashing monstrously with the deep active patterns on the carpet. Collectively the décor was a symphony of bad taste and unbridled expenditure.

The overbearing decoration and constant clamouring of voices made Samira feel like she was being smothered. With every minute that passed, she felt increasingly cornered and with that mounting pressure, she felt fear. Fear for herself and her cubs. She wanted to strike out, to bare her teeth and show that she was not to be trifled with. The joy demonstrated so verbosely by the others angered her, the men back slapping and boastful and the women cooing and full of hopes for the future. Each unaware of the terrible sin their celebration

311

condoned, only Abdul and she fully understood the extent of the proposed abhorrence. He supported it with all his will, she opposed it equally, only one could win and as things stood, she stood to lose.

Clear repetitive ringing of a crystal glass, struck by a silver knife or some other eating utensil, sounded long enough to gather the attention of the celebrants and to silence their diverse colloquies. All eyes turned to focus onto Abdul's father as the patriarch moved to the centre of the entrance hall. His face beamed with amour-propre, cheeks radiant and eyes bright and alive with an unaccustomed vigour. With faux modesty, he held his hands up and bowed his head as if trying to duck the silent respect they showed him.

"My dearest family, I welcome you all to my humble home. It is with God's blessed will, that we have come together today in celebration. Today we celebrate because my Granddaughter is betrothed to my dear Brother Mohammed's son, Al qasim."

On cue the assembled applauded, faces of all ages cracked with broad smiles behind rapidly enthusiastic hands, beating off their opposite twin. Holding his palms up, he silenced the hand clapping.

"This union will serve to make our strong family, stronger. It will cement us into an unbreakable tribe and with God's will the union will be blessed with another generation of our kin."

There was a murmur of hopeful approval through the crowd. Abdul's father raised his voice a little to maintain attention on his words.

"Please join me in congratulating the proud fathers."

With great aplomb, he beat his palms together and turned to indicate the bottom of the staircase where Mohammed and Abdul stood side by side, Abdul resting his hand on his Uncle's shoulder. They smiled and nodded their appreciation to all as the room filled with the clattering sound of taught flesh pounded together.

The Patriarch allowed the applause to die down naturally before he demanded the family's attention again.

"My wonderful wife has arranged a banquet befitting an occasion such as this. In the dinning room there are treats to

312

tempt The Profit, peace be upon him. Please help yourself then join us in the reception room where I hope we can persuade proud fathers and the euphoric Groom to be, to honour us with a few words."

Casting his hands high, he then gesticulated grandly that all should progress towards the dinning room. Content with his efforts, he watched the crowd move with a slow shuffling gait in the direction he had indicated and waited for his brother and son to join him.

With an undulating crowd motion, the relatives gradually filtered to the dining room in a chaotic mixing of colours, bright saris, silk shirts and shiny jackets mingling together as the beings within politely jockeyed for position. When the visitors had passed Abdul's Father, the proud fathers, of the moment, joined him. They stood either side of him, allowing him to place his chubby arms about their shoulders. Few words passed between them, as they preferred the unspoken language of looks, smiles and subtle squeezing of shoulders or hands.

People began to drift into the reception room, plates heaped with food balanced in one hand and glass of fruit juice in the other. The older females perched on the settees, younger females on the floor cushions. The males either stood about, drinks resting on any flat surface to hand and plates clutched as their forks delved, or sat on the hardback chairs, drinks on the floor and plates in their laps. Samira resented their arrival, sensing her sanctuary compromised she became uneasy. Clutching her children to her, she scanned the room for potential threats.

Distracted by food and interest waning in the principal characters of the occasion, the relatives began to reserve their fawning attentions. Abdul keenly felt the loss. Enjoying his local celebrity he was determine to resurrect his popularity with the gathered audience. Through the long grass of the crowded rooms, he stalked his prey. The feeding herd in the reception room parted briefly, allowing him a clear view of his quarry. She sat neatly on a floor cushion, her mother's arm about her in a protective cordon. Surreptitiously he moved about a group of large aunts, pre-occupied with settling their ample bottoms onto an equally grotesquely upholstered settee, then ducking swiftly past a pair of gossiping cousins he closed to within striking distance.

Registering the approaching threat too late, Samira snapped her head round in surprise when she heard his voice next to them.

"There you are, Daddy's little Princess."

Abdul crouched down by his daughter's side with his arm around her tiny waist. She tried to pull her child closer but he would not relax his hold. Fixing Samira with a steady gaze, he lifted the child to him and stood to pull her further from her mother. It was too late for the tigress to keep her cub without a public scene. Pulling her remaining cub onto her lap, she watched her husband recede into the throng with his captive daughter.

Holding his cherished trophy aloft, he moved amongst the gathered people, enjoying their renewed attention. Aesha looked dazed by the interest that she and her Daddy were drawing from the affectionate strangers. Her cheeks stroked, her hair touched and numerous and various adult hands clasping hers. Together they cut an erratic furrow of adoring platitudes through the field of family. A loud commotion spread through the party and the ubiquitous cameras flashed enthusiastically when Abdul handed Aesha to Al qasim. He took the child from her father and lifted her high before settling her into his right arm. Posed with an adoring look on his face he gazed at the child in his arms and allowed his relatives to snap photographs until their rapacious appetite for the captured image was satisfied.

From a floor cushion by the French windows, Samira's eyes burned, smouldering mahogany coals piercing the ether of the room, never leaving the male predator that held her daughter. Her frontal lobes fired demands for Aesha's safe return via the medium of sight. The dark corners of her mind conjured a chimera in which those that would threaten her child were eviscerated then torn limb from limb. As the rage blazed within, she realised that she was panting and perspiring, symptoms of the anxiety she felt.

Heart racing she kept her eyes fixed, cemented with hatred, on Al qasim as he approached with Aesha in his arms. He returned her hatred with goading indifference, returning compliments to the people he passed without eye contact. The air between them seemed to crackle with the static generated from the emotion flowing from her cerebral cathode into the sink of his malevolence. Silently he halted, standing over the tigress and her cub. Without breaking their connection of execration, he bent to allow the eldest cub to return to her mother.

Only when her child had returned to the relative security of her embrace did she break the optical challenge. With gasped gulps of air, she calmed her heart rate and fought to assume an air of reassuring normality for her children. Al qasim swaggered away, glad-handing any paw proffered by his self-perceived allies, taking with him any attention that Aesha or Samira had drawn.

She started when his voice sounded from behind her.

"May I bring you something, beloved?"

Abdul's adeptness at stalking Samira and her cubs, served only to stoke the furnace of her rage. With deliberate casualness, she turned to glare at him.

"No."

"What about our children."

"They need nothing from you."

"Ok, if you change your mind just call me."

He spoke with obtuse cheerfulness. She turned away sharply with a sickened gasp. After a hanging moment of awkwardness, he returned to the fawning attentions of his relatives, leaving his wife to her dark mood.

An expectant silence spread throughout the room when Abdul's father stood in front of a flattering portrait of himself, hung over the vulgar fireplace. Effeminately he briefly inspected his fingernails then clasped his hands before him. That was the cue for the party to give him their undivided attentions.

"The time has come my beloved family, for us to hear from our most honoured and important guests. First of all, I would ask the fathers to honour us with their thoughts on this magnificent day when we have all come together to celebrate the betrothal of Aesha to Al qasim."

As he spoke, he moved his hands in unison to indicate the subjects of his speech.

"Firstly I would invite you to give your attention to my beloved brother, Mohammed."
With overt graciousness, he applauded as he relinquished the 'limelight' to his brother.

Almost serenely, Mohammed took centre stage. With affected indifference to the applause the audience showered on him, he drifted to the spot Abdul's father had previously occupied and primed himself before delivering his speech. A monologue of pious gratitude to God for his blessings and a reminder to all that they should be equally grateful followed. He went on to ask the assembled guests to pray for the successful conclusion of the betrothal arrangements and for subsequent blessing. Some of the crowd showed signs of discomfort as his words grew, ever increasingly, evangelistic and there were hints of relief in the laudation that followed his conclusion.

His uncle wandered from the fireplace, hands clasped before him and eyes focussed vaguely on the middle distance. Abdul waited patiently for Mohammed to rejoin the assembled family then strode with his head held confidently high to take the position of orator. Sanctimoniously he re-iterated many of the gratuities Mohammed had pronounced. Then unctuously he craved their love and support for his wife and their children before delivering a comprehensive description of his delight with the betrothal of his daughter to Al qasim. He built a platform of lauding words for his cousin before relinquishing the stand and standing to the side where he bathed in the warm applause of his audience.

Natural arrogance radiated from Al qasim as he walked to the mark before the portrait of his host and smiled at the enthusiastically applauding family. His role of intended groom, assured him greater acclaim and he eventually had to hold his hands up to quieten his audience. He thanked all of the previous speakers before moving on to exhort the wisdom of the marriage arrangement and his absolute intention of honouring his duties as a husband. Then pausing he awaited further applause. When the anticipated hand clapping began, he held his hands aloft, again silencing the crowd, before continuing to speak.

316

"Beloved I ask your indulgence for a moment longer. May I ask my bride to be to join me up here with her beautiful mother Samira?"

All attention in the room turned to Samira, sitting on the floor cushion with her daughters. Abdul appeared by her side and took Zaynab from her, leaving her clutching Aesha. Initially she appeared terrified, then steeling herself she adopted an almost feral appearance as she stood up from the floor and carried her child towards the waiting Al qasim. He held his arm out to welcome them on to his metaphoric pedestal. As they approached, he moved his arm as if to take Aesha from her mother.

There was no warning, only swift and summary execution. Her right arm extended with super-human force to push the cold blade across Al qasim's throat, releasing a fine spray of pink into the air before him, turning to a spectacular fountain of crimson when the carotid artery severed. His initial incomprehension disassembling into terrified panic as he plunged his hand into the hot spurting plume of his blood. Mouth hanging open for a scream that would not come, red bubbles foaming at his open windpipe, he stared, eyes wide with terror, at the tigress.

Dropping the knife onto the vulgar carpet, she wondered why no one other than Al qasim had reacted to her action. Dispassionately she stood, waiting for the inevitable emotional eruption. Eventually the stunned silence, broken by an anonymous scream, was shattered and the family burst into action. Women screamed and lamented the evil that had visited the event. Men ran forward to intervene in the slaughter before the fireplace.

Aesha kept her innocent eyes on her mother as she and the other children were whisked from the room, shepherded hurriedly from the carnage. Samira looked to the ceiling where Al qasim's blood formed a fan of crimson droplets across the eggshell and gilt decoration. Strong hands grasped her upper arms and she looked down at the limp body, others were tending, at her feet. The tigress had done what she had to and her cubs were safe.

317

Detective Sergeant Bruce Willox chatted with the Custody Sergeant whilst he waited for the suspect to brought from her cell to the interview room. The Process and Detention Centre resembled the bridge of some starship from a TV show, the product of a Public Finance Initiative, the Force leased the building from a consortium of private companies who had designed, built and now operated the facility. The only Police Officers in the building were the Custody Sergeant and Willox, the arresting Officers now having departed to continue their duties after handing over custody of the suspect to the civilian Custody Officers.

From the vehicle 'airlock' to the processing suite, the custody kiosks, interview rooms and cells, the building built bespoke for purpose. Easy clean floors, unbreakable internal windows, panic alarms and immovable furnishings designed to last exactly twenty-five years, the period over which the contractual arrangement with the consortium would run. After this time, the facility would be the property of the Force, just as it would begin to fall apart. Debt repaid and all the profit drained from the project, private companies would have no further interest. The entire exercise having given benefit only to the private companies, profit, and politicians, the debt never having to appear on the Home Office's balance sheet, tax payers having to fund the massively overpriced facility for the entirety of the contractual life cycle.

The Sergeants chatted about the sterile environment they stood in, comparing it to the old facility. They agreed it was a great improvement even though it did seem to make the act of arresting a villain somehow impersonal and less satisfactory. Together they bemoaned the loss of job satisfaction and many of the old characters now retired from the Force. Draining the last of the coffee from a plastic cup Willox crumpled and tossed it towards a wastebasket on his counterpart side of the desk. The cup missed and one of the Custody Officers retrieved it from the floor, placing in the receptacle. "You're welcome," he said with obvious sarcasm. Ignoring the civilian, they continued their 'Police Only' conversation.

Incongruously a doorbell sounded, 'ding dong'. A Custody Officer behind the reception counter lifted a handset and spoke into it, then replacing the receiver he pressed a button and raised his head to catch the eye the Custody Sergeant.

"Serge that's DC Bridge, here for DS Willox."

"You let him in?"

"Yes he's in the airlock now."

The magnetic lock de-activated with a 'clunk' and DC Bridge pushed his way into the reception area. Recognising Willox he walked directly towards him.

"Hi Serge sorry it took a while, traffic's a pig, not what you would expect on a Thursday afternoon."

"Glad you could make it Dan. The suspect should be in the interview room now and one of the Custody Eagle's Civvies will have given her a cup of tea."

Bruce Willox indicated the Custody Sergeant with a flick of his head.

Pleasantries exchanged and administration confirmed complete, the two Detectives left the reception counter and moved towards a white door set in an equally unremarkable wall. The lock, released from behind the custody desk 'clunked' and they entered, pushing the door fully open. They continued down a corridor with a panic strip fitted to both walls until they turned a corner and found a Custody Officer standing opposite a door fitted with a large window. Through the window, they could see her sitting at a table, plastic cup before her. She made no movement as she sat dressed in a white paper suit, staring into her lap where her hands lay folded.

Turning to face the Custody Officer, Willox spoke quietly.

"Has she said anything?"

"Not a word."

"Done anything unusual?"

"Nothing, used the toilet in her cell once, other than that she has just laid on the mattress, staring at the ceiling."

"Is that tea in the cup she's got?"

"No she wouldn't answer me when I asked if she wanted anything so I just gave her water."

"Has she touched it?"

"Nope, it's still where I put it down."

Willox turned to Dan Bridge.

"Could have our work cut out here."

"Yeah Serge, doesn't sound like she's all that chatty."

"Well like it or not we've been handed this one. You worked a murder before?"

"No. First time for me."

"Well all I can tell you is that they are all different. Come on let's get started."

"Right behind you Serge."

She looked up from her lap to watch the Detectives as they entered the room silently. Without a word, they settled down at the table opposite her, the younger one took a small tape from his jacket pocket, unsealed it in front of her and then placed it into the machine fixed to the wall where the table joined it. The older Detective nodded and the younger man pressed the record button.

"I am Detective Sergeant Willox and this is Detective Constable Bridge. We are recording this interview. For the purposes of the tape, I would like you to confirm your identity. You are Samira Fatima Hadi?"

"Yes I am."

"You are being held on suspicion of the murder of Al qasim Mumar Hadi."

"Yes I killed him."

"Are you confessing to the murder of Mr Hadi?"

"Yes I did it."

"You understand that you are confessing to a very serious crime. A crime that can carry the maximum sentence of the law?"

"I killed him."

Willox cleared his throat and glanced fleetingly at Bridge, then returned his attention to Samira.

"In your own words can you explain what exactly happened?"

"We were at a family party. Al qasim was giving a speech and I cut his throat."

"Why did you do that?"

"I wanted to know how it felt."

"How what felt?"

"How it felt to kill a man."

"Did you intend to kill Al qasim Hadi when you arrived at the party?"

"I intended to kill a man."

"Any man?"

"Any man."

She sat placidly her eyes resting on the plastic cup in front of her. She gave no motion or gesture to support her statements, just spoke soft words in a resigned monotone. The Detectives exchanged glances to confirm their mutual surprise at the unexpected turn of events.

After confirming that she knew, what she was doing and having failed to establish any form of motive, Willox suspended the interview and left the room with Bridge. They read the case file together in a separate interview room and drank a cup of coffee each whilst Samira sat waiting.

The effort of talking had made her thirsty. The cup of water sat on the table before her and for a brief moment, she considered drinking it but decided to leave it untouched. She could hear the screaming distantly, like an annoyingly catchy tune in her head. Remembering the men trying to re-establish male dominance by strong-arming her unresisting body made her want to smile. It had clearly terrified them that a mere woman could slay a strong pious man like Al qasim with such comparative ease. Echoes of the trauma would ensure that in their vulnerable moments the family would be haunted by that demonstration of their feebleness, hopefully for the remainder of their lives.

The men had bundled her into one of the smaller reception rooms where they made her sit on a chair whilst three men stood guard. Standing around with their arms folded over their chests in as macho a stance as they could affect, they had stared in silence at the female demon that they guarded. She had heard some of the family suggest that they did not call the Police, instead she be taken to the garden and stoned or beheaded. To her it made no difference, she had saved her daughter and safeguarded the family's darkest secret. Any price would be agreeable for what she had achieved and as added value, she had enjoyed frightening the males. She remembered looking at them, their eyes wide in terror, trousers of some darkening with urine.

To her side she heard the door open and the Detectives return. This time she resisted the urge to look up, preferring to keep her eyes focussed into her lap where, through the gauze of time, she could picture the pathetic body of Al qasim lying in a pool of vital fluid. They sat opposite her, the tape machine clicked and the younger Detective announced the requisite pre-amble for the interview to resume.

"Samira."

"Yes?"

"You have told us that you went to the party with the intent of killing someone."

"No. I told you that I went to the party with the intent to kill a man."

"Is that important?"

"Yes it is."

"Why?"

"Men are pigs and they need to know."

"What do they need to know?"

"They need to know how it feels."

"How what feels Samira?"

"To be helpless."

"Did Al qasim make you feel helpless?"

"Not especially."

"Are you sure?"

"Yes."

Bruce Willox sat quietly, staring at the top of her head.

"I don't believe you Samira."

"Why?"

Willox sat back in his chair as Bridge leaned forward, the movement causing Samira to look up and directly at each of the Detectives in turn. The softer voice of Dan Bridge broke the silence.

"Because you never look us in the eye when you say it. You have two young daughters, a loving husband and a privileged lifestyle, why would you throw all that away for the momentary satisfaction of killing a man?"

"It's not momentary. I have the sensation in me and that will be with me forever."

"I think you are hiding something. What did he do to you?"

Samira stared Dan Bridge directly in the eye.

"I killed him because I wanted to kill a man. Happy?"

"No I am not, I don't buy it. You're hiding something from us."

"You may buy it or not buy it. If I am hiding something from you then that is because I do not want you to know what it is that I am hiding and so I will not tell you. I have given you all you need to resolve this case and gain retribution so why then do you wish to pursue matters further?"

"We are here to establish the true facts and to help you find the truth. You stand only to benefit from the truth."

"In your mind that may be so, in mine it is not."

The detectives altered their postures and Willox spoke.

"Samira, tell us again what you did today?"

With a loud sigh she set herself to answer, obstinately sticking to her invented rational.

"I wanted to kill a man so I went to the party and cut Al qasim's throat. I chose him at random and slaughtered him in front of all of them."

"And you will sign a statement to that effect?"

"Yes I will."

"I shall have the tape transcribed and you will sign it?"

"Yes I shall."

Willox read Samira her rights and formally charged her with the murder of Al qasim Mumar Hadi. Bridge announced the formal conclusion of the interview and terminated the recording. Both Detectives then stood; Willox gesticulated to Bridge for him to leave. Initially he looked perplexed then realising that the Sergeant wanted to speak with the suspect alone, he duly left. The Custody Officer looked uneasy as one Detective left the interview room leaving the other behind.

When Dan Bridge closed the door behind him, Willox leaned on the table and spoke quietly to his charge.

"Look Samira, I know there is more to this than you are telling us; why not tell the truth, it could only improve your position?"

"Why should I?"

"I have an old friend and colleague, he is one of the finest men I know and he would say something like this: 'Ah ken two wee lassies that need their Mummy, think o them'."
Willox felt embarrassed by his terrible Scots accent but hoped it might get through to her as if Mac Gregor himself had delivered the words. Samira sat motionless with a blank expression on her face.

Chapter 42

It had been a dreadful day. Distracted and unable to concentrate he had made numerous errors. None of his co-workers were surprised to see him sitting diligently at his desk as they packed up and left to enjoy the start of the weekend. They thought to themselves that he was probably trying to repair the damage his mistakes had done. He was tempted to join them when the Depot Manager left the office; he confirmed that Brian would lock up, then left. Every Friday evening the office staff would go to the Pub down the road for a few pints before going home and he had always enjoyed the weekly ritual, but tonight would have to be different.

Looking up from his keyboard, Brian said goodbye to the last of his colleagues to leave. Alone in the open plan office, he sat looking at the empty desks that surrounded him. Each desk had a large pile of folders stacked on the side, a telephone, keyboard and monitor. The glorious summer's evening sunlight shone through the dirty windows, set high on one wall. Ceiling tiles stained yellow from cigarette smoke, a legacy from the days when people were allowed to smoke in their place of work. Large pictures of landscapes or roads running off to some distant horizon, each with bold words of wisdom printed at the bottom, hung on the yellowed walls, paint flaking and dark scuffmarks lining the lower reaches. By the fire escape doors there was a key press mounted on the wall, its ancient wooden doors hanging open.

Distractedly Brian stood and moved randomly amongst the office furniture, stopping occasionally to look at items of interest on his work mates' desks. There was the usual tat, collected by some workers, gonks, postcards, ornate letter openers and stickers peeled from the fruit of choice for the desk's daytime occupant. The majority of his colleagues had photographs of their loved ones proudly displayed at their workstations. He did not. Casually he tried the door to the Depot Manager's office, as he had expected it was locked. He had no idea why the Boss locked his office, as he doubted there would be anything of any real interest contained within.

As he loitered by the Depot Manager's office door, he allowed himself a brief glimpse into the Pandora compartment within his mind. The pain and rage immediately coursed through his consciousness. Struggling, he managed to re-seal the compartment. It was not yet time to let it take over. Using the persisting afterglow to fuel his creativity, Brian refined the speech he had composed and would deliver that night, the moment he finally faced his demons. When he was satisfied with the words, the intonations and the timings of his planned oratory, he allowed a sickening smile to spread across his podgy face. Transformed from a portly unhandsome man to a gloating ghoul, Brian stood leering across the office at the images in his head.

The scraping crack of the building main door opening startled him from his dark reverie. Blinking into the present, Brian recognised the Depot Manager as he entered the open plan office.

"Good, you're still here Brian."

"I am Ralf, I was just thinking about something."

"Good man. I just forgot my wallet and it's my round in the pub."

He walked as he talked and passed Brian to his office door. Pulling a large bunch of keys from his pocket, he unlocked the door and entered. Brian returned to his own desk, sat down and waggled his mouse to re-awaken the monitor. Within a minute, the Manager returned, re-locked his office door and left the building, waving a wallet in the air as he went.

With overwhelming disinterest, Brian read a few e-mails prior to rising and locking the main door. Now locked into the office building he began to prowl the workplace, safe from any further unexpected intrusions. He wandered the unsecured areas of the building. He was not searching for anything he just needed to move. If he remained static for any length of time, he became anxious and agitated. Walking and navigating encouraged his thoughts to progress and not to stall into a short loop of infinity.

He thought of the infidelities his wife had recounted in painful detail over the internet. Staggered by the prevalence of her sexually inappropriate actions, all recorded in her e-mails to Debbie, he struggled to estimate the number of lovers she had taken over the years. They seemed almost to be keeping score and by his reckoning, Becky was winning by some considerable margin. Some of what he had read sexually excited him and some repulsed him. He had felt physically sick when he read about her seduction of the neighbour's son. Not only was she a slag, she was also a paedophile. He had married a paedophile and that was just another reason why he would have to end it.

It disturbed him that he was sexually excited by his wife's infidelities. From the moment he had walked in on a heavily pregnant Becky being ridden like a dog by that man, he had known that she would never be faithful. He had been prepared to tolerate the occasional sexual impropriety, provided she kept it well hidden and that it was not a regular occurrence. When he had eventually discovered that she was hunting sexual partners on the internet, something inside of him snapped. Her behaviour was intolerable and to compound the issue she appeared to have no sexual interest in him whatsoever.

Brian returned to his desk, moved the mouse and waited for the screen to come to life. A brief glance at the large clock on the wall informed him that he had been prowling about the building for nearly an hour. It was time to begin his preparations. Closing all the business applications on his monitor, he activated the web browser and logged on to Sophistidates.

Clicking through the explicit photographs of his wife, that she had posted and shared, he began to become aroused. His favourite shot was one that showed her bent over on their sofa at home, her hand was between her legs pulling the lacy knickers to one side, displaying her pussy and anus to the camera. He had always wondered who had taken the photograph, it might have been Debbie or it might have been one of her many lovers.

Having exhausted the visual medium of its capacity to arouse him, he decided to allow his imagination to carry him further into the realms of sexual fantasy. He began by re-reading one of the more lurid accounts she had shared of her sexual activities. When his mind had absorbed sufficient detail to sketch the scene he stood, undid his trousers, allowed them

327

to fall to his knees and pulled his pants down to join them. Taking his seat again, he massaged his stiff penis whilst he closed his eyes and ran the scenario through his imagination.

In his mind, Becky was gorging herself in the act of fellatio when he reached down to the bottom drawer of his desk, opened it and reached in for the box of tissues he kept there. With a wet gasp he climaxed into the wad of tissues he held in his left hand. He carefully captured all of his ejaculation in the paper and crushed the handful into a tight ball, which he laid gently on the desk before him.

Recovering from his orgasm, he began to feel, in a very real way that the end had begun. A pocket of effervescence in his stomach initiated sensations of terrifying anticipation. His world was now changing; the process he had begun was now beyond his control. He had a major part to play in the events that would change his world and play those parts he must. There was no choice, the course was set and he would have to ride this Nantucket sleigh.

The clock on the wall read ten minutes to seven. It was time for more direct action. Brian stood up and redressed himself, as he did, he checked his immediate surrounds for any wayward semen. He then logged out of Sophistidates and initiated the closing down procedure on his monitor. Picking up the clot of tissue from his desk, he went to the lavatory and flushed the evidence away.

When he returned to his workstation, the computer had switched itself off. Brian pushed his chair under the desk and went over to the key press. From the rows of vehicle keys, he selected a set for one of the recovery vans. Pocketing the keys, he scanned the open plan office to ensure all was as it should be, before moving to the rear door, which led to the vehicle yard.

Once outside in the yard he pulled his office keys from his trouser pocket and locked the rear door. He had selected the keys for one of the smaller recovery vans. They were parked overnight in the secured yard as each vehicle carried extensive and expensive tool kits. Finding the vehicle, he opened it and climbed behind the wheel. He adjusted the seat and the mirrors before starting the engine and slowly manoeuvring the van to the exit line. When the beam was broken, the heavy gates began to swing slowly open with a metallic dragging noise until with a resounding clang, they reached the extent of their articulation.

The traffic was light, mainly taxis and private cars; people setting out on a night of leisure: the cinema, drinks, a meal, some dancing and who knows, perhaps sex with a stranger. Brian muttered disapprovingly as he drove the van along roads lined with restaurants and pubs. There were groups of young girls, all legs and brightly coloured lycra, clinging to each other as they struggled to walk on enormous heels. Groups of young males pushed each other about and bellowed loutishly, their proclamation of manhood, a preamble to later courtship rituals. All the revellers pass unseeing as a filthy tramp settles dejectedly into a shop doorway. Cardboard tipping through all possible axis until positioned to the satisfaction of the manipulator to serve as protection from the hardness of the concrete.

From behind the wheel, Brian scanned the groups of people travelling the pavements. There were more mature groups and couples issuing directly from taxis outside of their intended destinations. The key to their immediate social ambition was the combination of their company. Groups of equal numbers of male and female were settled sexually and would seek only to enjoy the company of people in a similar circumstance. Groups with more men than women, would spend most of the night trying to pair off the unaccompanied men and thus, albeit vicariously, they could enjoy the trill of new sexual encounters. Groups with more female than men would spend the evening chatting about clothes and boyfriends because the males would almost certainly be homosexual. Single sex groups were sexually predacious. The women would wear provocative clothing designed for women many years younger than they were. The men would try to spend, obviously, as much money as possible. Both genders bathed themselves in powerful scents with which they hoped to attract the opposite sex and to cover the smell of their numerous bad habits. People were pathetically predictable Brian thought to himself. Well tonight, he was going to be anything but predictable.

He circled the block several times until a space at the kerb became available. The taxi driver received his next job over the radio and pulled away from the kerb as Brian approached in the van. Reacting quickly he flicked the indicator and pulled out of the traffic into the space left by the departing taxi. Parking manoeuvre complete, he checked the suitability of his vantage before switching off the engine. Releasing himself from the restraint of the seat belt, he looked through the windscreen at the Gastro Pub 'Bird Pie'. From the driver seat, he could see anyone approaching the rendezvous. He checked his watch and settled in his seat to wait.

Chapter 43

When I was Matt, I dwelt in the living forest. Back then, I had a match. I struck that match and set it to some kindling of leaves, twigs and bark. When the tinder caught, I blew my life breath into its base and fire was born. Its life grew as I fed it more and more kindling, then I graduated to branches, small at first, increasing to larger limbs as the dancing flames grew stronger. Waving my hands through the air, I caressed the child of free radicals that I had created, pushing waves of oxygen into the bottomless pit of its appetite. Radiating increasing amounts of heat, my bastard creation grew to suit my ardour.

At first, the fire warmed me in the calm nights of Bacchanalian bliss. Then the wind rose, giving sublime existence to my feral child. The flames grew in the driven air, blistering my skin and blinding my eyes with their emissions; wild fire, devouring the living forest, my demon, my destruction. No man can stop what has begun. No man can outrun the wind. In the teeth of my child I burned, flesh tuning to black cinder, bones charred to cracked splintered ends. Patricide, flaming Oedipus. It was then that I passed over. Waking, I found myself to be a dweller of the dead forest, Mortsylvan.

These years I have suffered the pains of purgatory, waiting patiently for the opportunity to pay my moral debts, divine retribution, universal reckoning, salary of sin. Signs sent and the tasking confirmed in the song of the Willow Monks, I took my opportunity and pursued the task with impressive zeal. Killing many of the vile creatures that my mission had targeted, I laboured for redemption.

Having proven myself worthy, I was given my final task, one that would require all of my courage and cunning. It had broken his covenant with the dead and now hunted beyond the confines of the Garden. Entities such as It, existential deviants, are required to co-exist only with the dead. His covenant clearly required It to remain within the boundaries of the Garden of The Dead, he went rogue and now hunts beyond his legitimate space. It is my warrant to hunt him, to bring It to compliance or destroy him in the trying, above all I must stop It

For many years, It has terrorised me in our garden. Prowling in the darkness seeking to feed from what remains of my life force. He has mauled me before, an experience that I have no wish to repeat. I have seen him do many worse things to others and for that, I am grateful it was to them and petrified that it could have so easily been me. Despite the obvious risk I run, I am glad that this mission has been given to me. I believe a task of this magnitude must be an ultimate challenge, on successful completion of this assignment I believe that I shall be delivered.

Many challenges face me. Firstly, I must find It. Secondly I must establish an advantage that will allow me to prevail. Thirdly, and potentially the most difficult, I must know when I have achieved the aim: in this instance, what does success look like? In many ways, the latter two are almost self-fulfilling in that either I do or I do not meet the challenge. The first could be unending or I could be damned to seek It for centuries.

It has only been a few weeks since I was charged with the task of stopping It and so far, I have not come close to my quarry. He is here. I sense his foulness. The living have seen and felt the results of his degenerate actions, they too seek him though they have no way of knowing the futility of their quest. Only I can find It and only I can stop him. Responsibility, amercement for my former malfeasance, holistic compensation; the toll demanded to pass from the dead forest to whatever lies beyond.

Whilst I have not yet come close to It, I do have a clear understanding of how I shall find him. It is necessary for me to have a plan, for without a plan, chaos will rule. When chaos holds sway, only the deceiver benefits, order brings clarity that defies the ambitions of those that would mislead. My plan will provide the order and nature shall do the rest.

Hating the light, he strikes in darkness. It is weakened by the pain clarity brings to his rancid soul. To find victims, he must come into the light, lure them to the shadows where he can feed. This cardinal premise therefore provides the opportunity for him to be hunted as he hunts in light, revealed as he moves with his prey, to darkness. I therefore have only to wait, concealed in the dark corners about an area of brightness, and he will be revealed to me. I sit in this doorway, observing people passing by, looking for the one without pleasure as he moves through the carnival of the urbane. Should It remain anonymous I shall move to a place of darkness and wait for him to come to me with his prey. I have sat here for over two hours, contemplating my quest and looking for It. Soon it will be time to go to the darkness where I shall need to keep my wits about me, for I know, only too well, how dangerous he is in the darkness.

Before me, the living parade in the warm night air. Recently it has occurred to me that my existence is not as I believed it to be. I have always imagined that my purgatory was a necessary phase that led invariably to my passing. Passing to eternal rest or an existence where we are liberated from the terrible curse of free will. Now I believe that I may have another future, one where I live again. My old life is gone and in that respect I am dead however, it could just be true that I can live again, re-born in my present form. I allow myself the luxury of hope and imagine myself walking with the living again. To have their desires and ambitions once more would be to confirm my re-birth. Simple pleasures: to be visible, to buy a pint of beer, to share a smile with a pretty girl, to feel the warmth of another's gentle touch, all of those things would be a joy to me.

To live again is my greatest wish. Perhaps that is why my suffering has been so great, greater than others, I am to be reborn from purgatory. Higher the prize the higher the price, I only have to frustrate, permanently, the ambitions of It. Should I be successful and should I be allowed to return to the world of the living I shall take with me the lessons I have learned. The greatest lesson is, when you die, those left behind mourn only for their loss not for yours. The selfishness of the living, they seek sympathy for their loss at the expense of the dead.

Driven by the desire to dwell again in the living forest, I struggle to my aching feet, gather up my cardboard groundsheet and shuffle onto the pavement. Only the occasional feral drunken youngster can see me, eliciting some poor humour or childish sniggering. The more mature revellers fail to sense me as they pass by, enthralled in their trite conversations.

A couple in their forties walk towards me, arms wrapped about each other. She giggles as he nuzzles her neck and quicken their pace as they pass. I recognise her, I have watched her having sex in a darkened doorway only days previous. Then her partner was a different man to the one she now walks with. Promiscuity, a long forgotten pleasure for me, could it be possible that I shall indulge again?

On the pavement opposite, a group of youngsters are talking with a Police Officer whilst his companion relays information from his notebook to a disembodied voice over his radio. The youngsters push boundaries in desperate attempts to impress each other. Tiring of their puerile posturing, the Officer raises his voice with threats of arrest and they are cowed to downcast children, awkwardly fidgeting as the authority figure continued his lambasting. When his partner called from the car, the Police Officer dismissed the youths and returned to the vehicle. I keep walking.

The pubs and restaurants I pass are busy, loud conversations and the percussion of glassware, crockery and cutlery issue from their variously lit interiors. The people within are enjoying themselves, raucous laughter frequently punctuates the night and the background noise periodically increases when parties open doors to enter or exit the many hostelries. Inhibitions banished by the alcohol consumed, now forgotten as the people begin to indulge their more primal desires. Boundaries are now being crossed, unlikely conversations are now commonplace and in this state these people will alter their lives, mostly for the worst.

Passing a narrow side street, I scan the darkness it holds. Four girls wearing tiny mini-skirts of various bright colours and small tops that expose significant cleavage and folds of fat, loiter near the entrance. One bends violently at the waist and loudly vomits against the wall, her friend rushes forward to grab her hair, only to have her bare legs spattered with puke rebounding from the wall. The other two burst into coarse laughter and point out their companion's misfortune in graphic detail. The largest of the girls pulls her skirt up then tugging her knickers down she squats and begins to urinate. They notice me watching them and chorus "fuck off you dirty old cunt." I walk on as they continue to screech insults and obscenities into the light, from the darkness.

Deciding to cross the road, I stand at the kerb and study the traffic, almost exclusively taxis and buses. The bright interior of the buses contain very few passengers, the occasional glum face peering out into the darkness at a universal party to which they are not invited. Contrastingly, the taxis are full, ferrying the more timid partygoers home and the adventurous, or unfulfilled, to alternative venues. A taxi halts in the road to allow its passengers to alight, blocking the flow of traffic and facilitating my safe passage across the river of transience.

This side of the street has fewer pubs and restaurants and commensurately fewer people. There are many closed shops and lights that will burn all night, illuminate goods the vendor wishes to draw the public's attention to, spill out over the littered pavement. I travel a short distance to a service road where I turn left and then left again to access the dark loading bays and refuse areas behind the shops. This is the ideal feeding area for It and in dark places such as this I might find him, giving me the chance to complete my mission and possibly return to the world I once knew, my forest re-born.

Using my burst shoes, I scrape the filth from the tiny alcove in the boundary wall of the shops' service area. With a degree of difficulty, I manage to fit the cardboard groundsheet onto the dirty surface in the darkened niche. Backing into the tight gap, I sit down on the cardboard and survey my field of vision. The shadow, darkness and alcove combine to hide me from any that would enter this area. I have an unfettered view of three service doors and two darkened areas, ideal for his feeding ground and for amorous couples with nowhere else to go. Fertile hunting ground indeed. There is every possibility It will reveal himself to me in this place and if he does not, I might be able to indulge my voyeuristic pleasures, either way I have great hopes for this night. I feel an optimism that has been absent for years. Hope abandoned me when I accused her of lying. Now she returns like a long lost friend to warm my desolate soul.

The black outlines of the buildings, silhouetted against the brilliant stars scattered across the velvet firmament, providing an intricate line my eye can follow as I pass the time. Distantly I can hear the mixtures of music coming from the livelier pubs and the babble of a thousand voices, combined to form an unintelligible choral symphony. Secure in my absolute invisibility, I wait.

Chapter 44

Twisting before the full-length mirror, she studied her reflected image with a vague frown. The knee-length black boots with substantial wedge heels flattered her ankles and fitted snugly about her calves. As her body moved, the pleated black mini-skirt flounced about her hips, teasingly threatening to rise high enough to reveal her bottom. The pleats fell into place when she stopped moving and placed her hands on her hips as she admired the black basque top adorned with cream lace that pushed her breasts into an eye-catching cleavage.

Flicking her hair with both of her hands, she turned and lifted the ornate handbag from the bed and slung it over her left shoulder. Stooping to scoop her jacket onto her forearm, she stepped to the door and left the bedroom. Her mother looked disapprovingly at her attire and then at her heavily made up face. Thomas looked up from his grandmother's lap and smiled at his mother as he extended the hand he held a small plastic figure in towards her.

"Yes darling that's nice", she assured him.

"It's a spaceman."

"Is it? That's good. Are you going to be a good boy for your Grandma?"

"Yes Mummy."

"Good boy."

She waited for her daughter to finish before she spoke.

"Is that you off then?"

"Yes the cab's outside and I need to get going."

"Are you going to be late?"

"You know Debbie we will probably have a late one."

"Debbie, really?"

"Yes really Mother."

"Does Debbie like you dressed like that?"

"Don't try to be funny Mother."

Becky stepped over to Thomas and kissing him on the head, told him that she loved him and that she would see him tomorrow. With a flourish she turned and leaving the room

337

with her backside wiggling from side to side, she announced, "Don't wait up" and was then gone.

The taxi swept her through the bungalowed streets to the duel carriageway and on towards the provincial town centre. Becky's excitement grew as she felt the shackles of her everyday existence dissolve. Becky the mother, daughter and wife was fading as Becky the sexy good-time girl returned. Her confidence boosted by the look that the cab driver had given her when she walked to the car and climbed into the back, she contemplated what reaction her appearance would solicit from Sean.

Becky experienced two distinct forms of excitement, when embarking on an evening of freedom and indulgence. The excitement of anticipation when she and her friends would go out, not knowing whom she would meet and what would happen or the excitement of knowing a particular man was waiting for her and that his penis would be inside her later that night. She looked forward to meeting Sean and hoped that he would not disappoint. The electronic correspondence they had enjoyed was overtly sexual and he sounded like an adventurous and broadminded lover. The photographs of his cock were impressive. She estimated he had at least nine inches, nine dark fat inches, stood proud and hard. She squirmed with moist sexual excitement on the back seat of the taxi.

Checking first that the driver had no visibility of her lower body in his rear-view mirrors Becky slowly parted her knees until they were as wide apart as she could comfortably get them. With her left hand, she lifted the hem of her skirt to reveal the tiny black Brazilian knickers she wore. They barely covered the thin strip of pubic hair she had sculpted that evening whilst grooming herself. Gently she stroked her clitoris through the sheer satin fabric of her panties whilst she impassively watched the streets and traffic roll by as the taxi carried her to Sean.

A large shopping mall marked the edge of the town centre. Recognising the grey concrete building, she straightened up in her seat and patted her skirt down onto her now closed thighs. She had enjoyed rubbing herself but had not intended to climax yet, Sean could have the pleasure of sexually, albeit briefly, fulfilling her.

The streets were busy with groups and individuals embarking on an evening of socialising, eating, drinking, perhaps dancing and possibly sexual opportunity. She lifted her bag onto her lap and prepared to find her purse as the taxi turned onto the street that contained her destination. Two loud bleeps informed Becky that she had received a text message. Immediately she panicked as she had carried the fear that Sean was going to cry off or worst still, just not turn up since she had began to prepare herself earlier that evening. She pulled her 'phone from the bag on her lap and checked the display, it was a text message from an unknown number. She could sense that it was from Sean, with some reluctance, she opened the message. Sighing with relief she read the message, it was from Sean but he was not cancelling their evening he simply wanted to change the rendezvous. Leaning forward she informed the driver of the change of destination and relaxed back into her seat as the vehicle passed The Bird Pie and carried on down the road to the traffic lights where it turned right.

Becky handed the taxi driver a ten-pound note and told him to keep the change. As she climbed from the car, she was careful not to expose more of her body than was necessary to allow her to gain her feet on the pavement. She slammed the taxi door closed and looked about, scanning the front of Café Chat where there were several small tables and chairs arranged in a roped off area. With the exception of one, couples occupied all of the tables. He sat with his legs crossed and his left arm draped casually over the back of the chair he occupied. On the second chair at his table, a folder Macintosh lay on the seat, clearly signalling that he was saving the chair for someone.

All uncertainty dispersed when she made eye contact with the man who was sitting alone and a broad smile spread across his handsome face. Becky made directly for his table. He stood to greet her and pulled the coat from the second chair.

"You must be Becky," he said in soft welcoming voice.

"You must be Sean," she replied as she held his eye contact and cocked her head slightly to the left.

Taking the hand she proffered, he gently shook it and leaned in to kiss her on the cheek. Obligingly she presented her right cheek to meet his lips. When he pulled away, he indicated the chair opposite with his open hand. Demurely she positioned herself in front of the chair with her heels together then clutching her skirt to her thighs she tucked it under as her knees bent and she gently set her bottom on the patterned metal surface. Once he was satisfied, that his companion was sitting comfortably, he took his own seat then with a wave of his hand captured the attention of a Waitress.

"I am sorry to have changed our arrangements at such short notice."

"I don't mind, it came as a bit of a surprise as it's the first time you've texted me."

"Yes, again sorry about that, I just thought that as it is such a lovely evening we could have a drink al fresco before taking our table for dinner."

"Are we going back to The Bird Pie?"

"No I have booked us a table here, this is a better restaurant. Now what would you like to drink?"

She order a vodka and tonic, Sean continued to drink from the glass on the table that appeared to contain orange juice. He wore a dark suite with an open neck shirt beneath. Becky thought he was good looking. He had a well-balanced face with fine features and a smooth light olive skin. He appeared as though he had spent quite some time in the sun, his tanned skin witness to that exposure. Hazel eyes, wide and friendly, gazed at her from under his narrow dark brows. The white of his smile contrasting strikingly with the dusky hews of his colouring.

When her drink arrived, they toasted each other and clinked glass over the table. Each time she held eye contact for longer than a moment she would flutter her eyelashes and with mock shyness, look away. He never took his eyes off her, if she had not been pre-occupied by her own image reflected in the restaurant window, she would have become uneasy with the optical attention he was paying to her every detail. They made small talk together, carefully avoiding any mention of the unusual circumstance of their meeting. She had decided earlier that she would not ask for any personal details of him and that she would offer no detailed facts about herself or her domestic life, curiosity however, did get the better of her.

"Have you been on holiday?"

"No, what makes you ask that?"

"You look like you have a tan."

He laughed at her answer for an unnecessarily long time before composing himself to continue the conversation.

"No it is just the swarthy colouring of the Celts."

"Celts, are you Irish?"

"Of Irish decent, yes."

"I suppose that is why you are called Sean then."

"My mother was born over here but her family come from Cork and my father is straight out of the bogs, County Clare."

"I thought all Irish people were ginger."

Again, he guffawed inappropriately.

"And I suppose you thought we all wore emerald green suits with funny hats?"

"No I'm not that stupid."

"The red colouring only came with the second immigration of Celts, the people we know as the Scots who settled up in Ulster. I am of the original stock, brothers and sister of the great Cú Chulainn."

"Wasn't he from Ulster?"

"Ah you know your Irish mythology?"

"No not really, only that he was taught how to fight by a woman."

"That's right he was given his war craft by a warrior Queen called Scáthach, who lived over the sea on a peninsula of The Isle of Skye."

"Didn't he get her pregnant?"

"Yes he did but that's another story. I think you know more than you are letting on. Shall we go to our table now?"

He stood and indicated the entrance.

Standing aside, he allowed Becky to enter the restaurant first, giving her a playful smack on the bottom as she passed. Pausing briefly, she gave him a light-hearted look of reprimand before smiling and continuing towards the interior. He watched her bottom, moving with an exaggerated wiggle, as she led the way to a pedestal where a smart young man stood, waiting to greet them.

Shown to a table near the rear wall of the premises, they navigated a smooth course through their fellow diners. Two places were set at the table and a long red candle burned, its base jammed into a wax encased wine bottle. A small posy of fresh flowers sat at the base of the candleholder. Casting her eyes about the room, Becky confirmed that the establishment was to her liking, very retrospective 1980's and that she did not recognise any of the people dining or serving. There was a delicious smell of frying meat and garlic, hanging in the air. Between the tables, several white shirted waiting staff hurried plates and trays in hand, as they facilitated the feeding of their employer's commercial guests. The walls were crimson, prints of works done by Lautrec hanging at regular intervals beneath the cream and gilt ceiling where a large chandelier formed a dominant centrepiece.

He stood patiently as the Waiter held Becky's chair for her then briskly moved to the opposite side of the table to hold Sean's chair whilst he sat down. Large card menus, too large for the relatively small tables, were set before them. He ordered a bottle of mineral water and she called for another vodka and tonic. The Waiter departed, leaving them to smile at each other across the table and to peruse the menus.

Studying the cards, they consulted with each other on possible choices. When he lent forward to point to a dish listed on Becky's menu, they opted to use only one list. Pointing and chatting, mingling hands and mingling glances, they came to a consensus.

A pretty young girl came to their table, notepad and pen held at the ready. He ordered their meals and a large bottle of mineral water. Becky watched him closely for signals of flirtation with the girl, pleased that he showed no signs of attraction, she asked for a bottle of the house white wine, confirming that was acceptable, with a glance to her date. The Waitress read the order back to them and with a broad smile departed.

The bottle of wine was half-empty when the starter plates were removed. Becky was feeling the warm glow of intoxication and their conversation had become increasingly sexual in nature. He had been so engrossed in her company Sean had barely touched his starter and appeared almost disappointed when the main courses were delivered. The Waitress topped Becky's glass up, placing his hand over the empty glass before him Sean declined the offered charge of wine.

"Do you not drink?"

"Not tonight, I want a clear head to enjoy you all the more later."

"Mmmmmm, do you think you are going to enjoy me?"

"Oh yes, I am getting stiff just sitting here watching you."

"I'm glad you like what you see."

"I do, very much."

Giggling like a girl, she turned her attention to the plate set before her. When she began to eat, he excused himself to go to the bathroom. As he squeezed passed her she lifted her hand and stroked the front of his trousers. Gently clasping her wrist, he slid beyond her reach and smiled warmly down at her. He had not lied, his penis felt almost erect in his suit, though she was slightly disappointed with its apparent size.

Becky found Sean very attractive, he was good looking, charming, sexy and judging from the obviously expensive suit, wealthy. In her temporary solitude, she reflected on the unthinkable possibility that he and she might someday be together. To leave Brian and begin a new life with a man worthy of her, someone who would be enough, someone she could devote herself to completely, someone to care and provide for her and Thomas. That was her dream, to be with one man, a man who could satisfy her and remove the constant need she had to find love in the arms of strangers or casual acquaintances. Temporary love she paid for with her body and dignity. Alcohol helped blind her to the pain that the price brought and bravado, shared with her friends camouflaged her pathetic vulnerability.

For her dream to become reality, two things would have to happen. She would need to win Sean away from his wife, to do this she would use her most powerful tools, her body and her sexuality. Brian would have to be persuaded not to inform the Police of the accident where she had run that poor man over. She could only hope that his involvement in the incident would be sufficient to dissuade him from that vindictive course of action.

A journey begins with the first step and tonight she would take many steps to begin the journey towards her dream. Becky had already determined that she would do anything for Sean, she would prove to him through sacrifice that he would find no other to satisfy him as she can. In time, she would demonstrate to him that she could love him like no other.

He returned to the table, arranged his napkin and adjusted the cutlery.

"I do apologise for leaving you."

"That's ok, you can make it up to me later."

"That I shall."

"And don't ever leave me again."

He froze for a second then looked up from his meal and smiled at her.

"Ok."

She held his gaze, puzzling over the meaning of his response, and then breaking the eye contact she picked up her glass and took a satisfying gulp of wine.

Watching him pretend to eat, she felt a surge of desire, desire not for sexual fulfilment but for a new life with the beautiful man sitting opposite her. Conscious of the intense silent attention she was paying him, he ceased re-arranging the food on his plate and held her in his gaze.

"What are you thinking about?"

"Your hard cock sliding into my moist pussy."

"Mmmmm, nice thought."

"What else would you like to do to me?"

"I don't know where to begin."

"How about you slip your hand under the table and finger me?"

"Not just now darling."

"Why don't you fancy me?"

"You know I do fancy you very much."

"Well finger me then, I want something in my cunt now."

344

"I want our first sexual contact to be just as we planned."

With a huffy sigh, she sat back into her chair and pouted.

"I suppose I will just have to wait then."

"Come on now, I thought we had agreed we would follow our plan."

Recovering herself to her previous demeanour, she sat forward again.

"Yes you are right, I just fancy you so much."

"Well think about my cock slipping into you from behind."

"Do you have a place in mind yet?"

"I most certainly do. I'll give you the directions when we leave."

The Waitress asked if everything had been ok when she collected the plates, his meal had been cut up and moved about the plate. Confirming that everything was fine and that they did not wish to see the desert menu, he asked for the bill. After a short wait a small black folder was placed in front of him, he lifted the cover and read the contents. Reaching into his jacket, he brought out a brown leather wallet, counted notes out, and placed them on the folder before closing the cover and handing it back to the Waitress. He asked for his raincoat and rose to seize the back of Becky's chair, sliding it away as she stood to join him.

His raincoat, returned to him at the door, hung over his left arm as he guided Becky out into the warm night. They moved with an air of excitement, like children eager to reach some promised destination. As they walked down the pavement, her arm in his, he detailed the directions to the place he had in mind. After she confirmed that she understood, he repeated the details of their plan. When they reached the street corner, he prompted her into action with a pat on the bottom. He then slowed his pace to a dawdle whilst she skipped ahead, giggling, smiling back at him over her shoulder and following his directions.

Becky crossed the road, clutching her bag and jacket as they bounced about with her quickening pace. On reaching the sanctuary of the far side, she slowed to normal walking pace and continued towards the row of closed shops, spilling their window illuminations out to form a pool of light across the pavement. Her heart was beating quickly. She felt a mixture of anticipation and sexual arousal. She was following the plan that they had developed during their sexually charged electronic correspondence. The night had an added poignancy as she now desired Sean as a long-term partner, tonight she would do whatever he asked of her but first she must play her part in the execution of the plan, faultlessly.

At the entrance to the service road, she paused only to check that she had not drawn the type of attention that would cause her to be followed, she left the street and cautiously walked into the darkness. The warmth of the day had ensured that the refuse bins were especially fragrant and Becky could hear anonymous creatures moving amongst the rubbish. Focussing on the plan, she put all thoughts of rats out of her mind and peered into the shadows. After a rapid reconnaissance, she confirmed that she was alone and identified the doorway where she was to meet her lover.

Gingerly she stepped into the dense shadow of the doorway. It seemed as though she had passed into another world. Despite the background noise from the pubs and restaurants, only metres away, she felt an isolation that was barely credible given her location. There was no time to contemplate her surrounding as she expected her man to join her very shortly.

Placing her feet carefully apart, Becky pulled her tiny knickers down to midway on her thighs. Leaning forward at the waist, she flicked the rear of her skirt up onto the small of her back and rested her hands on her knees. Face towards the darkness, Becky waited for Sean.

Chapter 45

In the darkness he felt more natural, relaxed and with purpose. Only with purpose to drive him could he release the rage, rage that served only to hurt him, no excitement, no heightened heart rate or respiration, just cold painful rage. Now he felt alive and free from the bonds of the expectations of others, able to seek enhanced sensation beyond his tedious existence.

He had been a sinner and he had made redemption for his sins, she had not. The opportunity for a new beginning squandered by her betrayal and further corrupted by her malignant machinations. It was clear to him that she had used her skills to manipulate him, to make him the guardian of an abomination. As a, truly skilled, deceiver always aimed to do, she had convinced him that her proposed actions were for the good of the family and as he wished to do good, he aligned himself with her ambitions. Unwitting affiliate of evil, he became as a vassal for Satan.

Cat-like he crept into the service area, dark with even darker shadows between the looming boundary wall, refuse bins and the deep pits of the rear doorways. Clutching the solid shaft of the hammer, he lets the raincoat fall to the ground, cold steel head issuing from the large hip pocket. Taking two further gentle paces his quarry came into view.

She had followed their agreed plan exactly. From the black rectangle of the doorway, her porcelain backside, incandescent against the shadow backdrop, stood out. The dark elongated triangular cleft running from her coccyx downwards to where her legs disappeared into the shadow, moving very slightly as she shivered with anticipation. Her knickers, taught between her thighs, formed a horizontal black line to complete the frame.

Impassively he observed Becky in her submissive pose. His wife had betrayed him and for that, she had to be punished. She had lain with another man, the night before marrying him. To compound her wickedness she had kept it from him until forced to confess. The illicit coupling had produced a child, which she carried into their union, the pregnancy demanding that she be truthful. He would not physically punish his wife; other women had to pay the price on behalf all harlots.

Initially he had paid prostitutes to allow him to hurt them. They unfortunately had boundaries that denied him satisfaction. He then took to attacking women he could seduce in the Champagne bars of London. Again, he could not sate his hunger for revenge. Eventually he had realised that he needed to kill in order to feel anything near satisfaction. Killing could not be gratuitous. Carefully selecting his victims, he targeted only those married sluts who would lie with a man other than their husbands.

The killings had been successful. It surprised him how many married women wanted extramarital sex and how easily manipulated into compliant sexual games they were. These factors had made his indulgence easier and in so doing, validated the legitimacy of his actions. Disappointingly, he found that the sensation of killing was not as intense as he had wanted it to be. He would have to find a greater thrill, perhaps abduction and torture.

With absolute conviction, he knew she lay awake at night dreaming of the liaison with her lover. It hurt him to know that she yearned for her illicit lover's return to her bed and to feel the joy she had felt when he had been inside of her. Whilst he would not harm her physically, he had planned to punish her. Thankfully, God had given him the opportunity to do that. He would give their abomination back to its creator, this time as his wife. Unfortunately, Satan was cunning and she had escaped that appropriate punishment.

Gripping the shaft with grim determination, Abdul stepped forward. He stood close by Becky she moaned slightly and gently wagged her bottom in anticipation. The air he drew through his nose, heavily scented with her perfume, filled his lungs and the sight of her well-formed backside aroused him. With an explosion of motion, he swung the hammer in a wide arc over his shoulder and down hard onto her head. The, now familiar, cracking thud marked the first impact. Tugging the shaft he freed the hammerhead, sensing the weak resistance of suction as it left her skull and drew it back over his shoulder again.

The impact came from nowhere, knocking Abdul off balance and causing him to lose the hammer. Struggling to regain balance and grappling with the person who had barged into him, Abdul tried to identify his assailant. Using his superior strength, he managed to swing his opponent onto the shop wall where he caught sight of his attacker for the first time. He could scarcely believe his eyes; he was wrestling a filth tramp. A filthy tramp was trying to vex his ambition, to stop him taking the vengeance he so richly deserved.

Hidden deep in the shadows, Matt had watched Becky take her position in the doorway opposite. His excitement grew when she adjusted her clothing and adopted a very erotic pose. Sensing the man enter the theatre, Matt held his breath and peered intently as the play unfolded. Initially he had though that he was about to witness two lovers copulating. As the man drew near the girl in the doorway, Matt saw the hammer, hanging at his side.

He had no way of knowing what was about to happen, just an immediate sensation of foreboding. The man's intent towards the woman became obvious when the hammer began to move. Before the tool had made contact with Becky's head, Matt was in motion, charging across the darkness towards Abdul. There was no plan just a desperate need to stop what was happening. Arriving in time to stop the intended second blow, he threw his body at the attacker and clung desperately to anything he could grasp. He was relieved to hear the hammer clank onto the ground as he furiously tried to resist the strength of the man he fought.

The killer and the tramp thrashed about furiously, the stronger and younger man threw the filthy older man about. Tenaciously Matt clung to Abdul, determined not let him land a clean blow on him. In the doorway, Becky rocked gently back and forth whilst emitting a low woeful moaning noise, oblivious to the frantic struggle behind her. Lifting his legs from the ground, Matt used his body weight to pull the killer to the ground where they rolled about, each seeking the advantage. Using his superior weight and strength Abdul rolled the tramp onto his back, pinning him there whilst he prepared to drive his fist into the dirty bearded face glaring up at him. With surprising speed and agility Matt, forced his knee upward with all the strength he could muster into the younger man's crotch causing him to cry out in pain as he instinctually relaxed his grip and crunched his body up to protect the injured area from further assault. Seizing the opportunity Matt wriggled from beneath him and gained his feet unsteadily.

Powerful hands grabbed Matt's arms, holding them behind him as the first blows landed. Caught in the desperate melee with the killer, he had failed to notice the two men entered the service area.

They had spent the evening in a particular near-by bar, flirting and chatting. The effeminate one waving his hands and forearms about like dancing egrets as he had explained to his macho companion why he had added another two men to his list of sexual conquests since their last liaison. The Macho one, happy to ignore the object of his desire's promiscuity in order to fully enjoy a night of freedom from his conventional heterosexual life, frowned then forgot all about it. Wife and kids at home, he sought out illicit congress to fulfil his true sexuality. They had decided to slip into the seclusion of the darkened area for sex before going their separate ways home.

Sounds of fighting caught their attention and they had approached cautiously. Scanning the scene, they saw a woman bending over with her naked bottom on display and an ordinary looking man fighting with a tramp.

"That's the dirty old fucker we caught spying on us."

"Looks like he's been at it again."

"You'd think he'd learn."

"Come on, let's lend a hand."

They waded in just as Matt re-gained his feet. Initially the blows were aimed at his head, then choosing the easier target they were directed at his torso in powerful and deliberate uppercuts.

Blood filled his mouth, causing him to choke as he tried to cry out in pain. His face burned as the hard fists pummelled the thin flesh, stretch across his skull. Granted the briefest of respites from the battering Matt allowed his head to roll forward and the blood and the teeth spewed out onto his beard and tatty coat. The beating resumed as the man to his front landed a devastating punch to his abdomen, causing Matt to fold forward, red bubbles briefly growing from his mouth before popping into crimson drool. His assailant stepped back to give himself room to increase the kinetic energy of the next blow, which he delivered after taking two steps towards his victim. Pain exploded inside Matt when the hard fist drove powerfully into his solar plexus, driving all the wind from his body, he felt something deep inside burst.

Abdul came out of the shadow, screaming, hammer held high.

"I'll fucking kill you, you bastard!"

The man holding Matt immediately relaxed his grip and pushed him away.

"Hey! What are you doing with that?"

"I'm gonna kill that fucking son of a dog!"

"No you're not, give it here."

The homosexuals closed on him, one wrestled the hammer from Abdul's grip whilst the other restrained him, ranting and thrashing in his arms.

"What the hell has been going on here?"

Realising that Becky had not moved from her position throughout the disturbance, they indicated her with their eyes.

"What's up with her?"

"Fuck that whore!"

"What have you done?"

"Fuck all of you. I have a right!"

"Jesus, what's been going on?"

The effeminate man, now in possession of the hammer, walked cautiously towards the doorway framing Becky's backside.

"Eh Miss are you alright?"

She continued rocking and moaning as he peered into the gloom to inspect her.

"Keep a hold of that mad bastard! I'm calling the Police."

Dropping the hammer, he fished in his jacket for his mobile. Pulling it from his inside pocket, he flipped the 'phone open and pressed the three-digit number.

After summonsing the Police, giving all relevant details and requesting an ambulance, he went to Becky's assistance. Pulling the back of her skirt down to protect her modesty, he then eased her from her position onto the ground before joining her and cradling her head in his lap. Only then did he notice the smell, she had messed herself and he had sat in a mixture of her faeces and urine.

It took only minutes for the patrol car to arrive, headlight banishing the shadows and illuminating the scene. The Police Officers leapt from their vehicle and walked purposely into the service area, assessing the situation as they went. The lovers took turns to relay the events, as they perceived them, to the Officers whilst Abdul continued to rant and rave. One of the Police Officers took custody of the incoherent killer, handcuffing him and imprisoning him in the vehicle, before returning to take statements from the two willing and able witnesses. The other Officer relieved the effeminate one of the casualty and began to administer rudimentary first aid.

When the ambulance arrived, two Paramedics rushed into the pool of light thrown out from the patrol car's headlights.

"Over here mate I think she's in a bad way," shouted the Officer tending Becky.

"What about this one over there?" The Paramedic indicated the prone form of a tramp lying next to the refuse bins, with and outstretched arm.

"Don't know, never noticed him," said the Police Officer as he craned his neck to look over.

The Medics spilt the workload and moved to both the casualties.

He lay on his side, perfectly motionless. The Paramedic checked his vital signs. Satisfied that he was breathing and had a pulse, albeit a weak one, the Medic slipped a blanket under Matt's head and began to unpack the equipment to measure his patient's blood pressure from the large bag he carried.

Sensing the benign presence, Matt groaned as he tried to form words through his smashed mouth. His mouth moved slowly, the blood that covered his lips and beard appearing almost black in the harsh lights from the Police vehicle. Noticing the movement the Medic laid a hand lightly on his shoulder.

"Hey there mate, you've been in the wars but don't worry we'll get you fixed up. What's your name?"

Encouraged by the caring voice, Matt re-doubled his efforts and whispered painfully to his carer.

"Did I stop It?"

"Come now, save your energy. Can you tell me your name?"

His breathe caught in his throat as the pain deep inside him wracked his body once more. Trembling in wretched agony, he gasped as he felt his life leaking into the warm night air.

As the pain faded and his life force diminished, Matt rolled onto his back.

"Careful now, try not to move," cautioned the Medic gently.

Staring passed the concerned face of the considerate stranger, to the stars he mumbled something incomprehensible. His carer leaned closer with his ear towards his casualty. Recognising the gesture as an invitation to repeat what he had said Matt spoke again.

"And so it ends."

His eyes grew dull and his mouth hung open.

With practiced efficiency, the Paramedic worked to recover life for the old tramp. Massaging his heart and breathing air into his lungs.

Chapter 46

The room was empty now of people. The last detective had carried a box of files, balanced on her left arm, through the door to the corridor beyond, passing Detective Sergeant Gayle. He stood with a smug expression of contentment on his face, surveying the tired dull green walls, from the doorway. He sucked air in through his nose and exhaled loudly. He scanned the desktops to confirm that they were clear of plastic coffee cups and redundant paperwork then walked purposefully towards the office in the far corner.

Knocking on the glass of the door-window, he turned the handle sharply and pushed into the office.

"That's it clear Guv."

Mac Gregor and Bruce Willox looked up at him from their conversation, and then both craned their necks to look beyond Tommo through the open door into the incident room. Recovering from their gesture of inspection, they returned their attentions to the new arrival.

"Thanks fir that Tommo, tak a seat."

He pointed at the only vacant seat in the office and waited for his subordinate to sit down.

Fine rain spotted on the window, light grey cloud-cover obscuring the summer sun giving the day an autumnal feel. Outside the usual sounds of traffic, mixed with the repetitive cooing of a pigeon, perched in the tangled bushes beneath. Inside the three Detectives sat silently. Mac Gregor appeared to be thinking. He sat back in his chair, fingers laced together on his stomach as he stared out of the window into the clouds. A dark stain on his tie, a legacy of his breakfast and damp patches under the arms of his shirt, testimony to the continuing seasonal temperature, the Inspector looked dishevelled. In contrast, Sergeant Gayle looked immaculate in his pin-stripe suit, fresh Egyptian cotton shirt, silk tie and shiny brogues. Bruce Willox looked to be somewhere between his colleagues in turnout and dress, better groomed than Mac Gregor but not as well dressed as Gayle.

Yawning loudly and stretching his arms out, giving the assembled Police Officers full view of the sweat patches in his armpits, Mac Gregor brought himself back to the impromptu meeting. As the case was now closed he felt it necessary to call an informal de-brief on recent events, the serial killer case and related cases. Having composed himself Mac Gregor looked first at one detective then the other.

"Well we goat the bastard."

"The tit 'eds got him Guv," corrected Gayle.

"Aye thanks fir pointin' that oot Tommo. Ah wiz referring tae the Guid Guys when a said 'us'."

"Sorry Guv."

Mac Gregor held Gayle in his gaze longer than was necessary before continuing.

"He's goin' wi the 'Diminished Responsibility' plea oan account o' his claimed mental illness."

"Is he denying anything," asked Bruce Willox?

"Naw he's bein' very compliant, tellin' us everythin' he kens, bit claims he wiz mad, citing everythin' frim drug abuse in his younger days tae, stress frim work and provocation frim his wife as the causes o' his illness. Even claims that a mysterious entity, a messenger frim Goad, telt him whit tae dae."

"A mysterious entity, Guv?"

"Aye he caws it 'It'."

"It, Guv?"

"Aye that's aw he'll caw it. Maybe the cunt is a bam after aw."

"Nah he's just trying for a cushy time in hospital and a cure few years down the line," interjected Gayle.

"That's as maybe, bit fir the moment he is charged wi five coonts o murder and wan o attempted murder."

After delivering the summary of charges, he sat back in his seat and fell silent.

Having left a pause long enough for the facts to sink in, Mac Gregor lent forward once again with a grim look on his face.

"The latest victim. She's alive bit only jist. Severe brain damage, bed ridden, incontinent, unable tae speak and takin' her food through a straw. Worse still, if she's ever fit tae face trial she'll be oan charges fir having sex wi someone below the age o' consent. We've the statement frim the neighbour an the evidence oan her computer. An gein whit she wiz up tae a wid say the cohesion o' her family is in doot."

This time he sat back and showed no sign of saying anything further.

The Sergeants looked at each other, attempting to agree who would speak next. Bruce Willox cleared his throat and leaned forward in his chair.

"Abdul Hadi's wife has changed her story. It would appear that she has some provocation for the murder of Al qasim Hadi."

"Dae ye think its enough fir them tae go easy oan her?"

"Doubt it Guv she did, by her own confession, premeditate the killing. The charge remains murder and she is likely to be convicted on the evidence. It will come down to the Judge on the day, on hearing the mitigation he may decide to give her a lenient tarrif. Your man Abdul has confirmed her statement."

"Seems a wee bit harsh fir the poor Lassie."

"True Guv, she was in a hard position. The two villains in the piece are out of the way, one dead and one in prison. The rest of the family have some very difficult thing to come to terms with. Good luck to them I say."

"At least we goat that prick o a husband o hers oot the way."

Mac Gregor gave Tommo Gayle a hard stare to dissuade him from any attempt at a correction.

A loud knocking on the door distracted the Detectives and all eyes turned to see who disturbed them. Recognising the Uniformed Constable, Willox leapt to his feet and opened the door. The Constable entered with a plastic tray carrying three cups.

"Sorry to disturb you Sir, Sergeant Willox asked me to bring you some coffee."

"Guid Laddie, jist pit them doon oan the desk."

He arranged the cups before the Detectives, leaned the tray against the wall and left. Mac Gregor pulled a cup towards him then produced a hip flask from the jacket hanging on the back of the chair. The Sergeants exchanged glances, Gayle showing open surprise, Willox resignation, followed by a shrug of his shoulders to dismiss the unspoken subject. The Inspector unscrewed the cap and poured a healthy dram into his coffee. Looking up at the others, he offered the hip flask to them. Tommo looked horrified, shaking his head vigorously, Bruce declined by casually raising a hand.

After taking a loud slurp of his fortified coffee, Mac Gregor began rummaging in his jacket on the chair. He slapped a pack of cigarettes on the desk and pushed his hand into his trouser pocket, holding cool and constant eye contact with Tommo. When he brought his hand out of his trousers, he looked down at the cigarettes and pulled one from the pack. When Sergeant Gayle drew breath to speak Mac Gregor fixed him with a hard stare.

"Keep your fuckin' mooth shut Tommo!"
Stunned by the senior officer's outburst, Gayle sat open mouthed and uncertain of what to do next. Mac Gregor maintained his icy stare, put the cigarette in his mouth and lit it. He blew a long stream of blue grey smoke into the room and turned his attention to his coffee.

Freed from the Inspectors powerful gaze, Tommo looked towards Bruce with incredulity etched across his face. He was seeking an ally but Willox could only give him a brief shrug and resigned smile. When he returned his attention to Mac Gregor his cold eyes greeted him, peering through the most recent cloud of exhaled smoke.

"Right Tommo, perhaps you'll be guid enough tae summarise whits goin' oan wi thae poofs."
Gayle took a moment to regain composure and his confidence returned.

"Well our heroic homosexuals would appear to have saved the victims life and to have captured the serial killer. Unfortunately, they beat a tramp to death in the process. Currently they are both in custody charged with manslaughter."

"And tell us why they beat the jaykie tae death."

"Well that's why we know they are homosexuals. They allege that they had caught him spying on them having sex some time ago."

"Does that hang teagether fir you Tommo?"

"Yes I think so. There is no evidence they had any other reason to attack him."

Mac Gregor moaned a thoughtful sound as he looked about the office.

He stooped out of his chair and pulled the metal wastepaper basket towards him, cigarette in mouth. Re-gaining his seat, he flicked ash into the basket and took a drink from his coffee. The cigarette packet spun on the desk as Mac Gregor fiddled with it. He appeared momentarily distracted before looking up to fix both Sergeants in turn with his eyes.

"And noo we come tae the man o' mystery, the tramp. The only wan o' the players in this sorry affair tae appear blameless. We dinnae ken anything aboot him, Nae ID Nae record o' his DNA or fingerprints. He disnae fit the description o' anyone reported as missing. He's no known at any o' the hostels or soup kitchens. Some people say that they have seen him wanderin' aboot in the streets and the poofs say he wiz a bit o' a Peepin' Tom. Other than that we ken nothin' aboot him. It's as though he came frim nae where or another world."

"He's just another filthy old tramp, probably slept rough, why bother," Tommo stated, with renewed confidence.

Mac Gregor turned his eyes on the Sergeant once more. This time they were feral, alive with fire and anger. Detective Sergeant Gayle froze in his seat, he went to look to his fellow Sergeant for reassurance but could not, gripped by the ferocity of Mac Gregor's glare.

"A man is aw men and his wretchedness is oor shame. Yed dae well tae remember that Tommo Lad."

He spoke in a low measured growl then held Gayle in his glare for a further few seconds before turning away quickly and extinguishing his cigarette butt in the basket.

The Sergeants appeared relieved when Mac Gregor recovered to his normal self. With a wry smile, he looked at them both and slapped his hands on the desk, elbows raised.

"Well much as a would love tae stay and chat wi you Gentlemen aw day, a have an interview withoot coffee in Forester's office."

He stood up, drank the last of his coffee, pulled his jacket on and walked from the room. When he was gone, Tommo Gayle sank back into his seat with a slight smile on his face. It took him a moment before he became aware of Bruce Willox's glare.

Printed in Great Britain
by Amazon.co.uk, Ltd.,
Marston Gate.